Burns
Burns, Jeremy
From the ashes : a novel /

34028079018942
CYF $16.95 ocn809543391
              10/18/12

L

W9-BBL-283

FROM THE ASHES

a novel by

Jeremy Burns

**fiction
studio
books**

This is a work of fiction. Names, characters, places, and incidents either are the product of the author's imagination or are used fictitiously. Any resemblance to actual events, locales, organizations, or persons living or dead, is entirely coincidental and beyond the intent of either the author or the publisher.

The Fiction Studio
P.O. Box 4613
Stamford, CT 06907

Copyright © 2012 by Jeremy Burns
Cover Design by Aaron Brown
Author Photo by Rachel DiDomenico of Imperial Photography

Print ISBN-13: 978-1-936558-32-2
E-book ISBN-13: 978-1-936558-33-9

Visit our website at www.fictionstudiobooks.com

All rights reserved, which includes the right to reproduce this book or portions thereof in any form whatsoever except as provided by U.S. Copyright Law. For information, address The Fiction Studio.

First Fiction Studio Printing: January 2012

Printed in the United States of America

For Becca,
Sister, Editor, Friend

Acknowledgments

Though it's been said that a writer's journey is a lonely one, there are many people to whom I am indebted for their assistance, support, and encouragement.

Becca Musil, for reading through every revision and offering me consistently useful suggestions that have been invaluable in bringing the novel to where it is today.

My parents, for raising me with the values and work ethic necessary to see this through, and for believing in me since Day One.

Meredith Curry, for your love and encouragement. You have no idea how much your belief in me has helped to spur me on.

Debi Bell, Keith Tischler, Kris Ryan, Travis Laffitte, Tim Manson, Martine Forneret, Kritika Lakhani, Pam Ahearn, and Harriet Epstein, whose comments and suggestions on earlier drafts of the novel helped shape it into the finished product. Your insight has been invaluable.

Lou Aronica, for falling in love with my story and taking a chance on an unpublished author. Thanks for sharing your vast reservoirs of experience and knowledge to get my story into the world.

Jackie Baron McCue, for helping give my book that final layer of polish.

Aaron Brown, for your friendship, insight, and assistance as we've embarked on our writing careers, as well as for the amazing cover design.

Authors Ethan Cross, Stephen James, Jeremy Robinson, Jon Land, Kathie Antrim, and Greg Mosse, for your encouragement and words of wisdom, as well as everyone who has helped put together ITW's consistently amazing ThrillerFest conventions the past three years.

D.B. Lyle, M.D., for his medical expertise.

Dr. Max Friedman, Dr. Jim Jones and Dr. Nathan Stoltzfus, whose university coursework was invaluable to the novel's historical backstory.

All the faculty and students at Universal American School of Dubai, for believing in the dream and cheering me on (as well as creating the first Facebook fan page for my writing).

And to everyone who has ever asked me "When is your book coming out?" for helping to light a fire under my butt and put in the work to make this dream a reality. You will never know how much your encouragement and support over the past five-plus years has helped make the lonely and often frustrating road from idea-for-a-story to published novel not so difficult. Thank you.

If you tell a lie big enough, and keep repeating it, people will eventually come to believe it. The lie can be maintained only for such time as the State can shield the people from the political and/or military consequences of the lie. It thus becomes vitally important for the State to use all of its powers to repress dissent, for the truth is the mortal enemy of the lie, and thus by extension, the truth is the greatest enemy of the State.

~ Joseph Goebbels

<u>Prologue – The Fatal Flaw</u>

Peace visits not the guilty mind.
~ Juvenal

Every guilty person is his own hangman.
~ Seneca

Manhattan, 1957

The frigid night air should have stung Roger's face, but it
didn't. Tonight, he noticed very little about his surroundings,
operating solely on instinct. All his faculties were taxed to the
limit with the battle that was raging within him, a battle that
had begun that afternoon, a battle that was steadily marching
onward to its inevitable conclusion.

A child! His weathered face contorted with his thoughts,
his natural, carnal self breaking through the years of carefully built-up training, the stoic facade that had somehow come
crashing down in one fateful moment. He had killed before.
He had killed his fellow Americans before. All under orders, of
course. All for the good of the country. But never before had he
killed a child.

What danger could a child really *have posed?* Roger's
thoughts continued, more a stream of answerless questions than
a real quest for understanding. It was obvious which side would
win his internal battle. He had decided its end when he left the
apartment. He had determined what its outcome would be when
he packed the heavy briefcase he carried at his side, its weight
hardly noticeable compared to the gravity of its implications
for Roger, for the Division, and maybe one day, for the country.

The rules were simple. Someone pokes their nose in the
wrong place, starts sharing "improper" ideas, ideas that get
uncomfortably close to that uncomfortable truth that he was
sworn to protect. A red flag goes up at HQ. Recon stakes out
the individual – or the "traitor" as the Division liked to call
such persons, for, according to Division protocol, anyone who

even entertained such ideas, decided years ago to be infinitely dangerous to national security, were considered enemies of the state, regardless of their intentions behind their quest for knowledge – then verifies the extent of the "ideological contamination." Elimination – or the "Cleaners" as they were sometimes colloquially called, as they removed the stain that the traitor made on the nation's integrity – moves in and removes the threat. Extra-Division Affairs, or EDA, then ties up any loose ends to make the whole thing disappear. Of course, if the Cleaner did his job properly, there wouldn't be anything to tie up. And after every one of Roger's missions, there never was. At least, not until today.

***

He had received the mission from one of the Division's special couriers this morning, the message itself encrypted to protect against interception. Short, to the point. The traitor's name, physical description, place of residence, and the like. Personal habits observed by Recon that could be used to help stage the scene. The usual requisite information that would allow Roger to do his job. He had been doing this for six years. For the military in Korea before that. And in the Pacific Theater of the Second World War before that. Death was nothing new to him. It was the same as going to the office for a banker or an executive: it was his job. No thrill of the kill, no sadistic pleasure from taking the life of another human being. Just the cold, stoic orchestration of death, as prescribed by his faceless superiors. Emotion of one kind led to hesitance; of another, sloppiness. The Division could not abide either.

Roger had thought nothing of the target's age. Billy Yates. Age: seven years. Forty-seven inches tall. Fifty-two pounds. A child, obviously, but none of this had struck a chord with the veteran assassin that morning. It was just another job. He'd never had to kill a child before, but he faced it as he would any other job: without emotion, without doubt. If the Division had decided the boy was a threat, then Roger would fulfill his duty without a second thought.

He had arrived outside the boy's school fifteen minutes before the students were due to be released. Sitting on the park bench across the street, an open newspaper in his lap, Roger stared intently at the photograph of the boy. It wasn't easy to get a decent photograph of each target taken and printed quickly enough to avoid increasing the lag time between the Division's initial awareness of the "traitor" and the actual elimination of the target, but, with the meticulous attention to detail and accuracy that they prided themselves on, it usually proved to be well worth the trouble. Roger, like all of the Cleaners within the Division, had been trained extensively in facial recognition, so that from his close study of this one picture, he would be able to pick out little Billy from a crowd of his peers. His knowing the route the boy would be taking home, as well as having a description of the clothes he wore to school this morning, would also be helpful. There was no room for error. There never was.

The boy's face was just a face, like many others he had studied before. Like many others he had seen right before death. A bit rounder, more cherubic, perhaps, but just a face nonetheless. It was just business for Roger. It had to be that way.

The ringing of the school bell jerked his attention from the picture and back to the park bench. He had allowed himself to lose track of the time, the plan having been to study the immediate area and its denizens at least five minutes prior to school being released. Now he had only seconds to survey the area for any potential interference or witnesses before the students began pouring out the front doors.

He subconsciously checked himself, something arising inside that had to be pushed back down. Fear about his need to rush? No, fear wouldn't have made him lose track of the time in the first place. It was something different. Something in the picture. Something far more dangerous than fear.

Roger sighted the boy. Blue jacket, buttoned up and covering the white shirt underneath, blue jeans, brown shoes, his reading primer tucked under his left arm, his right motioning wildly as he chatted with two other boys his age.

Roger cursed himself silently. He hadn't prepared for this possibility, a possibility that he should have treated as a likelihood. Of course the boy would have friends at school. A loner like Roger, a man who dealt in death and had long since left interpersonal relationships behind him – this was an alien world to him.

A world of universal acceptance and peace. Of wonder.

Of innocence.

Roger found the image of the boy's face, the close-up of his ingenuous countenance weaseling its way back into his mind. His well-trained subconscious went through the required motions to repress the subversive thought. He had made the identification. The picture was now superfluous. That face, that haunting face, was no longer any use to him. But, like the effects of subterranean tremors beneath a body of water, the usually placid surface of Roger's mind was no longer without ripples.

Slowly, cautiously, he arose, casually folding the newspaper in his lap and tucking it beneath his arm. Though he was focused on seven-year-old Billy, his senses still took in the rest of the scene: the girl holding her little brother's hand as they crossed the street to the park; the woman, ostensibly their mother, who awaited them on the next park bench, her youngest child sucking at a bottle in her arms; the middle-aged man – the principal, most likely – at the top of the steps to the school, watching the children disperse toward their respective homes; the elderly couple who sat on another bench in the park, the woman intermittently reaching into a brown paper bag to withdraw birdseed which she scattered at her feet; the young boy who clamored back and forth, whooping and laughing as he tormented the pigeons that had gathered for the free meal. Anything and anyone that could prove useful. Or that could potentially compromise the integrity of his mission.

Feeling assured that he was aware of all the variables in his scope, he began to follow the boys, walking across the street, just behind them, maintaining a casual pace while studying the children with his peripheral vision. As they walked, groups of students turned down side streets toward their homes. Most of the children came from poorer families that couldn't get by on just one income, so both parents were at work when the school day ended. Thus, the children walked themselves home. This would have made matters easier for Roger, but there was a caveat: *Billy's* mother was home with the flu. With each step homeward, the window of opportunity was closing. And with each passing second, echoes of that innocent face spawned more and more ripples in the long-stagnant waters of a long-forsaken corner of Roger's mind.

The crowd was thinning. The boys were alone now, a pair of older girls walking a few paces behind. One of the girls motioned in Roger's direction. Whispered something to the other girl. They giggled. He forced himself not to wince.

The cardinal rule: don't draw attention to yourself. He didn't exist. He couldn't. Standing out, being seen, being *remembered*: that was unacceptable for a Division agent. How had he been so careless as to draw their attention? What had he done that made the girls, children caught in their own little world, notice him? Everything was going awry when nothing could afford to.

The girls glanced in his direction again. He started to quicken his pace when a stooped-over hobo shambled past him, a tin can in his hand. He was waving the can around in the air, seemingly to attract attention by the clinking of the coins within, but no sound was heard. The can was empty. Thus, the hobo's relatively silent approach that Roger hadn't noticed. Thus, the girls' laughter, confirmed by the outstretched finger of one of the girls, pointing at the hobo who now ambled several paces ahead of Roger. Roger breathed a sigh of relief. He hadn't been sloppy. At least, not yet. He had to get his act together though, he told himself, or mistakes would be made. And he never made a mistake.

Billy and one of his friends reached a crosswalk, a line of taxis and town cars stopped at the intersection. They waved farewell to the other boy as he continued down the street toward his house. The girls turned the corner and headed in the opposite direction from Billy's house. And then there were two.

A policeman directing traffic blew a piercing whistle and thrust his palm out to stop the line of vehicles, beckoning to the boys at the corner with his other hand. As the boys crossed behind the policeman, Roger was sure the officer had glanced in his direction. *Why shouldn't he?* Roger tried to assure himself. A man didn't have to look suspicious for someone, officer of the law or not, to glance at him. Roger decided not to slow his pace, though. He had to turn the corner before the boys got there, to continue on the path that he knew Billy would take home. To loiter in view of the police officer, waiting until the boys had passed and then following them – that was just asking for trouble. He knew Billy's route, and walking in front of the boy instead of behind, that just seemed a better way to avoid suspicion. Especially now that it seemed he had no choice. Given, he wouldn't have a clear line of sight on the target while he walked in front, but his other senses, especially his hearing, would make up the difference. Besides, tricks of the trade he'd learned, like using reflections in storefront windows to get glimpses of the boy, would help fill in the gaps.

Turning the corner, he heard the voices of the boys coming up behind him. He couldn't tell which was Billy's, but he knew that for one of the voices, it would be the last conversation it was ever a party to.

The boys were yammering on about God-knows-what. Something from one of their lessons, it sounded like. "Hey guess what?" changed the subject. Now they were talking about... something about – *oh God, no*. Roger almost stopped dead in his tracks, his right leg stiffening with fear before he forced it to continue its downward motion into the next step. The boys were talking about the Operation. Not knowledgeably, of course, but they were poking in the right – or as it were, wrong – direction nonetheless. How in the world had *children* run across this seed of thought? If *they* had discovered something, what hope did the Division have of preventing the mass populace, distracted though they were with the Communist paranoia that still gripped the nation, from probing around and uncovering the truth? Roger's mind became a freight train of thoughts, both unbearably heavy and unrelentingly fast: Was this a test? He knew the Director and he had had some clashes in the past few months, but could this have been some sort of plant or something? Surely children couldn't have found this out on their own. Surely such a child couldn't pose any threat to national security. And yet he could hear the boys' voices floating down the street to him, uttering the very ideas that had proven the death sentence for many a citizen before them. Personal vendetta or not, neither the Director nor any member of the Division would ever risk giving information about the Operation to any member of the public. And this boy, this Billy Yates, aged seven years, forty-seven inches tall, fifty-two pounds, brown hair, brown eyes – this *traitor* was already starting to propagate his subversive truths. With one final burst of politically righteous indignation, Roger's subconscious pushed the image of the seraphic face – and its accompanying ripples – deep beneath the surface. The boy must die. And now, through his prying senses and loose lips, he had condemned his friend as well.

Roger pumped his right hand, trying to quell the tension and anger that had been sparked inside him. Technically, he wasn't supposed to eliminate targets other than the ones specifically approved and assigned to him by the Director, but this was different. If Billy had proven anything in these sixty seconds Roger had walked in front of him, it was that children couldn't be trusted to keep a secret. Especially a secret of this magnitude. Roger had to seal off the breach and eliminate the threat before it spread. Now.

Then Roger heard Billy's voice carry up words that were music to his ears: "Do you want to come over to play?" Moments earlier, this sentiment would have troubled him, bringing that accursed young face back to the forefront of his mind and adding the problem of getting the boys separated so he could eliminate the target without creating a witness in the process. Now, though, it removed the problem of having to eliminate the boys before they separated, which, considering that he had no idea who the other boy was or where he lived, was a huge boon to his mission. And he realized that the alley Billy was wont to take as a shortcut home, despite his mother's protestations, was just half-a-block ahead. "Come on, I'll show you a shortcut to my house," came from behind Roger, followed by an excited acceptance of the offer. Roger quickened his pace as subtly as he could. The alley was usually empty. The few windows that looked down into it were mostly shuttered and vacant. The perfect place for the kill. Both of them.

He turned into the alley about ten adult paces ahead of the boys. Quickly surveyed the area. Empty. Abandoned. A nook in one of the walls would prove a good spot for completing the ghastly deed, a large waste bin for industrial refuse, the perfect dumping spot for the bodies. No bodies, no crime. No crime, no investigation. Just the way the Division wanted it.

He heard the boys' voices approaching as he tucked himself into the nook, obscuring his body from view. Even as the boys moved down the alley toward him, they paid him no attention, enrapt in their own little conversation. Which was still about the Operation. Roger's mind began to reel. How many pedestrians had he passed since leading the boys down the sidewalk? How many ears had now heard the dangerous information these *traitors* were spouting? The founts of unthinkable thoughts, small though they were, had to be shut off.

The boys walked past the waste bin, and as they reached the nook, their conversation was cut short as two strong hands reached out from the shadows, gripping their necks and lifting them into the air. Roger shoved the boys against the brick wall of the nook, his eyes burning with rage at the impetuousness of these foolish boys. These vile *traitors*. And all the while, his grip grew tighter as the boys' struggles grew meeker. No more secrets would fall from their lips; no more treachery would their tongues weave.

And then he made his mistake: he locked eyes with Billy. That damned cherubic face came rushing up from the bowels of his mind, that face of innocence and wonder, of love and trust, of everything that had been so foreign to Roger for far too long. The face of the boy he was now throttling the very life from, twisted and purple in oxygen-deprived agony as it was. Those eyes, so happy and carefree in the photograph, locked with Roger's and spoke to a part of him deep within his being, the part of him that the Division hadn't been able to touch: the human part. Those eyes asked him but one word: why? Not accusingly, not in anger or fear, but with a solemn innocence, a quiet sadness that shook Roger to his very core. Then Billy's eyes rolled back in his head, and his throat stopped convulsing, gasping for oxygen that wouldn't come. The target, Billy Yates, age seven, forty-seven inches tall, fifty-two pounds, brown hair, brown eyes, bloodshot eyes, sad eyes, innocent eyes, dead eyes, was eliminated.

Mission accomplished.

Roger didn't remember dropping Billy's lifeless body to the pavement below. He didn't remember not disposing of the body as he had always been so meticulous in doing. He didn't remember leaving behind an eight-year-old witness, coughing and gasping for air, but very much alive, at the scene. All he remembered was running blindly from the alley, chased by a spectral pair of pleading brown eyes.

***

Roger turned east and began ascending the pedestrian section of the Brooklyn Bridge. An American icon, its strong steel cables and massive stone arches standing as a monument of a bygone era. A beacon of ingenuity and bravado, of innovation and work ethic. Everything like the America that stood up to Hitler, to Stalin, to despots and injustice worldwide, the great bastion of freedom she publicly considered herself to be. And nothing like the America he knew. At least, not anymore.

His footfalls echoed in the cold, dry air. It was quiet, but then, at this hour of the night, it should be. His breath came in short bursts, visible as puffs of smoke in the icy air. A haunting pair of sad brown eyes appeared in the mist and stared longingly at the breaths. Trudging onward, he tried to put it out of his mind. But failed.

Billy Yates was dead. The Division would ensure that his nameless friend would meet a similar fate, fixing Roger's mistake, his breach of conscience. They were perfect at what they did, if not as individuals, then as a unit, killing off any whispers of the truth behind the Operation. Billy and his friend had known enough of the truth to make them a liability. Never mind their age. Never mind their innocence. They had to die. And die Billy had. And die his friend would. But the face of Billy as he'd choked his last, the eyes that had locked with Roger's, opened the floodgates of the agent's mind, releasing an onslaught of the faces of the nameless dead, the Division's *traitors*, Roger's *victims*.

Officially, Roger's mistake had been leaving evidence, not disposing of the body, not killing the friend. The more faces rushed back into his memory, though, the more he began to wonder exactly what – and when – his biggest mistake really was.

Upon reaching the center of the bridge, the point with the greatest distance between the bridge above and the river below, he stopped and surveyed the area. A series of iron girders extended across the space between the central pedestrian bridge and the sides of the bridge itself. One of these led to a platform that jutted over the river. The intersection of two crossbeams in the vicinity completed the package.

The perfect spot.

Roger swung his body over the rail and onto the girder leading to the platform. He grabbed the briefcase and lugged it over the rail as well, careful not to let its weight throw off his balance and send him tumbling to the automobile section of the bridge some twenty feet below. He went through the motions emotionlessly, thoughtlessly. He was in mission mode, just as he always was before he made a kill.

He clambered across the girder and onto the platform, setting the briefcase down as soon as he got to its relative safety. From the briefcase he withdrew a length of steel cable, a loop at each end. Each loop was held by an apparatus bolted to each end that allowed the loop to loosen or tighten when the catch was released, but only to tighten when it was locked. He tied one loop around one of the supports of the bridge, threading the cable through the hole and pulling the knot tight, the catch set to secure the binding. The other loop he placed around his neck.

He hefted the cable in his hands. Heavy. Thirty-two feet of cable. Thirty-two. A symbolically fitting message, he felt. Thirty-two was where it began. Thirty-two was where it would end.

His suit jacket flapped in the brisk wind, his perfectly shined black shoes catching the light of the full moon above, that watchful orb that condemned him even now, as he stood on his self-prescribed gallows. He stared downriver, the lights of the Lower Manhattan harbors twinkling in the distance, the black expanse of the bay opening up beyond. And beneath him, the icy waters of the East River glimmered in the moonlight, beckoning him downward, calling him toward a descent that he would only be able to make partway. The cable would hold him back from completing the journey into oblivion, just as some uncrushed fragment of his humanity, lying dormant for so many years, numbed into nothingness by training and necessity, had prevented him from continuing his descent into depravity in the name of duty and patriotism. The icy wind bit at the exposed skin on his face, his hands, his steel-encircled neck, the flesh growing numb with the pain that Roger's occupied mind was already dead to.

The loop around Roger's neck was not a proper noose. A proper noose would have snapped Roger's neck the moment it drew tight: a merciful death. And Roger had decided that the monster he had become deserved no mercy. But although his noose would normally lend itself to a slow death by strangulation, in all likelihood, the speed his body would reach by the end of a thirty-foot free fall would more than provide the required force to break his neck. But the cable's thirty-two feet had more than just a symbolic purpose: that length would also ensure maximum visibility of his body from the city and from the river. Much shorter, and the underside of the bridge would obscure his body from many vantage points. Much longer, and the force of the noose stopping his free fall might decapitate him, his head and body plummeting to the inky depths below, being swept out to sea instead of remaining suspended from the East Coast's most famous bridge. A ghost dangling from an icon by a symbol. The importance of which most people would never fully grasp. But hopefully someone would. Someday.

A memory came to him as he stood on the precipice, ready to take the final plunge. As a boy, he had attended a Baptist church every Sunday with his family. He remembered Mrs. Booth, the bespectacled, grandmotherly Sunday school teacher who had taught the children about a "new life" in Jesus; a "second birth," as Christ Himself had put it. The irony was overwhelming. For Roger was not looking at a second birth, but a second death: the killing of a man already six years dead, buried in an unmarked grave in a country seven-thousand miles away. Maybe this would send ripples through someone's pond. Maybe this would rattle some cages.

That was part of the beauty of the whole operation: they didn't exist. Not as individuals, not as an organization. They were naught but shadows glimpsed from the corner of one's eye, ghosts that existed solely in dreamscapes. Dead men begetting more dead men.

Someday, the truth would come out, but not today. Not with the Cold War, as some were starting to call the tensions between the United States and the Soviet Union, escalating as it was. Just days earlier, the Soviets had launched a man-made satellite into space, broadcasting its ominous beeping as it traced a terrifying line across the night sky. No, the secret he guarded could not be revealed in this day. But by the same token, it would no longer be guarded by his hand.

His story, his secret, a secret that even his superiors would kill for, was in a safe place, even if its caretaker was unaware of its importance and potential implications for the nation, for the world. All of his loose ends in this life were tied up. All of them save one.

Roger gripped the cable in his hands, drawing the noose tight around his neck like a businessman tying his tie in the morning before going off to work. He was already dead, he told himself. He was just finishing what the Division had already done to him. What he had done to so many others in the name of freedom.

He took a deep breath, raised his eyes skyward in a last-minute plea for redemption, and, gripping the cable around his neck with both hands, stepped from the girder into nothingness. Three seconds and thirty-two feet later, the cord drew tight around his neck, lacerating the skin and muscle but leaving the head attached to its body. The eyes rolled back as the head lolled forward. A left shoe plummeting to the dark waters below, the body danced its brief fandango, a lifeless marionette held aloft by one fatal string.

On display for the city to see, a man six years dead was just growing cold. The Division had claimed its latest victim. One of its own.

<u>Part One – Ashes to Ashes</u>

The broad mass of a nation will more easily fall victim to a big lie than to a small one.
~ Adolf Hitler

Repetition does not transform a lie into the truth.
~ Franklin Delano Roosevelt

Chapter 1

Near Fallujah, Iraq

August 2010

Squinting into the late-morning sun, Sergeant Wayne Wilkins was doing his best to maintain his composure. The driver of the Humvee, Sergeant Price, was flying down the artillery-pocked road at a ridiculous speed, adeptly maneuvering the vehicle around potholes and debris as though he were playing a video game. But this was a real war zone, and there were no extra lives, no second chances here. And yet, despite all that, and despite the sweltering heat that had already claimed the day, the atmosphere in the vehicle was, for the most part, jovial.

"We're goin' home, baby!" Corporal Sedaris, a scruffy – at least by military standards – young soldier crooned from the front passenger seat. He had fashioned himself as somewhat of a bad boy, his longer-than-regulation hair and permanent three-days-growth beard mirroring his jocular and sometimes rebellious personality. It was his AC/DC mix CD that was playing on the boom box he'd brought along. He took a swig of illegal Iraqi moonshine from his non-regulation flask to celebrate.

"Dude, you're gonna be out of the country in just a few hours and you can't even wait that long to drink?" came the voice of Private Jenkins from behind him. The baby of the group at only twenty-two years of age, Jenkins's congenial and caring nature had long endeared him to Wayne. Raised by his grandmother on the streets of downtown Detroit, Jenkins had found God at an early age, and, under the guiding hand of a church deacon with a heart for impoverished youths, he had grown into a man full of compassion, rather than of the drugs and desperation that filled many of his peers. In the bunks at night, Wayne would often see him reading his Bible or praying for his family back home, for his brothers-in-arms, for his country, and even for the souls of those who had died that day – allies, insurgents, and bystanders alike.

"You sure you don't want some, bro?" Sedaris offered, dangling the flask just out of arm's reach for Jenkins.

"Dude, leave him alone. And you'd better not have any of that on your breath when we get to the airstrip or I'm disowning your ass," Price said. Price was the senior solider in the car, but even after fifteen years of service and eight tours of duty, his face still retained the boyish charm that had made him a hit with the ladies back in high school. A leader by example, Price had won Wayne's admiration and respect within days of their first meeting. Price, Jenkins, and even good old Sedaris definitely deserved this vacation. Their tours were up, and, just a few klicks down the road, an airfield waited to fly them to Kuwait, then to Dubai, and finally back to the U.S. of A. via Atlanta. If only things were that simple.

"Eh, whatever," Sedaris said. "We're almost home free." He took another swig, audibly relishing it for emphasis. "Mmm, mmm, mmm. Dee-lish."

Price bounced the right side of the vehicle through a pothole, jarring Sedaris and Jenkins in their seats.

"Sorry 'bout that, Jenkins," Price said with a mischievous smile, glancing at Sedaris in his peripheral vision.

All but oblivious to the goings on around him, Wayne stared out the windshield, the rocks and road rolling by too fast, too fast. The faster they traveled, the sooner they arrived, and the closer they got to that moment, the more Wayne felt his resolve slipping away.

"Hey Wilkins, what's eating you?"

The words barely registered, and he hadn't the slightest idea who had said them. Wayne continued to look at the road ahead with distant eyes, his mind too wracked with guilt and doubt, with sorrow and confusion, for any one emotion to emerge dominant and betray itself in his countenance.

"You carsick, dude?" Jenkins asked.

Wayne thought a moment. "Yeah," he said, only half-glancing at his compatriot, his friend. "Carsick."

Price moved his foot from the accelerator to the brake, lifting his eyes to the reflection of Wayne in his rearview. "Sorry about the driving, Wilkins. You know, just excited and all."

Wayne met his eyes in the mirror. "It's alright," he mumbled. His eyes drifted back to the road, the worst place for his eyes to be, carsick or not, but he just couldn't keep from staring. The road being eaten up, the miles ticking away, the time vanishing before his eyes. The twisted shell of an old roadside car bomb – a blackened and rust-ravaged corpse that had claimed human lives, an automotive suicide bomber – lay to one side of the road. The road surface nearby was buckled and broken. The gray and yellow, the sand and dirt, the desolation of the desert and the horrors of war stretched out as an endless canvas around him. He wanted to scream. He wanted to shout for Price to stop, to turn around. To tell them the truth, to tell them that he couldn't go through with it, that he needed to get out *now*. But it was too late for that. Powerful machinery was already turning, and he had passed the point of no return long ago.

It was too late.

"Aw, what the hell…" Price groaned from up front. A trio of Humvees – two of which were parked across the road – and four human figures appeared on the horizon. The markings indicated they were American vehicles, so they didn't have to worry about insurgents, at least, but it was still a momentary hitch. He motioned for Sedaris to kill the music, the scruffy Corporal complying with a scowl.

"They'd better not be trying to rope us in for more time," Sedaris said through his teeth. "I've got a flight to Vegas to catch."

"They wouldn't do that, would they?" Jenkins asked, his voice slightly less confident than he'd intended. "Grab us right as we're going on leave?"

"Sure they would, kid," Sedaris said. "Screw you over every chance they get."

"Sedaris, cool it, already," Price said. "It's probably just a routine checkpoint. The airfield's just a few klicks away. All they need is for some terrorists to get in there with a truck full of explosives and blow up the whole damn field."

"Whatever," Sedaris muttered, slumping down in his seat.

From the back seat, Wayne watched as the roadblock grew closer and closer, the vehicle decelerating as the men standing sentinel came into focus. Three of them brandished M16s – one on each side of the road, and one in the middle, in front of the roadblock – their expressions blank despite the beads of sweat that trickled down their faces. The fourth man, older and with more decorations on his uniform, approached Price's window with a clipboard in hand.

"Morning, soldier," came the booming voice of the man outside, the insignia on his uniform marking him as a Colonel. "Brown" read the fatigue's name tape. His face was red with sunburn, his hair graying at the temples. Yet, despite the man getting on in years, the way he held himself, the way he spoke, positively exuded power and confidence. If the three men standing at attention in the blistering heat were any indication, his leadership skills were impressive.

"Morning, Colonel," Price said. Brown offered a tight-lipped smile in response, then pulled out a folded sheet of paper. In the rearview mirror, Wayne saw Price's features tighten. *More orders*, Price must've been thinking. Sedaris scowled, keeping his eyes on the floorboards.

"I'm looking for a Sergeant Wayne Wilkins?" Six eyes turned toward Wayne, followed by the pair belonging to Colonel Brown. Wayne slowly turned his face to the Colonel, wishing he were somewhere, anywhere else but here.

"I'm Wilkins."

"Glad we got you before you left the country. We got word that you'd be leaving by this route, so we had to close it off. Sorry about the trouble. I've got orders here for a special debriefing for you. You need to come with me."

Wayne stared mournfully at his comrades, his motions trancelike, the look in his eyes even more distant than usual. He swallowed and slowly opened his door and climbed out of the vehicle, his feet sinking in the loose sand.

"You should be on the next plane out of here, Wilkins," the Colonel added. "Just a few loose ends to tie up."

Another soldier exited from the back of one of the Humvees and walked briskly toward Colonel Brown.

"Ah, I'd almost forgotten." The Colonel motioned toward the approaching soldier. "This is Private Jameson. He has an emergency meeting at the airfield in about thirty minutes. Now that we've found Sergeant Wilkins, our team will be heading to the debriefing, in the direction you boys've just come from. And since you've got another seat open now, I need you to take Jameson to the airfield." Price nodded in tacit consent. Sedaris remained silent, face forward, a guilty half-smile playing at the corners of his mouth. Jenkins looked at Wayne with genuine concern in his eyes. Wayne saw all of them but could not meet any of their eyes. Not anymore.

For a brief moment, as the Private moved to enter the Humvee, Jameson and Wayne stood next to each other. Jameson was about Wayne's height. About his build. In fact, their bone structures were almost *identical*. But everyone in the vehicle, now including Jameson, seemed to have his thoughts occupied with what had just happened and failed to notice the similarity.

The similarity did not escape Wayne.

"Look us up when you get back, man," Price offered out the window. "We'll have to get a few beers together. Maybe catch a few Broncos games."

"I'll save you a spot at my table in Vegas, dude. Have a few cocktails… maybe a few cocktail waitresses," Sedaris added with a coarse laugh, leaning toward Price's open window.

"Take care of yourself, brother," Jenkins said, looking solemnly at Wayne. Of all his compatriots, Wayne wanted to meet Jenkins' eyes, to tell him everything, but he just couldn't. He had crossed and burned his bridges. There was no going back.

One of the men with assault rifles raised his two-way radio to his lips, spoke into the receiver, and dropped it to his side again. The drivers of the two parked Humvees moved their vehicles to the side of the road, clearing the soldiers' path to the airport. And with one final glance out the window at Wayne, standing alongside the Colonel, Price gunned the engine, Sedaris cranked the stereo, and the Humvee zoomed down the road, whoops of elation mixing with the strains of AC/DC, fading as they sped off into the distance.

Wayne kept his eyes trained on the vehicle as it entered a small valley between the rising hills on either side. Suddenly, from positions hidden amongst the war-torn landscape, four plumes of smoke converged from all angles upon the vehicle, followed by four deafening explosions, all traces of '80s metal dying away and being replaced with the screams of his former comrades, nearly drowned out by the concussions but echoing in Wayne's ears nonetheless.

"Again," came the voice at his side, a two-way raised to the Colonel's lips.

Four more plumes. Four more explosions. No more screams.

Wayne wanted to look away, but he knew he couldn't. He had seen some truly horrible things in his time in the military. Two tours in Afghanistan, two in Iraq, all of them in some of the thickest fighting the campaigns had to offer. He had seen enemy combatants die in explosions he had been responsible for. He had seen his fellow soldiers die before his eyes, gunned down, blown to pieces, burned alive. But never before had he been responsible for the deaths of his brothers-in-arms. And certainly never like this.

Images of the men came flooding back to him: Price's calm leadership-by-example, his pictures of his twin five-year-old boys and their mother on vacation at the beach and waving to Daddy; Sedaris's gruff but generally good-natured attitude, his ambition to some day – when he finally got out of the military – write for Saturday Night Live; Jenkins's green innocence, his compassion that he bestowed upon all of his comrades, the prayers he said for the souls of those they'd had to kill in the name of freedom; and…

"Who was he?"

The Colonel looked at Wayne, wiping a grin off his face just a split-second too late for Wayne not to notice.

"Who?"

"Jameson," Wayne said, trying to remain calm despite the cacophony of emotions that was playing ever louder in his mind, in his chest. "Or whatever his name really was."

"Just a loyal soldier who was willing to die for his country." The Colonel clapped his hand on Wayne's shoulder and looked into his eyes in a not entirely successful attempt at reassurance. "As were they all."

Wayne turned his gaze from the Colonel, back to the burning wreckage of the vehicle that had been his compatriots' execution chamber. Despite the heat of the desert sun, growing warmer by the minute, and the raging heat of the flames that engulfed the Humvee, the look in Wayne's eyes, if anything, grew colder.

"Well, it's official," the Colonel said, squinting at his watch, then extending his hand to Wayne. "Wayne Wilkins is dead."

Reluctantly, Wayne took the hand of the imposing personality before him, struggling to keep his stoic resolve in place.

"Agent Wilkins," the Colonel said, looking firmly at Wayne as he shook his hand, "welcome to the Division."

Chapter 2

Blue Mountains National Park, Australia

March 2011

Friday

Michael's phone call was late.

Jonathan Rickner sat on the dusty ridge, gazing out at the thunderheads rolling across the valley, drenching the rocky landscape of orange and green in darkness, threatening rain that seemed reluctant to come. The previously picturesque view of the Australian wilderness had been transformed – the brightness of day seized by premature night, twisted into a dreamscape of encroaching darkness and shifting shadows.

Fitting, Jon thought. Still, his elder brother surely had good reason to be late. This evening – *Thursday* evening in Washington, across the International Date Line – was a big moment in Michael's life, and he couldn't be expected to put everything on hold just to make a phone call.

Yet here Jon was, waiting, sitting on the outcropping of rock he'd chosen for three reasons. First, it afforded a magnificent view of the valley. Second, it was one of the few areas within close proximity to his campsite that his cell phone got a signal. Despite the phone's international SIM card, the reception out here was far spottier than it was back at Oxford. But then, that was to be expected, especially as it aligned with reason number three – the main reason – he'd chosen this spot to wait for Michael's call: it was isolated. Jon could be alone with his thoughts, the vista of light and shadow, and his non-ringing phone.

He scratched absentmindedly the three-days' growth on his jaw – when camping with the boys, beard-growing was kind of par for the course. His eyes, normally a deep sapphire blue but prone to change colors depending on his mood, were currently on the gray side of the spectrum. He didn't know if he was ready for this. No, strike that – he simply *wasn't* ready. Michael was his brother, his best friend, his... He couldn't really put the connection they shared into words. Twenty-four years of life together, traveling around the world together with their archeologist parents, exploring, sharing, learning, dreaming together. Despite their differences, despite Jon's desire in recent years to get out from under his older brother's impressive shadow, theirs was an uncommon bond, a bond that had grown in depth and breadth for all of their lives.

Until now.

Jon didn't have a problem with Mara. Quite to the contrary, he liked her very much. She and Michael made a good match. He, like Jon, had a brilliant mind and was intensely curious about... everything, but he was prone to monomania, especially when it came to whatever historical or archaeological mystery had seized his attention at the time. Mara adored his genius and patiently helped him to keep the rest of his life on track while his primary focus was elsewhere. She was also very bright, and, though their fields of interest differed, they challenged and spurred one another on to bigger and better things.

The truth was, they made a great couple. And that made it even harder for Jon.

He took a deep breath. Blew it out in a sigh. He raised his eyes heavenward, but no answers presented themselves. Angry black storm clouds rumbled across the sky, turning day into night and blotting out the sun like a fire blanket. In a few hours, the sun would be setting on Friday here; the first appearance of

Friday's sun for Michael in Washington would still be hours behind that. Was there a metaphor there? Perhaps. An answer? No.

All Jon's life, Michael Rickner had been his rock, his best friend, and so much more. And vice versa.

The one constant in his life was about to do the unthinkable. Change.

What happens when your anchor abandons your ship? he mused. *At best, you drift at sea, never attaining that stability of being able to stay where you want again. At worst, you drift into a jetty and sink.*

He didn't hear the phone until a few seconds into the ringtone. He knew who it was without even looking at the screen. Deep breath. He answered with a grunt.

"Sorry, bro." Michael's words came quickly, betraying his excitement. "Did I wake you up?"

"No, no." Remain nonchalant. Don't sound needy. Nobody wants that.

"So, you want the long version or the short?"

"Both." Neither.

"Short version: she said yes!"

"Of course she did, bud. No surprise about that." None whatsoever.

Michael proceeded to tell Jon the long version – the beautiful, Hollywood-perfect engagement story where everything magically went right. Jon half-expected a downtown chorus line or random fireworks exploding overhead to come into the story at some point. He clenched his jaw as he listened, joy and betrayal, excitement and loneliness, clashing in his brain.

A rustling in the brush to his right caused Jon to turn around. A familiar form came into sight. Crap. Sam had found him. Had to finish this call off soon.

"I'm really happy for you, Michael." Lie. Well, half-lie.

"Thanks. You okay? You sound–"

"Tired." Nip it. "Just tired."

"Sorry. Hey, I wanted to tell you, too, my dissertation is really taking off."

Jon sat up. Sam was no longer an issue. "How so?"

"Hot lead. Hot *topic*."

"What did you end up changing your topic to?"

"You still coming out next month? I'll tell you all about the research then."

"Of course I'm coming. Why's it gotta wait until then, though?"

A tense silence on the other end. "Jon, I… I think I've stumbled onto something big. When I say 'hot topic,' I mean 'earth-shattering.' 'History-rewriting.' 'Instant career-making.'"

"And you're afraid that rival historians around the world are listening in even now with their sophisticated cell network monitoring systems that just about everybody in academia has these days?"

"Not academia, Jon. Bigger than that."

Jon scoffed, half-smiling. "Oh geez. You're a big dork, you know that?"

Silence.

Jon swallowed. "Wait, you're being serious?"

"When you come out here, Jon. All will be divulged. Of this you have my word."

"Alright, Mr. Dramatic, I'll hold you to that. And it had better live up to what you're hyping it up to be."

"It will, Jon. And so much more."

Jon raised his eyebrows. The wonder child had done it again. He stymied his jealousy for the time being, instead choosing to focus on the excitement of discovery that seemed to be rekindled. An excitement that the two brothers had shared many times over the years. Maybe the good old days weren't quite gone after all.

Michael cited the lateness of the hour, and they said their goodbyes. Jon held the disconnected phone in his lap as he stared at the landscape again. A flash of cloud-to-cloud lightning in the distance provided some illumination to the landscape of shadow. *Light in the midst of the dark,* Jon mused.

"No matter how bad things get," he said aloud.

"They can always get worse?" came the voice at his side.

Jon started, turning his head toward the figure that was looking down at him with a curious expression. "Geez, Sam. You scared the crap out of me."

"Sorry." Sam dropped to one knee next to Jon. "So Michael and Mara?"

"Yeah. Engaged."

"Cool. They're good for each other."

Jon bit his lip. It was true. But all he could muster in agreement was a terse little grunt.

"Oh, boy," Sam huffed good-naturedly. "What's going on? Jealous?"

Jon grimaced at the valley before him. "Yeah, maybe."

"Look, Paul and I found some real cuties a couple of campsites over. Sorority sisters or something. Let's go meet–"

"It's not that, Sam."

"'Not that'?" Sam cleared his throat. "Geez, you ain't goin' gay on us, are you, bro?"

Jon finally turned to face his friend, a steely glint in his eyes. "*No,* Sam. It's Michael. I'm..." The glint faded as his eyes drifted toward the ground. "I guess I'm jealous of Mara. Maybe a little afraid of losing my big brother."

Sam raised his eyebrows, and breathed in through barely parted lips. "Oh."

Jon nodded his head slightly, grimacing at the dirt. "Oh."

Neither of them spoke for a long moment. In the distance, Jon could see the clouds begin to let loose their cargo, sheets of much-needed rain falling to nourish the parched earth. Change,

Jon reflected, was an integral part of nature, of life. If there were no rainy days, there would be no plant life; no plant life, no animal life. And so on. Death and rebirth, sun and rain, the inevitable cycles that kept the world alive and beautiful. But then, like flash floods and hurricanes, not *all* change was good.

"Paul's grilling some burgers. That's why I came to find you. We invited the sorority girls over. Four of them, three of us. Good odds, good food, good times, you know?"

"I'll be there in a minute. Thanks."

Sam stood, dusted off his knee, and clapped Jon on the shoulder with a meaty hand. "Take your time, man. And don't worry too much, okay. Michael's still Michael. No matter what happens, he's still gonna be your brother, you know?"

Jon looked up at Sam with a weak attempt at a smile. "Yeah. I know. Thanks."

Sam made his way back through the woods, leaving Jon alone on the ridge. With his thoughts, his now-silent cell phone, and his view of the gathering storm. The lightning was growing nearer, but the gray curtains of rain remained at a distance, a dreary backdrop to the scene. Lightning flashes would fill the valley intermittently, but, Jon could see, the contours of the terrain shielded pockets of ground from direct lighting altogether. Places where neither the bright of day nor the flash of a thunderhead could ever penetrate the darkness. Places where sunny days and happily-ever-afters didn't exist.

But perhaps Sam was right. Of course Michael was still going to be Michael. People didn't just change who they were because they got hitched. Well, maybe some people did, but surely not Michael.

Not Michael.

Chapter 3

Washington, D.C.

Michael Rickner awoke with a start. Eyes wide open, seeing nothing but darkness. Ears straining for unknown sounds that would not betray themselves. He sat bolt upright, the bed-springs creaking beneath him, and he turned his head from side to side as he took in the scene, trying to orient himself.

He was still in his bedroom, in his bed, under the covers. Ambient light from street lamps toward the front of his apartment building spilled through the window blinds and into the room – a dim, soft light, slatted with the blinds' shadow, giving the room an ethereal, ghostly glow. He held his breath as he listened for whatever sound might have pulled him so abruptly from his slumber. A dog, probably a Chihuahua or another small breed, yipped in the distance. The slow, steady drip of the toilet filling, a sound that Michael had become so accustomed to that he automatically tuned it out – except for now, when he was endeavoring to hear any and every sound, no matter how small or ordinary. A police siren – no, make that two sirens – wailed in some nearby part of the city, just reaching his ears. And… nothing else. Yip, drip, wail, and nothing else but silence. All mundane, far too ordinary to disturb his sleep. But something had.

What had he been dreaming before he had awoken? A nightmare or some particularly exciting dream that had been the impetus for his sudden awakening? Perhaps it was merely something in the dream world that had disturbed his slumber?

No, he would have remembered that dream, or the last part of it at least, upon returning to his conscious mind. But he remembered nothing of his dreams tonight.

He yawned, an open-jawed eye-scruncher of a yawn. He *had* to get some more sleep. Tomorrow – or rather, today – could be the pivotal moment in his dissertation research, and indeed in his entire academic career. A day that so much hinged upon was not one to go into sleep-deprived. He would be pushing it as it was, but every minute of rest counted tonight.

He reached over to his nightstand and fumbled for his phone, his eyes still trying hard to focus. Laying hands upon it, he pressed a button to bring up the backlighting. *1:47.* He'd only been asleep two hours? It felt like it had been much longer, probably because he was so fatigued from the stress and excitement of the day before, full of thoughts and emotions that his mind needed to convert into long-term memory. He definitely wanted the previous day's events – his engagement to the love of his life – filed permanently in his long-term memory: an afternoon never to be forgotten.

As he set the phone back on the nightstand, its light still providing additional illumination, every muscle in Michael's body suddenly tensed. He could not explain why, for no audio, visual, or other sensory stimulus seemed to have caused it.

His mind immediately flashed back to a moonless night, years ago, in the bush country of Mali. He and Jon were sleeping in one tent, their father and mother in another. Both Jon and Michael had awoken at the same moment. A preternatural tingle of fear, inexplicable at the time or afterward had yanked them from their sleep and permeated both of their bodies. They had sat up and looked at one another, the darkness obscuring their faces but able to see each other, nonetheless. They listened, hearing nothing but the natural sounds of night: wind whispering through the tall grass, jackals snarling at the edges of their territory, owls hooting and calling as they hunted their nocturnal prey. Nothing out of the ordinary, but the two brothers felt strangely convinced that *something* was out there, *something* had awoken them, even if not by normal sensory means. And, upon scrambling from their tents, carbines in hand, they had found their intuition to be correct – within five minutes' time a small war party of tribal natives had descended on their camp, and only their rifle fire, quickly joined by that of their now-awake parents, had driven the tribesmen away in search of easier prey.

What he sensed that night in Mali was death approaching. He hadn't felt that way before or since – until now. And that frightened him tremendously.

Finally he heard something. A creak coming from the living room. It could have been the building settling, water in the pipes, a noise from a different apartment, a figment of his imagination, or any number of a hundred other things, but Michael knew better. He looked around his room, eyes darting from place to place in search of something, anything, to use as a weapon. *Of course*, he thought as his eyes settled on his choice.

It would be a shame to damage the seventeenth-century rapier, the heirloom once wielded by one of his ancestors, the Earl of Arundel, but that was the purpose for which it had been crafted. It had been over two hundred years since it had last been used in a fight, but it had served his forebear well, and he prayed it would do the same for him. Actually, as long as he was praying, he wished that whatever agent of death seemed to be approaching would just disappear without the need for an altercation. But, he knew, there was little hope of that happening.

He slipped from his covers as quietly as he could, and padded barefoot on the threadbare carpet to the sword's case atop a small bookshelf near his closet door. He unfastened the clasp as quietly as he could, and opened the glass lid. As he hefted it in his hand, he realized how very different fighting would be with this sword – weighted and forged to kill back in the 1600s – compared to the fencing foils he and Jon had learned and practiced with as youths. But then, whoever his unknown assailant might be, his unseen bringer of death, it was unlikely that he would also be coming at him with a sword. A fencing match this would not be. A visceral, high-adrenaline, one-hit-wins brawl seemed more likely to transpire.

Michael crouched behind his still-closed bedroom door and waited. And waited. Not daring to turn on a light to check his watch, and not wanting to give up his position to go check his cell phone clock – which also would have entailed turning on another light – he had no idea how much time had passed since he had first grabbed the sword and begun waiting by the door. Had it been one minute or twenty? Had he just imagined the whole thing? The creak could have been any number of things, and his inscrutable sense of death approaching… could that have simply been the product of an overtaxed mind? Yesterday was a big day in his life, and today stood to possibly become equally big. Could all that have been the cause of his strange feelings tonight? He hadn't heard anything else since that solitary creak, and the muscles in his legs were growing sore, his feet going numb from crouching.

He stood up, still slowly, and exhaled deeply but quietly. He waited for another minute or three, gripping the sword loosely by his side. Nothing.

How much *more* sleep had he now lost because of his overactive imagination? Sleep he truly could not afford to lose. After he got back from New York, he would have to take a personal day of sleeping until noon, relaxing and unwinding. As exciting and wonderful as all these new developments in his life were right now, he still had to take time for himself to just chill, lest his mind would just shut down when he really needed it.

He had just lifted his right foot to begin walking back to replace the sword in its case when he heard the doorknob to his bedroom, just a foot away from him, begin to turn. He froze. He drew his foot back, and stood at the ready. Instantly his mind flashed through a dozen different possible plans. He could return to bed and pretend to be asleep, hoping to catch the

intruder off-guard. He could hide in the closet and either pop
out to catch the intruder unawares or simply remain hidden. He
could try to go out the fire escape and— no, there wasn't time
for that now. He could try to pad the covers so it looked like he
was still in bed, then leap out from the shadows to attack the
intruder— no, no time for that either. He could yank the door
open and stab the sword into the intruder's head. Or...

The door began to open toward Michael, who stood by the
hinges at the ready. A shadowy torso, several inches shorter
than Michael, started to snake into the room. The shadow was
halfway through the gap between the door and the jamb when
Michael shoved the door with all his might, shouting out a
"Yah!" as he slammed into it. The shadow grunted and slumped
slightly against the jamb, but seemed to quickly recover its
footing.

"*What do you want?*" Michael screamed as he slammed
into the door a second time, this time catching the shadow in
the spine. Michael immediately followed up with a blow from
the hilt of the rapier to the intruder's head. The shadow fell to
the ground in the doorway. Michael slammed the door into the
shadow once more, this time just using his hand on the doorknob as leverage. "*What do you want?*" he screamed again, his
voice turning into a screech on the word "want," a feral animal-
ism having taken over his being, a primal survival instinct having been triggered in his mind.

The shadow rolled over onto its back, facing the bedroom.
A pair of black eyes, blazing with indignation in the spectral
light of the room, bored into Michael. Then a third eye, black
with a slim silver iris, appeared near the shadow's chest, pointing right at Michael's head.

"*Sólo esto,*" came the shadow's voice at last. *Only this.*

The third eye's black pupil flashed white. The sharp sound
of a report.

And then – nothing but darkness.

Chapter 4

Blue Mountains National Park, Australia

Saturday

Hanging from the side of a cliff, four hundred feet off the canyon floor, generally did good things to clear Jon's mind. This morning, it was working, but not quite as well as he'd hoped.

He found himself half-wishing he'd taken the first part of his vacation in Europe, or maybe somewhere in the Middle or Far East. The wealth of historical sites and archaeological treasures those regions held could have easily distracted Jon from the Michael-Mara issue. Instead, for this first chunk of his seven-week break between Hilary Term and Trinity Term at Oxford, he found himself in Australia. Given, it was a beautiful country, and he was sharing it with friends. But the natural beauty, the company of friends, even the sorority sisters from the previous night – four attractive and convivial friends from UCLA spending their term break in the Blue Mountains – hadn't managed to cheer him up. His sleep was sporadic at best, and now, as he clung to the rocky edge of the cliff, scaling the mountain with little more than his bare hands and a belay line, his brain was still fixated on the problem.

Jon knew, deep down, that his bond, his relationship with his brother, wasn't going anywhere. Come hell or high water, they would always be tight. It was impossible to go through what they had together and not be. But that didn't change the fact that, since he and Mara had started going out, Michael seemed to have much less time for Jon. And the fact that Jon would probably see even less of him after they officially became Mr. and Mrs. Michael James Rickner.

The rock he had just chosen for a foothold turned out to be less solid than he'd thought. The sandstone surrounding it crumbled under his weight, the chunk of rock directly beneath his foot dislodging from its position and plummeting to the canyon floor below. Jon dug into the cliff with both hands, forgetting about the handhold he had been maneuvering toward and simply trying not to follow the fallen rock to the bottom of the gorge. The last cam he'd placed was a dozen meters below; a six-story fall awaited him if he fell, and that was only if the cam held out. He felt the belay line tighten against his harness, but he didn't want to rely on it. As distracted as he had been, he had serious doubts about how securely he had placed the last few cams into the rock.

"Jon!" Paul shouted from forty meters down the cliff, making his own path up the rock face. Even if he could have helped a precariously dangling Jon without endangering himself, Paul was too far away to lend a hand. All he could do was tighten the belay rope and pray he didn't have to hold the weight of a six-foot-two, one-hundred-eighty-five-pound free-falling partner.

Twin beads of perspiration snaked down from Jon's short, sweat-soaked brown hair and into his eyes, forcing him to blink away the painful saline – and the dust his frantic clawing was kicking up. Jon huffed as he scrabbled his left leg along the cliff side, half-looking, half-feeling for a new foothold, all while doing his best not to put too much pressure on his other leg. All he needed was for the purchase his right leg still held to disappear, either from his foot slipping off of it or from accidentally sending the rock down the cliff to join its brother. Which would leave him literally hanging on for dear life, his handholds and a sketchy safety line all that stood between him and a four-hundred foot drop into the gorge.

This was a bad idea.

First rule of any sort of life-risking diversion: don't do it when you're overly tired or when you're mentally or emotionally preoccupied. If it applied to driving, it sure as heck applied to dangling from the side of a mountain. And Jon was three for three.

His left foot finally found the purchase it sought. He just hung on for a few moments, catching his breath and allowing himself to get his wits about him.

"You okay?" Paul called.

"Yeah," Jon replied with a grunt. "Never better." He looked up the cliff. About twenty-five feet to the top. He should have waited for Paul to reach him, but he had some rope left, and he really didn't think it wise to spend any more time than necessary without the safety of solid ground beneath his feet. Then he'd see if he couldn't find a way down from the top that didn't involve putting his life in danger. In the meantime though, those twenty-five feet still remained to be climbed.

Jon took a deep breath. Slow and steady wins the race.

He shoved a cam into another crack in the rock face, fastening it as securely as possible. His eyes found the handhold he'd been moving toward when he'd lost his footing. He tested his footholds and both of his current handholds. Sturdy. Safe. Time to move forward. As he moved his hand toward the rock, he heard a familiar tune emanating from his jacket pocket. The *Indiana Jones* theme song. Michael's ringtone.

He knew he shouldn't answer it, especially in light of how close he had just come to falling to his death, but he couldn't help it. He missed his brother, and if he waited until he got to the top of the cliff, there was no guarantee that Michael would still be available to talk. He seemed to be incommunicado a lot these days, and the ten-hour time difference that separated them right now didn't help. Instinctively, his hand went to his jacket pocket and answered the phone.

"Jon?" came a soft voice as soon as he'd answered. Not Michael. Female. Sounded like Mara, but… different.

"Mara? That you?"

Silence. Labored breathing. Sniffles.

Jon furrowed his brow. "Mara?"

"He's dead, Jon."

Jon huffed a nervous, disbelieving laugh. "What? What're you talking about?"

A deep high-pitched intake of breath from the other end. "Oh God. Michael's dead, Jon. He's gone."

Jon's head was suddenly filled with helium, light and compressed all at once.

No.

No no no no.

Not possible.

His head rolled back, eyes fixed on the unforgiving blue sky, staring but not seeing. The rising sun, warming his skin until just a few moments earlier, had turned cold and empty. Sobs and undecipherable entreaties continued to emanate from the phone Jon held in his tenuous grasp, but all he could hear was the relentless whisper of the wind, rushing through the canyon as it had all morning, now transformed from an enjoyable bit of atmosphere to an all-consuming wall of noise.

All-consuming. Everything Jon had been worried about regarding himself and his brother now seemed petty, ridiculous. Marriage wouldn't have changed anything, but this…

Jon just clung there, dazed, as the phone finally slipped from his grasp, tumbling unanswered four-hundred feet into the darkened chasm below.

He had been mistaken, he realized. Most things, "high water" included, wouldn't have been able to change his bond with Michael. But "hell" *had* come, and it had changed everything.

Chapter 5

Washington, D.C.

Sunday

The view out Jon's window was dismally sunny. The daylight, the fluffy white clouds, and the shimmering waters of the Chesapeake taunted him as the plane began its final approach into Dulles. Crossing nine time zones, the International Date Line, and the equator was generally enough to screw with a person's faculties, but Jon's faculties had been screwed up long before he ever set foot on the plane.

Michael. Dead.

He had called Mara back at Los Angeles International Airport, halfway through his trip from Sydney. Told her he was coming to Washington. For the funeral. For Michael. For her. And for Jon himself.

He felt immeasurably guilty about his jealousy now. And for the distance he had put between himself and his brother these past few years. Not that he blamed himself for Michael's death. Not really, anyway.

The phone call to Mara had raised more questions than answers, and his mind was already full of unanswerable enigmas. But what Mara had told him was particularly suspicious. He prayed it was just emotion on Mara's part, but he was far from confident that would be the case.

The whole thing just kept getting stranger and stranger. If what she said was the truth… well, Jon didn't want to think about what that might mean.

He had boarded the plane and found a window seat to hide himself in. Shortly after boarding, his seatmate – a middle-aged German businessman bristling with Teutonic efficiency – had asked Jon if he was okay

"My brother just died," came Jon's terse reply. The man muttered an uncomfortable apology and didn't bother Jon for the remainder of the flight. And now, so many hours and time zones later that Jon had no idea what day or time it was, the plane was at last descending toward Washington, D.C. A city renowned for corruption, deceit, and smoke-and-mirrors as a matter of policy. Jon had come in search of answers, of closure, yet he had the unmistakable feeling that things would get far worse before they got better.

If they ever got better.

Jon checked himself and stopped that line of thinking in its tracks. He reminded himself that he wasn't alone in this. He had company in his misery, and, if he could, he had to try to be strong for Mara. Less than 24 hours after she became engaged to the love of her life, he ends up dead. Under suspicious circumstances, no less. And poor Mara had to be the one to find the body.

He swallowed as the cityscape below grew in detail. He couldn't be selfish with his feelings here. Somehow, he had to pull himself together. For Mara.

And for Michael.

Fifteen minutes later, the jet touched down on the tarmac at Dulles International Airport. Jon continued to stare out the window, watching the baggage handlers and ground traffic controllers going about their business. Just another day in the life. Business as usual.

The plane taxied to its gate, and the other passengers began to unload their belongings from the overhead bins. Jon took a deep breath.

Journey of a thousand miles. One step at a time.

After most of his fellow passengers had filtered out, Jon grabbed his carry-on from the overhead compartment and filed down the aisle to the exit, nodding a forced half-smile to the pilots and flight attendants who met the exhausted passengers at the door.

He drifted through the terminal, the barrage of advertising posters and duty-free signs passing by unnoticed. He walked as though in a trance, bumping into people and being jostled in return as he trudged blindly through the terminal. His body was in one place, his mind somewhere else entirely. Through passport control, through the baggage claim, through customs, and on toward the exit.

Jordan Wagdy, Ms. Saibani Lakhani, Lloyd Reissig, Aya Gawdat, F. Moodley, N. Lawrence; the placards with waiting drivers or hosts went on and on. None bore the name "Jonathan Rickner." Jon wasn't surprised, as he hadn't arranged for anyone to pick him up from the airport, but he was somewhat disappointed nonetheless. His sense of aloneness increased in seeing all these people waiting to greet, wine, dine, and just *be* with these arrivals who they had likely never met before. *They* had company; he was alone.

Then a familiar face, not bearing a placard but simply a somber, grateful countenance pointed in Jon's direction, appeared in the throng near the exit. At the sight, Jon smiled.

It was Mara. At twenty-five, she was a year older than Jon and a year younger than Michael, but Jon imagined that the past twenty-four hours had aged her more than all of the previous two years since Michael had first introduced her as his girlfriend. Her medium-length auburn hair, slightly less perfectly styled than usual, framed a face both familiar and not. Her hazel eyes were rimmed in red, her normally porcelain complexion tear-stained and ruddy, her lips free from lipstick and faintly tremulous. Still beautiful, but broken, like a war-torn cathedral. He hadn't told her when he was arriving, just that he'd call her once he was in town. How she had discovered his flight information, he had no idea. But he was glad she had.

"Mara," Jon said in a soft voice as he reached her, dropping his bags and wrapping his arms around her. She responded with an equally strong embrace, burying her tear-stained face in his chest. She began sobbing into his shirt, and he held her even tighter, rubbing his hand across her upper back in a comforting gesture.

He realized that this was the first time he had hugged or been hugged since he'd gotten the news. He needed the hug more than he had thought. It felt so good to feel the life of another pressing against his body, particularly the life of someone else close to his brother. The deep embrace, the touch of mutual sorrow and mourning, reminded Jon that, no matter how hard everything could get, life went on.

Mara nestled into his chest – small, alone, and scared. Her best friend and lover was gone, and everything she'd known and believed in was suddenly in danger of being devoured by fear and anguish. She was not yet his sister-in-law, and ultimately, would never be so, but Jon vowed right then, in this embrace, that he would do what he could to help her through this crisis in Michael's stead, playing the protective brother role that he'd never officially have with her.

"Jon," Mara said, loosening her grip on Jon and looking up at him with red-rimmed eyes. "How are you doing?"

"Honestly? I have no idea. I think I'm just on automatic right now. The shock stage of grief or whatever."

"You mean 'denial'?"

"Yeah, that one." Jon took a deep breath. "What about you?"

Her face tensed up like she was fighting back a flood of tears. He pulled her into a tight embrace, trying – unsuccessfully – to hug the tears away.

She sighed as she buried her face into his chest. "I'm glad you're here."

Jon felt the wetness of her tears begin to soak through her shirt. "I'm glad *you're* here, too. I'm still reeling. God knows I would have probably forgotten how to hail a cab."

Mara let out a little grunt of a laugh, her head still resting on Jon's chest. They stood in silence, immune to the hustle and bustle of commuters around them.

Jon sighed, the movement in his chest spurring Mara to lift her head.

"So what now?" she asked.

"I'm famished. What time is it here anyway?"

"A little past nine."

"You eaten yet? I could really go for some breakfast. My treat."

"Not much of an appetite yet, I'm afraid," she said, sniffling. "But okay." Then she glanced at the bags to his sides. "Where are you staying?"

"I was gonna get a hotel. Somewhere over near Foggy Bottom."

"No, you're not. Come stay with me. My roomie's gone to Florida with her boyfriend for the week. I... I could use the company."

He sighed. "Alright. Thanks."

"So, my place, then breakfast?" Mara asked as she grabbed his carry-on for him.

"Sounds like a plan," Jon nodded thoughtfully, though a real plan for where to go from here was nowhere in sight. But, he reflected, even though his life may have been in turmoil, he at least had some solid company along for the ride.

Chapter 6

Langley, Virginia

In a small corner of land officially allotted by the federal government to the CIA, the headquarters of the Division sat unassumingly, just another building lost in a much larger complex. The concrete-and-mirrored-glass facade bore no sign or other indication as to what the building housed, as even the privileged few who were granted free reign to explore the campus of the CIA's headquarters were not allowed inside the building. Fewer than a dozen people in the entire country, not including Division operatives and staff, knew of the organization's existence or purpose. The clearance required even to set foot inside the building was *exclusive* to those specifically granted license by the Division's director.

Exiting from his black Mercedes sedan, a well-built Latino man, clad in a black double-breasted suit and sporting wraparound sunglasses, his dark hair shining in the sunlight, headed toward the small, two-story building. Though his head remained set on his shoulders, facing forward as he walked at a brisk pace toward his destination, his eyes swept from side to side beneath his dark sunglasses, scanning his surroundings as he always did. No matter where he was, no matter what he was doing. Being a field agent with the Division, Enrique Ramirez had found, was more than just a job; it consumed your whole life. Which, he realized, was fitting considering how the Division quite literally had taken his old life, as fire consumes the phoenix, and rebirthed him from the smoldering ashes of his staged death.

He climbed the half-dozen stairs to the front doors of Division HQ, his sweeping eyes noting the chewing gum stuck underneath the left-hand rail, and ticking off another day in his mind that maintenance had neglected to clean it off. Enrique was glad the maintenance guys weren't responsible for the more important parts of the operation. As it was, the Division's fate, and thus the fate of the nation, was in much more able hands – hands like his.

As the only child of first-generation American immigrants from Honduras, Enrique Ramirez had had a rough childhood. The inner city of Los Angeles and the cycle of poverty that afflicted so many of his peers plagued his upbringing, but it was his father, Juan Pablo, who he feared the most. When Enrique was fourteen, he had come home to another of his father's drunken rants, the paper-thin walls of the apartment ensuring that the family's dirty laundry was no secret to their equally despondent neighbors. Juan Pablo was in the kitchen with Enrique's mother, Luisa. Normally, his mother would try to calm him down, to placate him somehow until he sobered up. To yell back would only infuriate him further, and that was when he turned violent, as both Enrique and Luisa had found out more times than they could count. On this day, however, Luisa neither yelled nor placated. The voice that Enrique heard as he entered the house was fearful, pleading as though for her very life. And as he discovered when he approached the kitchen, he realized this was, in fact, the case.

His back to the entrance to the kitchen, Juan Pablo stood over the crumpled body of Enrique's mother. Luisa's blue gingham housedress was splattered with the crimson that leaked from her nose and mouth, and a pool of blood was beginning to form on the yellowed linoleum. Attempting to curl into a fetal position, she was shaking with fear and with the onset of shock.

And Juan Pablo continued to yell, punctuating his hateful tirade with kicks to the shins, kidneys, arms, and face.

Enrique didn't remember picking up the long cutting knife from the counter; it was just there, in his clenched fist, ready to help him dispense justice. Juan Pablo was so consumed by his drunken fury that he didn't even notice Enrique come up behind him until the knife was already driven into his spine, almost to the hilt. The man whirled in surprise, flailing about to defend against his teenage son, but Enrique stabbed him again and again, pummeling him with his free hand in between thrusts. After his father had finally fallen to the ground in a bloody, dead heap, Enrique finally dropped to his knees beside his mother, who was still quivering on the floor. She looked at Enrique through blackened eyes that were already beginning to swell shut. Her lips seemed to form the word "why" as she exhaled a soundless bubble of blood from her mouth. Whether that questioning word was directed at him or his father, Enrique never had been able to decide.

Luisa died from internal bleeding on the way to the hospital. Juan Pablo had been dead before the paramedics even showed up. Enrique Ramirez, fourteen years old, was alone in the world.

After an investigation into the affair, the authorities decided not to pursue charges against the teenager. Between the history of abuse, the boy's age, the motive of defending his helpless mother, and the passionate nature of the crime, the police wrote it up as self-defense, the justifiable homicide of a man no one would miss.

Months of counseling and years of revolving door foster families followed for Enrique. Social workers and guidance counselors described him as somber, angry, and lacking direction. But the day he turned eighteen, he discovered the direction he was destined for: the armed services.

When Enrique joined the United States Army in the build up to NATO's invasion of Yugoslavia in 1999, he immediately stood out as a formidable soldier. Fearless and cunning, his instincts on the ground would often lead him to improvise changes to his missions – changes that always either granted surprisingly successful results or avoided the massive casualties that the ill-conceived original plan would have incurred. Even his senior squad members listened to his advice with an open mind, usually opting to follow the rookie soldier. But when one of his improvised missions took a turn for the worse, forcing him to separate from his squad and find his own way back through enemy lines to base camp, he got his first taste of operating solo. No squad mates' backs to watch, no predefined mission parameters, a license to kill, and a lot of bad guys to use that license on. Not only did he make it back to base camp alive, but he also managed to kill seventeen of the enemy by himself: with only an M4, a pistol, one extra clip of rifle ammo, and a knife. The last four kills, apparently, had been made after he had run out of ammo, and judging by stories that circulated later on, the families of the deceased would have had no chance of holding open casket funerals.

He had risen quickly within the ranks, being put on special assignments, and eventually, due to his loner tendencies and his ability to make operational magic happen when given a long leash, he was assigned solo assassination missions: taking out high-profile or tactical targets as a splinter cell – for the United States neither condones nor partakes in assassinations of foreign leaders… officially, at least – backed up only by minimal reconnaissance and intelligence members with whom he rarely interacted, save for the occasional radio contact. He came to like it that way. Just him and his target. His guidance counselor back in high school would have said that he was channeling his anger at his dead father toward these surrogates, the enemy combatants he so efficiently dispatched, but Enrique didn't buy into that. He was simply good at killing people who needed to be killed. Very, very good.

Enrique slid his plain white entry card through the reader next to the entry door – a door that, like the rest of the building, appeared to be made of mirrored glass, but was in fact constructed of two inches of steel, with the glass merely covering its exterior. In fact, all of the building's windows concealed either a foot of concrete, six inches of steel, or both, immediately on the other side of the glass. Entering the building, Enrique removed his sunglasses and glanced at each of the five closed-circuit cameras trained on the small entryway; at each of the thirty-two tiny nozzles connected to pipes filled with cyanide gas that would be released should some unauthorized person try to gain admittance to their sanctum; at the vent in the ceiling used for sucking the gas away after the unwelcome guest had been taken out of play.

On the numeric keypad to the right of a heavy steel door – the only features in the otherwise stark concrete room – he punched in the 8-digit code, prompting the pad to slide back into the wall, then up, revealing another console with a small camera lens, a microphone, and a large LCD touch-pad. He pressed his right palm to the touch-pad, a red light-bar like that of a copy machine passing over his hand and recording his fingerprints, handprint, and pulse – in case someone might try to use the hand of a dead agent to gain access. He enunciated his agent identification number into the microphone, and centered his left eye in front of the camera lens, which image-captured his retina.

When the security computer had checked the passcodes and biometric data against the agent files in the system, verifying that he was indeed supposed to be in the building, a small green light next to the camera lens lit up. One last step. Enrique backed up two steps, turned his face and body to the center camera, cognizant of the other four that were also focused on him in his current position, and stared patiently into the lens. The operator on the other side saw that it was a living agent – and only that agent – and pressed the button to buzz him through. Rushing to push open the door before the lock reactivated – and he had to go through the whole process again – Enrique entered the brightly lit headquarters of the Division.

Some people found the security measures to be a bit over-kill, but not Enrique. He was glad for anything that would pro-tect this great nation of his from the treacherous subversives who would see its downfall. And he was proud to be an impor-tant cog in that powerful machine. It was the current director, Harrison Greer, who had taken an interest in Enrique's abili-ties – and lack of personal connections. Enrique's background fit the profile that Greer had found produced exceptional field agents, and after contacting Enrique and making his proposal, Greer had arranged for him to be one of the first casualties of the war in Afghanistan. According to the official report, Enrique Ramirez had been blown apart by a land mine – left over from the Soviet occupation of the country in the eighties – while on patrol. He had gone off alone, as he was wont to do, and never came back. An explosion was heard, and *somebody's* body was found, though it had gotten such a good blast from the land mine – and the second land mine that the torso had convenient-ly landed on – that identification was all but impossible. Just the way the Division liked it. After months of training, he had undertaken his first assignment, excelled, and the rest was his-tory. Albeit unwritten history.

He turned a corner, walked to the end of the stark, tile-floored, white-painted concrete-walled hallway and stopped. Lingering, he stared at the gray steel door, which displayed a copper nameplate bearing the single word: *Director*. He had always relished being summoned before the man who held this office. Greer was the father he had never had, the mentor and leader he had always needed, and Ramirez had always been his golden child. But things with Greer lately had been… different somehow. Ramirez took a breath and rapped twice on the door.

"Enter," came the gruff reply from within. Ramirez did so.

Enrique had heard it said that you could tell a lot about a person by the way they decorated their "space," be it their home, their office, or even the interior of their car. The centerpiece of the office was a shiny aluminum desk about the size of a pool table; a desktop computer, a legal-sized pad of paper, a black mesh pencil cup, and a Civil War-era cannonball, held in the bowl of a specially constructed display stand, were all that graced its top. Three framed pictures hung behind the desk. In the center was the standard portrait of the current President of the United States. Flanking him were the pictures of the two former directors of the Division: Harrison Greer's father and grandfather. Nepotism was generally looked down upon these days, especially when it came to public office, but this office was anything but public, and every Greer that had held this position had proven more than competent.

Other than the portraits, the walls were whitewashed and unadorned. No nonsense, no superfluous distractions. Ramirez liked that dedication, that single-mindedness that Greer, as his mentor, had in turn instilled in him. The only features in the room other than the desk were the two filing cabinets located on the left wall opposite the entry door, a closet behind the desk that Ramirez had never seen open, and a three-foot-long bombshell that stood in one corner behind the desk. No one within the Division, save Greer himself, really knew whether it was a real, live bomb or not. When Ramirez had once inquired, Greer had told him that it was a reminder of the explosive nature of the secret they were sitting on. Like the bomb's unknown danger potential, each subject slated for elimination by the Division, given time and freedom to pursue things further, *might* never discover enough to really pose a threat to the nation. But,

Greer would finish the metaphor, is it really worth the risk to let someone whack the tip with a hammer just to find out?

Harrison Greer was hunched over his desk, flipping through some documents in a manila folder. His piercing gray eyes turned toward the door. His tanned face sat on a muscular neck. His thick head of brown hair belied his forty-eight years of age, the salt-and pepper at the temples and the sun-weathered wrinkles around his eyes the only indications of his age. His body was that of a weightlifter, tugging at the seams of his gray suit.

"Ramirez," Greer said as he placed the file on the desk and stood, extending his full six-foot-three frame. Ramirez, being five inches shorter, had long fostered the joke, privately of course, that Greer was someone he 'looked up to.' "Have a seat."

Ramirez eased himself into the chair opposite the desk while Greer walked over to the filing cabinets and extracted another folder. Returning to his chair, the Director adjusted the folder on his desk, folded his hands, and fixed Ramirez with a stare.

"Ramirez, last night's mission…" Greer pursed his lips, as if the next words held an acrid distastefulness. "It may have been premature."

Ramirez raised an eyebrow but remained silent, his hands folded in his lap.

"I don't want to say anything else until I know more, but that's where I need you again." Greer took a deep breath, and shook his head once, like he were shooing away an obtrusive thought. "Apparently Rickner had a laptop that he kept at home. He may have kept his most sensitive discoveries there."

"I didn't see a laptop when I was there, or I would have grabbed it then." Ramirez made a face. "Why didn't Recon pick up on this before?"

"Apparently he never connected it to the Internet. Cautious, I suppose, especially after he realized what he'd stumbled across. We found his student account, and thought that was it. He must've paid cash for the laptop and forgone any warranties. No record of the laptop, until this morning when... well, never mind the particulars. The fact of the matter is I need you to get that laptop. It should be at his apartment. Perhaps hidden somewhere. Find it and bring it back."

Ramirez waited. Greer was silent, his eyes locked back on the contents of the manila folder. "Anything else, sir?" Ramirez asked.

Greer swallowed, looked up. "Sorry. No. Not yet. Just report back as soon as you have that laptop. It is paramount that we get the laptop and the information it contains immediately."

"Yes, sir." Ramirez stood to leave, conscious of the fact that Greer was distracted by something he wasn't telling him. "Sir, permission to speak freely?"

"Granted."

"Are you okay?" Ramirez tilted his head to the side. "I mean, you seem a little–"

"Distracted?"

Ramirez nodded. "Perhaps."

Greer leaned forward over his desk. "You know the feeling you get when your ticket matches the first five numbers in the Mega Lottery? You're incredulous at your luck and tingling with anticipation, waiting for that last number, the Powerball, to come up?"

"Not personally, but I can imagine."

"We may have a winning lottery ticket on our hands, Ramirez." Greer jabbed a meaty finger at the intel lying on his desk, still locking eyes with Enrique. "And this laptop may be our Powerball. Go get it."

Chapter 7

Washington, D.C.

Some things in life never seemed to change. Vacations were planned and canceled; engagements made and terminated; brothers and fiancés killed. But the omnipresent golden arches of McDonald's were always around. During his travels around the world with his brother, Michael had often joked that, if the world were plunged into nuclear holocaust, cockroaches and McDonald's – along with the odd Starbucks – would be all that survived. And in this spirit of constancy and familiarity, Jon and Mara approached the restaurant that remained the same despite the tumultuous state of their own lives.

Jon was now free of his luggage – he and Mara had dropped his bags off at her apartment, then walked the five blocks to the nearest of the ubiquitous restaurants in the Washington Metro area. The pair was walking close, Jon at times sliding his arm around Mara's shoulder and squeezing her side against his in an attempt to comfort her, to comfort himself, and, in some small way, to absolve himself of some of the guilt he felt over his recent jealousy toward her.

The breakfast rush was tapering off, and Mara grabbed a booth while Jon ordered their food. Five minutes later, Jon returned with two sausage-egg-and-cheese biscuits, two orders of hash browns, a coffee, and a Coke.

"Breakfast of champions," Jon announced as he set the food on the table.

Mara stared at him. "Uh huh."

"Eat up," he urged as he grabbed a biscuit from the tray.

Mara took a hash brown from the tray and began to pick at it, putting the morsels in her mouth in slow, detached movements. Jon was halfway through his biscuit – he hadn't even realized how hungry he had been – when he noticed Mara's demeanor.

"Not hungry?"

"Hungry." Mara dropped her hash brown onto the tray. "Just no appetite."

"Mara, you gotta eat. When Mom died, Dad just retreated into his research. Didn't eat, didn't let Michael and me help him through the pain. He just isolated himself in his misery. He lost twenty pounds that he didn't have to lose, and he almost had to be put in a hospital to boost his electrolytes intravenously. If we're gonna get through this, we're gonna have to keep our strength up. Emotionally and mentally we're shot, but if we start wasting away physically..." He let the thought hang in the air between them. Hoping it would give her some impetus to keep pushing on. But, as Jon knew all too well, it was damned hard.

"I know. I just..." She drifted off. An uncomfortable silence filled the void.

Jon looked at his biscuit, then back at Mara. "You want to talk about it?"

"God, Jon, it was horrible." Her words tumbled out in an avalanche of emotion. "I was supposed to drive him to the airport. Eight A.M. My first morning as an engaged woman, sending my husband-to-be off on a big adventure. But when I got there, he didn't answer. The apartment was quiet, and the peephole was dark. I figured he had gotten another ride, or perhaps overslept, but he would have let me know if he didn't need me to pick him up, and he never would have missed this trip. I tried calling his cell, but there was no answer. And I heard his ringtone from inside the apartment. I thought he might be in the shower or something, so I used my key to get in."

Jon raised his eyebrows and took a long pull of air. All this was too much for him, but regardless, it was where they were. And as distasteful as the story's ending was sure to be, Mara needed to tell it. And Jon needed to hear it.

"But everything was wrong," she continued breathlessly, as though the story had been kept inside her for too long and now was forcing itself out of her mouth. "It was too dark, like some supernatural shadow had been draped over the room. I called his name, making my way toward the bedroom, and then my voice caught in my throat as I gagged on a scent I'd never smelt before. One I hope never to smell again. I wanted to run away, just flee that apartment and never look back. But I couldn't. So I went to the bedroom. Forced myself not to gag as the smell became stronger. I opened the door and... His head... so much blood. Blood everywhere." She took a few quick heavy breaths, as though she were beginning to hyperventilate. Then she composed herself and continued. "The police are calling it suicide, but—"

"But no freaking way," Jon finished her sentence through a mouthful of sausage, egg, and biscuit.

Mara snorted a quick laugh despite herself, which quickly gave way to the prevailing frown. "Yeah. No way."

Jon swallowed and shook his head. "I didn't even know Michael owned a gun."

"He didn't, at least not legally. Certainly none that I knew of, but the cops say he could have gotten it from any number of illegal dealers around the city. Which I don't doubt that he *could* have, but I have serious doubts that he would. But there was a gun in his hand – the murder weapon, they said – when I found him."

"But the cops didn't know Michael so they didn't factor that into their *official* assessment." He exhaled sharply through his nose. "So what *evidence* pointed the cops to a conclusion of suicide?"

"They say there was no sign of a struggle, no sign of forced entry, no evidence of anyone else in the apartment that night. They matched the bullet that killed him with the gun found by the body. And the gun was fired through the..." She paused, cringing. Her hand went instinctively to the small silver cross that hung around her neck, which she rubbed between her fingers.

"Take your time."

"No, no, I'm fine." She stared at a spot on the table and started picking at the chipping Formica with one fingernail. "The gun was fired from under his jaw through his b..." She looked like she was about to vomit, then regained her composure. "...through his brain. Typical suicide shot."

Jon made a face. "Not Michael."

"No, Jon. Not Michael at all. Especially what with everything that was going *right* in his life. He was really stoked about this new dissertation topic he had started a week or so ago. Some real breakthrough that was supposed to have helped 'all the pieces fit' and 'make his career.'" She looked down at her hands resting on the table. "And of course, there was me..."

Jon tilted his head at Mara, fixing her with a compassionate gaze. "There still is you, Mara."

"Yeah, I know. I know." Mara raised her eyes to Jon, looking as though she were on the verge of tears. "Geez, Jon, how in the world are you holding up like this?"

"I'm not. My jet lag is probably disguising how I'm feeling. Believe me, I'm pretty screwed up right now. I haven't really lost anyone that close to me since Mom died. I was thirteen, Michael was fifteen, and the four of us – Dad, Mom, Michael, and I – were down in Mexico working on a Mayan dig site. Mom was the ancient linguistics specialist, and some mysterious glyphs had been discovered at some ruins a few miles away from our site. So she went off into the jungle with a pair of guides and a grad student of my Dad's who was kind of serving as her assistant. Michael and I were content to explore our site and help Dad out with some of the less mundane aspects of the dig – we were teenagers after all – and..." Jon stopped and gave Mara an apologetic look. "Sorry, you've probably heard all of this before from Michael."

"Not all of it. Michael didn't like to talk about it very much." She gave him an encouraging smile. "And, please, let it all out. I'm sure it's good for the healing process."

Jon exhaled a shuddering breath and nodded. "Okay. So Michael and I are exploring the main ruins while Mom's a few miles off in the jungle to decipher these new glyphs. She's gone for a several hours, and when sunset arrives, and we still haven't heard anything from Mom's party, we start to worry. Just as Dad, Michael, and I start grabbing our flashlights and machetes to go looking for her, one of the guides stumbles out of the jungle, wide-eyed with fear. Dad grabbed him as he collapsed. The guide shivered violently, as though wracked with bone-chilling cold, even though the temperature was well into the nineties."

Jon stopped for a moment to gather his thoughts. Mara waited patiently.

"'*Muerto.*'" He shook his head at the table. "'*Todo muerto.*' That was all the guide would say. He repeated it over and over again, like a mantra. *All dead.* The three of us all spoke Spanish, but the man wouldn't elaborate on what happened. He died a few minutes later, still muttering his fearful mantra, still shivering violently, still wide-eyed in mortal terror.

"Michael was the first to call for a search party. Dad and I were also thinking it, but Michael beat us to the punch. Dad wanted to wait 'til the light of morning. Said the jungle was too dangerous at night. And though the evidence of the danger of the jungle was lying dead at our feet, Michael insisted on beginning the search right then. I sided with Michael, partially because I knew I wouldn't be able to sleep anyway, and partially because… well, it was Michael."

Mara smiled a little. She knew what Jon meant. Michael's influence on his brother, and the esteem Jon held him in, were no secret.

"So we searched through the night, past sun-up, and all through the next afternoon. I don't know how many miles we trekked through the jungle that day, but I do know what we found. Nothing. No trail to follow. No scrap of clothing or drop of blood or anything that might explain what happened. Dad called in a favor to the Director of the INAH – the Mexican National Institute of Anthropology and History who oversee archaeological sites and whatnot – who in turn managed to get a squad of Mexican troops to help comb the jungle for Mom and her group. The search party turned up absolutely nothing. Death certificates were drawn up, but Dad never lost hope that, somehow, Mom was still alive out there somewhere.

"And that, until now, was the worst moment of my life." Jon looked up at the ceiling and took a deep breath. "Dad immersed himself in his work and got through each day solely on the blind hope that Mom was alive and would some day find her way back to him. And Michael and I were left predominantly to our own devices, forced to mourn our mother in a foreign country with no body, with no support from our father. So Michael was my rock, and I was his. We talked. We cried. We helped to distract each other from the pain. We explored and adventured and forced ourselves to do the things we knew we loved. Because we knew that's what Mom would have wanted. She would have wanted us to keep on living all the more." He stopped and bit his lip. "Michael and I wouldn't have gotten through that without each other. And now that someone else has died, the one guy I relied on to get me through it the last time isn't there anymore."

Mara placed her hand on Jon's arm. "Well, I'm here now, Jon. And vice versa, I think."

"Yeah," he said, thinking guiltily of the jealousy he'd felt for her just a few days before. And of the way he'd abandoned his brother when, apparently, he'd needed him most. "Definitely." A brief pause, a silence that seemed to echo the emptiness they felt, the void Michael had left, the absence of any sense of the future.

"So what was so interesting that he ran across?" he said, trying to change the subject to something more productive than wallowing in grief. He took another bite of his biscuit before continuing. "I mean, the Mafia of the 1950s is great fodder for Hollywood, but I don't see how shedding new light on the relationship between the press and the mob half a century ago could have the implications he hinted toward over the phone."

"He said he backdoored into something. In his research, he stumbled across a mob-blamed shooting that didn't add up. And it led him to the threads of something much bigger. A government cover-up or something."

Jon put the remains of his biscuit down. "A government cover-up? And what, some G-men killed Michael because he was the man who knew too much?" He shook his head. "C'mon Mara, this is real life, not a Robert Ludlum novel. The government goes around spending money they don't have and covering up sex scandals, not murdering their own citizens to keep some grad student from publishing his allegations about a sixty-year-old murder charge."

Mara's face flushed. "Well, Michael's dead, isn't he? So we're left with two options: he killed himself, or someone else killed him."

Jon cocked an eyebrow. "But the government?"

"I never said the government killed him. *You* said that. I was just telling you what he was working on. Like you asked."

Jon looked at her hand, which was caressing her pendant again. A comfort object, he supposed. A fitting choice for someone who had majored in Religious Studies like Mara had. "You're right. I'm sorry. My mouth got away from me there."

"It's alright." Mara gave him a crooked half-smile. "We're both a little messed up right now. I think an extra dose of patience might be in order."

Jon nodded. "Sounds good. So did he say exactly what this government cover-up or whatever was supposed to be?"

"Not to me. I think he might have been a little afraid… for me, at least. He didn't want the ideas to get out before he could back them up." She chuckled softly. "I thought it was kinda cute. Nice and chivalric and all, defending me from enemies unknown." Then she fixed him with a gaze that seemed curiously cold. "He was really excited to tell *you* about it though. Figured you'd be proud of him. His adventuring buddy."

Jon blinked, cocked his head querulously, but the look in her eyes was gone just as soon as it had appeared. Or maybe it had never been there at all. He sat quietly, looking pensive as he furrowed his brow and stroked the stubble on his chin.

"What?" Mara asked. No trace of the coldness. *Must've been my imagination*, Jon thought. *Too much, too soon.*

"Can I borrow the key to Michael's place?" he asked.

"Sure, but why?"

He pointed a thumb toward the door. "I wanna go over there and check it out. See what he was working on. Research-wise."

"Okay…" Mara reached into her purse and withdrew her keys. "The cops cleared out pretty quick. Declared it a suicide, took the… took *him* to the morgue, and cleaned up the scene. Shouldn't be any issues."

"Do you want to come with? You've been there since I have… you could show me around and stuff."

Mara shook her head vigorously. "Not yet, Jon. I can't go back there just yet."

"That's fine." He nodded and patted her hand. "I understand."

"Michael's research should be on his laptop and in a red notebook he keeps either on his desk or in his backpack."

"The old beige one?"

Mara smiled a little. "That's the one."

"Ha! He's still using that… oh," he said, suddenly realizing that he'd used the wrong verb tense. Across the table, Mara frowned.

"Alright," Jon said, "I'll meet you back at your apartment, then? Say in an hour-and-a-half?"

"Yeah, that works." The pair disposed of their trash and headed for the exit. Stopping just outside the restaurant, Mara grabbed his arm and gave him an anxious look.

"What?" he asked.

"Just…" She looked away briefly, then met his eyes again. "Be careful, all right?"

Chapter 8

Langley, Virginia

Harrison Greer tightened his grip on the receiver, his palms beginning to sweat. He was pacing his office aimlessly, too nervous to stand still, too full of pent-up rage to sit down.

"I want a second opinion," he bellowed into the phone.

"I *am* the second opinion, Mr. Greer." The doctor's voice was calm and measured. It wasn't the first time he'd had a conversation like this. And it wouldn't be the last. "Several of my colleagues have looked at the results, and the conclusion is, sadly, indisputable. I'm very sorry, sir. But there are options for cases such as yourself."

Greer tried to swallow away the growing lump in his throat, but to no avail. "You say it's inoperable and chemo and radiation therapy won't do any good. What the hell options are there, in your *esteemed* second opinion?"

The doctor's voice was measured as he ignored Greer's sarcasm. "Well, sir, we can put you in touch with a very good hospice service—"

Greer cursed at the man through the receiver and hung up. He flung the phone onto his desk, cursing again as he punched the side of one of the filing cabinets, leaving a large dent in the metal. He stopped when he realized he was damaging Division property. Took a deep breath, exhaled, slowly wobbled over to his desk, and sank into the seat.

Cancer. He was forty-eight years old, as fit as most college athletes, and he was about to be killed by an invisible mutation in his own body. He felt fine. But, as his father found out the hard way, cancer could seem dormant until it reared its ugly head all at once, striking down even the healthiest with shocking speed. But Greer would not be caught with his pants down. And he wouldn't be caught dead whiling away his final days in some old folks' death camp filled with nurses who couldn't cure and patients who never checked out. No, he would choose his own way.

Unlike his father and grandfather before him, Harrison Greer had no progeny to pass the mantle of Director on to. He and his wife, Lucinda, had never had children. Once, shortly after they were married, Lucinda had gotten pregnant, but she had miscarried three months in. The doctor said that there was something wrong with the way her uterus was set up – Greer had cared less about the medical mumbo-jumbo and more about the bottom line – and told them that she would never have children. And, sad though Greer was not to be able to have any children of his own, he refused to consider adoption, primarily because that would entail agencies not privy to the secrets of the Division poking around in his life and background. That, and with the advances of DNA testing these days, you never knew when the kid you adopted was going to try to find his birth parents, stage some sort of reunion, and… again, it was way too much potential headache for Greer and his commitment to secrecy.

But one of the perks of being Director instead of a field agent was that he could have some semblance of a life. His death had never been staged; hence, the doctors knew his real name. But not, of course, his profession. Officially, he just worked for some top secret division of the government, one for which the line "I could tell you, but I'd have to kill you" was actually appropriate.

And he had Lucinda. He swiveled in his chair and opened one of his desk drawers. A framed portrait of his wife lay inside. He kept it inside his desk so as to always have it accessible, but to keep his love for her separate from the work he did at the Division. The task of defending the nation's integrity could often get ugly – as any soldier could attest – and Greer didn't want the image of his beautiful wife to be tainted by the horrors that performing his duties required.

The portrait had been taken years ago, back when they were both younger, back before the news about their inability to have a baby. He had taken the photograph himself, a vacation Polaroid that had turned out to be his favorite picture in the world. The way the sunlight sparkled in her eyes, the way a beach breeze made the tips of her curly black hair dance around her tanned, slender face.

The Bahamas. That's where they would go. He had some money saved up. A lot of money, actually. He had never been much of a vacationer; the Division had always been his number one priority. The fate of the free world always seemed a more noble purpose than riding roller coasters in Florida or sipping Mai Tais on some bikini-laden island. But he would make up for that now. He would take the money and his wife to the Bahamas, where they would live out the rest of his days in tropical bliss. The doctor had said weeks, maybe months – who could tell – but Greer certainly wouldn't see another Christmas. He would have to be sure to take a gun with him. Or perhaps just buy one there so as to circumvent Customs authorities. He was looking forward to spending some time away, with his beloved wife, but when his health started to deteriorate… Well, he'd been there when his dad had started crashing, seen the misery and dehumanization that comes with the long slow death of cancer. Greer didn't want any part of that. When *his* health started to deteriorate, when he actually saw the end upon him, he would choose his own way to end things.

But before his vacation, he had one last thing to take care of. A rather big thing, actually. His legacy. The legacy of his father and grandfather before. He would complete their work and find what they had been searching for since day one of the Division's existence. Though Greer had chosen his replacement already, he would not entrust this great task to someone else. He had to see it through, for his father and for his father's father. He had been trying for years, but to no avail. And now time was running out for him. But fate, with its curious sense of irony, had also just dropped a wild card into his lap. A piece to the puzzle that had previously remained hidden, a key that could unlock everything Greer needed to know, a map that could lead them right to the prize he sought. It all depended on what was on Michael Rickner's laptop.

Greer stood abruptly and began to pace the office again. He wished Ramirez would hurry. Time was running out. For them all.

Chapter 9

Washington, D.C.

Despite the bright daylight outside, Michael's apartment was dark, dismal even. Or perhaps it was the eyes that Jon looked through that made it appear so gray and lifeless. Eyes that knew this was the site of one of the two great tragedies of his life, that had had their color-sensing abilities shocked into numbness. Eyes that beheld the scene through the gray-tinted lenses of sorrow.

Jon locked the door behind him, not out of safety, despite the somewhat shady neighborhood, but because he didn't want anyone to intrude and violate his time with what lingered of his brother's spirit. He flipped the switch by the door, and the room burst into light. The apartment looked much the same as Jon remembered it from his last visit over the Christmas holidays. A few new photographs and pieces of artwork adorned the walls and tabletops, several new books on the shelves... and a *plant* by the door? Probably Mara's doing. Wasn't dead yet, though, but Jon suspected Mara had probably been sneaking over to water it during Michael's recent monomania. No, that wasn't quite right – Michael would have had *two* great passions in the weeks before his death: his research, and Mara.

The room felt cold. At first, Jon figured this must've been the psychosomatic effect his feelings about this place were having on him before he realized the apartment itself was completely silent. No heater running. The cops must've turned it off after they left. Or a penny-pinching landlord who didn't want to get stuck with an unpaid utility bill charged to a dead man. Jon turned to the thermostat, just to the right of the entryway, and flipped on the heat. Michael's memory, and his home and possessions that served as reminders of the man's life, deserved better than some cheapskate cost-cutting move that turned his home into a meat locker.

Jon's eyes lit upon another incongruity with his last visit. Michael's backpack sat near the door – instead of on his shoulder or by his side. He hesitated, then picked up the backpack. It was of rugged, sturdy beige cloth, and had been put to the test on many an archaeological trek in sites around the globe. Michael's constant companion for nearly a decade, the very sight of the bag triggered a flood of memories – a grass stain from Finland, a muddy smear from Indonesia, a spot of blood from an unfortunate run-in with an antiquities thief in Peru. Adventures that the brothers had shared together. Yet another thing that could never be the same again.

Jon slid his arm through one strap, then the other, taking a deep breath as he shrugged the straps into position over his shoulders. The whole thing felt... weird. It was almost as though Jon were defiling something important to his brother, taking his most often-used possession before his body was even in the ground – the funeral having been postponed until Jon and Michael's father could be reached at his dig in a remote corner of the Brazilian Amazon. Yet at the same time, wearing the backpack felt good, as though Jon were taking on some sort of mantle that his brother had left behind – like by picking up and wearing something that was so closely associated with his brother, Michael was able to live on through him. As though Michael were passing on some sort of torch from beyond the grave. Or perhaps Jon was just being sentimental.

He took the backpack off, unzipped it and peered inside; the red notebook was there, along with the rest of his kit – camera, digital voice recorder, iPod, a smaller palm-sized notepad, and a worn paperback novel – John le Carre's *The Spy Who Came In From The Cold*. Some of the other items the brothers would often take on their adventures – such as lock-picking kits and Swiss Army knives – were notably missing, probably due to Michael's upcoming flight and the security checks through which his luggage would have to have passed. Jon closed the bag; he would have time for rifling through the notebook soon enough. Michael's spirit still clung to this place, he felt. He needed to find out why.

Reshouldering the backpack, Jon walked through the living room toward the room he felt he most needed to visit, the room he most dreaded going into. The bedroom. The site of Michael's violent death. And, unless he had changed the furniture around since Christmas – which seemed unlikely considering the relative similarity of the living room's arrangement – the location of Michael's desk – and laptop.

He paused in the hall at a picture of Mara and Michael in front of Cinderella's Castle at Disney World. A wry grin crossed his lips. Memories of happier times that never again would be. As was the next picture: Michael and Jon himself smiling and laughing in the Andes as they indulged in their favorite pastime: exploring. Growing up with renowned British archeologist and historian Sir William Rickner and the brilliant American linguist Dr. Anna Calvert Rickner as their parents, traveling across the globe as a family in search of ancient mysteries, served to strengthen their passion for adventure and discovery, as well as cementing their bond with one another. *But the great duo is no more*, Jon thought, a somber look in his eyes, a heavy feeling in his chest. Everything he loved doing with his brother, everything they would never do again. His brother, his mentor, his inspiration, his best friend – gone. Forever. And forever was just too damn long.

Pursing his lips and taking a deep breath of the stifling air through his nostrils, he turned from the pictures and continued down the hall to the bedroom door. The door hung off-kilter on its hinges, there being a slight discrepancy in the gap between door and jamb at the top and the gap at the bottom. Old door? Or… The scuffs on the door itself, as Jon inched it open – and corresponding ones on the jamb – told Jon it was damaged through force. Impacting something. Had Michael accidentally slammed it on a ladder or a chair or something? Strange. Clenching his eyes tight and taking a deep breath, he pushed open the door. Slowly, fearfully, he opened his eyes and peered into the darkened room.

And sucked in a sharp breath as he beheld the scene of horror.

To the dispassionate observer, it wasn't much as far as scenes of horror went. The stripped and disposed-of bloody sheets where Michael had bled his last were gone, revealing only a small, dark stain at the foot of the mattress. Some blood spray was splattered on the ceiling between the door and the foot of the bed, and a few drops of crimson could still be seen on the carpet. The body was long gone, but the musty scent of death remained. For Jon, no Hollywood slasher gorefest could have been more horrifying. Not only was this one actually real, but it also cut far deeper and hit much closer to home. How he wished this nightmare would just roll credits and be over and done with, but it was not to be. This was one nightmare he couldn't wake from.

He walked over to the window and looked outside. The closed and shuttered windows of the neighboring building were like unseeing eyes across the alleyway. The frame of the fire escape just outside the bedroom window was mostly brown with rust, a few scattered chips of the original black paint still clinging to the metal. Nothing much else to see, but Jon didn't care. It was something other than the horror in the apartment, the sight of his brother's lifeblood, spilled and splattered like wine from an upended glass. He opened the window, which stuck at first, then acquiesced to his tugs after a moment. The air from outside smelled... urban. Exhaust, garbage, pigeon droppings. But it masked the coppery smell of blood, the acrid stench of death he feared he'd never rid his nostrils of, so he inhaled deeply and left the window open. From the street, Jon could hear the sounds of car engines revving and horns honking, reminding him that, despite the horrible presence of death in this room, life went on.

Returning to the doorway, Jon's eyes swept the room, squinting though they were in a futile attempt to keep out any disturbing images that might haunt him. A room with Michael's blood sprayed on the ceiling and pooled on the bed, but without Michael himself, already held more than enough horrors to haunt Jon for a lifetime. The bloodstained bed was directly in front of where he stood in the doorway, the outside window to his right, the closet, desk, and bookcase to his left. As he glanced to the left, he saw the black trolley-style suitcase – carry-on sized – sitting next to the desk. *All packed up and nowhere to go*, Jon thought. He walked over to it and unzipped the main compartment. Underneath a weekend's worth of clothes was Michael's laptop, the power cord coiled next to it. Jon withdrew the computer and set it on the desk, then froze. His eyes shot to Michael's rapier, perched slightly off-center in its case. Jon moved closer; one of the jewels from the hilt was missing. Not a large one, probably not terribly valuable. But missing nonetheless. Stolen? Then why hadn't the whole sword been taken, or, at least, the remaining jewels? Broken off? By whom? And how? Michael surely would never have resorted to using the heirloom as a tool or a weapon.

Jon blinked. As a weapon. If it were an emergency, might Michael have–

Scritch.

Jon started, his outstretched hand hovering between his body and the display case.

Scritch scritch scritch.

What the hell? Jon thought. The sounds seemed to be coming from back in the living room. Like a cat scratching at a sheet of metal. No, not a full sheet, and not quite scratching. It was more like—

Click. Several clicks actually, but they were so close together that they sounded as one. *Strange,* Jon thought, poking his head into the hallway between the bedroom and the living room, *that sounded just like a—*

The doorknob to the apartment turned. He *had* locked the door, hadn't he? Yes, definitely, he reassured himself. Though what that ultimately meant was somewhat less than reassuring. Not only was someone coming into the apartment; someone was coming into the apartment who had no business in here, someone who had to pick the lock. A burglar who had heard about Michael's death – and thus the unoccupied apartment and untended belongings? He closed the bedroom door to a crack, peering out to catch a glimpse of whoever was coming into the apartment unannounced. He shot a glance at the open window, his only other means of egress from the apartment. This was fight or flight time, but Jon had no intention of surrendering Michael's sanctum to this intruder without a struggle.

His eyes darted to the sword in the case. *Had* Michael tried to use it as a weapon? Jon couldn't see him using the heirloom, a priceless piece of family history, to fight with someone or something. Not unless it was a matter of life and death... Of course, considering what had happened, perhaps it had been. Perhaps Michael had tried to defend himself, and died in the process. But why? And against whom? Was the intruder who was now entering the apartment Michael's killer, coming back to tidy up the scene, to collect some fiber or fingerprint left behind, to finish some part of what he had started? All these questions, and dozens more, flew through Jon's mind in a matter of seconds as he stared at the sword. Then, as the apartment door opened, his attention was jerked back to the widening crack, and the figure that entered through it.

A Hispanic man – well-built, in his mid-thirties, and dressed in a black hooded sweatsuit – slinked through the opening, and paused immediately, tilting his head to the side slightly as though he were listening for something. *The lights!* Jon had left the lights on in the living room. That, coupled with the recently activated heating system, betrayed the recent, if not current, presence of someone else in the apartment. *Might as well have written the guy a sign*, Jon cursed himself silently.

Seemingly content that he couldn't hear anything out of the ordinary, save for the heater whirring in the icy room, the intruder closed the door quietly, cautiously, behind him. And pulled a pistol from his coat pocket.

Damn! Jon winced. Talk about bringing a knife to a gun-fight, he thought as he straightened up and padded over to the sword case, lifting the lid and soundlessly withdrawing the rapier. Despite the damage to the hilt, the sword seemed to be in working order, the balance only slightly thrown off by the new weight distribution. Jon returned to the door. As the man screwed a silencer onto the end of his weapon, his eyes probed the room, ignoring the PS3, the TV, and the other easily fenced items. He was looking for something in particular. He wasn't some stupid crook out to make a few quick bucks off a dead guy. He was here with a purpose. And he composed himself like he had done this before. Like this wasn't the first time he'd been here uninvited.

Silent intruder, gun-in-hand, two times in the same apartment in one weekend. What were the chances, unless it was the same guy? And immediately, Jon was filled with a rage like none he had ever known. He was certain he was looking at his brother's killer, picking his way through Michael's life as nonchalantly as a window shopper browsing through a store.

Jon gripped the sword's jeweled hilt so tightly his knuckles began to turn white. Was this what the guy was after? No, if Michael had used it to defend himself, if the hilt had been damaged while attacking the intruder who had ultimately murdered him, he would've been swinging it for dear life, not placing it back in its case. The cops would've put it in evidence if it had been on the floor of the scene. The intruder must have replaced it, he realized. And now, Jon had obscured any fingerprints that might've been on the hilt. But no, he thought, catching a glimpse of the man's black-gloved hands. This guy was too smart, too careful, to leave behind fingerprints. But Jon would see to it that the killer left something behind this time. His blood.

The man left the living room and began moving into the hallway. Toward the bedroom. Toward Jon. Jon took a deep breath through his nostrils, stepped behind the door just out of sight of the opening, and set his feet in a fighting stance, steeling his resolve and trying to calm his nerves and anger. He knew he was being brash by even trying to put up a fight, but Michael's honor had to be defended, his death put to rights. He only had one shot at this, or *he* might be the one shot. It was show time.

No sounds of footsteps reached Jon's ears, no audible indications of where the intruder was, what he was doing. Still coming toward the bedroom, checking out the kitchen, doubling back into the living room? But Jon waited. And waited. When the bedroom door in front of him started to inch open into the room, Jon started, his breath catching in his throat. The door stopped moving. *Damn*, he thought. Had he given himself away? What to do now? Yank open the door and rush the enemy like a Visigoth? Stay where he was and confront his enemy when the opportunity for a surprise attack presented itself? Or turn tail and climb out the window and down the fire escape to safety, to live to fight another day?

The decision was made for him as the door began to inch inward once more. The black metal end of a silencer peeked into the room. The intruder was leading with his gun. Not good.

Jon made a snap decision, yelled, and slammed his body against the door, catching the intruder by surprise and crushing his gun-toting hand against the jamb. He tried to wrench the gun from the intruder's hand, but the grip was too tight. The man kicked the door from the other side, and Jon stumbled backward. A pair of dark, determined – and now, angry – eyes greeted him, the man clutching his injured right hand with his left. The intruder raised his gun and paused briefly, a flash of surprise crossing his face as his pallor blanched slightly – almost as though he felt he were seeing a ghost. Jon took advantage of the opening and swung the sword at the man's outstretched hand, whacking his wrist with the blade's dulled edge and sending the gun flying as the intruder's hand flinched in pain. The man's eyes were momentarily fixed on the gun that fell behind him in the hallway, and Jon used the opening to kick him squarely in the chest. The intruder sucked a mouthful of air as he stumbled backward. Jon raised his sword and charged forward to deliver another attack.

The intruder glanced toward Jon, some new thought flashing through his mind, and then reached for his gun on the ground. Jon got to him first and stabbed at his torso. The man twisted his body in an effort to avoid the blade, but it pierced his side. He cried aloud in pain, the fury in his eyes growing, both men losing all reserve and fighting for their lives like feral animals.

The intruder grabbed Jon's right hand and squeezed his fingers in an iron grip, wrenching the sword from Jon's grasp. The weapon tumbled out of reach – through the open bathroom door, just off the hallway. The intruder threw a slow left jab at Jon, who moved his head to the side just in time, the wind from the punch brushing his ear. *My turn*, Jon thought as he kept his momentum from the dodge going and delivered a left to intruder's solid jaw, followed by a right to the solar plexus. The intruder wheezed as he fell to the ground, Jon panting with rage and exertion at his feet.

Then the tables turned. The intruder sucked in a deep breath of air, gripped his pistol between his feet, and flicked the weapon through the air and into to his left hand, wincing at the pain in his side. And just like that, the man had a gun in his hand again. Jon's eyes widened as he saw the weapon pointed directly at his face. A voice in his head, barely audible over the pounding of blood in his ears, screamed one word: *run*.

So he did. White drywall dust rained down on Jon's head as the bullet intended for him passed through the space his face had occupied just moments earlier and pierced the ceiling overhead. He darted into Michael's room, kicked the door closed, ran to the window, and hoisted himself over the sill with one hand, landing hard on the rusty fire escape outside. The bolts fastening the escape to the building seemed to give way as his weight hit the structure. A horrendous creaking, groaning sound emanated from beneath his feet, and Jon was all but certain that the whole stairway was about to let loose from the building, that he was about to plummet fifty feet to the alley below, to be mangled in a gruesome mess of blood and twisted steel.

But it held. Jon scrambled down the rickety stairs, swinging himself around the corner of each flight by pivoting on the inside handrail, a smudge of rust being driven deeper into his palm and fingers with each momentum-propelled turn. A *ping* of metal on metal ricocheted from somewhere near him. The bastard was still shooting at him! Jon instinctively lowered his head as he hurtled down the steps. Each time his feet hit the metal flooring, the rusting hulk creaked louder, seemed to lean further into the alley as its bolts were pulled from the brickwork. His footfalls crashed and echoed as he thundered down the derelict zigzag. Another *ping*, this one sending sparks from the handrail right next to Jon. Leaping down the last three stairs, he hit the final platform. The ladder was up, and one look at its rusted grooves told Jon that it wouldn't lower in a hurry. And he didn't have the time to fight with it, trying to get it to break free of its months or years of neglect.

Still ten feet above the ground, Jon scrambled from side-to-side on the bottom platform – mainly to find another, quicker way down, but the additional perk of presenting a moving target for the gunman above didn't hurt either. He spotted a closed dumpster a few feet down the alley from the fire escape. Another *ping*, another spark. This time the shot had hit the ground right where Jon would have been standing had he continued his stride before he had halted to look at the dumpster. The dumpster had saved his life once simply by distracting him, he reasoned subconsciously in the span of milliseconds. Perhaps jumping onto it might provide a more long-term salvation.

Another *ping*, this one hitting the floor of the level just above him, right over his head. It was now or never. He got a running start of a few steps, grabbed the rusty metal railing with both hands, hoisted himself over, and flew downward, fearing both a bullet from above and a broken ankle or leg from below. He received neither. As soon as Jon hit the lid of the dumpster, he collapsed his legs and let his momentum carry him into a somersault. Relieved that his move actually worked – on his first try and while wearing the backpack that he had all but forgotten about in the excitement – he heard a *crack* from just behind him as a bullet penetrated the thick hardened plastic of the lid. Reaching the edge of the dumpster, he rolled off, landed on his feet, and hit the ground running, bobbing and weaving as he ran in an effort to throw off the gunman's aim. One more bullet hit the ground behind him as he kept flying down the alleyway until he reached the corner of the building.

He turned, briefly, in mid-stride, to see if his attacker was following him down the fire escape. The gunman was still in

Michael's apartment, his upper body stuck out the window Jon had exited from, loading another magazine into his pistol. Even from that distance, Jon could see the fanatical look in the man's eyes, a look he wouldn't soon forget. And then the look changed to one of intense concentration as the gunman extended his arms and aimed his pistol at Jon.

A split-second later, the muzzle flashed and a shard of brick exploded from the corner of the building. But Jon had already darted around the corner and down the street.

Chapter 10

Enrique Ramirez cursed in Spanish, then pulled himself back into the apartment. With his good hand, he pulled the window closed, and latched it shut. There was no use going after the guy now. He had too much of a head start, and Enrique wouldn't be able to keep pace with the bleeding wound in his side. With his tongue, he probed the inside of his mouth, sweeping around the teeth on the right side of his jaw, trying to find the source of the blood he tasted. No teeth knocked loose or out, but the inside of his right cheek was raw where it had been sandwiched between knuckles and molars. He slowly made a fist with his right hand. It hurt like hell, but he hadn't broken anything. Thank God. But it had been enough to screw up his aim, enough to make him the first Division agent in fifty years to leave a witness.

A photograph on a bookshelf caught his eye. The target from last night – Michael Rickner – smiling for the camera alongside the guy Enrique had just chased from the apartment. He thought the guy had looked familiar. At first, he thought he might have been the ghost of the other day's kill. Was this Rickner's brother then? What was it with this apartment, with this *family*? *Twice* he had been caught unawares by the brothers. Never before, in nine years with the Division, had he made a mistake. Now he had made two in as many days.

He stumbled to the bathroom, stripped to the waist, grabbed a blue towel from the rack, and pressed it to his injured side. It was bleeding pretty badly, but the damage seemed to be superficial. Seeing that there was no medicine cabinet in the room, he bent down, mindful of the tender muscles in his side, and rummaged under the sink for a first-aid kit. Finding one, he stood, set it on the counter, opened it, and procured a handful of cotton balls, a bottle of hydrogen peroxide, a roll of gauze, and a package of butterfly bandages. After cleaning the wound with the cotton balls and the peroxide, he closed the wound as best he could with the bandages, then wrapped the gauze around his torso, covering the slice in his side with four layers. He tossed the bloody cotton balls into the toilet, pocketing the rest of the gauze roll and another handful of cotton balls for later.

Then he walked back into the hallway to survey the damage. Bullet hole in the ceiling, two in the bedroom wall above the bed. Nothing a little toothpaste – the poor man's spackle – wouldn't fix. He'd have to ditch the gun soon enough, anyway, and by the time the bullets in the ceiling and wall were found – *if* they were found – the weapon that had fired them would be long gone, with nothing for Ballistics to trace the projectiles to.

And then there was that unsightly blood trail. That much blood in an apartment, especially one that was so recently the scene of a police investigation, was bound to raise some questions. Add that to the fact that the blood belonged to a military veteran who was supposed to be dead, and some real red flags would start to go up. Enrique felt his face growing hot, his indignation with the Rickner brothers mounting, his anger at himself and his carelessness reaching a fever pitch. He kicked the sword at his feet, which flew across the floor and bounced off the baseboard. Releasing a deep sigh, he bit his bottom lip and shook his head in disappointment. How had this happened? But now, more importantly, how would he put it right?

First things first. Take care of the scene. From the bathroom, he grabbed the toothpaste – which, thankfully, was white, so it matched the walls and ceiling. From the kitchen, he got a small butter knife, which he then used to apply the toothpaste-spackle to the bullet holes, wincing as he stretched to reach them. That taken care of, he returned the toothpaste to its place and pocketed the knife.

And now, for the blood. He toweled the blood off his shirt, then put both the shirt and the towel in the bathtub. Using a bottle of bleach he found under the bathroom sink, he poured it liberally along the hallway, the bedroom, and everywhere else he had leaked. Returning to the tub, he poured the bleach over the towel and the shirt, rinsed the pinkish runoff away, then repeated. When he was content that they wouldn't leak color or DNA, he wrung them out, then poured bleach around the tub and down the drain. More bleach went into the toilet and the blood-soaked cotton balls floating within. Then he flushed the whole mess down the toilet and poured still more bleach around the bowl, flushing again to make sure all the blood was gone. Next, with a scrubbing brush he found under the kitchen sink, he rubbed the bloodstains on the carpet into oblivion. He scoured the walls and other surfaces to ensure that no arterial spray had been missed.

Except for the faint chemical smell, and the soon-to-be faded splotches of carpet, his tracks were covered. The bullet holes in the alley would be attributed to gang warfare or a drug deal gone wrong, and nothing more would be thought of it. Enrique was safe. He found a few unscented tea candles in a kitchen cupboard and lit them, hoping to burn away most of the scent. Staring at the sword lying on the floor, he made a snap decision to take it with him. That would accomplish two things: remove potentially critical evidence, and, at least symbolically, disarm one of his enemies. He wanted to snap the sword in half, but he restrained himself. *Focus your anger*, he told himself. *Channel it*.

Next order of business: finish what he had come here for in the first place. He walked back to the bedroom and saw his prize. The laptop sat on the desk to the left of the doorway, just waiting to be taken. *This* was how easy it should have been. Pick the lock, walk in, grab the laptop, and leave. And it would have been that easy, if only Rickner's brother hadn't—

Enrique took a deep breath. He'd get to dealing with the other brother. One thing at a time. He didn't need to be distracted and make *yet another* mistake. The laptop was unplugged, but, looking around, he spotted its coiled power cord lying in the open suitcase nearby. May as well take it too, Enrique decided, although the model was common enough.

He flipped open his cell phone and punched in a number.

"Yes?" replied Greer's breathless voice on the other end.

"The package is secure."

"Excellent." Enrique thought he could hear a car horn in the distance on the other end of the line.

"Good to hear," Greer responded. "I knew you wouldn't let us down. Corner of Massachusetts and Eighteenth. Black Lexus with Nevada plates. Front passenger window will be cracked. Password exchange Bravo-Three-Seven-Romeo. After identity is verified, pass package through window to female EDA officer inside."

"Massachusetts and Eighteenth. Black Lexus, Nevada plates. Bravo-Three-Seven-Romeo. Pass package through front passenger window. Understood. When, sir?"

"One hour. And Ramirez?"

"Sir?"

"You've done your country a great service. And loyalty like that will be rewarded. Sooner than you know, my son."

Enrique swallowed. "Thank you, sir."

"Until tomorrow morning at nine, then."

The line disconnected, and the agent stared at the floor for a moment. It hurt him to lie to Greer – even if by omission – but revealing the truth of what had just transpired with the Rickner brother would hurt even more.

He took a dark blue sweatshirt from Michael's closet and put it on, an attempt to hide the bloody wound his torn undershirt exposed. The sleeves were too long, Michael having been two inches taller than Ramirez, but it would do. He grabbed two plastic grocery bags from the recycling bin in the kitchen, placing the laptop and power cord into one, the wet sweatshirt, towel-wrapped sword, and scrubbing brush in the other. He snuffed out the candles, poured the liquid wax down the kitchen sink, and wrapped the rest of each candle in the towel in the bag. There certainly was no reason to tell Greer about his little slip-up. Something big was brewing over at the Division, and Greer didn't need this as a distraction. No, Enrique Ramirez cleaned up his own messes, before they became problems for anyone else. He had sanitized the scene himself, and done a darned good job of it, all things considered. There was just one last loose end to tie up, and he would do that on his own. No, there was no reason to inform Greer, or even officially involve the Division at all.

Enrique would take care of the other Rickner brother himself.

Chapter 11

Blocks away from Michael's apartment, Jon ducked into a clothing store, trying to catch his breath as he wandered around the store, pretending to browse through the racks of designer shirts. Looking around him, he verified that he was almost alone in the store. The lone sales clerk was helping the only other customer in the store, a college-age kid sporting spiky hair and already wearing designer threads. Satisfied at his relative privacy, Jon whipped out his phone and called 911. After reporting the incident in the apartment as best he could, he hung up and dialed Mara's cell number.

"Hello?" she answered hesitantly.

"Mara, it's Jon."

"Oh, sorry. Haven't programmed your number in my phone yet. Did you—"

"Listen, I was just in Michael's apartment and some guy broke in and tried to kill me."

"What?" she replied incredulously after a moment of stunned silence.

"A guy, a pro from the looks of it, just broke into Michael's apartment while I was there. He was looking for something. I got the jump on him, injured him I think, and I managed to get away, but barely."

"Wh— Jon, what— Are you serious?"

"Absolutely. Mara, I think this guy might've been the one who killed Michael." Mara replied with silence, a silence Jon figured held a battle of emotions: relief at the affirmation of her hope that Michael had indeed not committed suicide, anger, and a new wave of grief at the thought – or rather the apparent confirmation of her suspicion – that he had been murdered. Jon was undergoing a similar emotional battle himself, now that the blind rage that had consumed him at the apartment was abating.

"Oh God, Jon…" she started, the whole sordid affair starting to sink in. "Are you alright?"

"I'm fine. A little sore after the James Bond moves I had to pull off, but I'm still alive." He winced as soon as the last words had left his mouth, realizing that his brother hadn't been as lucky in *his* encounter with the intruder.

"We have to go to the cops, Jon. They've got it all wrong. They're calling Michael's death a suicide. And if this guy's still out there, he has to be caught."

"I've already called them. They said they'd send somebody. I'm going to meet them outside the building."

"I'm leaving now. See you there."

***

Jon was pacing outside the building, waiting for the cops to let him know it was safe to come up, when Mara walked around the corner. His face brightened slightly when he caught sight of her, and he ran to meet her.

"I parked around the corner. What's going on?"

"They're up there right now clearing the scene. Apparently the guy who attacked me is long gone, but they're checking neighboring apartments and stairwells and such."

"Michael's backpack," Mara said in a tone that didn't seem to expect any sort of response, brushing her fingers affectionately over the bag that was slung from Jon's shoulders.

"Yeah, I'm fine too; thanks for asking."

She chuckled and gave him a smug smile. "Glad to see you made it out in one piece. Any permanent damage?"

"I've had worse. Bruised and banged up a little. But he was bleeding all over the place. I cut him with Michael's rapier. His DNA's gotta be all over that apartment."

"You attacked him with a *sword*?" Mara didn't even try to suppress a laugh. "You are *so* your brother's brother, you know that?"

Jon managed a smile himself. "Adventurers born in the wrong century. No more blank spaces on the map."

"Maybe maps aren't the only things with blank spaces."

Jon grunted. "True enough. And filling in the blanks is just as dangerous as it's always been. But with all the evidence our fight left behind, I'd say Michael's killer is as good as nabbed."

"Knock on wood," Mara said, lightly rapping her knuckles against her own skull.

"Mr. Rickner?"

Jon turned to see a tall female officer with dirty blonde hair standing in the doorway of the building, beckoning to him.

"Yeah?" Jon's eyes were wide, a hopeful expression on his face. "Did you find him?"

"Sir, I need to verify your statement." The officer was stone-faced. "Could you go through what happened again?"

Jon took a breath in exasperation. "Just like I told the 911 operator. I was in my brother's apartment when a Latino guy picked the lock and broke in. He moved like he was looking for something, and when he realized I was in there, he drew a gun and started creeping toward the bedroom, where I was hiding. I defended myself with a sword my brother kept in his room."

The officer, whose name badge identified her as G. Mabry, cleared her throat. Jon paused and looked at the officer, but it was clear she wanted him to continue his statement.

"I cut him across his midsection, and he started bleeding everywhere. He shot probably a dozen times at me, both in the apartment and as I was running down the fire escape and out of the alley."

"Uh huh."

Officer Mabry studied Jon, her arms crossed, an eyebrow raised quizzically, like she was trying to figure out what kind of game he was playing, as though his complaint was a distraction for some unknown offense of which he was guilty.

"What's the problem?" Jon raised his hands in front of him, palms up, in frustration. "That's the same statement I gave the 911 operator. Why are you looking at me like I've grown a second head?"

"Come with me, please, Mr. Rickner." Officer Mabry turned to go back into the building.

Jon looked at Mara. "Can she come–"

"I can't, Jon." Mara's hand was on her cross again, polishing the silver between her thumb and forefinger. "I just can't go in there yet. It's still too fresh."

"Mr. Rickner?" Mabry was tapping her thumb on her belt, waiting.

"I'll be right back," Jon told Mara, squeezing her shoulder. He entered the building with the officer, lost in thought. The building was a little run-down, and it lacked security guards and closed circuit cameras. The chances of getting this guy on tape were negligible. The apartments next door and across the hall were vacant, and Jon didn't remember hearing many day-time noises from Michael's floor at all earlier. Everyone was probably at church, at work, or sleeping off a late-night bender. No witnesses, except Jon and the evidence. And, as he followed Officer Mabry up the stairwell, he got the distinct impression that even that wouldn't help catch the intruder.

Exiting the stairwell, they approached the door to Michael's apartment. Another officer, a rotund yet muscular man with a shaved head, stood outside the door.

"We finished the door-to-door," the officer, whose badge read J. Rioux, told them. "No one saw or heard anything."

Jon gritted his teeth as Mabry led Jon into the apartment. Another cop was there, writing something on a pad of paper. Michael's bags were still by the doorway. The PS3 and TV were still in the living room. But what surprised Jon was not what was there, but what was missing.

The blood trail, the sword, the bullet holes, all of the evidence was *gone*. A faint chemical smell hung in the air, but none of the cops seemed to take any notice of it. Jon looked around the apartment with wide-open eyes and a gaping mouth, dumbfounded. *Had* he imagined the whole thing? *No, no way*, he thought, feeling the soreness in his upper back from where he had rolled over the backpack while on the dumpster lid. He walked through the scene of the fight, but no bloodstains were visible. No rapier covered in the assailant's DNA. No bullet holes in the ceiling. Nothing.

Surprised but undaunted, Jon stalked down the hall to the bedroom and scoured the room for bullet holes. There were two roughly round patches in the wall above the bed that were a slightly different color than the white-painted drywall around them. Bullet holes?

"There!" Jon pointed to the wall, and Mabry slowly trudged into the room, expecting to be disappointed. "Bullet holes."

"Bullet holes? Come on, Mr. Rickner. Please stop wasting the department's time and resources."

"They're bullet holes. He shot at me and the bullets ended up there."

"I see two holes where some former occupant hung a picture or two and spackled over them before he or she moved out."

The glass rapier display case yawned open, visibly empty. Jon pointed to it. "I fought back with the sword that was in that case. It's gone now. I cut him with it and he took it with him."

"And why did your brother have a sword, exactly?"

"It was an heirloom."

"So you grabbed this priceless heirloom and fought this alleged intruder with it?"

"Yes, that's exactly what happened. The empty display case–"

"Is proof of nothing. I've got empty display cases at home. It doesn't mean that some swashbuckling intruder stole a sword from it."

Jon kicked the foot of the bed in frustration. This lady did just didn't want to find a crime scene here. And then Jon saw the desk.

The laptop was not where he had left it. The intruder must have taken it. *That* was what he had been looking for.

Mara's words came flooding back. *Michael's research should be on his laptop.* His *research*? That's what this guy had been after? That was why Michael was killed?

When it finally came, Jon's voice was hushed, awed. "He took the laptop."

"Hmm?" Mabry asked in an impatient tone.

"The guy who was here, the guy who shot at me, he took the laptop. That must've been what he was here for."

"Sir, there is no sign of forced entry, and no evidence of the sword fight you claim took place. If you want to report this as a burglary, then I need you to write out a list of what was taken, and we'll see what we can do to recover your property." She whipped out a pad of paper and a pen from a pouch on her belt. "It is extremely important, however, that you tell us exactly what actually happened if you want to maximize our chances of finding the culprit."

Jon narrowed his eyes in frustration. "I already *told* you what happened. The guy just… cleaned up after himself."

Officer Mabry made a face that indicated she didn't believe him. "Okay, how long were you out of the apartment before you called 911?"

"I don't know." Jon shrugged. "Maybe ten, fifteen minutes?"

"You waited fifteen minutes between being shot at by an armed burglar and actually calling the police?"

"I don't know how long it actually was. The guy was following me down the fire escape. I just wanted to make sure I was safe before I stopped to call anyone."

Officer Mabry tilted her head forward and raised an eyebrow. "Fifteen minutes."

Jon fixed her with a steely glare. "It happened."

"It sounds pretty darned suspect, if you ask me."

Jon shook his head in disbelief. "Are you going to help me or not?"

"Look, Mr. Rickner—"

"Jon."

"Fine. Jon. I assume you realize filing a false police report is a crime. However," she continued with an insufferably condescending air, "you've suffered a loss, and it's not uncommon for the loved ones of suicide victims to try to rationalize the seemingly inexplicable."

"But—"

Officer Mabry held up her palm to cut him off, then continued as if Jon hadn't tried to interject. "So as long as you don't send our department on any more wild goose chases, we won't press charges." She placed her hand on the young man's shoulder, and it took every ounce of Jon's self-control not to shove her hand away. "I'm sorry about your loss, Jon. I really am, but you're going about your grieving the wrong way. Don't grasp at false hopes and *Three Musketeer* fantasies, and don't involve the authorities in your delusions."

Jon bit his lip, repressing the words and tones he really wanted to deliver. "Fine," he finally huffed through clenched teeth. "I won't."

And he meant it. He would get to the bottom of this himself.

Chapter 12

Langley, Virginia

Blumhurst.

The name was as distasteful to Harrison Greer as it was shrouded in mystery. The agent who went wrong. The one flaw since the Division's inception seventy years ago. The man who had, for all intents and purposes, betrayed Greer's grandfather, Walton Greer. And, perhaps, the key to finally getting what the Division had been seeking for the better part of a century.

Greer cursed himself for not catching this earlier. As much as he would like to, he simply couldn't personally keep up with all of the intel on everyone that the Division had dealings with. While the Division was still necessarily small, especially by the standards of the traditionally bloated bureaucracies of Washington, the amount of information they had to pore through these days was simply massive. Gone were the days when simple phone taps and manual surveillance would suffice to glean the needed intel on a subject. The means for communication these days were infinitely diverse, quick, and vast. Cellular phones, text messaging, the Internet, email, social networking. Viral videos, tweeting. These would have been the realm of science fiction just a few years ago, yet today, they were a very real fact of life. And it made the job of controlling the flow of information incredibly difficult. Once an idea hit the Internet, it was all but impossible to stop. One user uploads it to his website, his Facebook status, or tweets it to a few friends, and within milliseconds, the great unwashed masses, from Belgium to Bangladesh, from Jordan to Jamaica, would have access to the idea, could add to it, expound upon it, flesh it out with evidence and speculation. Today, one bullet might not be heard around the world, but one idea could certainly incite revolutions around the world. Even now, revolutions were spilling across the Middle East, promulgated largely by the free flow of ideas, often inspired by people and situations in wholly different countries.

Yes, an idea was a dangerous thing, but, thankfully, Greer and the Division only had one particular idea to keep under wraps. One secret that had been successfully swept under the rug for nearly a century. And every time someone threatened to come too close to that idea, it was the Division's job to eliminate that threat. Unfortunately, Greer realized, in their zeal to snuff out threats before they had a chance to dispense even a whiff of the unspeakable truth on the Internet, they may have destroyed their best hope in years at finishing off the mission that Walton Greer, first director of the Division, had started.

But then again, maybe not. Greer turned the next page in the folder of intel that Recon had put together for him. He smiled despite himself. Michael Rickner had been good. Very good. According to information Recon had pulled off his computer, Rickner had uncovered a lead Greer thought the Division had covered up years ago. But Rickner found a back door into the truth. Or the beginning of it, anyway. The first breadcrumb that could ultimately lead Greer to what he so desperately sought. The culmination of his family's legacy. The one thing he absolutely needed to finish before the cancer finally claimed his life. And that first bread crumb lay with the secret of a man dead more than half a century, a man of whom Greer had heard stories from his grandfather, and later, from his father.

Agent Roger Blumhurst.

In 1957, Walton Greer had given Blumhurst a special, somewhat unorthodox mission. To reclaim the one substantive loose end, the only evidence that could ever prove the horrible secret that the Division was tasked with protecting. The Dossiers, as the Division referred to them. The only problem was that the Dossiers were guarded, as they had been for decades, by a man with more power and influence in many circles than the President himself. And this powerful man, despite decades of pleading from top government officials – many of whom he considered friends – would not relinquish control of the evidence. In fact, all he would say was that they were in "a safe place." Safe from whom, he never bothered to elaborate, but Walton Greer, realizing the man was not long for this world, decided the time for decisive action was upon them. So he summoned his most trusted field agent, Roger Blumhurst, to undertake another mission in addition to his regular duties. Beg, borrow, steal, or kill, Blumhurst was to recover the Dossiers. At any cost.

In September 1957, Blumhurst began a recon mission on one of the most powerful and famous men of the day. He followed him everywhere he went – covertly, of course – and, when that failed to provide any clues as to where the man might have hidden the Dossiers, he turned to violence. In the cloakroom during a ball at the Waldorf Astoria, Blumhurst managed to isolate the man and rough him up in one of the stalls. Yet even when faced with the business end of Blumhurst's revolver, the man maintained his silence. It wasn't until the man rejoined the party, blaming the soreness Blumhurst's beating had given him on fatigue alone, that Blumhurst realized the tack he should take. The man wanted the past covered up as much as the Division did. Yet he was too wracked by guilt to bring himself to fully destroy the evidence. And it was that guilt that Blumhurst trusted would lead him to the Dossiers' hiding place.

When the man was away on business the last week of September, Blumhurst took the opportunity to break into his home. The mansion was a miniature palace, yet, thankfully, the servants in residence were few and not on the estate at the time. Jimmying a window open, he made his way to the great man's study, where, hidden behind a false partition in the bookcase, he uncovered a wall safe. Blumhurst had the skills to crack the safe if need be, but, on a whim, he tried the first combination that came to mind. The day, month, and year it all started. The day the great man had made the fateful decision that would haunt him for the rest of his life.

The safe opened.

After that, the story got murky. Blumhurst originally reported that he found some sort of journal inside, and he took it with him. Then he changed his story, saying that it was merely a ledger, and after he had thumbed through it, he left it behind. He eventually told Walton Greer that it was a dead end. And Walton, thinking he might have chosen the wrong man for the job after all, ended Blumhurst's special mission and put him back on elimination duty. Walton planned to give the agent the third degree about what he really found in that safe, but Blumhurst killed himself before he had the chance. And, for some reason, Blumhurst chose the most conspicuous place and manner of suicide that he could. Which was very bad press for the Division. Or could have been if they hadn't begun their cover-up immediately. And it was this very cover-up that young scholar Michael Rickner had inadvertently stumbled upon.

Rickner had all sorts of intel on the cover-up, and was beginning to unravel the threads of the original conspiracy itself. But it was less his work on the conspiracy that had piqued Harrison Greer's attention; it was his work on finding the Dossiers. Michael Rickner had the right leads, the proper drive, notable discretion about prematurely publishing anything, and, above all else, the brains to finally uncover the great man's hiding place for the Dossiers. The only problem was, thanks to the Division's characteristic efficiency in eliminating potential threats, Michael Rickner, perhaps the greatest asset to finding the Dossiers in decades, was dead.

Greer turned the page. He smiled again, this time with teeth showing. Things might turn out alright after all. The caution that Michael Rickner had shown would be exacerbated in his replacement. As would his drive to find the Dossiers. By all reports, the replacement had a similar thought process as Michael, and was, if it were possible, even more brilliant. All the replacement needed was the proper leads. And Greer would make sure that those leads – closely controlled, of course – were extended.

Until Greer finally took hold of the Dossiers and completed his final service to his country. Until his family's legacy was completed and his grandfather's betrayal by Roger Blumhurst avenged. And then, the replacement would join Michael Rickner in death. Buried, along with the truth, forever.

Greer grabbed the phone off his desk and placed two calls. His hands were shaking with excitement as he replaced the receiver. Then he stood, stretched, and headed out the door. He was too full of energy to stay cooped up in the office today. All the pieces were finally coming together, and tomorrow the game officially began. But today he needed to get out, to move. As he locked up his office and headed down the hallway, he decided he would walk around the National Mall in Washington. The expanse of man-tamed nature commingled with the rich history of their nation to form one of Greer's favorite places for reflection in the area. Though the weather was still a bit chilly, the sky was brilliantly blue today, and Greer realized that he didn't have that many blue skies left to enjoy.

But even though he knew the cancer was there, a slowly ticking time bomb within his own body, Greer didn't feel sick at all. In fact, thinking about the promise that tomorrow held, he realized he had never felt more alive.

Chapter 13

Manhattan, New York

Despite the decade that had passed since the attacks of 9/11, the site of the former World Trade Center, also known as Ground Zero, still largely looked like a hole in the ground. A quiet, reverent place where pilgrims traveled from all around to pay homage to the victims of the devastating attack, to pray, to reflect. New towers were beginning to arise from the site, half-finished skyscrapers that would always have the ghosts of their predecessors lingering in their very foundations. A high chain-link fence surrounded the site, construction equipment and personnel visible through the gaps in the tarpaulins and boards that covered much of the fence. At the northern edge of the site, peering through one such gap, stood a man who had come here every day in the two weeks since his six months of training had finished. Brainwashing might have been a better name for it, he thought, but here he was, finished and free again. Until he was called up, of course. Which, Wayne Wilkins feared, would be sooner than he was ready for.

To say the past few months of his life had been a soul-searching, introspective experience would be not wholly untrue, but there is only so much probing of one's own thoughts and beliefs one can do while new thoughts and beliefs are being shoved in on a daily basis. But if there was one thing the Division had underestimated about Wayne, it was his mental ability, both in its acuity and in his ability to shut off certain stimuli, certain parts of his brain even, in order to be able to think for himself. Something he felt he was just beginning to do for the first time in a long, long time. And he was here today – and every day – in remembrance of that moment, nine-and-a-half years ago, when his world had been turned on its head, and Wayne had drastically changed the course of his life.

One sunny Tuesday morning in September, nineteen terrorists hijacked four commercial jets and used them as weapons of mass destruction against the very people who had created the planes, the business bigwigs in New York and the military honchos in Washington. Destroyed one world icon and damaged another. Stole three-thousand lives and crushed countless others through injury and disease, the loss of loved ones, the faltering of the economy. Brought international terrorism, that unpleasant experience that *those* people in *those* countries *over there* had to deal with on a regular basis, to the doorstep of the American homeland, a wake-up call for top policy-makers and common citizenry alike. One of the countless Americans directly affected by this catastrophe was Wayne Wilkins, and he had been hit worse than most. Two of the dead from the World Trade Center attack were Edward and Martha Wilkins: Wayne's parents.

Martha had been secretary to the CFO of a major brokerage firm that had its offices on the ninety-fifth floor of Tower One. Right where the first plane hit. Had she seen it coming, stared as the plane came far too close to the tower, felt the shocking realization that it was going to hit them? What were her last moments on earth like? Did she run for the door, hide under a desk, scream and panic? Wayne had often returned to those painful questions in the years after the towers fell. No, knowing his mother, she would have undoubtedly warned as many of her colleagues as she could, attempting to drag them to whatever safety she could find. Which ultimately was none, but that wouldn't have stopped her from doing all she could. It never had.

Ed Wilkins had been a lifelong firefighter. Four months from retirement, but he had planned to continue on with the volunteer program, despite his relatively advanced age. Saving and protecting people and their well-being: that had always been his greatest passion in life. He had already brought two groups of civilians to safety from within Tower Two and had gone back in, against advisement, to try to rescue some more. Minutes later, the tower's structure gave out and collapsed into a mass of steel, drywall, and human flesh.

Wayne, then a scholarship student at Stanford who was just starting his sophomore year of undergraduate study, was just heading to the gym for his early-morning workout when he heard the news. All that day, he sat in his apartment, glued to the television, watching the nonstop news coverage on every network. He called all of his friends and his parents' friends and his friends' parents: every number he had for everyone he knew in the New York City area. Left messages and called back ten minutes later. No one had seen or heard from either Ed or Martha. Air traffic was grounded, and Wayne was stranded on the other side of the country from his parents, unable to do anything to help them. And being powerless was a feeling Wayne could not abide.

When the death tally came out, Ed and Martha Wilkins were counted among the victims. Wayne considered that his name should have been on that list as well, for a part of him, a *huge* part, had died along with them, had fallen along with the towers, was buried under dust and ash like the bones of his parents.

Whether dropping out of college to join the military was a conscious decision or just a knee-jerk reaction of rebellion against the world that had betrayed everything he held dear was a question Wayne had never really started to ponder until just recently. He still didn't have all the answers, but what had happened, happened. When the invasion of Afghanistan was announced, the Taliban having been linked to the attacks that stole his family from him, Wayne had enlisted in the Army. And had almost instantly made a name for himself.

Even before he had completed basic training, his commanding officers had taken special note of him and had flagged him as Green Beret material. When he got on the ground in Afghanistan, he had exceeded their already lofty expectations. He was put on a special detail that carried out covert missions, including assassinations of key targets, infiltrating high-security compounds, and other projects that intentionally never made the news yet were essential in winning the war.

Wayne killed to numb the pain. It took his mind off of the loss he had recently suffered. And these were the bastards who had been responsible for that loss. Maybe not directly, but that didn't really matter to him. *They* were all the same. Weren't they?

He escaped from the painful familiarity of life as he had known it, from the impotence he had felt when trapped three-thousand miles away from his parents when they had needed him most. The military allowed him to escape the normal life that was no longer normal for him, to take action against those who had taken his family from him. His anger and hatred for the terrorists, now dead with their victims, spilled out to those he killed on the battlefield. Yet every face inside his crosshairs that resembled those of the terrorists, every efficient kill that he made and mission he completed – kills and missions that eventually, with his lack of familial ties and loner lifestyle, turned the Division on to him as a potential candidate for their exclusive ranks – he felt his parents, their memory, and what they had stood for, getting pushed further and further away. No amount of blood, no number of vengeful killings could fill the void that that fateful Tuesday morning had opened inside of him. He closed himself off to his brothers-in-arms, suffering his grief and guilt on his own. Until one day, when everything changed again.

Through an emissary, Harrison Greer, director of a mysterious extra-governmental organization known simply as the Division, contacted Wayne. Greer had expressed admiration at Wayne's exceptional mission success rate – and killing prowess. He wanted Wayne for a top-secret mission, one that would last the rest of his career, would have him stationed in his hometown of New York City, and would require him to sever all personal relationships – of which Wayne had none of any consequence at this point. A mission that was of the utmost importance to the nation's future.

Wayne had mulled over the proposal long enough for Greer to send another message, following up on the first. On one hand, he had a lot of questions about this long-term mission, questions that would likely remain unanswered unless and until he officially accepted the assignment. It would mean moving back to the States, to his hometown, no less, the site of the happier days of his life. Where dreams were once born, and where they had died in a noxious cloud of asbestos and screams.

On the other hand, it was a change, a change in a method that very much was not doing anything to ease the pain, to heal the wound he had been trying to salve with the blood of insurgents for the better part of a decade. Perhaps here he would find the answer to his big unanswerable *why*s, to finally being able to put his parents' ghosts to rest, and his insatiable guilt along with them.

He had chosen the path less traveled, and almost immediately it had made a difference. The deaths of four good men, three of whom he had been as close to as he had been to anyone in recent years, were required in order to plausibly kill him for the official record. Even his superiors in the military didn't know the true story behind what had happened that day. Price, Sedaris, and Jenkins. All dead. All because of him. And their screams, echoing up the valley to his benumbed ears, still rang loud in his dreams.

"Jameson" had been an English-speaking Iraqi who Greer had recruited off the radar and away from any scrutiny. The military had no record of Jameson existing, of him getting in the Humvee, of Wilkins getting out. Only the Division, and the select few who were aware of its internal workings, had any idea that Wayne Wilkins was not only still alive, but had also returned to his old stomping grounds. The extensive facial reconstruction surgery he had undergone as part of his training eliminated the chances of his being recognized by anyone from his old life, while his acquaintance with the city itself would prove an invaluable asset when carrying out his missions. But those were far from the only changes he was forced to endure.

Immediately after Iraq, he had been brought back to the States, to the Division's secure facility in Virginia, officially just an annex of the CIA, but with security so tight that even the director of that more well-known agency didn't even have access to the building or knowledge of what went on behind its doors. Wayne's training program commenced immediately upon his admittance to the facility. Wayne already knew how to infiltrate almost any sort of building, how to remain undetected in all sorts of situations and surroundings, and, of course, how to kill effectively and without reservation. The vast majority of his training was psychological, impressing upon him the importance of keeping a certain government secret a secret. The necessity of killing one man to preserve the lives of a million. Pruning the bushes, controlled burning, a dozen metaphors were used to illustrate the importance of their mission.

Wayne had listened, learned, and absorbed the lessons they fed him. Externally, he was the obedient soldier he had always been. Inside, however, something didn't click. Or rather, something that hadn't clicked in a long while, but perhaps should have, finally did. He had killed in Afghanistan and Iraq because *they* were the people who had killed his parents. *They* were the ones who threatened to destroy the country he loved, the life his forefathers had died for. To him, *they* were all the same. Middle Easterners, Muslims, *they* all hated America, *they* all were part of the problem that had stolen his family from him and wanted to steal everything else he held dear. But now, hearing his new assignment, the targets being people who he actually considered people, his fellow Americans, he paused, privately of course, to reconsider. He had joined the military partly out of anger. Anger at the Middle East, that backward region *over there* that was the embodiment of everything he thought he hated, the people who were all alike, who had all conspired to kill three thousand innocent civilians on September 11th. This aimless and blinded anger was honed by the military to make him more effective in his role. After all, his job wasn't to rescue or assist innocent Afghani or Iraqi civilians, those people whose liberty and well-being had ostensibly been the military's goal in the invasions. No, his job was to blow up what he was told to blow up, steal what he was told to steal, kill who he was told to kill. And he had done that beautifully.

But there was something else that had inspired him to join the fight. The anger had been tapped far more often during those past years, keeping it fresh and well-fed, constantly on the surface. But below the anger, another element lay dormant, but alive: love. Love for his parents, love for his country, love for greater humanity, a love that had been a large part of his life right through September 10th, 2001. And in his new training, in hearing the argument for killing his neighbors and fellow countrymen, it finally rose to the surface in protest.

One night after training, lying in his bed at the Division's complex, he reflected on the past nine years, something he had never done during that whole chapter of his life. They had all been dedicated to killing people. But he had never really thought of them as people. *They* were targets. *They* were the enemy. *They* were terrorists who would kill him, would slaughter millions of innocent Americans, would try to bring America to its knees. It was kill or be killed, a thousand times over. At least, so he was told. But who were *they*, really? As he lay on his mattress, a flood of images came back to him, images he didn't consciously remember, but saw nonetheless: a child's doll, discarded among the rubble; a photograph of a smiling Iraqi family, singed and fluttering through the bomb-riddled streets like an autumn leaf; the shriek of a little Afghani boy as he saw Wayne kill his father, a Taliban general, then turn the blade on the young witness, the boy's shriek ending in a gurgle of blood. That night in his bed, years after the fact, Wayne was hit with the implications of all he'd done, and for the first time since the ceremonies honoring his father's sacrifice, he cried. Emotions, not just anger and hate, had come back to him, riding on the wings of his rediscovered humanity, his love for his fellow man, his sense of right and wrong.

Truly, the old Wayne *had* died in Iraq, not inside the burning Humvee, but while watching it. And the new Wayne had arisen from the smoldering ashes of that horrific attack, much as the smoke and fire of the falling towers had forged the hardened soldier that he had become. Only time would tell, though, time and trials that were sure to come in the near future, what form this new Wayne would take, and what destiny he would choose. There were still far too many questions swarming in his head, like a kettle of vultures circling over the corpse of his former life, deciding what to do with the carrion, and how, and when. Questions about his mission, about his government, about humanity, about his parents' legacy, about national security and terrorism, about himself, about his past, his present, and his future.

As though on cue, his cell phone beeped in his pocket, signaling a received text message. Reluctant to be drawn from his musings, he pulled his phone from his pocket and checked the message. Unknown number. Not good.

Report to HQ. 0900. Tomorrow.

Wayne stared at the message for a moment after he'd finished reading it, his lips pressed tightly together in resignation. He took a deep breath, deleted the text message as per protocol, repocketed his phone, and, with a final longing glance toward Ground Zero, turned his back on his parents' unmarked gravesite, beginning the long walk back to his apartment to pack his day bag for the trip. *The* trip.

And so it begins, he thought as he trudged northward. But the question remained: how would it end?

Wayne was still figuring that one out.

Chapter 14

Washington, D.C.

"This is nuts," Jon said staring out the window of the corner cafe. He and Mara were eating an early dinner, trying to make some sense of everything that had happened thus far. Mara's apartment had made Jon feel claustrophobic, so they went out to eat. But even the change of scenery didn't seem to be helping much.

"Which part?" Mara asked wryly.

Jon turned from the window and met her gaze. "All of it. Michael's death, the police's calling it a suicide, the guy in the apartment, and the police again being useless."

Mara tilted her head and swallowed a bite of her pastrami sandwich. "They're not *useless*. The police just... Well, would you believe it? I mean if you were one of those cops, would you have reacted much differently to your story than they did?"

Jon, with a mouth full of a turkey club, stopped chewing mid-bite, furrowed his brow thoughtfully, then started chewing again. "I guess you're right," he admitted after swallowing his food. He looked at the ceiling, then back at Mara. "What in heaven's name have we gotten ourselves into?"

"I don't think heaven has anything to do with what happened to Michael," Mara said with a frown. "So what do we do now?"

"What now?" Jon's mind flashed back to the disbelieving face of Sergeant Mabry. "With or without the authorities' help,

I'm gonna get to the bottom of this whole screwed-up mess, that's what."

Mara knew his angry tone was not directed at her, but she winced nonetheless. "I meant *how*. What's our next step?"

Our. The word was a comfort in itself. Jon sat in silence for a moment, looking pensive. "His research," he said suddenly, lifting his eyes to meet Mara's. "The laptop was what the guy took from the apartment. What he was presumably after in the first place. He must've been after the 'world-changing' research Michael was working on for his dissertation. Unless you can think of some other reason why a trained professional would be after his laptop?"

"No, none," she replied after a few seconds of probing her memory. "He wouldn't even hook that computer up to the Internet. Afraid of hackers getting in and stealing his work. Or sabotaging it."

"I'd say someone's sabotaged it pretty badly now." The pair sat quietly, immune to the Sunday evening commotion in the restaurant around them.

"I miss him," Mara sighed. "So freaking much."

"Me too. I guess you're just about the only person who understands just how badly."

"Probably." Mara allowed herself a small smile. "I swear, you two were closer than any brothers, heck, any friends, I've ever known."

Jon grimaced. "Michael and I traveled all over the world together. All our lives. I imagine I am who I am today largely because of him. After Mom died and Dad drew within himself and his research, Michael kind of stepped in. He helped me get a date with the first girl I think I ever loved – this French beauty named Martine – in Marseilles back when we were both teenagers. He saved my life on multiple occasions – from spear-wielding natives in Papua New Guinea, from drug lords in Colombia, from a particularly angry hippo in the Congo. We challenged each other to bigger and better things – not just in the one-upmanship of most guys, but also in becoming better people. He was the one who led me to my Christian faith when I was a boy. And he was the one who helped me remain in the faith during the turmoil of Mom's death. His inspiration, his mentorship, his companionship, his encouragement…" His voice drifted off, and he pressed his lips tightly together, breathing heavily through his nose, wishing once again that he could rewind time and do the last couple of years a little differently.

"It's okay," Mara said, her eyes sympathetic. "We're in the same boat here. He was an anchor for me, too. After my parents' divorce when I was in high school, my Disney-inspired dreams of a dream come true with my own personal Prince Charming were all but shattered. I figured I'd seen enough of the dysfunctions of marriage to last me a lifetime. If I ever found myself able to give my heart away to someone, to ever trust someone that much, I wouldn't marry them. Maybe a long-time boyfriend or something, but marriage just ruins things. It was great for other people, maybe, but not for me. Or so I thought until I met Michael. My Prince Charming who came along even after I'd stopped believing in such things."

She stopped, absentmindedly rubbing her cross pendant again. "We met at church. A young professionals' Bible study. Michael already told you this before, I'm sure, but he couldn't have told you the way he made me feel. His eyes were full of warmth and understanding and… It was as close to love at first sight as I imagine exists outside of Hollywood. And I don't mean that Michael was perfect or anything, as I'm sure you well know he wasn't."

Across the table, Jon's lips curved in a private smile. "I can't tell you how many pairs of earplugs I went through bunking or sharing a tent with Michael over the years. The man snored like a grizzly bear with a head cold."

Mara smiled sadly. "But the love he had for me," she continued, "and for you, and for those he cared deeply about; the passion he had for learning; the zeal for squeezing as much out of life as he possibly could; all that was as real and as genuine as they come. He was truly a gentleman and a scholar in every sense of the phrase, and he was about to be my husband. My husband..."

She broke down into sobs, holding her head in her hands as her hair fell into her eyes. Jon started to reach out and put his hand on her shoulder, but then realized that sometimes you just needed to cry. He just wished – privately of course – that she had chosen a less public venue to do so. After a few moments she calmed down, wiped her eyes dry with a corner of her napkin, and forced a weak smile. She was going to make it. They both were. Somehow.

"So, Michael's research," Jon abruptly began again, trying to push emotions to the background for the time being. "Any idea what he was working on?"

"Nope..." Mara sniffled, once. "Didn't you ask me that at lunch?"

"I probably did." Jon frowned and rubbed his temple. "Sorry, a lot's happened since then."

"*That's* an understatement. So the guy took the laptop, then. What about the notebook?"

"The notebook? Oh, in the backpack?"

"Yup. And you were wearing the bag at Michael's. Was the notebook in there?"

"Shoot. Yeah, it was, but I left it at your apartment. When I was getting cleaned up."

"It should be fine," she tried to assure him. "If the laptop was an afterthought, then the notebook should be completely off their radar... whoever 'they' are. We'll thumb through it when we get back. Should be something in there worth looking into."

Jon nodded. "Definitely, although knowing Michael, it'll be mostly notes and references to other sources. His conclusions about where it all led would be on his laptop."

"Lucky we've got you, then," Mara said, "since you're probably the only person on the planet who thinks like Michael." Jon was conscious of her omission of the verb 'did' from the end of her sentence, which would have been an admission that Michael would no longer do anything in the present tense. She smiled encouragingly. "You should be able to reach the same conclusions as Michael."

He winced. *Hopefully we'll avoid the conclusion that found him.* "So, beyond the notebook and the laptop, what else do we know? He was going to New York this weekend. Why?"

"I'm not really sure. An interview or something, I think."

He raised his eyebrows. "An interview? With whom?"

"I don't know… But I know who might."

"Who?" Jon asked before the realization dawned on him.

"Dr. Leinhart." Their voices were as one as they exclaimed the name of Michael's major professor simultaneously.

"He would know what Michael was working on, wouldn't he?" Jon asked.

"I would assume so. It's kind of his job."

He looked at the date dial on his watch. "Tomorrow's Monday. What say we pay the good professor a little visit?"

Mara tensed and hesitated a moment before agreeing.

"Mara, if you don't want to come with, that's fine. But this is just something I have to do."

She nodded. "I understand. It's hard for me, it is. But I think it's something I need to do too. For Michael. And for myself. And Lord knows you could probably use all the help you can get."

He smiled. "That I could." Then his expression sobered. "But you *do* realize how dangerous this could potentially be, right?"

"Jon, my fiancé is dead because of this. Which makes me realize both how dangerous *and* how important it is. I'm in."

***

Twenty minutes later, Jon and Mara were back in her cozy two-bedroom apartment. They sat on the edge of the love seat, Michael's worn, red-covered, spiral-bound notebook open on the coffee table in front of them.

And they were both hopelessly lost.

The notebook was full of print-outs and photocopies, glued to the pages, accompanied with Michael's scrawling in the margins, and, at times, on the copied manuscripts themselves. Statements issued by top politicians. Major foreign policy decisions. Earnings reports of mega-corporations. Philanthropic enterprises and awards.

All from the 1930s.

Even with Michael's commentary, Jon and Mara could find no links between the articles, reports, and other research crammed into the notebook. It was like trying to solve a 5000-piece puzzle without the picture on the box as a guide. With no idea of what their finished result was supposed to look like, they were going at it blind. Michael's conclusions – the bigger picture into which all of these puzzle pieces fit – must have been on his laptop.

Jon turned the page again. A photocopy of a German-language newspaper was pasted just below a note in Michael's handwriting, identifying it as being from the March 24th, 1932 edition of a periodical called *Die Stimme*.

"German?" Mara turned to Jon. "Do you know German, too?"

"*Jawohl, fraulein*. Just one of the many languages Michael and I learned in our youth," he answered in a deep, pretentious voice dripping with mock arrogance.

"Well, then read it, Mr. Worldly."

Jon peered down at the clipping. The copy quality wasn't the best, and the fact that it was printed in a gothic font and in a secondary language for him didn't help his reading. A few lines in, though, he drew in a sharp breath.

"What?" Mara asked from his side, impatient to find out what the article said.

"Strange... It says that the NSDAP received a large sum of cash for campaign support from an undisclosed foreign benefactor."

"*What?* Pretend I don't know as much about history as you do and explain, please."

Jon shook his head quickly, as though shaking an idea out of his head. "Sorry. Um, let's see, where to start…"

"How about what the NSDAP was," Mara offered. "Or is."

"No, no, it's 'was.' In this incarnation at least." A grim look crossed his face before he continued. "The *Nationalsozialist-ische Deutsche Arbeiterpartei.* English translation: the National Socialist German Workers Party. Often shortened to National Socialists, what we, today, know as—"

"The Nazis."

Jon nodded solemnly. "Bingo. Before they were the scourge of the Western world, they were a subversive political party in Weimar Germany."

"The Weimar Republic was the government that ruled Germany after World War I, right?"

"Yep. That was one of the requirements of the Treaty of Versailles: the Imperial government had to abdicate its rule and give power to a new democratic system. The new constitution was written in the medieval town of Weimar. Hence, the Weimar Republic."

Jon paused, stroking his chin with one thumb. "How much do you know about the Treaty of Versailles? Specifically about how it related to Germany."

"I know Germany was forced to sign it after World War I by the victors: Britain, France, and Russia – also known as the Triple Entente. And I know Germany thought they got screwed over by it."

"They kinda did get screwed over. Part of the dictate of the treaty forced the German Empire to change their system of government to the first democracy in the region's history."

"Kinda ironic, isn't it?" Mara said. "I mean, democracy, 'rule by the people,' being forced upon a people by outsiders."

"Indeed it was. And that was one of the reasons it ultimately didn't work. Many in the new Germany resented the new government and its being put there by foreigners. As punishment, no less. Some went so far as to accuse the Weimar government of simply being a puppet of the French or British, or even the Soviets."

Jon got up from the couch and began pacing the room. It was a habit he picked up from Michael, being unable to sit still when weaving a tale from history. "But there were plenty of other reasons it failed. And most of them traced back to the Treaty of Versailles. The French, ticked about how badly their country had been ravaged by the Germans during the war, and in fact, several times in the previous generation since the Franco-Prussian War in the 1870s, decided that Germany should A: remain weak so they couldn't rise up and attack France again as they had been wont to do over the past century, and B: should be forced to make reparations payments to the Allied powers, specifically France, to make up the damage that had been done. Never mind the fact that Germany's economy and infrastructure were as devastated as any in Europe and they could hardly afford to repair the damage their own country had suffered, much less the exorbitant sums that France charged them. The U.S. argued against the payments; the British, not wanting to anger their allies across the channel, took a relatively neutral position. Eventually the reparations payments made it into the treaty, albeit with a lessened amount."

"A compromise?"

"Yeah, pretty much, although it essentially still had the same effect as the original French proposition. German failure. But, thanks to intervention by American Big Business, it happened a little differently from the way the French might have expected. But now I'm getting ahead of myself." He forced himself to stop pacing and sat back down next to Mara. "Where was I?"

"The Treaty of Versailles?" Mara said, adjusting herself on the loveseat's cushions.

"Oh yeah, right. Another clause that the French demanded be in the treaty basically said that the Germans were responsible for World War I, the infamous 'War Guilt Clause.' Of course, Germany only entered in because they were allied with the Austro-Hungarians, who, in fact, did start the war. And this was one of the things that pissed the Germans off most, having to accept full responsibility for a war that was, at most, only partly their fault."

She shook her head. "But it *was* Germany who was the biggest threat to France, both during the war and throughout history."

"Yeah, which is why France came down so hard on them. Now bear in mind that the Germans were forced to kick out their own imperial government and instate a democratic one. Guess what the new government's first act in office was?"

"Signing the treaty?"

"Bingo." Jon's left leg was bouncing up and down nervously, his body's only outlet for the restless energy that had him pacing just moments earlier. "They had to sign the Treaty of Versailles, taking full responsibility for all the damage that the war had done, both in principle and in cash. Almost immediately, citizens started calling for the new leadership's head.

They claimed that the Weimar government had sold Germany out, that the Jews had infiltrated the halls of power and were trying to sell the nation into the slavery of foreigners—"

"Wait, they blamed the Jews? And this was pre-Hitler?"

"Well, Hitler was around, but he hadn't found the Nazis just yet, and made them into the powerhouse that they would soon become. No, anti-Semitism had been around for centuries in Europe. And with the recently published *Protocols of the Elders of Zion* that claimed to reveal the evil subversive conspiracies of the Jewish race, anti-Semitism was at a peak. Besides, everybody loves a scapegoat, and the Jews provided a historically acceptable one. Hitler just capitalized on the established fears and prejudices of the populace to promote his message."

Mara crossed her arms and sat back in the loveseat. "Bastard."

Jon quickly nodded in silent agreement before continuing. "So anyway, from the get-go, lots of people felt the Weimar Republic would fail. Some *wanted* it to fail, and worked actively to try to ensure its failure, creating public discord and sowing malicious rumors about the government. And the first few years were quite rough. The reparations payments were yet another thorn in the side of an administration trying to create and maintain the first democratically elected national government in German history. All the cards were stacked against them: the reparations payments, the enemies within, the widespread feelings of betrayal by and distrust of the government, the inexperience of the people and culture with democracy, the critically damaged infrastructure that had to be repaired. And in 1923, the country's economy almost collapsed entirely.

"In rushes the American cavalry, only instead of John Wayne on a white steed, it's banker and political advisor Charles Dawes with a proposal to rescue Germany economically." Jon stood and began pacing again, this time gesticulating with his hands to illustrate his points. "The international committee he chaired proposed a series of loans from American banks to German companies, who were able to increase the GDP, enabling Germany to make the reparations payments to France and Great Britain, who in turn were able to pay the Americans back on the loans that helped sustain them throughout World War I. And around and around it went. A tremendous circle of money that saw a lot of unscrupulous American bankers getting filthy rich."

"Wait, tell me about those loans that we gave Britain and France."

Jon stopped pacing for a moment and looked at her. "Well, you know the First World War began in 1914, right?"

"Yeah, with the assassination of Archduke Franz Ferdinand. Of Austria. He was killed in Sarajevo by a Serbian nationalist, right?"

He nodded. "'The shot heard 'round the world,' they called it. One bullet that started the most destructive war the world had yet seen. That happened in 1914, but the United States didn't enter into the war until 1917, a year before it finally ended."

"Just like in World War II: we wait until our allies' situation is sufficiently desperate," Mara said with a smirk, "then we swoop in to save the day."

He shrugged, still standing but resisting the urge to pace. "Eh, not quite. Up until 1917, U.S. banks had provided our allies with massive loans to fund the war effort. Then, three years in, we finally joined the war militarily, despite the protests of many Americans over getting 'involved in foreign entanglements,' to quote the famous admonition of George Washington.

"In truth, there were a lot of reasons why we finally got involved. First, our key allies in the Western world, namely France and Great Britain, were in danger of falling to the Central Powers. Second, Russia had all but pulled out of the war, the country having been thrust into civil war. This hindered the Allied war effort, but also added the danger of communist revolution, one that American policymakers feared might spread to neighboring countries like an infectious disease, eventually taking down some of America's key trading partners and allies, as well as possibly disrupting the capitalist system in America herself. In fact, did you know that immediately *after* World War I, we stationed soldiers in Russia to try to ensure that the communists failed in sustaining their revolution?"

She made a little O with her lips. "You're kidding."

"No joke. And let me tell you, it pissed off the Russians, especially after Wilson made all his famous promises about the right of every nation to self-determination of its leaders, type of government, type of economy, and so forth. Our government denied it for a while, but the Russians knew from the beginning. Later, when the Nazis were besieging Leningrad and other Russian cities during World War II, Stalin alleged that the American and British reluctance to open a second front in Western Europe was a deliberate attempt to have the Nazis and the Soviets finish each other off, and then sweep in and take over whatever was left. He was probably right, too. I'm guessing you already know about the Red Scare in the post-war years, right?"

"Yeah, with McCarthyism and all that?"

"That's it. Senator Joe McCarthy's fear-mongering had people seeing communists in their closets, under their beds, in every school, every public office, every person of influence, great and small. The arms race was taking off, the space race was about to start, and tensions between the nations were escalating, so it was natural that someone would take advantage of the fear for their own benefit."

Jon smiled mischievously, as though he were letting her in on a secret that not everyone was privy too. "But there was another Red Scare thirty years earlier. Shortly after the Bolsheviks seized control of Russia and created the Soviet Union, Americans were just as fearful of a communist plot to overthrow the government taking place in their own nation. In fact, really, from the October Revolution in 1917 until the fall of the Soviet Union in 1991, many Americans were absolutely terrified about the possibility of a communist revolution in the good ol' U.S. of A."

"And this has to do with the loans... how?"

"Oh, right. Sorry, got sidetracked there, didn't I? So yeah; the third, and perhaps most controversial reason that we entered the war officially in 1917 was to protect the interests of Big Banking."

"Protect their interests how? To end the war quickly so our allies could pay us back?"

"Partially, yes. But we'd lent Britain and France a buttload of money. What happens to all that money if Germany conquers them?"

Mara lifted her hands as though in acquiescence. "The American bankers can kiss it goodbye."

"Exactly. You think Germany would pay back loans that were used to finance weapons that were used against them? Hardly. Britain and France lose, all of Big Banking's investment is lost as well. So we entered in, the Allies won, and Big Banking got its money back. But victory was not without a cost. More than a hundred thousand American soldiers were killed in the nineteen short months we were fighting. The resultant public outcry, especially over allegations that the real reason for the invasion was to safeguard Big Banking's investments, all but guaranteed the isolationist stance the United States would largely take on foreign affairs for the next two decades, right up to Pearl Harbor."

"War-for-profit, huh?" Mara raised an eyebrow incredulously. "Sounds like a conspiracy theory."

"You'd be surprised at how often those conspiracy theories turn out to be true. Of course, the vast majority are bunk, but there have to be some that are true in order to inspire the false ones. The U.S. has participated in its share of real conspiracies, especially within the realm of international politicking. The Cold War was just one long series of secret operations conducted by the CIA and KGB behind the scenes, the truths hidden from their respective citizens for years, decades even. Who knows, maybe there are still some more secrets that we don't know about."

"Maybe like what Michael found."

Jon's jaw tightened involuntarily. "Yeah. Like what Michael found." He plopped down on the loveseat next to Mara, some of the wind suddenly gone from his sails.

"So the article," Mara prodded, pointing at the open notebook. "You were saying about the Weimar Republic—"

"Right, yeah, sorry. So Germany gets their loans, France and Britain get their reparations payments, and American bankers are growing fat and happy. And best of all for American policy-makers and financiers, Germany didn't fall to the dreaded communist conspiracy that they believed threatened to move west from the newly created Soviet Union. The USSR was shaky at this point, to be sure, but the Germans were desperate, and God forbid the industrial heart of Europe, which also happened to be roughly the geographical center of the non-Soviet part of the continent, should fall to communism. Instead, after the Dawes Plan went into effect, Germany actually looked a lot like America in the Roaring Twenties: young people rich quick off investments, parties, movie stars, living the high life, everything glamorous and flashy. Of course, it was American money that financed the whole system. And like America's high-rolling lifestyle in the 'twenties, the whole system crashed and burned."

Jon took a deep breath, then continued. "July of '29, Germany's economy is faltering, and the powers-that-be held another meeting in Paris. The plan they came up with this time was called the Young Plan, named after American banker Owen Young who chaired the commission, like Charles Dawes before him. It basically said that they would continue the loans to Germany, and the payments to France would be lessened. Of course, with the reduced payments, Germany would have paid France reparations until 1988."

Mara looked shocked. "Geez."

"I know, right? Lots of crazy ideas that to us don't seem very practical, but France had their vendetta, America had their prosperity to keep bolstering, and Germany had to get out of their slump somehow. Plus, we've got the benefit of hindsight.

"So the Young Plan looks like it'll fix things again, but before it can be put into effect, Germany gets hit with two big blows: Foreign Minister Gustav Stresemann, the architect of much of the nation's economic and political stability, a symbol of hope for his people, dies; and then, just three weeks later, Black Thursday hits."

"The stock market crash?"

"Yup. Thursday, October 24, 1929 – and the weeks thereafter – saw the market plummet, banks fail, investments vanish. You've seen the pictures and heard the stories about how bad things were in America. Well, when America's money dried up, so did its loans to Germany. And if you think America was hit hard, consider the fact that Germany's economy was already starting to falter before October, and that virtually *all* of their money dried up – especially when, after America tried to call in their loans, they couldn't pay their lenders back. Bad credit."

"But that wasn't the end of the Weimar Republic, though, right?"

"No, not quite, but it *was* the beginning of the end. Unlike America, which had been around for a century-and-a-half and had attracted millions of immigrants from across the globe, many in Germany didn't want Weimar to continue. It was only a decade strong, and that had been a turbulent decade at best. This was proof positive for many of its detractors that this democratic, free-market capitalistic state wouldn't work. So several groups, including the Nazis, took it upon themselves to take advantage of the situation and try to uproot the system once and for all.

"Now the Nazis, an insignificant group of a few dozen members until 1919, when it was first lent the charismatic oratory skills of a young disillusioned veteran named Adolf Hitler, had been known as nothing more than a band of rabble-rousers in the early 'twenties. Trying to stir up dissent and public discord, acts of vandalism, hate speech, threats against Jewish business owners; that sort of thing. But after the failed Beer Hall Putsch in 1923, when Hitler and the Nazis unsuccessfully tried to overthrow the government by force, Hitler decided that the group wouldn't go that route again. When he got out of prison, he stated the new direction of the Nazi Party: politics. They would win seats in the Reichstag – the German parliament – and other governmental bodies to bring down the system from within.

"People didn't take them seriously as a political force at first, and, in 1928, during the first national election where the Hitler-led NSDAP was on the ballot, their showing was fairly pitiful. Their 2.6 percent of the national vote landed them a few seats in the 491-seat Reichstag, but they were nothing more than a footnote, with no real power to speak of. The centrists held most of the power, and it kept things mostly even-keeled. But the fact that they had won *some* seats inspired Hitler, and thus, the party, to keep it up. So they campaigned like crazy, Hitler himself touring much of the country and presenting himself as a man of the people, angry in true Hitler fashion with the corruption that he claimed had seized the government and culture, the corruption that was destroying the German ideals of life and art, the subversion that was most often, for Hitler, embodied in the Jews."

Mara shook her head in disgust. "Easiest way to unify a people: give them a common enemy. And Lord knows the Jews have had their share of it."

"Of course, the Nazis weren't the only ones villainizing the Jews then: they were just the best at it. And then they get their biggest boon: Black Thursday. The country was plunged into economic chaos again, and, just like in 1923, the extremists, like the Nazis and the Communists, seized the opportunity to stir the populace into even more of a frenzy. Only this time, the American cavalry lost their horses on the stock exchange, and their rifles had been confiscated by public isolationist sentiment. Germany was left to deal with the chaos on its own, and radical groups, left- and right-wing alike, skyrocketed in popularity.

"The radicals promised drastic changes, and it was obvious to the German people, witnessing economic, political, and social chaos, that major change was needed. Given, much of the political and social chaos was abetted, if not orchestrated, by some of these radical groups, but that was beside the point. The people wanted major change, and the far-left and the far-right were there to deliver."

Jon took a drink of water from one of the glass tumblers on the coffee table before continuing. "The Nazis saw a huge jump in governmental representation after the elections of 1930, both at the local level and the national. In one fell swoop, they had virtual control over many regions of the country, especially in places like Bavaria, where the movement had gotten its start. Even more importantly, they were the second largest party in the Reichstag, having won over a hundred seats. Thanks to the stock market crash and its ramifications for Germany, the Nazis had gone from footnote to force-to-be-reckoned-with in less than two years. But they weren't done yet. Hitler had his eye on total Nazi domination, and he would stop at nothing less than the ultimate power to assert his vision upon Germany and indeed the whole of Europe.

"A massive campaign was launched in the build-up to the 1932 elections. Between Hitler's passionate orations and Joseph Goebbels's masterful use of propaganda, the Nazis' popularity continued to soar. The fact that the Chancellorship was a virtual revolving door as the faces inhabiting the top tiers of the halls of power kept changing, another sign that the Republic was in serious trouble, didn't hurt either.

"The Nazis received substantial funding from industrial magnates like Fritz Thyssen and Alfred Krupp, who had a lot to lose if the country should fall to the *other* radical camp, i.e. the Communists, and the seizure of their vast assets in the government-controlled system they would instate should they come to power. There were rumors that the Soviets were sending money to the Communist Party of Germany, the KPD, but the Nazis? Until Hitler came to power in '33, the Nazis really didn't have many supporters internationally. Certainly none who would give them significant campaign funding. Nobody took them seriously as a political body. As a group not to be crossed, sure, but capable of efficiently running a country? Hardly. That's really weird…"

"Maybe it was propaganda by the newspaper? Trying to show that the Nazis have the support of the international community, established allies if they come into power?"

"Or maybe the other way around, maybe trying to say that they're not as purely German as they claim to be, taking funding from outsiders and thus being beholden to some foreign beneficiary?" Jon shook his head. "But Michael didn't seem to think so. It looks like he took the international funding seriously, like it was real, like it was important." He sighed, his brow furrowed, his eyes a mixture of confusion and concern.

"Well, thanks for the history lesson."

"What? Oh yeah, sure. Anytime."

"Of that, I have no doubt," Mara said with a smile, which Jon half-returned.

He turned the page again. This time, a tourist map of modern-day Manhattan was pasted to the page. Hand-drawn circles designated various spots on the map – the United Nations, Radio City Music Hall, the Metropolitan Museum of Art, the Museum of Modern Art, Fort Tryon Park, the Cathedral Church of St. John the Divine, and a few other locations around the city that hadn't made it onto the tourist circuit, thus remaining unlabeled on the map. Below the map, Michael's handwriting: *'Where did he hide it?'*

"Hide *what*?" Mara asked the page in exasperation. "And who's *he*?"

Jon just stared at the map. A connection was there, between those locations. He should know it. He *did* know it. It just wasn't coming.

After unsuccessfully wracking his brain for the answer, he turned the page once more. The final page with Michael's research, his handwriting. Four newspaper articles, all four labeled as coming from the *Brooklyn Herald*, a newspaper Jon had never heard of. Probably long defunct. The dates on the articles were from nearly two decades after most of the others: October 1957.

He started to scan the first article, then, reading Michael's notation, began reading again, this time paying closer attention to detail. Mara read along beside him.

The article reported the suicide of a man who had killed himself by *hanging* himself from the Brooklyn Bridge. Lots of people had jumped to their death – hitting the surface of the water from that height was enough to break every bone in a person's body, and if the impact didn't kill you, it was hard to swim to safety, even if you wanted to, with broken arms and legs – but *hanging* yourself, with a length of cable no less, from the Brooklyn Bridge. That had to be to send a message. About himself, about what drove him to his death, some sort of statement that *someone* was supposed to get. Had they?

Then his eyes reached another startling statement. This man matched the description of a soldier who had supposedly been killed in Korea in 1951, a Roger Blumhurst. Blumhurst's identification papers had been found in the pocket of the suit coat the suicide victim had been wearing. And Blumhurst's estranged daughter, one Catherine Smith, had confirmed that the recently deceased man was indeed her father.

The second article was a sidebar to the first, relating the vicious murder of a young schoolboy on his way home from school, and the attempted murder of the boy's schoolmate, who had been walking with him. After receiving medical treatment for wounds to his neck and the back of his head, the schoolmate told police about the attack and gave a description of the assailant. The article noted the striking similarity between the mysterious assailant and the suicide purported to be Roger Blumhurst.

The third article was from a few days later. Short and blunt, almost as though the paper's management didn't feel it warranted column inches at all, it reported that the schoolboy who had survived the mysterious assailant's attack had died of injuries sustained in a hit-and-run automobile accident while walking to school.

Jon sighed heavily, shaking his head in awe.

"Wow," Mara intoned from his side. Jon didn't know which article she was on, but it didn't matter. The whole thing was just plain eerie.

The final article, dated six days after the first one, completed the circle. It was an obituary of sorts, with a plea for information regarding the alleged mob-related murder of *Herald* reporter Jim Torrence. It seemed somewhat off-topic from the rest of the articles until Jon looked at the earlier entries and discovered the connection: Jim Torrence had written the previous three articles, covering stories that, judging by the absence of corroborating evidence from other periodicals in Michael's notebook, no other paper, no other journalist, had reported on.

'This is the key to breaking the whole thing open!' read Michael's script in a hurried, excited font, scrawled next to the collage of *Herald* articles.

Maybe so, Jon thought. *We just have to figure out what lock it fits.*

Chapter 15

Rockville, Maryland and Washington, D.C.

Monday

The home of Dr. Richard Leinhart, esteemed professor and world-renowned historian, was surprisingly simple. Just another house in suburbia, a concrete drive cutting a swath through its perfectly manicured lawn – which was still beautiful in March, if less green than it would be in summer months – to the double-car garage housing the professor's silver Audi. It could have belonged to any one of the two-parent, soccer mom families with 2.3 children, a pension and a mortgage who populated the neighborhood, any of the young business-minded couples who were several years – and promotions – away from starting a family of their own who lived up and down the street. But this house belonged to one of the most highly respected academics living in the D.C. area – single, no kids, dedicated more to the advancement of his field than to keeping up with the Joneses. And, this morning, he was having a great deal of difficulty in gathering the strength to go to work.

All weekend he had been wracked with guilt, with fear, with sorrow. Why had this happened to Michael? Michael Rickner, one of the brightest, most dedicated, most insightful and perceptive individuals he had ever had the pleasure of mentoring. His work, had it been completed, could have rewritten much of the history of the twentieth century. And not just from an academic standpoint. Textbooks from the grade school level on would have had to have been rewritten, the government would have issued their typical denials, then apologies on behalf of their long-gone predecessors, the world would have changed the way they thought about one of the darkest periods in human history, rethought America's white knight image as it pertained to that era. *If* Michael's new theory proved to be true.

But had Michael committed suicide? He couldn't see that, but then, didn't everyone say that about suicide victims? They were so happy, never saw it coming, just weren't the type. "The shadow," Carl Jung had called it, the dark part of self that we fought to deny existed. The part that, in failing to acknowledge its existence, can be given power by our unconscious. Not that he bought into that psychobabble claptrap, but it did provide a possible answer to the unanswerable. And yet, even then it didn't quite fit. Michael was cognizant of his dark side, his humanity, and his flaws despite his largely genial nature. He didn't deny his "shadow"; he just always strove to rise above it.

In his long academic career, Dr. Leinhart had known students who had later committed suicide. Sadly, it was all too common among students at elite universities, especially at the graduate level. The pressure to succeed, the constraints on time, energy, and finances just proved to be too much for some students, and they sometimes took the easiest, hardest way out. And even though the professor had known several suicide victims, and had felt the requisite I-never-saw-it-coming reaction, the truth was, considering his proximity to the students and their workload, there was usually something in their actions, their speech in the weeks, days, leading up to the tragic decision that was simply not there with Michael. This one wasn't stressed; he was elated. His life, professional and personal, seemed to be taking off in the right direction. He had committed suicide right between proposing to his girlfriend – who, knowing the both of them, Leinhart was certain had said yes – and going off to get the first eyewitness conclusive evidence to support his revolutionary theories? Not likely.

Which left an even more chilling alternative. He had been killed. By professionals, judging by their ability to stage the scene like a suicide. No one had held a personal grudge against him. Who could? He was far too likable. And he was genuine. Always genuine with his sentiments. But had his research managed to piss somebody off? Had he gotten too close to discovering something that someone, someone powerful, wanted to stay hidden? That was what his research alleged, wasn't it? That was what he thought the Blumhurst guy from the article was supposed to be a part of. That was what he was about to follow up on, right before he was killed. If anything, his death seemed to lend credibility to his theory. And that terrified Dr. Leinhart.

The professor was surprised to find himself sitting in his car, key in the ignition, ready to back out of the driveway. His mind solely focusing on the inner debate that he had been going over and over since he'd heard the news, his body had been on autopilot, going through the morning ritual it had been trained in over the years. He grimaced, aware of how much this situation was bothering him, taxing his faculties. He should really think about taking a day off, maybe a week. A mini-sabbatical to get his head together. Deep breath. But no, not today. He was already ready. Press on, and make it through. He'd take it relatively easy today, but if he couldn't make it all the way through the day… well, he'd just cross that bridge if he came to it. In the meantime, he'd just have to focus on the immediate task at hand and not let his mind wander into the fearful labyrinth of questions bouncing around in his head. And right now, that task was driving.

Forty minutes later, he pulled into his parking spot in the faculty lot, grabbed his briefcase, and started walking toward his office in Phillips Hall, its stark plate-glass exterior and seven-story height standing in contrast to the brick and stone buildings that composed much of the historic campus, making the building look more like a modern business building than the haven of academia it truly was. Upon exiting the elevator for the third floor and turning toward his office, he was greeted with a conflicting sight. The visitors who awaited him were welcome faces, but ones that had already plunged his mind back into the labyrinth.

Jon Rickner and Mara Ellison.

Leinhart forced a smile at the pair as he approached the door to his office. "Mara, Jon, how are you?"

Jon looked at Mara, then back at the professor. "We're making it through, all things considered," Jon answered. "Yourself?"

Leinhart sighed. "The same. You two want to come in?" he asked as he unlocked his office door.

"Very much so," Jon said. "Thank you."

***

Leinhart led the way into the room, closing the door behind them, and motioning for them to take the two seats in front of the antique oak desk while he moved to his own chair behind it. The walls of the mahogany-paneled office were adorned with myriad commendations, awards, and degrees. A framed map of the world drawn by famed Renaissance cartographer Gerardus Mercator hung prominently on the far wall. A large varnished bookcase lined the wall behind the desk, shelves of old leatherbound tomes and contemporary reference books – some of which bore the professor's name on the spine – standing at the ready for consultation. His briefcase set to the side, Dr. Leinhart folded his hands atop the desk, leaned forward on his elbows, and frowned.

"To what do I owe the pleasure of this visit?"

"You know about Michael, Professor?" Mara started.

"I do indeed. I can't believe it. Such a tragedy."

"Dr. Leinhart," Jon said, "I went to Michael's apartment yesterday and was attacked by an armed intruder. An intruder who then stole Michael's laptop. I think – *we* think – that this guy might have killed Michael because of his research."

Across the desk, a flicker of something flashed in the professor's eyes.

"He was working on something big," Jon continued, "something revolutionary, something that somebody might not have wanted to be discovered, right?"

"He was." Leinhart had a mournful look in his eyes as he stared at his hands, folded in quiet resignation upon the desktop.

"Can you tell us what he was working on? What his theory was?"

"It was…" The professor's eyes drifted to the closed office door, then back to Jon and Mara. "Are you guys sure you want to hear about this? If it got Michael killed…" His unspoken admonition hung in the air like a storm cloud.

"Yes," Jon answered.

"Definitely," Mara chimed in.

"It was about some government cover-up from the 'thirties. Something involving the secret funneling of American dollars into the coffers of the Nazi party in 1932, and then, when Hitler became Enemy Number One for our allies in Europe, the government tried to cover it up by killing anyone who knew too much, or tried to find things out. God, if that wasn't enough of a warning to Michael to tread carefully, I don't know what would have been."

Across the desk, Jon and Mara's eyes grew wide, jaws slackened. Of all the international financiers to fund the Nazis, they never would have guessed it could have been Americans. Franco's Spaniards, maybe. Mussolini's Italians, perhaps. But not Americans.

"Seriously?" Jon spoke up. "But why? And how on earth could the government justify sending taxpayer dollars abroad – for *any* reason, much less funding the Nazis – when the economy here at home was still in shambles?"

"I have no idea, but that was the premise for his work. Outlandish, I thought at first, but he seemed to have a nose for hunting down obscure truths and piecing them together into a cohesive whole."

"That sounds like Michael," Jon agreed. He and his brother had made something of a pastime of digging for elusive truths in the mists of history and legend. And now it had gotten Michael killed. Jon bit his bottom lip, then forced himself to continue. "What was this interview he was going to do this past weekend?"

"Oh, that," the professor began. "A witness, he believed. Not to the American funding of the Nazis but rather to the cover-up years later. He thought there was an office somewhere in the government responsible for keeping this potentially explosive secret under wraps. An office that employed assassins. He was researching the relationship between the Mafia and the press in the late 1950s, when he found a mob killing that didn't fit the bill. The hit was right, but the motives were all wrong. The guy had never written anything about the mob, about money laundering, about any of the vice trades that the Mafia had interests in. But what he had written about just before he was murdered was a very strange series of events, beginning with a guy who was supposed to have died in Korea years earlier. Somehow, this long-dead veteran managed to jump off the Brooklyn Bridge with a noose around his neck."

Jon's eyes lit up. He reached into Michael's backpack and pulled out his notebook. Flipping it open to the final entry, he plopped the article face up on the professor's desk.

"This one?"

"That's... that's it. Where did you?"

"Michael's apartment. That's what I was doing there when the… assassin? …whoever he was, attacked me."

"But he made off with the laptop?"

Jon sighed. "Yeah."

"Shoot." Leinhart said. "Most of Michael's stuff was on there, I think."

"Had he backed it up anywhere else?" Mara asked.

"Nowhere else that I'm aware of." Leinhart shrugged. "He said that he didn't want too many people to find out about it yet. If someone found out that he had that info, and his theories were true…"

"Sounds like they found out anyway." Mara's voice, the cold, bitter ire behind it, surprised even her.

Jon looked at her, an expression of sadness and concern on his face, before turning back to the professor. "Who exactly did he plan on meeting in New York, Professor?"

"One Catherine Smith, estranged daughter of Roger Blumhurst. Still alive after all these years, apparently."

"Estranged? So how much would she have known?" Mara asked,

"I don't know. Sometimes people, when they're on their proverbial deathbed, try to make amends before the end. Maybe he tried to reconnect with her shortly before he killed himself. That's what Michael was hoping. That's what he was going to go find out."

"Then that's what we're going to find out," Jon chimed in. Dr. Leinhart looked at Jon in disbelief, then at Mara. They were both meeting his gaze with confidence and firm resolve.

"What? Why? You saw what happened to Michael. …I'm sorry, that… that was crude."

Jon slapped his palm on the professor's desk. "How many more people have to die, how many brothers and fiancées left to mourn because of this secret? If Michael was wrong, then we've got nothing to fear. If he was right… we've got to stop the cycle somehow."

"Geez, Jon. But how? I mean, Michael was working on this for weeks. And he still hadn't found conclusive evidence to bring the conspiracy into the light. He still hadn't made any huge breakthroughs, nothing beyond conjecture and speculation. *Educated* conjecture and speculation, given, but nothing to make people take it seriously."

"I don't know, Professor, but I do know that it's something I—," Jon glanced at Mara, who gave him a nod, "—that *we* have to do. For Michael, for his memory and legacy, for all the other people who've died over the years and for those who can still be saved."

Dr. Leinhart smiled softly despite the tightness he felt in his chest. "My God. You really are Michael's brother, aren't you?"

"Yes sir."

"He would be proud of you, Jon. I'm sure he would. He talked about you all the time, you know."

Jon took a deep breath, and the professor picked up on his sign of discomfort.

"Sorry, I… I didn't mean to make you uncomfortable. I hope I didn't—"

"No, no, it's fine," Jon answered, giving Mara a thankful glance in response to the hand she had placed gently on his arm. "It's hard, but I'm fine, really."

"So when are you two planning on embarking on your little expedition?" the professor asked.

"This afternoon," Mara answered before Jon could.

"So soon?"

"No time like the present," Mara chimed more cheerily than might have been appropriate.

"I'm on break from Oxford," Jon explained, "and Mara's got bereavement time from her job. Dad's somewhere in the Amazon, miles away from the nearest electrical grid or cell phone tower, so the funeral's on hold until they can track him down, and it'd be great if we could clear this whole thing up for Michael by then. If this wasn't suicide, which I think all three of us can agree that it couldn't have been, then we want to set the story right by the time his eulogy is delivered."

Dr. Leinhart nodded. "Good point…"

"Plus, Jon has a ton of frequent flyer miles," Mara added. "Forty-five minutes and we're in NYC."

The professor raised his eyebrows. "Wow. You guys are serious." The pair nodded at him, a cool confidence carved into their faces. "All right, I'll tell you what; let's swap cell numbers. That way we can stay in touch while you're in Manhattan. You find anything, let me know, and I'll try to work on it from this end. And I'll let you know about anything I can dig up."

"Professor—" Mara started to plead.

"No, no. I want to. It's the least I can do."

"Okay." She smiled gratefully. "Thanks."

Jon handed Professor Leinhart a prepaid cell phone, one of three they'd paid for in cash earlier that morning. "Untraceable. Just in case. Our numbers are already in there."

The professor nodded slowly, his eyes growing worried as he seemed to be realizing the gravity of what was happening.

Jon started to stand up. "Well, I think we've probably taken up enough of your time this morning. Mara and I have some packing to do."

The professor blinked, then stood in turn. "Any time, Jon. Mara," he said as he shook each of their hands. "Just please, watch your backs out there."

Chapter 16

Langley, Virginia

Enrique tried not to let the worry he felt show on his face. He sat patiently in the chair across from Greer's desk, conscious of the heavy tension around them, waiting for his boss to speak. Greer, reading through a sheaf of papers on his desk, seemed animated – but reservedly so, as though he'd just found out a secret that he was aching to tell someone, but couldn't yet. Finally, he sat back in his chair and interlaced his fingers across his stomach.

"I was on the fence about something, Ramirez. Your run-in with the younger Rickner brother yesterday has helped me make up my mind." Greer sniffed to himself. "So, I suppose, thanks are in order."

How could he have known? Ramirez was going to resolve the issue himself. He had an opportunity to do so this morning, but Greer had insisted on his being back at HQ. So he'd missed his shot. And now Greer knew.

The shock of the revelation must have registered on Ramirez's face, for Greer continued, "Yes, I know about the incident. The young man was predictable enough to attempt to file a police report. Nothing for them to follow up on, of course. You did your job quite well in that regard. However, the incident report was logged by the Washington Metro PD yesterday, and our boys in Recon picked it up on the channels." Greer shook his head. "I thought there were no secrets here, Ramirez."

Ramirez got his breathing under control. "Sir, I had every intention of taking care of it myself. I didn't want to involve the Division with this little... annoyance."

Greer smiled to himself. "I'm sure you didn't. But why would this be your job rather than the Division's? Don't you think an incident like this would necessarily concern the Division?"

Ramirez realized he could take two different tacks here. One would be apologetic and conciliatory. But Greer knew him well enough to see right through the lie that that would be. He settled on the second course of action.

"Sir, I believed – and truth be told still do believe – that I can do as good a job cleaning up my own messes as the Division could. Small and cohesive though we are, multiple people working on a single project can lead to miscommunication, disagreements, the loss of critical time and resources. And something like this didn't go through the normal sequence of departments. Recon didn't discover the target. I – a field agent – did. I created the incident. And so, especially considering that I have the most at stake in seeing that the Rickner brother is eliminated, I decided–"

"What do you have at stake?" Greer interrupted, his face still unreadable.

Ramirez blinked. "I'm sorry?"

"You said that you have the most at stake in making sure the Rickner brother is eliminated. What, exactly, were you referring to?"

"Well, the Division's integrity for one. Preserving the mission–"

"No!" Greer interrupted again. "That's what we all have at stake. What do *you* have at stake? Don't second-guess yourself; just answer. Now."

"Pride," Ramirez blurted. "My pride, sir. For my skills, for the mission, and for our country."

Greer smiled broadly. "Thank you for your candor, Ramirez. I'm removing you from field duty effective immediately."

Ramirez felt his stomach plummet through the floor. His throat seized up, but eventually he was able to croak out, "Why?"

"Because, my dear boy, of how very much you do take pride in your work. Because of your relentless dedication to the Division."

Ramirez felt the room begin to tilt on its axis. He was being punished because of his pride and dedication to the mission? It made no sense at all.

Again seeming to read his agent's mind, Greer continued. "No, you're not being punished here." He paused and looked down at the desk. He brought a fist to his lips and swallowed deeply. "You're being promoted."

Ramirez couldn't believe what he was hearing. The hierarchical structure of the Division was completely flat. Three tiny sections – Recon, Elimination, and Extra-Division Affairs – all presided over by a single Director: Harrison Greer. Unless Greer was changing the very structure of the Division, the only thing he could possibly mean was…

"Yes," Greer said, "I'm stepping down as Director. You, Ramirez, will be my replacement."

"But, why?"

"Why am I stepping down or why did I choose you?"

"Both," Ramirez said.

"I'm not going to stroke your ego any more than I already have in answering your second question. You're simply the best man for the job. As for the first question, I'm afraid my father's killer has come for me as well."

Ramirez blanched. "Cancer."

Greer nodded. "The same. I feel fine, but apparently it's progressed to the stage where there's not a thing the doctors can do about it. I'm going to step down before things get bad, but before I can do that, there's some unfinished business I need to take care of. To wit, the Dossiers."

Ramirez involuntarily blew a short burst of air from his nostrils. "Sir, no disrespect intended, but how do you intend to find them? We've been trying for decades, but to no avail."

Greer bared his teeth in a malicious grin. "Not like this we haven't."

For the next fifteen minutes, Greer went over the details of his plan with Ramirez, including his rationale for pulling him out of the field even before he could take over the Directorship. Ramirez hung on his every word. He realized it was the most ingenious, most terrifying plan he'd ever heard. If it worked.

And that, Ramirez feared, was a big if.

***

Halfway down the hallway, Wayne Wilkins encountered fellow agent Enrique Ramirez, stalking his way toward him, shaking his head at the floor. Wayne's stoic expression, the one he had built up over years and years of walling up his true thoughts and feelings, and barricading out everything and everyone else, was shaken by the glare Ramirez gave him as he passed him. The look – one that seemed to say, "don't screw this up, rookie, or I'm coming after you" – jarred him. Wayne had been with the Division only six months, and almost all of that in training. Their paths had rarely crossed, and no interaction of any note had ever transpired between the two. The look of contempt on Ramirez's face seemed both unmerited and foreboding. Strange.

So much for first impressions, Wayne thought ruefully as he reached Greer's office door. He rapped sharply on the door, twice.

"Come!" boomed the voice from within.

Wayne opened the door and entered the office.

"Ah, Wilkins…" Greer stood to greet Wayne with a strong bone-crushing handshake. "Please, sit, sit."

Wayne did as he was instructed, still surprised by the greeting Greer offered. The seeming geniality and warm handshake from a superior officer was a far cry from the business-only saluting that he was used to from his military days. Yet despite the familial treatment, Wilkins never could get the memory of their first face-to-face meeting out of his head. Dressed in his old colonel's combat uniform from his Army days – albeit with a different name tape – Greer had been right there deceiving his compatriots so convincingly that Wayne himself had almost been taken in. Greer was the one who had arranged the whole thing beforehand; he planned it, called in the attack, and orchestrated the follow-up that resulted in an official death certificate for Sergeant Wayne Stephen Wilkins. The point of the whole darned exercise. But a man who lied that convincingly, a man who had led his countrymen to their fiery deaths with a smile on his face – for however noble a purpose… could he truly be trusted?

That August morning would forever be burned into his mind. The waiting – as he listened to Price, Sedaris, and Jenkins chatter excitedly about the vacation they would never get to take – was almost as bad as the actual attack on his fellow soldiers, his… yes, they *had* been his friends. Or at least the closest to friendship he had had in these past years. But the guilt, the guilt he lived with daily, the image of the billowing smoke, the deafening explosions, the roaring flames, the haunting death knell screams of his friends. All his fault. All his fault. That was worse than the waiting and the actual event put together. And it never, ever ended.

"Wilkins?"

"Sorry, sir. Mind drifted a bit."

"Mind that it doesn't, Wilkins. This is a top priority assignment and we can't afford any mistakes." He fixed Wayne with a look. "*Any*," he reiterated. "This assignment is perhaps the most important one we've embarked on since the creation of the Division. It can finally root out and destroy the Achilles' heel that has threatened us for so long."

"The Dossiers, sir?"

Greer smiled. "Good, so you were paying attention in training. I know you were trained for Elimination, not the Recon teams searching, among other things, for leads on the Dossiers, but, well, let's just say this mission is a bit unorthodox. There isn't really a department here or a training program for something like this, so we have to think outside the box. Are you ready to think outside the box, Wilkins?"

Wayne tried to figure out where Greer was going with this, but it was all he could do just to follow along. "Yes sir."

"Good man. As you know, I've been the director here since Clinton was in office, and I've had the privilege of having some of the best operatives in the country working under me. That's given me what I like to think is a pretty decent take on operatives and their capabilities. Are you following me?"

Wayne nodded.

Greer nodded once in response and continued. "I've been watching you. In Iraq with your unit, in training with us. It is my opinion that you are an ideal candidate for this mission. Are you up to undertaking a mission that might be a little unusual in its methods, but immeasurable in its rewards?"

"I think so, sir."

"You *think* so?"

"Yes sir, I am up to it," Wayne revised.

"Excellent." Greer walked back around to his desk, pulled open a drawer, and removed a file. *Operation Anglerfish* was written on an orange label on the tab. He opened the folder on the desk, shuffled through the contents and spread them out before him. Computer printouts containing educated conjecture and speculation about a government conspiracy, mentioning the

NSDAP, top American politicians and businessmen from the early 1930s, Roger Blumhurst's suicide, and something called Operation Phoenix, the name "M. Rickner" appearing next to the page number at the top of each sheet, filled most of the file. Greer laid hands on one page and placed it at the top of the pile. It was not a computer printout, but rather a photocopy of a police incident report. The person instigating the investigation: Jonathan Allan Rickner. The name of one of the other involved parties in the investigation: Mara Christine Ellison. Both names were circled several times in red ink from Greer's pen.

Greer spread his hands over the papers and leaned across the desk toward Wayne.

"Okay, here's how my little plan is going to work…"

***

In his black sedan outside Division headquarters, the engine running, heater on full-blast, Dvorak's *Symphony in G Major* playing on the stereo, Enrique Ramirez sat, mulling.

What Greer had devised was brilliant. It was indeed the best chance the Division had had in half a century to once and for all smash the last real threat to the public charade they'd enshrined in history. Without the Dossiers, anything anyone said tried to say was mere conjecture. Perhaps the government would even shut down the Division – no, the government only got larger, never willingly paring itself down. And besides, the few people in Washington who knew of their purpose would hardly risk closing down the only tangible safeguard to that unspeakable truth from so many years ago. But retrieving and destroying the Dossiers would certainly allow Ramirez and everyone at the Division a little more peace of mind.

But Greer's plan also came with tremendous risk. And the very prospect of discovering the Dossiers in the first place – was it perhaps better that they stayed as they had, hidden for all those years? When hidden, they were almost as harmless as they would be if they were destroyed. But no, there would always be the possibility that someone, somehow, would discover them on their own. Better to snuff things out now, while the Division was still in control. Or so Greer's thinking had gone.

Enrique smiled as he realized that Greer had given him an out. Even though Greer had chosen the rookie Wilkins for this assignment – a necessity Ramirez had created with his altercation back at the apartment – Enrique realized he still had a role to play. He was caught in limbo between being pulled off of field duty – which meant no new assignments – and assuming the Directorship. His time – for the first time in a long, long while – was his own. And nothing could be a better use for his time than shadowing Wayne Wilkins and seeing through Greer's bold scheme. If Wilkins was able to do what was necessary and everything went as planned, then great. If not, Ramirez would be there ready to clean up the mess, ensuring the integrity of the Division that he himself would preside over very, very soon. And regardless of the outcome, when the time came, Ramirez would make sure that it was his bullet that killed the younger Rickner and his female companion. His pride would allow for nothing less.

The front door to the building opened, and, as if by divine providence, Wayne Wilkins emerged. Enrique took a deep breath, murmuring a quick prayer of thanks as he watched his fellow agent cross the parking lot to his own vehicle.

Showtime.

Chapter 17

Washington, D.C.

"Last call for Continental Flight 8736 to Newark." The firm female voice echoed through the halls as Jon and Mara dashed through the terminal at Reagan National, carry-ons in hand and flinging wildly about with their frantic pace.

"I *knew* we should've left sooner," Mara huffed between strides.

"Then why did you *pack* so darn much?" Jon retorted as he hurtled alongside her. "We're cutting it *way* too close."

"Then quit your yammering and keep up." She started to pull ahead, but Jon was having none of that. He picked up his already rapid pace and passed her, immune to her shouts of "hey!" from behind.

They skirted their way around some crowds, jostled through others, all the way to their gate. Reaching their gate, gasping for breath, they managed to stop the gate attendant before he shut the door to the jet bridge.

"Cutting it a little close?" asked the young man, raising an eyebrow but not his eyes as he checked their boarding passes.

"Yeah, you know," Jon quipped. "Living life on the edge."

"Two more, heading down now," the attendant spoke into a telephone receiver mounted on the check-in counter.

Mara smiled weakly at Jon. He returned her grin. They had made it.

"Mr. Rickner, Ms. Ellison, enjoy your flight. Please hurry, your flight is about to depart."

Jon snatched their boarding passes from the outstretched hand of the attendant and led the way as they hurtled their way down the tunnel toward the waiting plane.

"Boarding pass?" asked the brunette flight attendant waiting by the door. Jon presented their boarding passes again, and the attendant directed them to their seats. Jon found a half-empty overhead compartment, a few rows up from their seats, where he placed his bag, then Mara's.

"Such a gentleman," Mara said as she followed him to their seats.

"Yes I am… I get window!"

"Hey!" she laughed. "That's fine. I wanted the aisle seat anyway."

"Yeah, on a little puddle jumper like this, nobody gets stuck with the middle seat." The Embraer jet had only 22 rows of four seats, two on each side of the narrow aisle. And, despite the economic crisis, the short driving distance from Washington to New York for those with cars and the rather cheap bus or train fares for those without, the plane was almost completely full. Racking up those frequent flyer points, he guessed. Especially considering the number of business suits on the plane. Which made sense; the two termini of the flight were the political capital of the country and the financial capital. The number of organizations – lobbying firms, law firms, research institutes, corporations, and groups from other fields in which business and politics invariably met, mingled, and walked hand-in-hand – jetting representatives back and forth had to be tremendous.

One standard greeting message from the pilot on the speaker system, one safety regulation demonstration by the flight attendant, and one long taxi to the runway later, Continental Flight 8736, its jet engines whirring loudly, accelerated to take-off speed and left the ground, bound for New York City and all the secrets – and dangers – it held.

Jon looked over at Mara and noticed she had her eyes closed, her fingers clenching the armrests as though she might float away should she let go of them. He grimaced. If she was scared about taking off... The fact was they had no idea what they were up against, how to go about their quest, or even exactly what it was they were looking for. They would have to start with tracking down and talking to Catherine Smith. Tomorrow. At her age, she would probably be in bed before Jon and Mara even got to their hotel room. But after that? If nothing *definitive*, if no real leads came out of that meeting, then what? A sinking feeling in the pit of Jon's stomach, as the plane lurched through an air pocket, still less than a thousand feet off the ground, but he couldn't attribute the sensation solely to turbulence. They were leaving Washington behind. New York lay ahead. And it was clear to Jon that they were now passing the point of no return.

Two rows behind them, in the window seat on the other side of the plane, Wayne Wilkins would have agreed.

Part Two – The Burning Secret

The problem to be solved is, not what form of government is perfect, but which of the forms is least imperfect.
~ James Madison

We must be the great arsenal of Democracy.
~ Franklin Delano Roosevelt

Chapter 18

The short flight to New York had proven uneventful. Two hours after touchdown, having made their way through the Newark airport and via train to Penn Station, Jon and Mara checked in to the historic Hotel Pennsylvania – the hotel that inspired the classic Glenn Miller song "Pennsylvania 6-5000" – and settled in. Due to several large conventions booked into the hotel – and its proximity to Madison Square Garden, Penn Station, and much of Midtown Manhattan – the rooms were nearly all booked. Jon and Mara had taken a spacious two-bed room, which, though potentially awkward, allowed them to keep an eye on each other – both in their grieving and should something more sinister befall them.

After unpacking, Jon suggested they grab some dinner.

"Definitely," Mara agreed. "But I'm choosing the place this time."

Jon conceded and, after changing into more formal attire – he in a deep red long-sleeved button-up with black slacks and a charcoal gray sports coat, she in a dark blue dress and black pea coat with black tights –they made their way through the crowded twilit streets to Mara's restaurant of choice.

Del Frisco's Golden Eagle Steakhouse was a three story affair smack dab in the middle of Midtown Manhattan. Located in the McGraw-Hill Building of the Rockefeller Center complex, the glass-fronted establishment looked out on the throng of pedestrians and motorists bustling down the Avenue of the

Americas. The atmosphere was formal, but cozy, the kind of place professionals might take a prospective client for a little wining-and-dining, or where they might go with some of their colleagues for lunch. Considering all the towering glass and steel skyscrapers that surrounded the restaurant, it was not surprising to see all the suits and work attire. The tuxedos and dresses comprising a good chunk of the rest of the patrons were likely headed to catch a show in the nearby Theater District, or perhaps in Rockefeller Center's own legendary Radio City Music Hall. Directed to a table on the second floor, Jon felt somewhat out of place. He and Mara hadn't just gotten off work from their six-figure executive job. They weren't going to a hundred-bucks-a-pop performance afterward. They were just here to eat. And talk.

"Nice place," Jon commented after they had been seated.

"Yeah, it is. Michael took me here once." Her eyes started to glaze over. "Shoot, I didn't think it would be this hard."

Jon looked concerned. "Do you want to leave? Too many memories? We can go somewhere else if you want."

"No." Mara shook her head forcefully, as though she were trying to convince herself as well. "No, this is fine. It's not like anywhere else we go will make me think of him less. And, honestly, I think I do want to think about him tonight."

"He is the reason we're up here, after all."

Mara screwed up her face and nodded. "Yeah. He is."

"Isn't this place a bit ostentatious though?" Jon changed the subject. "I mean, if we're trying to stay under the radar?"

"Jon, you're a grad student, and I'm a brand new family counselor at an underfunded charity out of my church," Mara said as she unfolded her napkin and placed it in her lap. "A place this cushy is the *last* place anyone would be looking for us. Besides, considering your restaurant choices of late, they're probably combing the local Burger King for us right now."

"Hey, now," he countered with a smirk.

Their waiter approached the table, introduced himself as Ted, mentioned the soups and entrées *du jour* and offered his suggestions, then took their drink orders.

"Water for me," Mara said.

Jon eyed her, then turned his attention to Ted. "Water for me as well. And two glasses of this Merlot, too, please," he said, pointing his selection on the wine list. Mara looked at him with surprise, but he pretended not to notice.

"Very good, sir. Madam." Ted tilted his head in a slight bow. "I shall be back shortly. Please take your time looking over our menu."

"Will do," Jon said, still looking at the waiter and ignoring the stares of his dinner mate. "Thanks, Ted."

Ted nodded with a polite half-smile on his lips, and turned to leave. Jon started to study the menu, a smile creeping up on his face in response to Mara's surprise.

"Merlot?" she finally asked.

"I think a good-luck toast is in order. Besides, I know *my* nerves could use a little calming."

Mara sighed, sinking back into her seat with something like resignation. "Yeah, sure, why not."

They thumbed through their menus, Jon deciding to go with the filet mignon, Mara setting her mouth for the shrimp scampi. A few moments later, the waiter arrived with their water and wine.

"Are you ready to order?"

Jon motioned for Mara to go first. After they had both ordered their entrees, Jon added, "And could we have an order of those crab cakes you suggested for our appetizer?"

"Of course. Just one order?"

Jon looked at Mara across the table. "How hungry are ya?"

"Just *one*, thank you," Mara told Ted.

"Very good, madam. Anything else?"

"No, that'll do it for now." Mara forced a smile. "Thanks, Ted."

"You're quite welcome. Sir, madam." And Ted made his retreat, leaving Jon and Mara alone.

Jon grabbed his wine glass, held it aloft, and waited for Mara to do likewise.

"And to what shall we toast?" Mara asked, mirroring Jon with her wine glass.

"Well, for starters, how about Michael?"

She pressed her lips together, her eyes sad but resolute.

"To Michael." She raised her glass toward Jon's. "The most amazing, most loving, smartest guy this world ever saw. He was taken away too soon."

"Hear, hear. To Michael. The best darn brother and friend anyone could ask for. May he forever rest in peace." *Clink.*

"What else?"

Jon raised his glass toward Mara's again. "To Michael's memory and legacy, may his character never be forgotten, the lives he touched, the hearts he blessed, may he live on forever in our hearts, and may his life be lived out in our own."

"Amen. Hear, hear." *Clink.*

"And to truth. Michael and I were always big on digging deep and finding the truth behind the mystery, or, as the case may be, the deception and conspiracy. May we finish his final quest for truth and bring justice and peace to his spirit."

"To truth." *Clink.*

A pause. Mara broke it.

"What about for protection?"

"From... the guys who got Michael? The cover-up guys?"

"Yeah. From them. According to Professor Leinhart, they might be after us, too, right?"

"They're already after *me*," Jon said, rubbing his shoulder, still sore from his encounter with the intruder at Michael's apartment.

"Well, for protection, then," Mara said as she raised her glass.

"You don't toast *for* something. You toast *to* something."

"To a safe, successful quest for truth?"

"That'll work." *Clink.*

The crab cakes arrived, and the pair dug in.

"Better than a Big Mac?" Mara jibed between bites.

"Oh, hush. It does beat meat pies back in England, though."

"Do you eat haggis over there?"

Jon made a face. "*Please*, Mara, I'm trying to eat. Haggis is disgusting. And decidedly Scottish. Oxford is in England. Different places, different foods. Thank God."

Mara paused between bites and looked around the room, her eyes seeming to focus not on the room as it currently was but rather on how it had been in her memory.

"This place hasn't changed a bit since Michael brought me here. Must've been about six months ago…" She counted on her fingers. "Yeah, it was. Last September. He wanted to take me to the Rainbow Room – iconic, historic, romantic, great view, great dancing, the works. But it was booked solid. A three month waiting list, if you can believe it."

Jon chuckled. "It's New York. I believe it."

"Yeah. So anyway, he just broke everything the Rainbow Room would have held for us into smaller chunks." Mara smiled, staring misty-eyed off at some point over Jon's shoulder and six months in the past. "We came here for a romantic dinner in the Rockefeller complex, then to a musical – *Phantom*, of course – and then he took me up to the top of the Empire State Building. Not the main observation deck, but the higher one, the one just below the antenna. It was just the two of us up there for a bit, and we… we danced. No band, no music. Just us, the stars above, and the far-off beat of the city, alive beneath our feet." She shook her head slowly, her eyes sinking to the table, seeing nothing but the irreclaimable past. "It was… just perfect."

Jon pressed his lips tightly together, nodding silently while fighting off a rush of emotion. "He was a heck of a guy," he finally said after a reflective pause. "He and I both were kinda following in our parents' footsteps. The love of academia coupled with a restless spirit of adventure. But as much as my parents were an influence on us, Michael had an even greater impact on me. I mean, he double majored in history and archaeology at UNC; I did the same at Harvard two years later. He went to GW for his doctorate in history; I went to Oxford. Different places, but very similar interests. He was more into American history, whereas I fell in love with European history and the archaeology of the ancient world. Hence, him being Stateside, and my studying over in the old country." He paused, broke eye contact, and slowly shook his head, almost mournfully, at the table. "And I left him. He was…"

Across the table, a look of concern crossed Mara's face, but she remained silent.

"It was stupid jealousy. All my life, all both of our lives, we'd grown up in the shadow of our father, the great archeologist Sir William Rickner. Given, Dad never tried to force history or archeology on us as far as our career choices went, but growing up in that environment, seeing and experiencing the things Michael and I did, it was all but impossible not to fall in love with it. So it was just our fate that we would necessarily begin our own professional careers in the shadow of a giant who also shared our family name. Probably why we both decided on getting our doctoral degrees in history rather than in archaeology, although we've always been just as active in the latter as we had ever were. And then Michael, being older, begins to make a name for himself." He sighed and looked at the table for a moment. "Another shadow to live in. First my dad, and then my brother."

He looked back at Mara, meeting her eyes, wanting her to understand, to somehow absolve him of this guilt he felt and tell him that he wasn't to blame. Because right now, he sure as heck couldn't stop blaming himself on his own. "I still loved them both, and nothing would ever change that, but somewhere along the way, Michael got "rival" added to my mental list of relationships we held for each other. And so I refused to attend the same university as him, even going so far as to attend school on a different continent for grad school. It was stupid, I know, but..." Jon furrowed his brow at Mara's bemused expression. "What?"

"It's just funny. Not funny, ha-ha; funny, ironic." Mara smiled almost maternally at Jon. "Michael felt the same way about you. Even though he missed the heck out of you, he kind of wanted to distance himself from you professionally. So he could make his own mark, so to speak."

Jon was visibly shocked. "But he was older than me. He started his university career before I did."

"And he was firmly convinced that you were the brighter of the two Rickner sons. He would tell me stories about some of your adventures growing up. About how impressed he always was about your ability to figure things out that no one else seemed to be able to – not even him."

Jon sat dumbly, staring at Mara with a mixture of relief and disbelief. He wanted to laugh and cry all at once. Instead, he just sat, his face twitching into one emotion, then the next, blinking away tears that wanted to come and swallowing laughter that threatened to pour forth in the middle of the restaurant. Finally, he mustered up the control to ask a question. "Really? Then why didn't he..."

"Tell you?" Mara picked up the end of the trailed-off question. "He wanted to. But really, how do you broach a subject like that? 'Hey little bro, just wanted to tell you that you're smarter than me and that's why I'm glad we don't go to the same school'?"

Jon chuckled softly. "Yeah, good point. But even still... Gosh, we were both so stupid. I mean, we weren't even focusing in the same field of history. We could have been an asset to each other, and instead we just wasted the precious time that we had. If only I'd known..." He drifted off, trying to control his breathing, the tightness building in his chest. Then he shook his head abruptly and looked up at Mara. "Sorry, I'm rambling here. Maybe it's cathartic or something. What?"

Mara had put down her fork and stared out at the street.

"What?" Jon repeated, afraid he'd somehow offended her by monopolizing the conversation.

"I..." She slowly turned her head back toward Jon. "I miss him. It's still hitting me how very much I miss him. I don't know what I'm gonna do without him."

"Hey, hey, hey, don't worry about that right now." He reached across the table and took her hand, which she didn't pull away. It was time to switch roles, from consoled to consoler. Mara's pain was every bit as real and fresh as Jon's was. "I know, Mara. I miss him like anything. And I know you do too. He's left an empty spot in both of our lives, but we can't let that keep us from living. We've gotta keep on living all the more now that he's gone. It's what he would've wanted. You know that."

"Yeah." Mara sniffed as she wiped a tear from her eye with the back of her wrist. "Yeah, I do. It's... it's just hard."

"Of course it is, Mara. But, at the risk of sounding cliché, anything worth doing usually is." Jon almost couldn't believe that, just seconds earlier, he was the one struggling through and she was the one encouraging him. But then, that was the way of emotions sometimes. Especially when you have to help someone else through the pain as well.

She picked up her fork and began to absently poke at her half-eaten crab cake. Her eyes, so recently sad and mournful, began to grow dark with something approaching anger. "Why weren't you there for him?" She didn't look up, but a strange coldness had crept into her voice.

Jon blinked. "Excuse me?"

"Why weren't you there for him? Why'd you have to run off to England for graduate school? Why'd you... abandon him?"

"Mara, we *just* had this talk." Was this new wave of sorrow she was experiencing messing with her memory? Or was her pain suddenly making her less sympathetic to what they were talking about? After all, Jon wasn't the one who had just been killed.

She shook her head at the crab cake, her voice still soft and filled with quiet tension. "He'd still be alive if you had been here."

"What are you talking about?"

"If you hadn't left, if you had been there for him, he would have backed down. He would have realized the danger in what he was doing. He wouldn't be dead."

Jon was stunned into silence. Then he broke out of his shock and responded, trying to keep his voice low despite the emotions raging within him. "Holy crap. Are you seriously trying to blame me for Michael's death?"

"Well," she said, her gaze still lingering on the table, "I mean, if you had been here... You've both done this sort of thing before. You knew the dangers. You could have talked him down."

Jon felt his face growing hot, fighting to not explode at Mara here in the restaurant. After all they'd just talked about. After all she knew about Michael, Jon, and the nature of their relationship. *The audacity. The sheer freaking audacity.*

"If you think Michael would have backed down from this," he said through clenched teeth, "you didn't really know Michael at all. He never would have backed down from a good mystery. He never would have forsaken a quest for truth, especially one where people were dying. He would have given everything he had to stop whatever injustice, whatever deceit, he had found." Not to mention the fact that Jon would have been infinitely more likely to join in with Michael in his quest than try to talk him out of it.

"Yeah, the old Michael perhaps." Mara's eyes had left the table and were now meeting Jon's, a surprising glint of anger-tinged confusion behind the welling tears. "But Michael wasn't just living for himself anymore. He was about to be a husband. And in a few years, a father. The head of his own family. Not a stupid teenager running around chasing legends. A grown-up who people depended on."

Jon laughed humorlessly. "You women. Thinking you can change a man's basic personality when you rope him into marriage."

"We *women*?" Mara's voice went up and her face flushed. She scrunched up her face as the tears began to trace their paths down her cheeks. "You pigheaded idiot."

Jon hated himself and hated this situation, knowing full well that they were both emotionally frazzled, and that Mara needed a friend right now, not an adversary. But for some reason, he couldn't stop himself from defending the Michael he knew and loved. "Fine, maybe not fair to the whole sex, but *you, you're* incredible. What Michael got killed doing was nothing less than his most fundamental passion. And if you didn't understand that about him, if you wanted to change him, change that passion that made him my best friend and exploring buddy, then you didn't understand him *at all*."

A tense silence descended upon the table, the murmurs of conversation and clinks of dinnerware from neighboring tables unnoticed as Jon and Mara's eyes bored holes into each other.

Finally, it was Mara who broke, starting to sob as she lowered her head. "I'm sorry. I'm sorry. I…" She clenched her jaw. "Dammit!" she said as her fist hit the table, sending silverware flying and wine sloshing. This drew some stares, but the pair remained oblivious to their surroundings. The very fact that she'd broken from her normally conservative abstention from cursing spoke volumes to the level of her emotional turmoil. Her right hand grabbed her cross pendant and began rubbing its well-worn silver surface. "This is too freaking hard. I… Why did he have to be so brash and adventurous? Why did he have to be a hero? Why couldn't… I loved him for his standards, for his adventurous spirit, for everything that got him killed. But when we were getting engaged, moving toward married life together… Why now? Why couldn't he just stop before it was too late?"

Jon let her vent, each word, each moment he wasn't locking eyes and horns with her another notch his anger lessened. When she lapsed into silence, he waited, then spoke.

"I'm sorry, too. I… You're right. I wish I could have been there for Michael. I'd give anything to turn back the clock, but I still stand by what I said: nothing I said or did would have changed Michael's determination to see this through. Just like nothing you or anyone else say or do will stop me from finishing what he started."

Mara wiped the tears from her eyes with a thumb. Thankfully, she tended to wear minimal eye makeup, so didn't she have mascara trails drawn down her cheeks. She sniffed and half-nodded, half-bobbed her head in agreement.

Jon looked at her thoughtfully. "Why are you here, Mara?"

"Because Michael didn't tell me enough to get me killed, too," she said automatically, looking upward as she tried to stave off another wave of tears.

"No, no, why are you *here*? New York? If you hate this 'chasing legends' nonsense, then why aren't you back in D.C.? Or with your family in Oregon? Why are you *here*?"

"Because I have to be."

"Why?" Jon pressed.

"Because I have to find out what happened to Michael. *Why* I don't have a fiancé anymore. *Why* the love of my life is dead. That's why."

"And exactly how far are you prepared to go in order to do that?"

She met his gaze with a steely determination he had yet to see from her. "As far as I have to."

"Even putting your own life on the line?"

Mara paused, not a good sign in Jon's opinion. Either she was committed to this or she wasn't. Either she would be an asset to finishing Michael's research and to bringing his killers to justice, or she would be a hindrance. And her hesitation didn't portend the kind of determination and nerve that Jon knew would be necessary to see this through.

"Yes," she finally said. "Even putting my own life on the line. Michael cared enough about exposing this secret to risk his life. I care enough about him to risk mine."

"You're sure? This is real, Mara. Real bullets, real death."

"I found his body. Believe me, I *know* how real this is."

"Fine." Jon's mind was far from at ease, but he decided to let the issue rest for now. He was tired. They were both grieving. He had to focus on the task at hand. That presented enough to worry about on its own.

Ted returned with their entrées. As they dined, they swapped half-hearted stories about Michael, reminiscing about the good-old-days that would never be again – Jon and Michael discovering a new temple complex buried in the jungles of Indonesia; Mara and Michael spending a romantic weekend getaway at the beautiful Biltmore Estate in the mountains of North Carolina; Michael's foibles – like loudly cracking his neck at inappropriate times, and snoring; and his strengths – his intelligence, his wit, his compassion. Sad though the situation was, the conversation was strangely healing, and Jon found himself more grateful than ever that he was blessed with a partner in all of this – both for the mourning of Michael and for what would come next.

"So what's our game plan?" Mara finally asked during a lull in the reminiscences.

"Well, we're working off of what Michael was doing, right? Finishing what he started, following in his footsteps, that sort of thing."

"Yeah."

"So I guess the next step is what *his* would have been," Jon said, feeling purpose returning to him. "Talk to Catherine Smith."

"And you plan on finding and talking to her… how?"

"Oh. Right." Jon gave a sheepish grin as he offered, "Um, phone book?"

Mara had a "Jon, this is New York City. Eight million people. Even *if* she's still in the same place with the same name, how many Catherine *Smiths* do you think might be in the book?"

"Yeah…" He made a nervous sucking sound between his teeth. "Maybe we should go back to the notebook. He probably had some sort of clue or thought process written down there that he used to find her."

"And you can find it?"

Jon shrugged, but his expression was hopeful. "If it's in there, I hope I can. Our minds worked in pretty similar ways."

"And if Michael was right about your mental prowess, we should be doing just fine." Mara smiled at Jon. "The student who outgrew his master."

Jon felt the warmth of blood rushing to his cheeks. "Meh. I don't know about that. I'll do what I can, though."

"And after we talk to Ms. Smith?"

"I don't know. I'm kinda banking on her being the lead we need to point us in the right direction. If that doesn't pan out… well, we'll burn that bridge when we come to it."

Mara raised an eyebrow at Jon's deliberately misquoted idiom. "Well, Michael seemed to think that she was key to unraveling this whole thing, and since he knew more about this than either of us do—"

"Then Catherine Smith probably *is* key," Jon finished. "Alright, I guess we'll just have to find her, then go from there."

After Ted's offer of dessert had been politely declined, the waiter brought their check. They argued about who would pick up the bill, guilt and anger from their fight still tainting the atmosphere, each trying to be the bigger person and pay for the dinner. Jon eventually won, but he allowed Mara to pay the tip.

Picking up their coats, they headed down the stairs and into the chilly night air. The drone of engines and blaring of horns, the shuffle of pedestrians and jingle of coins, the soulful croons of a street musician's saxophone, and the nasally pleas for charity donations greeted their ears as the soundtrack of the city. Out in the open, in the dark, Jon was cognizant of the weight in the backpack slung from his shoulder. The notebook. Legal-size paper, college-ruled, 80 sheets, spiral-bound. Not really heavy – but it was weighty. Or at least, its contents were. Worth more than its weight in gold to the right – or wrong – person. What clues had Michael left behind? He couldn't have known he was going to die, but something in that notebook *had* to hold some sort of answer for Jon, to hold some importance that would lead him to the truth that both brothers sought.

As they crossed the plaza to the sidewalk and started walking south down Sixth Avenue toward their hotel, Jon turned to gaze at the towering spires of the iconic skyscrapers around him. Historic buildings from the 1930s, buildings that would have stood witness to the suicide of Roger Blumhurst in '57, and, presumably, countless other deaths like Michael's associated with this alleged conspiracy. Buildings that had been built by magnates like Woolworth and Chrysler – men who built and ruled empires, steered economies, held tremendous power over millions of people's lives.

And suddenly, the connection he had been sure that he knew came rushing back to Jon. The connection between all of the locations on Michael's map of Manhattan. It was quite literally staring him in the face.

Years ago, all of the locations on the map had either belonged to or received tremendous funding from the same incredibly wealthy, incredibly powerful man.

John D. Rockefeller, Jr.

Chapter 19

Tuesday

The night had been long. Mara's sobbing in her sleep had kept Jon awake for nearly an hour, her tears stirring something within him, steeling his resolve even further. This was about more than just finishing Michael's work or unveiling the truth. This was about retribution, setting right wrongs perpetrated against all those who loved Michael – and against however many other victims of this purported cover-up before him. As he had lain in bed, staring at the dark ceiling above, he realized that it wasn't just Michael's death he was setting out to vindicate; it was the deaths of everyone who had dared to ask questions someone didn't want asked, the nameless – dozens? hundreds? thousands? – before him, and perhaps countless more afterward if Jon and Mara should fail.

No pressure or anything.

He had finally fallen asleep after midnight, awakening hours later to the morning sun peeking underneath the drawn curtains. Daylight. The day of reckoning. Or so Jon hoped. He sat up in bed, checked his watch, and swung his legs off the side of the bed. Glancing across the room at Mara's bed, Jon froze. Her bed was empty.

Had she been abducted during the night? Had the bastards come in and taken her away, maybe trying to use her as a bargaining chip for Jon, the notebook, and everything they knew? But Jon was right there. Wouldn't he have heard them? Or, more likely, wouldn't they have taken or killed him, too?

His breaths came in quick, heavy bursts. He leapt to his feet, darted across the room to her bed. The sheets were tossed aside, her suitcase open. Her toiletries bag missing from its conspicuous spot in an easily visible mesh pocket. The sound of water running from the other side of the wall. From the bathroom. The shower.

Jon rolled his head back, clapped his hand on the back of his neck, and squeezed, massaging the tension from his muscles. He was getting jumpy, paranoid. Given, his brother *had* been murdered, and someone *had* broken into Michael's apartment, attacked Jon, and stolen the laptop, but that didn't mean there was a conspiracy lurking in every corner. He had to be careful, cautious, but not paranoid. That could backfire.

He sat down on the end of her bed, took a deep breath. Stood again, walked over to the window, drew back the curtain. *Great view*, he thought sarcastically, the window opening onto another row of the hotel's rooms just across the small alleyway. He couldn't even see the ground, sixteen stories below, from this vantage point. Most of the windows he could see had their curtains drawn. But then, it was just after seven a.m., and there wasn't much to see anyway. Jon thought he saw a figure, its features hidden in shadow, peering down at him from a window across the way, but it disappeared behind the curtain before Jon could get a good look. Someone spying on him? Was it "*them*"? Had "they" followed them here, to New York, to their hotel, to their room? *Stop that*, he admonished himself. He was letting his fears, the bloody scene and the gunman he had encountered in Michael's apartment, run away with him.

His paranoia wasn't the only issue plaguing him this morning. Nor was the jet lag that was beginning to catch up to him. He missed his brother. Not just because he was dead, although that obviously weighed on him. Growing up with archaeologist parents, traveling around the world, often being the only children within miles, had led Jon and Michael to develop an uncommonly strong bond. When their mother had met her mysterious and ostensibly bloody end in the jungles of the Yucatan, the then-teenage brothers had grown even closer together. The hole Michael's death had left in Jon's life, and would continue to leave, was tremendous.

What Jon had set out to do – solving this mystery steeped in history and conspiracy – was nothing new for him. He and Michael had embarked on their share of Indiana Jones-esque adventures throughout their youth, probing the four corners of the earth, like their father, for truths obscured by the mists of time and the shrouds of men. But those adventures had always been shared by the brothers: Jon *and* Michael. For this mystery, possibly the biggest challenge he'd yet to face, Jon was on his own.

Which brought him to Mara. That Michael loved her, he had no doubt. That she loved him was equally unquestionable. Undoubtedly, they would have made a happy, romantic married couple. But would Michael have brought her into the field? Into the dangers that his family seemed to have a penchant for attracting? The fact that she had, inadvertently, been brought into this latest danger, was immaterial to Jon's internal debate. Was she fit to be a sidekick, assistant, co-adventurer in solving Michael's murder? In bringing his killers to justice and exposing the truths that they apparently were willing to kill to protect, that Michael had given his life to discover and reveal? Jon had his doubts, and last night's verbal dustup hadn't helped. The odds were already stacked against him, and he didn't need an emotionally distraught, unstable sidekick to further hinder his chances. Nor, he reflected, did Mara need to be dragged along through whatever perils and mayhem awaited them. But ultimately, the decision was out of his hands; the choice was hers and hers alone.

"Enjoying the view?" Jon jumped at the sound of Mara's voice behind him. He hadn't even noticed that the sound of falling shower water was now gone, and here she was, dressed and ready for the day, save for the towel she had wrapped around her hair.

"Not really. Just thinking."

"Shower's all yours if you want it." She took a step toward him and made a face. "Whew! And, please, *want* it."

"Thaanks..." Apparently she'd chosen to put last night's argument behind her. He'd try to do the same.

"Just kidding," she said, slapping him playfully on the arm. "Hurry up."

Jon grabbed his toiletries bag and a change of clothes, and slipped into the bathroom. After a quick shower, he shaved and brushed his teeth. Although he and Mara had talked about how to actually get to Catherine Smith and find out what she had to share with Michael, they hadn't come up with much of anything concrete. Jon had pored through Michael's notebook and quizzed Mara for any little clue Michael might have inadvertently given her, but to no avail. Blame it on the shock of his brother's death, on the attack at the apartment, or on everything moving so very very fast these past few days, but mentally, Jon had hit a major brick wall. But then, staring at himself in the mirror – toothbrush in mouth, froth overflowing – he hit upon an idea.

"The article!" he said to his reflection immediately after spitting in the sink. His reflection seemed to agree, its excitement matching Jon's. "Mara!" he called into the hotel room as he opened the door and rinsed out his mouth.

"What?" she called back, appearing a moment later with a worried look on her face.

"The article! Maybe if we go to the original article, or the issues on the days after its publication, we'll find something else about Catherine Smith."

"Okay. Do you know where Michael found it?"

Jon shook his head. "No, I don't. I've never even heard of the *Brooklyn Herald*."

"And *you're* a history buff."

"Michael never mentioned where up here he found it, then?"

"Nope. 'fraid not." Mara frowned and shrugged. "Part of his whole protecting-me-from-'them' thing, I guess."

Jon scratched the back of his head. "Well, if the paper's not around anymore, their non-existent headquarters won't have any archives for us to search."

"Well, Michael found it *somewhere*."

Jon snapped his fingers. "Leinhart."

Mara's lips widened into a satisfied smile. "He'd know."

"Glad we swapped numbers. I'll call him before we head out to breakfast."

"Good idea. My hair's still drying anyway." She started to head back into the main room, but stopped short, turning back to Jon. "Oh, and put on a shirt before we head out, if you would."

Jon looked down at his bare torso, embarrassed, the muscles of his chest and stomach glistening in the steam of the bathroom. Thank God he'd put on his *pants* before he called Mara in. He threw on a gray long-sleeved button-up, grabbed his toiletries, and headed back to his nightstand, and the cell phone that rested atop it.

He dialed the professor's number, hoping he wasn't waking him up. Knowing what Michael had to say about the man's work ethic, though, he doubted he'd be sleeping in on a Tuesday morning. The professor picked up on the third ring.

"Jon!" Leinhart's tone was energetic and excited. "How are things in New York? Found anything yet?"

"Whoa, whoa," Jon said into the mouthpiece as he sat down on the bed. "Goodness, sir, you're awfully… well, for lack of a better term, perky, this early in the morning."

"No, sorry, Jon. Not perky. Just nervous. For you guys." Leinhart made a noise that sounded like something between a sigh and a horse's neigh. "Hell, for me, even. I guess we're all in this together now, huh?"

"Yes sir. I guess so. Sorry."

"Don't be. I figure I was neck deep in it before you even got on this side of the ocean, simply through my association with Michael's work. So have you found anything yet? Did you meet with Ms. Smith?"

"Not yet, sir. We're still trying to figure out how to find her. Michael didn't mention how he was going to meet with her, did he? Like a phone number or an address or something to help find her in a city full of 'Smiths'?"

A pause. "No. Sorry, Jon, but I can't remember him saying anything about that. He had just told me about her on Friday. Right before…" The professor drifted off.

"Yeah, I know. Kinda screws with your head, doesn't it?"

"It does, Jon. Besides, the older I get, the more… scatter-brained I get. Of course, we academic types prefer the term 'eccentric.'"

"Of course, sir," Jon said with a chuckle. "We were thinking about that article that Michael found…"

"The one with… um, what was his name, Blumhurst—"

"That's the one. The one that mentions Catherine Smith. Do you happen to know *where* Michael dug that up?"

"He said he found it at the main branch of the New York Public Library."

Jon's eyes lit up. An answer? A tangible lead. Excellent.

"In print or—"

"Microfilm," Leinhart interrupted. "I'm fairly certain he said it was in microfilm. He'd been scouring newspapers for days when he found this one. The weekend before last. Had to get to a seminar the next day or he probably would've chased Ms. Smith down right then and there."

"And he didn't check it out or anything, right? It's still there?"

"I don't believe they allow you to check out microfilm. Unless it's an academic loan through a university in the city or something like that. Either way, no, Michael didn't check it out. Just made a print of what he found. It should still be there."

"Thank you so much, Professor." Jon's voice was full of enthusiasm and excitement, the restless night and crappy window view now a million miles away.

"Not at all, Jon. You two take care of yourselves out there, alright? Remember, everyone else who has ever tried to do what you're doing... well, they're not around anymore. Watch yourselves."

Jon swallowed hard, exhaling a thick breath from his nostrils. Slowly. "Yes sir. We'll be careful."

"And let me know of any developments. Anything I can do for you from this end, you let me know. I've got a feeling time may be against us here, so the more hands we have working on this thing, the quicker we should succeed."

"Will do. Hopefully you'll hear from us this afternoon."

"I'll be looking forward to your call, Jon. Give my best to Mara, and Godspeed to you, son."

"Thanks, Professor." *Click.*

Mara turned from the suitcase she was digging in toward Jon as he finished the call. "You got something?"

"New York Public Library. The main branch on 5th Avenue. Michael got the article from there."

She took a deep breath, exhaling in a sigh. "Good. Breakfast first?"

"Yeah." The pair grabbed their belongings, Jon taking the backpack he was already beginning to think of as his, Mara her purse, and the pair went downstairs to breakfast at Lindy's, the café by the Seventh Avenue entrance to the hotel. After an aptly named "Big Breakfast" apiece, they made their way up

Seventh Avenue, across 34th Street to Fifth Avenue, then north eight blocks to their destination. They passed between the famous stone lions, Patience and Fortitude, who stood sentinel at the entrance to the library. More classically sculpted figures looked down at the pair from atop the triple arcade, unflinchingly guarding the repository of information as they had for the past century. Jon and Mara walked up the stairs, feeling strangely secure under the watchful gaze of the stone guardians, and into the historic Beaux Arts-style building.

Just inside the entrance, a dark-haired man in a black suit and blue tie with a briefcase tucked underneath his arm, thumbing through a day planner, bumped into Mara, almost knocking her down.

"Hey!" Jon exclaimed in concern.

"Oh, so sorry," said the man.

"I'm fine," Mara said, slinging her purse back over her shoulder. She locked eyes with the man. Briefly. His ice blue eyes made her shiver. He broke eye contact and nodded before continuing on his way out the door.

"You okay?" Jon asked.

"Yeah. I thought he was after my purse at first, but I guess he was just too caught up in whatever he was reading."

"Your wallet still in there? These pickpockets can be pretty crafty."

She checked her purse. "Yup, still there. Besides, how many pickpockets patronize the library in a business suit?"

"It's New York," Jon said with a sideways glance at her. "I bet there's at least one."

They made their way down the hall to the Microform Room – where the library housed its extensive collection of microfilm, microfiche, and other pre-digital age periodical archive mediums – without further incident. A pair of tables stood to their left, and rows of microfilm readers spanned the length of the room. The far end held a series of tall filing cabinets, and an expansive set of large, professional looking volumes filled the bookshelves on the right. Behind the counter to their right, a man in his mid-thirties sporting a stylish goatee, shoulder-length hair, and a green turtleneck, wearing a name badge that identified him as library staff, sat in a chair and stared at the clipboard he held. He looked as though he would fit right in with the crowd of beatniks at a Greenwich Village poetry reading.

"Excuse me," Jon said.

"Mmm?" asked the man, whose name badge identified as Eli, pretending he hadn't noticed them before.

"Can you help us find a certain newspaper? We're a little lost in here."

Eli sighed impatiently as though he had just been asked the most inane question in the world, a question he was far too busy to be expected to deal with. Jon shot a look at Mara, who already had one eyebrow raised.

"Which newspaper would you care to see, sir?"

"The *Brooklyn Herald*."

"The *Brooklyn Herald*, eh?" said Eli, starting to walk toward one side of the room, apparently intending for the pair to follow him. "That's an obscure one."

"Oh, you've heard of it?" Jon said, he and Mara falling in next to the library staff member.

"Please. I work in the Microform section of one of the most expansive libraries in the world," Eli retorted, his voice dripping with haughty indignation. "Of *course* I've heard of it. Although I do believe that we are the only institution to archive that particular newspaper. As I said, it's extremely obscure."

"Uh huh," Jon replied, fighting the temptation to slap the man across the face.

"You need to fill out this form."

Jon looked at the form and thought back to the date on the article Michael had printed and pasted in the notebook: October 10th, 1957.

"Can you do the whole month of October 1957?" Jon asked with an attempt at a friendly smile plastered on his face.

"I imagine so. The dailies were rather short back then. Most rolls have at least a few months on them. And the *Herald* went out of business… You said you wanted October '57?" Jon nodded. "Heh. That should all be on one roll then. The paper went belly-up right before Halloween. IRS shut 'em down or something. Not that they had that much of a readership, of course."

Jon met Mara's disbelieving gaze, another piece of the puzzle coming together a little too clearly, although the finished picture on the box was still blurry, amorphous, a continually shifting portrait of phantoms and shadows. The beatnik employee cleared his throat and glanced at Jon, then at the form, motioning with bored eyes that he had better things to do than wait for patrons to fill out forms. Jon turned to finish the form and handed it to Eli. Eli tore off the carbon copy beneath, handed the copy back to Jon, and turned to go in the back.

"Wait here," Eli said with his back to Jon and Mara, his air of superiority still being laid on thick. "I'll be right back." And he disappeared through the door.

Jon spoke first, whispering louder and more quickly than he intended to. "The paper got shut down by the government just a few weeks after they report on the public suicide of a U.S. soldier who had supposedly died in combat six years earlier. The only witness to a murder the soldier seemingly committed just hours before his real death is run down in the streets two days later, and the reporter who dared to cover the stories is mown down in a hail of gunfire just days afterward. Coincidence?"

"Creepy, is what it is, Jon. Downright creepy."

Jon nodded his solemn agreement. "Michael was certainly right. Something is rotten in the State of Den—"

"Where the hell is it?" Eli demanded in a fury, a split second before the "Staff Only" door slammed against the doorstop. His finger, jabbing in the faces of Jon and Mara, shook with the rest of his hands. Fury and panic warred in his eyes.

"Where is what?" Jon asked in a deliberately hushed tone, more suited to their library surroundings than the tone Eli had just used, eliciting the stares of several patrons throughout the room.

"The— the microfilm is gone."

"Gone, like checked out?"

"No. Gone, like stolen. *Somebody stole the archives for the whole damn paper.*"

Chapter 20

Wayne's pale blue eyes were now shielded from the sun's rays by the reflective lenses of the Ray-Bans he had extracted from his suit pocket. A brief reprieve, to be made unnecessary as soon as he set foot in Grand Central Station, just a few short blocks away. He walked east along 42nd Street, squinting into the morning sun despite the added protection of the sunglasses.

He had already had quite a busy morning. Monitoring the targets' conversations, ascertaining their next move, and staying one step ahead of them. It was something he had been skilled at in war zones. From just a few pieces of information about a man's character and personality, from just a few minutes of observing him in his natural habitat, Wayne could draw up a fairly accurate profile of the man, a profile that would allow him, more often than not, to figure out what the target's next move would be even before the mark himself knew.

The game of cat and mouse was far more complex here though. For one, there weren't millions of potential witnesses in the villages and insurgent strongholds in Iraq and Afghanistan. The sites of his previous missions were in officially declared war zones, not in an iconic American city, the same city that had suffered the attacks that had sparked the "War on Terror." And this mission couldn't be accomplished with just a well-aimed bullet. Both the carrot and the stick had to be employed, driving his targets where he needed them to go, to do what he needed them to do.

If you knew the right strings to pull, the marionette would do almost anything.

After leaving his room on the eighteenth floor of the Hotel Pennsylvania, Wayne had walked to the New York Public Library, sneaked into the Microform archives via an "Employees Only" entrance, and absconded with all eight years' worth of the library's microfilm collection of the *Brooklyn Herald*. Dumped in a black plastic trash bag and hidden inside the briefcase he carried under his arm. He didn't want to *destroy* any information just yet. Greer wanted him to, but he had too much of a respect for learning and knowledge to destroy what seemed to be the only remaining copies of the newspaper in any library in the country. Somehow it got missed in the purges, and now he was supposed to finish the job. Well, for all intents and purposes, it *was* purged now. And his purpose for taking the microfilm had nothing to do with information containment; he simply wanted to draw in all the leads so that only one remained: him. Hello, carrot.

Fear remained a good stick for the time being. If that scuffle Jon had had with Ramirez at the apartment didn't have him looking over his shoulder, he would be soon. In fact, that was probably why Ramirez, Greer's golden child, hadn't been given this assignment. He left a witness. The fact that Greer hadn't ordered Ramirez's immediate dismissal spoke volumes about their relationship. But if Ramirez had been given any hint of the kind of mission his mistake had deprived him of, and if Greer had told him who was getting the assignment that otherwise should have been his, he surely would have been furious. Thus, in all likelihood, explaining the contemptuous stare he had drilled Wayne with as they passed in the halls.

And so, for whatever reason, Greer had given this mission to Wayne. Perhaps he really did admire his skills; Wayne certainly wouldn't deny that thus far, his skills had proven more than sufficient. Perhaps it was because New York was Wayne's backyard, despite all the emotional baggage the city held for him post-9/11; he didn't need a street map to figure out which streets led where, nor a compass to navigate the more expansive parks of the city. Or perhaps Greer just didn't have anyone else who *quite* fit the bill. So he settled for the new guy. And even though Wayne told himself he was more than up to the task, the truth was, he was in uncharted waters here. His was a terribly important yet precarious assignment. Made all the more risky by factors of which Greer, seemingly blind to the real world outside his single-minded dedication to the Division's mandates, hadn't the slightest inkling.

As Wayne approached the entrance to the world-famous Grand Central Terminal, he looked up at the looming statues of Mercury, Hercules, and Minerva, perched around the clock that read 10:21. Mercury, the fleet-footed messenger of the gods. Hercules, the powerful demigod who used his physical strength, and the gullibility of others, to accomplish his ends. Minerva, the embodiment of wisdom and moral turpitude. Was there some symbolism there? Greer would be Hercules, to be sure. Fierce, manipulative, bloodthirsty, cunning; all the attributes the Greeks and Romans loved in their heroes, a far cry from the selfless valiance that more recent heroes in Western civilization represented – a result of the influence of Christian teachings and values in European society throughout the intervening centuries. Minerva: well, Wayne *hoped* that for once in his life, he was using the wisdom he'd been given – he needed it now more than ever. And Mercury? The instant information relay of the digital age. More precisely, satellites.

Wayne pulled out the pocket-sized GPS receiver he had tucked in his suit jacket. The little red dot near the corner of Fifth and 42nd told Wayne that Jon and Mara were still at the library, probably just now realizing the fruitlessness of their quest there. Unless Mara had discovered that his bumping into her hadn't been an accident, and she had found the tiny GPS transmitter he had dropped into her open purse. Considering how much stuff women seemed to carry around in their purses, especially the fashionably large ones like Mara was carrying, he seriously doubted the transmitter was in jeopardy of being found.

Indeed, the pair had been careful about not being tracked, even going so far as to ditch their cell phones and buy prepaid ones with cash. But Jon, apparently meticulous about keeping track of his money – a strangely all-too-rare characteristic in today's world plagued by credit card fraud and identity theft – had held on to the store receipt from the purchase. And even if he did realize that the receipt for the cell phones was no longer with the others in his bag at the hotel, he would have likely thought nothing of it. Besides, he was too busy solving his brother's murder and uncovering a national secret to do much book-balancing right now. Wayne, on the other hand, had plenty of use for the receipt. With the timestamp on the slip, coupled with the store's hacked inventory records, he had ascertained the numbers of the three phones the young scholar had purchased, careful observation of Jon and Mara allowing him to figure out which phone belonged to whom. Because, ultimately, he would only need one.

Wayne rented a locker inside the station to store his briefcase in; there was no reason to lug it around all day. When this was all over, he'd probably come back and retrieve the briefcase, go back to the library, and catch up on a little reading. Probably. You could never know how these things would end, and there were too many variables to rest on your laurels and bank on any kind of success. Laziness begat sloppiness. And whatever people might have said about Wayne Wilkins, lazy and sloppy were two words that would never have been used to describe him.

Locking the briefcase in the locker and pocketing the key, he entered a tunnel and descended the first staircase, following the signs for the Number 6 line to Brooklyn. He had one more meeting to make, one with a person who the Division had kept on file for years but had been all but certain that the lead had been pumped dry – until Michael Rickner had backdoored his way into the nation's secrets and changed the game. Just this one last stop, keeping a step ahead of Jon and Mara, before he was ready to put the next phase of the plan into action.

And as plans went, this one was a doozy.

Chapter 21

"Gone?"

"Gone," Jon told Dr. Leinhart on the other end of the line. He and Mara were standing outside on the steps of the library. A chorus of sirens – fire truck klaxon and ambulance wail – sounded from the east. "The librarian had no clue where they went. He was as shocked as we were."

A distorted noise as the professor sighed into the mouthpiece. "I— God, Jon I don't know what to say." Silence, then, "One thing this does tell us, though."

"What?"

"It's real. Someone doesn't want anyone to find what Michael found. I'd say, between this and the guy at the apartment, Michael's theory was legitimate. Or at least close enough to ruffle some feathers."

Jon shook his head abruptly. It was both good news and bad. They were, in fact, on the right track. But that track, as Michael had found out the hard way, was extremely dangerous. "Any suggestions as to what to do next?"

Another pause. "None from this end. I'm still plumbing my resources for anything that could shed some light. On my way to class right now actually, so I'll be out of touch for about two hours. I'll keep looking, but you guys dig deep. Maybe go back to the notebook. If anyone can pick up the trail, you can, Jon. Michael had nothing but praise for your intellectual acuity and insight. Make him proud."

Jon allowed himself a small smile. "I'll try, Professor." He glanced at Mara beside him, and revised his statement. "*We'll* try."

"Good. I'll let you know if I turn up anything. Good luck."

"Thanks. Bye."

"Goodbye, Jon."

Mara stepped closer to Jon as he pocketed the cell phone. "Any luck?"

"He didn't have any new info. Suggested we go back to the notebook. He figures the missing microfilm proves that the conspiracy Michael was researching was real, though."

"Yeah, I guess it does. Well, I suppose that's *something*."

"Something you can't really follow up on." He grunted in frustration. Turned and looked up at the library behind him. "Library," he said, snapping his fingers.

"Yes, it *is* a library," Mara said with a slightly sarcastic edge. "We just went in there, remember?"

"No, no, we need to go back in. Surf the Net, google what we know, see if we can track her down that way."

"If they've purged everywhere that's *hard* to find, why wouldn't they have purged the Internet? It'd be much easier for them to find the evidence against them with a search engine than in the dark recesses of some old library. Besides, the Web's only been around the past twenty years, and this article—"

"You got a better idea?" Jon cut in.

"No," she admitted after a tense pause. "Let's give it a shot." Her voice and body language were lacking enthusiasm and confidence in this course of action, but she followed him back inside nonetheless.

They found an empty computer station, pulled up an extra chair, and set to work. "Catherine Smith" returned thousands of hits. "Brooklyn Herald": none that referred to a newspaper of that name; most were "Brooklyn heralds blah blah blah" – not what they were looking for. "Roger Blumhurst": only a handful, all but one of which referred to men who seemed to have been born years after the Roger *they* sought had died, the exception being a website listing Korean War Veterans who had given their lives in combat. Roger Blumhurst, 1951 – *not quite*, Jon reflected. "Catherine Smith" with "Brooklyn Herald": zilch. "Catherine Smith" with "Roger Blumhurst": nada. "Catherine Smith" with "1957": nothing useful. Another dead end.

"Wait a sec," Mara burst in. Jon turned his head from the screen at her sudden show of enthusiasm. "We've been looking for phone numbers and street addresses all this time, right? I mean, she's an old lady by now and all, but what if she's moved into the twenty-first century?"

"You mean email?"

"Exactly. My Great-Uncle Roland is eighty-four, and he talks with his grandkids across the country via Skype. Very modern for an old guy."

"Michael's email. Of course!" Jon pulled up Gmail and typed in his brother's login and password. Login successful. Jon smiled. Michael still used the same password that the pair had coined years back for access to their "secret hideout" in an abandoned mine in Ecuador, near where their dad was working on an anthropological/archaeological team with some of the tribal natives in a remote mountainous region. Jon himself still used it as his password for some of his accounts. The memory, and the bond it signified, brought a tearful smile to his face.

Even in the few days it had been since Michael's death, the emails had already started to pile up. A few pieces of junk mail, some newsletters from campus organizations, bank statements, bill reminders, frequent flyer points updates, and the like. Facebook notifications, invites to coffee from colleagues and friends who had fallen by the wayside in recent weeks. Nothing from Catherine Smith. Another dead end.

"Wait a minute," Jon said, mostly to himself. He pulled out Michael's notebook and thumbed through to an entry he had just glanced over before. Scribbled in the margin, halfway covered by a newspaper article that had been glued onto the page, was an email address. One Jon had never seen before. *Of course.*

Jon logged out of Michael's personal Gmail account, then logged in to the new account, using the same password as before. It worked. According to the welcome page information, the account holder was one Michael Smith. *Oh, the anonymous wonders of free email services.* Michael had created another account, one not associated with himself at all, exclusively for the purpose of investigating this conspiracy he'd stumbled upon. He was paranoid about anyone finding out about his work, so of course he'd be careful and put some distance between it and himself. And a new email account under a false name – and probably a false date of birth and zip code as well – would have been the ideal tool to use. The most recent email in the inbox was an email sent Sunday evening. Two days after his death. Status: *Unread*. Sender: *Catherine Smith*.

Jackpot.

Jon clicked on the subject line – reading "re: Visit" – in the inbox to open the exchange. Both he and Mara hunched over in their seats, leaning closer to the screen, their breaths coming more quickly now. The page loaded with an innocuous message, simply inquiring about the visit Michael was supposed to have paid her the day before, a visit he never turned up for, prevented by causes she apparently wasn't aware of. She didn't realize he was dead. Of course she didn't. How would she have found out? The only one who knew how to find her was Michael, and he wasn't likely to send her an email from beyond the grave telling her that he had been unavoidably detained and couldn't make their appointment.

Nothing else in that message, but Jon scrolled down. Michael thanking her for the opportunity to meet with her, and saying that he looked forward to meeting her "tomorrow." That part must've been sent on Friday.

Jon scrolled down more. Bingo. Meeting time (and her long-winded reasoning behind the time she had chosen), conditions on her talking with him (including not having to testify in court and not being quoted in "anymore damned newspapers"), and other particulars. Including her home address.

Mara grabbed Jon's hand and squeezed. He looked from the address on the screen to her, beaming. He jotted it down on a piece of scrap paper sitting next to the monitor, pulled the address up on Google Maps, and, after checking which subway station was nearest the woman's home, he logged out of the computer and they headed for the door. They finally knew where Catherine Smith – their last remaining lead – lived.

In Brooklyn.

Chapter 22

Jon and Mara exited the library and stood perched at the top of the steps, looking down on Fifth Avenue and consulting the tourist map they'd picked up from a sidewalk stand.

"Well, there's a Metro station right down there," Mara said, pointing west down 42nd. "*Or*, we could hoof it to Grand Central a few blocks thattaway."

"We'd have to change trains at Grand Central anyway," Jon chimed in. "Let's hoof it."

"Sounds good to me." Mara pocketed the map, and the pair climbed down the steps, walking north down the sidewalk. They crossed 42nd and made their way east toward a side entrance for Grand Central near Madison Avenue. At the top of the staircase, Jon froze.

Mara was two steps down when she looked back at Jon.

"What?" she asked, oblivious to the Latino man who stood at the foot of the stairs, returning Jon's look of disbelief.

"*Run*," Jon breathed, grabbing her hand and tugging her up the stairs. The Latino recovered himself and started up the stairs after them.

The pair dashed across Madison, right in front of a bus, effectively slowing their pursuer. And they kept on running, Jon wrestling with the probability that his assailant had followed him to New York, Mara trusting in Jon's seemingly impetuous judgment. Weaving and pushing through the hordes of sidewalk patrons, Jon chanced a glance back over his shoulder. It *was* the same guy. Latin features, embittered eyes, eyes that recognized and despised Jon. He was wearing a black jogging suit, warm but easy to maneuver in. And to help hide in the shadows, Jon thought. The man was running after the pair, no further than thirty feet behind. And gaining.

"We've gotta ditch the bags. They're slowing us down!"

"No way!" Mara shouted in response. "Besides, that's *Michael's.*" Jon knew she was right. He could never just throw away Michael's bag like that. But he had to do *something* to put some distance between them and their pursuer.

How did they do it in the movies? Knock over stuff behind them, impede their pursuer's progress, right? Worth a shot, Jon thought as he saw a lightweight folding table on the sidewalk, piles of flyers advocating some social cause littering its top. A few volunteers stood behind it, shouting at passersby and entreating them to support their cause. A donations box sat at the back of the table, its lid partially open. It'd have to do.

When they reached the social cause advocates, Mara kept on running, but Jon grabbed the cheap green tabletop and flung it to the ground behind him. Shouts of "Hey!" and "What the hell?" chased after him as he slid out of the grips of grabbing hands and beat a path down the sidewalk after Mara. The volunteers, as well as several passersby, bent down in the middle of the sidewalk to pick up the contents of the donations box, and to collect the errant flyers that were already starting to disperse with the breeze and be trod upon by the feet of the unaware. Just like Jon had planned. And on the other side of the diversion, their pursuer was forced to slow his pace and alter his course. Jon met his eyes, and the man's vengeful stare deepened and darkened. Jon shivered, and quickened his pace to catch up with Mara.

"What was that?" she asked in between breaths.

"Diversion."

The iconic main entrance to Grand Central began to loom in the distance before them. Darting between cars, they crossed Vanderbilt Avenue. Horns blared and tempers flared as they finally reached to the safety of the sidewalk. A glance behind told

Jon that their pursuer had maneuvered past the diversion and was nearly at the intersection himself.

"Keep going! Into the station!" Jon shouted at Mara, who was two feet away and already moving as fast as she could. Mara flung open the door as she and Jon hurtled inside down the ramp.

An intersection. Jon glanced left and right as he ran, scanning the signs for the subway, for the Number 6 line. Left to the gift shop. Right to the train station and dining concourse. No sign for the subway. They ran straight.

The next archway did read "Subway." They dashed through the entrance and into the main concourse of Grand Central Station. Jon halted briefly, lost in the cavernous room, entries and exits in every direction. The squeal of sole rubber sliding on marble behind him caused Jon to look over his shoulder, his feet already in motion again as his mind registered their pursuer rounding the corner behind them.

Directly in front of them, travelers waited in line to purchase their train tickets. Jon smelled a shortcut and another diversion. He and Mara shoved their way across the four lines, knocking people down and drawing the lines into an indignant cluster. Jon shouted an apology over his shoulder and smiled. He saw that the cluster of bodies required the Latino to go around them, a change in route that would cost him a few seconds. And every second counted.

At the end of the concourse, Jon and Mara headed into the tunnel that headed to the Number 6 line.

Jon and Mara's clamorous footsteps slapped the tile floor and echoed off the walls, the crowded tunnel already full with foot traffic becoming all the more tumultuous with their pushing and shoving to get through. A woman with an oversized Macy's shopping bag received a particularly strong shove from behind, mainly directed at the arm that held her purchases. Jon could hear her cursing above the din as the contents of her bag spilled onto the floor.

"Sorry!" Jon yelled back without turning around or missing a step. Another diversion. Excellent. They needed all the time they could get. Turned right. Back toward 42nd Street.

"Crap!" Jon huffed as daylight poured through the exit doors at the end of the hall. "Where the hell is the subway?"

"There!" Mara shouted, pointing in stride toward a pair of staircases on the left.

Jon shot another look behind him, their pursuer still hot on their heels. He felt his fatigued muscles stiffen, burst forward with renewed drive.

The pair shoved their way down the stairs, drawing the protests and accusatory glares from shoppers, executives, and protective parents. After they finally extricated themselves from the angry mob, Jon glanced back to check on their pursuer. He was already starting down the stairs. How had he caught up with them so fast? Regardless of the desperation that might have been setting in, Jon strove onward, his lungs threatening to explode in his chest. Mara, her chest heaving and eyes wide with fear and exertion, kept right on running with him.

On the other side of the turnstiles, a sign for the Number 6 line to Brooklyn beckoned. The recognizable screech of brakes resounding just beyond told Jon that their train was just arriving – and thus, about to leave again.

"Hang on, I've gotta find my MetroCard," Mara gasped as they approached the turnstile.

"Screw the MetroCard!" Jon yelled, putting both hands on the sides of the turnstile and swinging himself over. A nearby police officer yelled a creative "Hey!" at the pair as Mara swung herself over after Jon.

"Sorry!" Mara called behind her, catching a glimpse of the irritated cop on the other side of the turnstile. And of the black running suit and hate-filled eyes behind him, shoving past the cop, knocking him aside as he hurtled the turnstile with one hand.

"He's right behind us!" Mara screamed at Jon. He didn't have to ask whether she meant the cop or their original pursuer. The fear in her voice made it all too evident.

The subway train sat on the platform, waiting. The inviting open doors that Jon knew would close in a matter of seconds. If the doors closed before he and Mara got there, they would be royally screwed.

"Hold the train, hold the train!" he shouted in vain as they tore down the stairs. If anything, the people on the already crowded train wanted *fewer* passengers, not more. And especially not sweaty ones with a crazed look about them, like this pair of youths who were running down the stairs like wild animals.

Jon and Mara swung around the banister and threw themselves into the train, not even attempting to arrest their forward momentum until they were past the threshold and safely aboard. Startled cries tittered about them, followed by a heavy sigh of relief breathed simultaneously by both Jon and Mara. They were aboard.

Glancing out the doors, they saw the legs of their pursuer appear, flying down the stairs. A police officer behind him, gesticulating indignantly at these offenses to the public order he was charged with keeping.

Jon's eyes widened in fear. Surrounded by people in a subway car, he had reached a dead end from which there was no escape. And then, as though the fates were intentionally waiting until the last minute to grant his thudding heart a reprieve, Jon heard the most beautiful sound in the world.

"Please stand clear of the closing doors." The pneumonic hiss of the doors closing. Right in the bastard's face.

The seconds seemed to slow, the doors taking a thousand times longer to close than they should have. The expression on their pursuer's face tightening, darkening with anger and hate. The useless cries of the cop, the shouts of subway patrons upset by the ruckus the chase had caused, all seeming to slow to a crawl yet being yelled far too quickly for Jon to make any sense of it. His brain had been drenched in molasses, its processing speed slowing to match the scene around him. Rooting him to the spot, little more than an impotent observer, helpless to exact change on his dire circumstances.

And shut. The doors now closed, the airbrake was released and the train started down the tunnel, leaving the scene of chaos behind them. Confusion reigned on most of the faces that could be seen from the window. Except for one face, the face Jon couldn't seem to take his eyes from.

The face of their pursuer held not a trace of confusion. Only a strengthened resolve, fueled by fury and fanaticism. A freeze-frame in time, where their eyes met and something, some preternatural message seemed to be passed from the mysterious assassin to Jonathan Rickner. A solemn promise passed from hunter to prey.

This is not over.

Chapter 23

Enrique Ramirez cursed himself silently as he pushed his way through the throng and disappeared into the faceless crowds of Grand Central Terminal, shucking off even the Metro cop as he blended and milled with the unwashed masses on their daily commute. Not only had he once again let Rickner catch him by surprise, but he had also caused a scene. So much for being done with fieldwork.

He knew why he had pursued them. It was instinct, pure and simple. Jonathan Rickner was the one that got away. And, even though Greer had other plans for how Rickner's eventual elimination was to play out, the shock at accidentally running into – and being sighted by – his quarry, combined with his own damaged pride at having been taken by surprise yet again, caused Ramirez to kick into pursuit mode.

And then, while chasing them through Grand Central, Ramirez had realized how to turn this meeting to his advantage. He ran, he chased, he scared the crap out of the young pair, but he did not catch them. On purpose, though they would never know that. And because of his pursuit, Jon and Mara would not rest until they found what they – and the Division – sought. Which moved up everyone's timetable, just like Greer – a man with a ticking clock of his own – wanted.

Ramirez glanced over his shoulder as casually as possible. Because he was now moving back toward the exit – the last place someone who had jumped the turnstile for a free fare would be heading – the Metro security personnel seemed either to be looking elsewhere, or to have given up the chase altogether. And though Ramirez was well aware of the closed-circuit cameras set into the walls and ceilings of the terminal, he was unworried by the prospect of someone finding him on a grainy black-and-white CCTV monitor. Besides, he had probably been little more than a blur when he'd run past the guards earlier, and he had enough practice blending into a crowd, becoming all but invisible, that he knew he had nothing to fear.

Just to be safe, he avoided the main concourse and instead headed for one of the many alternate exits, emerging into daylight on a street corner a block away from Grand Central. Making his way through the midday pedestrian crowds, he realized that he did have one other option. Even though he'd lost track of Rickner and Ellison, Ramirez did have one way of tracking them. By following the man who would be following them.

Ramirez pulled a small black device from his pocket, slid out the tiny keyboard, and began to punch in a query. He'd taken it from Recon before leaving Division HQ the previous day – he didn't have authorization, but as the soon-to-be Director of the Division, he didn't particularly care. It would be used for the benefit of the Division's goals, as was everything Ramirez did. The object was a GPS tracking device, capable of tracing the signal of any cell phone to within a 10-yard radius. The problem, as Ramirez had already found out, was that Rickner and Ellison had left their phones back in Washington and were now using prepaid disposable phones – ones apparently bought with cash, as neither party's credit card records showed any such purchases. Thus, Rickner and Ellison's phones were virtually untraceable, even with the technology and resources Ramirez had at his disposal. But Wayne Wilkins's phone – invisible to every telecommunications company, government agency, and third party besides the Division – was not. And as the tracking device returned the query with a display of Wilkins's current position, direction, and speed, Ramirez began to move to intercept.

As he walked purposefully down the sidewalk, Ramirez vowed to himself that he would not be caught unawares a third time. The plan that Greer had devised was terrifyingly ingenious, and with both Ramirez and Wilkins there to make sure it came to fruition, Rickner and Ellison didn't stand a chance.

The next time Enrique Ramirez's path crossed with that of Jonathan Rickner, the young scholar would have no idea he was being watched, stalked from the shadows. And by the time he did, it would already be far too late.

Chapter 24

Brooklyn, New York

Except for wheezing to catch their breath again, Jon and Mara were silent until they reached their stop in Brooklyn. Partly from shock, partly from exhaustion, partly from embarrassment of the scene they had caused, and partly from fear of who might overhear them. As soon as they were off the train and on the street again, Mara broke the silence.

"That was the guy from Michael's apartment?" Mara asked in a hushed tone.

"Yeah," Jon said, his eyes darting around for any sign that, *somehow*, their pursuer had managed to track them here. "I'd say he's pretty pissed about our little scuffle."

"Geez, Jon. You think he works for *them*?"

Jon nodded forcefully. "I'm sure of it."

"Then we're probably on their hit list by now, huh?"

"Oh God." His forehead creased with concern as he placed a hand on her shoulder. "Oh, Mara, I'm so sorry to have dragged you into this."

"Forget it. Let's just do what we came out here to do," Mara said halfheartedly, but the concern on Jon's face was also etched into hers.

A block later they turned onto Higbee Place. Checked the address. It was a townhouse just up the way. The home of Catherine Smith.

The pair spotted the house, climbed the narrow staircase – limestone or some sort of inexpensive masonry – and rang the buzzer. The long-dead husks of what once were flowers sat withered and forgotten in terra cotta pots on either side of the door. The olive-green paint of the door itself was chipped and peeling, faded by the sun and torn away by the relentless march of time.

The screech of a deadbolt sliding across metal sounded from the other side of the door. The knob turned, and the door cracked open, a security chain drawn tight across the opening. A single gray eye, surrounded by wrinkled and weathered flesh, appeared in the aperture.

"Yeah?" asked the eye's owner in a raspy female voice.

"Ms. Smith?" Jon inquired.

"Who's askin'?"

"I'm Jonathan Rickner, Michael Rickner's brother. This is Mara. We need to talk to you."

"Michael's brother, huh?"

"Yes ma'am. It's really important."

Catherine Smith grunted. "Always 'really important' with youngsters," she mumbled. "Gimme a second. Stand back, stand back."

Jon and Mara took a step back from the closing door, heard the chain being removed from its slot, and the door opened again. The figure of an old woman, hunched and gnarled by time and a lifelong addiction to nicotine, greeted them. Well, not quite greeted, for the scowl on her face held an entirely different message. Her outfit was a simple, threadbare linen dress that may have once been something close to white, with tiny blue flowers patterned sporadically upon the cloth. Now, the flowers were a sickly green and the dress itself was nearly as yellow as the old woman's remaining teeth. The cause for the yellowing was likely the smoldering unfiltered cigarette that she held limply between the fingers of one hand, and the thousands like it she had smoked in her sixty-plus years with the habit.

"Well, don't just stand out there," she urged. "You're letting the heat out."

The pair hurried through the door. Ms. Smith looked outside, her eyes darting around quickly as though expecting to see something that she didn't *want* to find, then closed the door, locked the deadbolt, and slid the safety chain back into place. When she turned around again, she had her scowl back in place, and she ushered the pair into the living room with such time-honored traditions of hospitality as shooing flips of her wrist and calls of "Livin' room. G'won!"

The living room would have been a quaint little affair fifty years ago. The sofa where Jon and Mara took their seats was upholstered in flower-patterned fabric, yellow stuffing leaking from holes and entire seams that had ripped over time. A tattered crocheted afghan was draped over the back of the varnished wooden rocking chair where Ms. Smith took her seat. Atop the coffee table sat a half-full pack of cigarettes; an ashtray filled with butts, two of which had a faint trail of smoke still rising from the end; and a soggy, used teabag rested in an otherwise empty teacup, the Lipton tag still dangling from the string over the rim. Hundreds of little Precious Moments figurines with innocent blue eyes in oversized heads stared down from the many shelves lining the walls. At a glance, Jon could see that some were chipped, a few even missing limbs, but there they stood. Watching. It was like a ceramic version of *Children of the Corn*, and it creeped the heck out of Jon. But like everything else in this room, probably like everything else in the whole house, their innocent little white faces and wardrobes were yellowed by the pervasive smoke of their owner.

Jon coughed, no longer able to stifle the reaction his lungs had been screaming for ever since he'd entered the home's carcinogen-filled air. Mara looked at him, a grimace on her face as she too struggled to deal with the smoky atmosphere.

"So whaddya want?"

Mara nodded to Jon; he nodded back, and began.

"I realize this might be a painful subject, Ms. Smith—"

"Cat."

"I'm sorry?"

"Call me Cat. Short for Catherine. You know, like a *nickname*."

"Yes, ma'am. Cat then. We're here about your father."

"My father's dead."

"Yes, ma'am, we know—"

"Goddammit, don't call me ma'am. It makes me feel old."

Jon and Mara traded incredulous glances as Cat pulled another cigarette from the pack on the coffee table, lit it from the stub that she had been smoking, and set the still-smoldering stub on the rim of the ashtray. She took a drag on the new cigarette, gazing with bleary-eyed contentment at its glowing end, and blew the smoke from her lips in one long breath like the fiery exhalations of some mythical dragon.

"Well, what about him?" she demanded, her attention returning to her guests.

"What kind of work was he in?" Jon asked.

"Military. Espionage, infiltration, something like that. I don't know exactly. My mother left him when he was in the Pacific in '42. Dear John letter and all that. I was just a girl at the time, but Mother always told me to avoid the man. So I did. Wouldn't talk to him. And then he up and dies in Korea… the bastard."

"Your father's name was Roger Blumhurst, right?"

"Yeah, that's him."

"What *really* happened in 1957?"

Catherine's distant gaze, staring through the coffee table as though it were some sort of time portal to reclaim opportunities lost, regained focus at Jon's query. She turned her eyes to her inquisitor and frowned, the canyons time had etched into her face growing deeper, her loose jowls growing somehow tighter.

"You know about '57? Egh. Of course you do. You're Michael's brother. Egh. Alright, dammit. I'm too old to be keeping secrets anyways. You hear me, you bastards? Try and come get me if you want!" She shook her fist at the ceiling, scattering ashes from her cigarette upon her dress and the carpet. Then she turned her gaze back to toward her guests and fixed them with an intense stare. "Two conditions."

"Name 'em," Mara said, finally finding her breath in the hazy room.

"No subpoenas to get me to testify. 'Cause I won't. You can't make me, ya hear?"

"No subpoenas," Mara nodded. "Got it. And the other?"

"No more of those damned newspapers. They quoted me back in '57, and my life's been hell ever since. Reporters coming to ask questions early on, then the damn G-Men. Bastards give me nightmares. Still afraid to answer the door some days. The assholes can all go hang themselves for all I care."

"Agreed," Jon said quickly, trying to stave off another rant and get to the story they sought. "No subpoenas, no newspapers."

"Alright, then." She took another long drag, held it in for a moment, then sighed it out. "1957. *October 9th*, 1957. God, I'll never forget that night. Knock on my door at two-in-the-stinkin'-morning. Real impatient-like. This is just after my husband, Jim, got himself killed, you see. Worked in the Empire State Building. Division Manager, on his way up in the world. Walking to his car one night and some asshole up and kills him. Just like that I'm a widow. Three months after I'm a blushing bride, and I'm a stinkin' widow. God, that kills me. Well, I figure the knocking must be about him. They caught his killer, and the cops are out there to tell me about it. So I show up in my nightdress, a robe wrapped around me and all, but I didn't change inta somethin' more decent 'cause the knocking was so darned urgent. I answer the door thinkin' I'm gonna get some closure, but when I get there, it's just another old wound, opened back up and smilin' in my face. Well, he wasn't exactly smilin', but—"

"Your father?" Mara asked.

"Yeah." Catherine took another long drag of her cigarette and blew it out the corner of her mouth. She coughed, breathed deeply, then coughed again before continuing. "Never really knew him as such, him being gone in the wars so much during my childhood, and then his 'dying.' Well, here he was, right out that door, same as you two were a few minutes ago. Alive in the flesh. I was shocked to say the least, but I invited him in anyway. I asked him what the hell was goin' on, and he told me that he was really sorry about what had happened and that he hadn't really died in Korea. Well, I told him I had eyes in my head to tell me that, and I asked him what in the world really happened. My first thought was that Mother had lied to me, that she just wanted him out of our life so she told me he had died, but he told me that wasn't what happened."

Jon swallowed, wondering where this flood of loquacity had come from, and where it was going. Catherine leaned forward in her rocking chair, as though she were imparting a secret. Despite the fact that her volume didn't decrease correspondingly, her interviewers leaned forward on the sofa as well, if only to display their interest and to encourage her to keep talking.

"What *really* happened is the government set the whole damn thing up." She was nodding now, giving them a knowing look as though the three of them were members of a secret society based upon this shared knowledge. "They made it *look* like he died in Korea, and then put him on some special assignment over here. In New York."

"Did he say what kind of assignment it was?" Jon asked.

Catherine flicked her cigarette, sending some more ash to the carpet. "No, he didn't. He seemed to be in an awful fright about something. Like he had to go do something real fast. Like someone was after him, maybe. He just apologized for all the hurt he'd caused me and said he'd done a real bad thing and made too many mistakes but he just wanted to come by and set things straight one last time. He told me he loved me and he was so sorry and if he could've done things differently, he would've." What might have been tears were materializing in the corners of her eyes, but it was hard to tell through the smoke, and if her voice was choking up, her already raw vocal cords made it impossible to tell the difference.

"Then he gave me this sealed envelope. Said it was incredibly important it *not* get in the hands of the wrong people. He didn't tell me who they were, but I figured it was the people he was hiding from. He said don't give it to anybody from the government, either. He said someday it'd be the key to setting right everything that he'd done wrong. Kisses me goodbye, leaves, and the next I hear, he's hung himself from the goddamn Brooklyn Bridge." She shook her head solemnly, her gaze lost in the mists of time. "Hello, goodbye, I'm dead for real now. Gee-zus, I swear I'll never understand men."

"Ms. Sm— I mean, *Cat*…" Jon started.

"Yeah?" Catherine croaked, not turning her eyes from the empty patch of yellowed, peeling wallpaper behind the sofa she had focused on.

"Do   you   still   have   that   envelope?"
"Yeah, I've kept it all this time. Never opened it, but kept it just the same. A last little way to hold on to him, I guess."

"Can we see it?" Mara asked.

"Well, no, I don't still have it *now*," Catherine said, then turned to Jon, "but you can ask your brother about it."

"My- my brother? You met with him before he—"

"Well, of course I met him. Don't you guys talk? Gave him the envelope and all. I'm no spring chicken, son, and I'm gettin' sick of lookin' over my shoulder all the time. My father told me to keep it safe, that I would know the right time and person to pass it on to. Something in your brother's emails told me that he was the right man."

"When was this?" Mara asked. "When did you give him the envelope?"

"I dunno. An hour or so before you guys showed up, I guess."

"An *hour*?" Jon and Mara exclaimed together.

Catherine started at their exclamation. "Well sure, give or take."

"Ms. Smith, what did this guy look like?"

Catherine threw her hands toward the ceiling, letting them fall back to her lap. "Geez, son, he was your *brother*, for crissakes! You know what he looked like better than I can tell ya."

"Ms. Smith, Cat," Mara said, her voice beginning to quiver, "Michael has been dead since early Saturday morning."

"I— He what…? Well, the guy said he was Michael Rickner. Tall fella, 'bout like you, son, dark hair, light blue eyes. Wore a suit. I dunno. He said he was Michael. How the hell should I know the difference?"

"It *couldn't* have been Michael," Jon said, his face etched with worry.

Catherine Smith stabbed her cigarette butt out in the ashtray, her scowl returning in full force. "Well, then who the hell did I give that envelope to?"

Chapter 25

Langley, Virginia

Harrison Greer was restless. The moment he'd been waiting his entire life for was nearly upon him. The reclamation of the Dossiers. The demise of the only true threat to the Division. The redemption of his grandfather's legacy. The fulfillment of his own.

His grandfather, Walton Greer, had decided not to kill Roger Blumhurst's estranged daughter, Catherine Smith. Whether out of some misguided respect for her father's years of service or in hopes of eventually gaining some lead on what had really happened during the last weeks of Blumhurst's life – his special Dossiers-reclaiming mission for Walton, his later insistence that the mission was a dead-end, his flubbed elimination mission, and his symbolic public suicide – Harrison Greer couldn't say. He liked to think that Walton knew that one day, leaving Smith alive would result in an opportunity like the one Michael had created. Like the one his brother was now an integral, if unwitting, part of. How fitting that it would be Blumhurst's own daughter who would be so unconsciously instrumental in the righting of all the errant agent's wrongs.

The Director paced his office, waiting for the phone call from Wayne Wilkins that would ensure the last piece was in place. And then...

Greer had been out of the field for years, but his skill with a sniper rifle had never been sharper. There was a private range in rural Virginia an hour from his home that he frequented every week. Targets set up across a valley, where both wind and distance provided a constantly changing challenge for even the most able marksman. And he was about to take his deadly shooting skills to the most populous city in the nation.

For too long, the Dossiers and Rockefeller's refusal to give them up had plagued the Division and Greer's family. For too long, the Operation's one Achilles' Heel had haunted him and predecessors. But now, Greer was going to put them to rest. The unspeakable truth, finally buried once and for all. And Greer himself would be the one to destroy the Dossiers and eliminate the traitors Rickner and Ellison. Soon. Very soon, indeed.

He walked to the closet door, unlocked it, and withdrew a canvas bag from the shelf within. He moved back to his desk, shoved the chair out of the way, and opened the bag on the desktop. His fingers flew as they assembled the weapon from the parts from within the bag. They knew every step by heart, every motion practiced hundreds and thousands of times before. Greer had two true passions: the Division, and shooting. And, for the first time in far too long, he would be able to combine both of those loves in one life-defining moment. Considering the short time he had left on this earth, and considering the gravity of what he was about to do, he couldn't think of a better time to step back into action.

His plan would work. It had been in the back of his mind – only as a hypothetical, of course – for some time. A way to finally beat the old Tycoon at his own game. To unearth his blackest secret and destroy the threat it presented to the country. But it was impossible. Too risky, too many ways it could go wrong. And then Jonathan Rickner had fallen into his lap. The missing piece that would make everything work out just right. Rickner was perfect. The circumstances were perfect. And with Greer's own days numbered, the timing was perfect as well. Greer had never been one for religious beliefs or spiritual leanings, but as fortuitous as everything was turning out for him and the Division, it was almost tempting to think someone up-stairs was giving him a hand. Almost.

The gun was now assembled. Greer hefted it in his hands, affixed the scope to the weapon, and chambered a round. Then he swung the barrel around to the filing cabinet, where the files on Jonathan Rickner and Mara Ellison were kept, pressed his eye to the sight, and envisioned the moment that was to come.

"Bang," he whispered to the empty office. Everything he'd ever worked for was about to come true. With his plan and his sniper rifle, Harrison Greer would finally finish the secret mission that the United States had begun seventy years before. His legacy, and that of his family, would no longer be the betrayal of Roger Blumhurst, but of securing the Dossiers; not of kill-ing countless overly inquisitive citizens but rather of saving the nation from the threat that the Dossiers held. It was almost too good to be true. And it was almost here.

Greer smiled as he ejected the unspent bullet and began to disassemble the weapon for transit. He was one phone call away from New York City. Where his plan would finally bear its glorious fruit.

He could hardly wait.

Chapter 26

Manhattan

Still in Brooklyn, Wayne thought to himself as he checked his GPS receiver again. Although there hadn't been snow on the ground for weeks, the grass of Central Park was still much less green than it would be later in spring. A group of teenage boys played a game of baseball on the field across the way from Wayne's bench. After reading the page from the envelope again, he would glance up from the sheet and watch a play or two of the game, smiling at the carefree innocence of youth. How we always think things will be easier, smoother when we get older, when we can finally strike out on our own, Wayne reflected. He knew, better than most, the folly of such arguments, propagated for generations by young people desirous for greater freedom, denied by adults who had lived through both phases of life, but never believed by the youth until they themselves had reached adulthood – and the stresses and sorrows it held.

For example, Jon and Mara, right now in Brooklyn, probably just finding out – or at least still reeling from the realization – that the prize they sought, the prize Michael had sought, was long gone. Go back a step further, even, with the death of Michael in the first place. The older you got, the more time began to devour the ones you loved. Wayne had been younger than Jon when the towers fell and his world crumbled into a burning ash heap along with them. But Jon was conducting himself, at least from the observations Wayne had made thus far, in a rather different manner from how Wayne had reacted.

Though further disappointment, like the disappearance of the articles and the envelope, hadn't made the guy's loss any easier.

Wayne knew the importance of what he held in his hands. It was huge. And he knew enough Division lore – of which Blumhurst was legendary in the good-agent-gone-awry department – to put a few more pieces into place. Why the agent had chosen to kill himself before he completed the mission Greer's grandfather had him working on the side was something Wayne couldn't quite understand. No matter how dark Roger's soul had gotten, this project, this sole loose end that hadn't been tied up from the Operation certainly seemed like an engaging and worthwhile task. Wayne was captivated by it. It was exactly what he needed, exactly what he hoped he would find. The key to everything he hoped to accomplish, the pivot point of this silent war that both invisible factions – the Division, and the too-inquisitive dead-men-walking – would kill to get their hands on. That the Division *had* killed to try to find. And, in all likelihood, would kill again for before it was secured. He was a wily one, that Rockefeller, and how in the world Roger Blumhurst had managed to discover the magnate's most carefully guarded secret, Wayne hadn't the foggiest. Nothing short of breaking into one of Rockefeller's residences and digging through his personal papers would uncover the page Wayne now held in his hands. But then, perhaps that was just what Roger had done.

Wayne knew what he was about to do would go down in history. Of course, the official story would never include his name. The official story said he had died in Iraq seven months ago. They couldn't give credit to a dead man for actions that he performed posthumously. But Wayne would know. His involvement would be swept under the rug like the powers-that-be knew how to do so well, but *he* would know that because of him, the country was a better, safer place.

As Wayne read the page again, he felt satisfied that he knew what he needed to know. About the past. About the present.

And about the future he was about to shape. It was time to draw in his quarry to usher in Phase Two. He pulled out his cell phone and began to compose a text message.

A message that would, one way or the other, change history forever.

Chapter 27

The bright sunlight, now on the other side of high noon, seemed somehow darker than when Jon and Mara had entered the home of Catherine Smith. The hope had died, the lead had dried up. And the worst part was that it was real. The lead was *there*, but they had been beaten to the punch by someone who knew a whole lot more about all of this than they did. Someone who had managed to stay two steps ahead of them this whole time. And now they were left with nothing but a vague description that would match any one of thousands of men in the city. A man who, as keen as he seemed to be thus far, wouldn't allow himself to be just picked out of a crowd.

The despondent pair didn't know whether to draw hope or further fear from the fact that Ms. Smith's description didn't seem to fit the Latino man who had seemed to make Jon's demise at his hand his top priority. On one hand, the fact that the pursuer whose eyes had burned at Jon with murderous intent was *not* the one who had snatched their one lead away from them brought *some* comfort; Jon's previous adversary wasn't the one anticipating their moves. In fact, it had almost seemed by chance that the black-clad man had found the pair, though the fact that he was in the city at all, ostensibly having tracked Jon here, didn't bode well for their future. On the other hand, they not only knew that the conspiracy and cover-up was real, but that there were *at least* two of these guys after them – one behind and one ahead. And with no clue as to where to go next, the likelihood that one of them would catch up to them soon was steadily growing.

Despite the relatively pleasant weather, Jon and Mara had opted to eat indoors instead of on the patio of the Green Moon Café. Snipers' bullets had a harder time penetrating – and aiming through – walls than in open air. A NY Giants bobblehead perched atop the cash register across the room seemed to be agreeing with everything Jon and Mara were saying. But their conversation was one that they didn't want anyone, five inches tall and made of plastic or not, to listen in on.

A basket of chicken fingers and fries lay largely untouched in front of Jon; Mara's Cobb salad looked just like it had when the waitress had brought it out five minutes earlier.

"There's *got* to be something else," Mara was saying.

"We've gone through the notebook over and over. It looks like Michael thought Rockefeller entered into this somehow, that he'd hidden something, but, Mara, the man owned, or had dealings with, half of Manhattan. How in the world do we search half of the most populous city in the country without even knowing *what* we're looking for? We don't even know *who* we're going up against here."

Mara frowned. "Ms. Smith seemed to think it was the government."

"So did Michael, according to Dr. Leinhart, but *who* in the government? And for what purpose?"

"Jon." Mara's voice softened to cool down the conversation's tone. "Call him."

"Who? Leinhart?"

Mara nodded. Jon rolled his head back and forth on his shoulders, cracking his neck – an unconscious habit he'd picked up from his brother years back – then pulled out his phone and dialed the number of the prepaid phone he'd given Dr. Leinhart. He didn't answer. Considering how cheap the phones were – and that they weren't tied to any account – Jon wasn't entirely surprised that no voicemail was included. But it was a disappointment. He decided to risk a call to the professor's office phone.

One ring. Two. Three. Four. "Hello. You've reached the mailbox of Dr. Richard Leinhart…"

"Machine," Jon mouthed to Mara.

"Leave a message," Mara mouthed back.

"…I'm obviously away from my phone right now, but if you'll kindly leave a message, I'll get back to you as soon as I'm able. Thank you." *Beep.*

"Professor, it's me. We found…" He hesitated, trying to sanitize what he was saying in case someone was listening in, while still providing sufficient info for Leinhart to go on. "…the person we were looking for," he settled on, "and it's a dead end. We're trying to figure out what to do next. Hope you're having more luck on your end and can give us something to work with. Give me a call back from your other line as soon as possib–"

"Your recording time is up," an automated female voice chimed in. "To review your message, press—"

Jon punched the End Call button and slammed the phone down. His left elbow on the table, he rubbed the heel of his hand across his eyebrow, fingers dragging through his hair. Mara gently touched her fingertips to his forearm. Jon looked up.

"It's gonna be alright. We'll figure something out."

"How?" Jon asked in a tone harsher than he'd intended. "It's a dead end. If we hadn't been so slow, if only—"

"Jon, we can't do anything about that now. We are where we are. We can't deal with *what if*s and *if only*s. We just have to figure out where to go from here. As Michael would say, the only way now is forward."

"I know. And I'm trying to figure it out, Mara. I am. I'm sorry for snapping and all. You're just as frustrated as I am, I'm sure…"

Mara raised her eyebrows knowingly. "I've just got a lot of experience dealing with excited Rickner boys."

Jon looked up at her and caught her comforting, almost motherly smile. "No wonder the ancients attributed the voice of wisdom to their female goddesses," he said.

"Hey, somebody had to step in to keep all those battle-hungry warriors from killing everybody off." Her eyes grew serious again. "We'll figure something out. I have faith in that. You're Michael's brother. If he can get this far, I have no doubt we can make it the rest of the way."

"Wherever that is…"

"Hey, what's that?" Mara pointed behind him, a shocked expression on her face. Jon turned around and looked toward the entry door at the front of the café, half expecting to see Death come to greet him, personified in his tireless Latino pursuer.

"What?" he asked, seeing nothing obvious. "What is it?" He turned around to see Mara stuffing her face with fries from his untended basket. "Hey!"

"Bwhut?" Mara asked through a mouthful of half-chewed spuds, a smile teasing the edges of her bulging cheeks. Jon half-repressed a smile and slowly shook his head back and forth at her.

She swallowed. "That's what you get for being negative, Mr. Grumpy Gills."

Jon raised an eyebrow at her, then let it fall. "Eh, you're right. Sorry. I just can't figure out where to even start for what we should do next. I feel like we're about three steps behind the starting line, and we don't even know where the goal is or how to recognize it when we find it."

"Oh, I'm sure we'll recognize it when we find it." She smiled mischievously. "See, you said, 'when,' not 'if.' My fry-stealing's already having a positive effect on your thinking."

"Take a chicken finger. Maybe that'll trigger some other mental miracle."

Mara shrugged, and reached for a chicken finger.

"Hey!" Jon said with a laugh, catching her wrist en route back to her mouth. She passed the chicken finger to her other, unimpeded hand, and stuffed it in her mouth whole. Her eyes lit up, eyebrows arched, smiling lips hiding the prize she'd captured. Jon couldn't help laughing, and Mara almost spit out the chicken finger when laughter seized her.

When he caught his breath, Jon closed one eye and tightened his facial muscles, as though concentrating on some inner thought. Another fit of laughter grabbed Mara, who thankfully had swallowed most of the chicken finger by now.

"Alright then," Jon said, loosening his face slightly. "Where's my miracle?"

Beep beep. Jon's cell phone, still face down on the table, vibrated as the tone indicated a text message had been received. The only reason he had gotten phones with text messaging capability was so they could be used if and when Jon, Mara, or Leinhart were unable to communicate audibly – such as on a crowded train or while being followed by someone suspicious. But he hadn't been expecting to actually receive one, especially with Mara sitting right here beside him. Jon looked from the phone to Mara without moving his head. "Tah-dah?" she suggested.

"We'll see." He turned the phone over, the illumination from the screen casting its glow on the green Formica of their table.

'One new message,' read the screen. Jon pushed the button for 'Show,' and the message appeared.

Sender: *Number Withheld.*

Message: *Your brother's death was no suicide. I've got the answers you seek. St. John the Divine, St. Saviour Chapel. 4pm. Come alone.*

"Holy moley."

"What, what?" Mara slid her chair closer to Jon so she could read the message. He still stared at the screen, thumbing up and down so he could reread the whole thing. "Um... miracle?" she asked.

"I don't know. Maybe. Or maybe it's a trap."

He started keying in a response. 'Who are you? How do you know about my brother?' *Send.* A few seconds passed. '*Message sending failed.*'

"What?" He tried again.

'*Message sending failed.*'

"Crap," Jon said, bringing up the received message on the screen again. "The line's blocked or something. Well, what do you think we should do?"

Mara took a deep breath. "It's all we've got, isn't it?"

"Yeah, I guess it is. Besides, nobody's gonna knock us off in a church, right?" A pause, as Mara continued to look at the screen. "Right?" Jon repeated.

"What? Oh, yeah, I wasn't thinking about that. I don't think it'll be *us*, though."

Jon made a face. "What do you mean?"

"Well, it says come alone, right?" Mara pointed to the phone in Jon's hand. "And it says 'your brother.' So it's obviously addressed to you."

"But we've been doing this together from the beginning. Surely, if whoever sent this knows I'm after the truth about Michael's death, then they know that you're with me in all of this."

"I guess so, but he seemed pretty specific about coming alone." Mara shook her head. "What if he doesn't show because you're not alone?"

Beep beep. The phone buzzed in Jon's hand. He backtracked to the main menu, which prompted him to see the newly received message. *Show.*

Sender: *Number withheld.*

Message: *Bring Mara. 4pm.*

"Frea-ky…" Mara said after reading the message, eyebrows raised in surprise.

Jon bit his lip. "Yeaahh… So, do you want to come then?"

She nodded. "I'm in if you are."

He looked at his watch. "Alright, it's 12:47 now. Three hours and change to get to… that's up in north Manhattan, right? Up near Harlem?"

"The Cathedral of St. John the Divine? Yeah, I think so. Near Columbia."

"Well, it won't take three hours to get there," he said. "What should we do in the meantime?"

"Well, first, I suggest we finish our lunch. We'll probably need our energy for whatever happens next." She paused, looked at Jon, and grabbed another fistful of fries. "Besides, you should probably hurry up and eat. Your food keeps disappearing."

He laughed and shook his head at her. "Waitress!" he called over his shoulder. "We're gonna need another basket of chicken fingers over here!"

Chapter 28

Even in its unfinished state, the Cathedral Church of St. John the Divine, Episcopal Seat of the New York Diocese, was enormous. Composed of stones hewn by hand and built with largely medieval methods of construction, the edifice evoked images of the great churches of Europe. Despite the fact that the towers and transepts had yet to be built, a process that would take yet another 50 years, the 119-year-old building presented an imposing sight. And that was just from the outside.

Inside the nave, the ceiling rose to a height in excess of one-hundred feet, and the distant altar seemed to be leagues away from the western entrance through which Jon and Mara had just passed. Although the slightest sound could undoubtedly echo loud enough for all to hear – one of the reasons behind the use of Gothic architecture in ecclesiastical buildings during the pre-electronic-amplification days of the Middle Ages – the room was quiet, a reverence that worshippers and visitors alike seemed to hold, if not for the God worshipped within these halls then at least for the awe-inspiring artistry and dimensions of the church itself. Even to the unbeliever, the church, like most so-called "great churches," held an aura to it, a spiritual significance that seemed to resonate from the very stone and glass that had been fashioned and forged into a place of reflection and soul-searching.

The pair of young visitors were not in search of answers for their souls, but for other answers, answers to questions that couldn't be found in a Bible or book of liturgy, questions that Jon and Mara themselves didn't even know how to phrase. Jon had to take a moment, a few steps inside the nave, to stop and breathe, letting the ambiance of the church, of the architectural, historical, and spiritual significance that pulsed from the buttresses to the basement, sink in to his being. He'd been to New York plenty of times, but for whatever reason, he had never made it to this grand cathedral before. Eyes closed, mouth shut, he tilted his head back and breathed the charged air into his lungs. He loved churches. Thrived on them. Especially the older, more historic ones. And although this one was relatively young, especially considering how much of the construction was almost brand new, the soaring heights and classically decorated ornamentation would normally have given off an atmosphere that Jon lived for.

But today, in this cavernous, largely empty hall, he felt not peace but trepidation. The greatest and most fearful mystery this church currently held was neither ecclesiastical nor carved in stone. And thus far, it had proven lethal for all who had sought to discover its truths.

The pair started walking down the length of the nave, taking time to gaze at the ornate sculptures and brilliantly colored stained glass that graced the walls. Some sections of the walls still bore the black of smoke and ash from the terrible fire that had ravaged the church in December 2001. It was a miracle that the fire hadn't been worse, that the church was even still standing. Like the miracle that *Jon* was still standing after all that had happened. And the worst, Jon feared, was yet to come.

When they reached the front of the church – the bishop's pulpit, the altars, and the empty choir loft all in attendance – Jon checked his watch: 3:57. They needed to hurry. Although the chapel they sought lay only a few dozen yards away on the other side of the choir loft, he was well aware that, if he allowed himself to, he could take an hour walking that short distance, entranced as he was wont to be by the artistry and mystery that surrounded him, and nervous as he felt about what they might find in the chapel. Worried about what fresh terrors the truth might bring.

They walked to the right of the altar, and began to traverse the south side of the ambulatory, slowly making their way eastward. On their left, the choir rose above them with fifty-foot granite columns stretching upward behind an ornate lattice of wrought-iron fencing. On their right, a series of chapels passed by in a heart-wrenching flurry, each likely to hold historical and cultural particularities that Jon was dying to explore. But they had a job to do first. There would be other times to explore, to indulge, to immerse. The church, having been around for nearly twelve decades, probably wasn't going anywhere anytime soon. And, if nothing went awry in the easternmost chapel today, Jon and Mara would hopefully be around for a while longer as well.

An intricately sculpted bronze gate was set inside the stone entrance to the Chapel of Saint Saviour, the site of their date with destiny. Angels paid homage to a golden cross set against a green and red wreath, and a stylized Alpha and Omega provided a backdrop to the beautiful metalwork. Alpha and Omega. Beginning and end.

Or the beginning *of* the end. Whatever end that might be.

They walked into the empty chapel. Empty save for the haunting stone stares of angels and saints above, of bishops interred, of Christ and the apostles looking holy in a giant stained-glass window as the bright of day lit them from outside. None of whom, presumably, could have sent the text message summoning them here. Jon poked his head into an alcove on the left of the chapel. Nothing but a locked door, leading to some other place in the church, inaccessible to all but clergy and lay staff. He glanced at his watch. 4:01. Their mysterious summoner was mysteriously absent.

"It's after four. Where is he?"

Mara shrugged in reply. "Maybe his clock is running slower than yours?"

"Egh." Jon walked to the altar, stared at the elaborate stained-glass artistry.

"Beautiful, isn't it?"

Jon spun on his heel toward the voice. Mara, who had been studying the details of the altar, whirled around just as fast. The voice belonged to the third person in the room, a person who had entered as stealthily as a jungle cat stalking its prey. A man the pair had seen, briefly, earlier that day. It took Mara a second to recognize him as the man who had bowled into her at the library that morning.

Jon broke the nervous silence. "Are you the—"

"One who summoned you here? Yes."

"Who *are* you, exactly?" Mara asked, her face contorted in a combination of apprehension, distrust, and curiosity.

"*That* is an excellent question, Mara. Oh yes," he went on, Mara's eyes opening wide with surprise right on cue, "I know all about you. Both of you. And I'm here to help you get what you want."

Jon narrowed his eyes. He felt defensive of both Mara and their mission, and he wasn't going to just let some outsider purporting to have all the answers into their circle without due scrutiny. "And what do we want?" he asked the man.

"The truth." The man raised his hands skyward as though a televangelist preacher, exhorting heaven itself to rain its blessings down on him. "The liberation and vindication that only pure, unadulterated truth can provide. A truth that I am here to impart."

"Who killed Michael," Jon said, his eyes still narrowed with suspicion. "The conspiracy."

"Precisely." The man was cool, his voice and tone even as though he had been rehearsing this speech for quite some time. And yet, strangely, there didn't seem to be a bit of falsehood about him. Not that Jon could detect, anyway. "Michael understood a great deal. More perhaps than he realized. More than *we* realized. But then, in order to understand all that, you must understand the big picture."

"You still haven't answered my question," Mara broke in. Jon looked at her with a combination of pride and concern. She was stepping up, but whether or not that was wise remained to be seen. "Who are you? And who is this 'we' you speak of?"

The mysterious stranger let his eyes drift to one of the heavenly warriors flanking the room. "Who I am, who I *was*, is a tricky question." The man's speaking pace quickened as he returned his gaze to Jon and Mara. "One that will be answered in due course, but one that will only add confusion if I attempt to explain now. Time is of the essence, and the answers you seek are far from simple."

"Can you at least give us your name?" Jon returned, his tone somewhat hostile. "Or would that take too much explaining, too?"

"You may call me Wayne. But my name is of little significance to your quest. You need to understand the truth of how this whole mess got started. Before people like Michael were killed in the ongoing cover-up. Before soldiers like myself were killed in foreign lands and resurrected back home in America for the purpose of slaughtering the curious in order to hide the truth. Back to the original conspiracy, almost a century ago."

Wayne swallowed audibly and took a deep breath. "The truth about Operation Phoenix. From the beginning."

Chapter 29

Manhattan

January 1932

The knock at the door was unexpected at this late hour. John D. Rockefeller, Jr. had just sat down in his favorite reading chair, the rich leather cushions seeming to absorb some of the stresses and worries of the day. The West 54th Street mansion was replete with classy furnishings, not overly lavish, but in a style that Mrs. Rockefeller had deemed "tastefully grand." Mr. Rockefeller's den was no different: the antlers of a trophy deer were mounted on one wall with assorted stuffed waterfowl; two of the other walls were lined in bookshelves, filled with thick leatherbound tomes and copious ledger books representing years of records for the many business enterprises in the Rockefeller empire. A solid but quietly elegant desk – a green-shaded reading lamp perched in one corner, a pocketwatch holder resting near the other edge – was positioned in the middle of the room, facing the door, its back to the chilly, snow-addled world outside the room's only window. Between the desk and the door, nestled between the towering walls of books that met in the far corner, were two leatherbound chairs, one of which held the man who was a household name, while the other sat empty.

He didn't arise immediately when he heard the knock, assuming that it was some drunk who had gotten lost on the way home. Prohibition, he thought to himself, was long in need of repealing. Although he himself was a lifelong teetotaler, he knew the eighteenth amendment was causing more problems than it was fixing. If these poor bottom-feeders who populated the city, destitute in every sense of the word, needed anything, it was a pick-me-up. And it wasn't like they couldn't get it anyway; the prevalence of speakeasies in the city was at a record high, and the fact that they were generally run by mobsters, running all sorts of underground criminal enterprises on the side, just added to the problems he found with the ban. It didn't quell the amount of alcohol people drank; it just moved it to the shadows, a far more dangerous place for secret vices to dwell. It was a good idea in theory, but simply untenable on the ground. Pass all the moral and idealistic laws you want; human nature would always win out in the end. Get the vices out there in the open, Rockefeller felt. Secrets and lies only breed more secrets and lies, and often more criminal ones at that.

Rockefeller was yanked from his thoughts by the opening of his den door, followed by the entrance of two men. As soon as he saw one of the men, he stood up, partly in knee-jerk courtesy, partly in surprise. The knock was not from a lost drunk, after all. The man who his butler, Robert, let into the house was just as unexpected as the knock he had been responsible for. He was dressed in a woolen overcoat, which Robert took as the man shed it, the heated mansion providing a warm refuge from the cold January night. A business suit, with a gray tie and black wingtip shoes, completed the ensemble. His graying hair and mustache gave him an air of wisdom, adding to the decades of experience, both in high-ranking political and military positions, that glinted in his eyes. The man was Henry Lewis Stimson, Secretary of State to President Herbert Hoover.

"Henry," Rockefeller began, his voice and demeanor far less sure than was customary for the industrial giant. "What brings you here at this hour? I haven't seen you since... what, that White House dinner last summer?"

"The Independence Day dinner, I think, yes. How are you, John?" The Secretary seemed calm, at ease, ready to play whatever cards he had, whatever purpose for which he had come, at his own pace, with his own timing.

"I'm well enough." The tycoon shot a thumb at the window. "Can't say the same for those poor saps down in the soup kitchen lines, but hey, somebody's gotta run things." A twitch at the corner of Stimson's mouth portended a smile that never came.

"Indeed," the Secretary said. "These are tough times. As you know with your having to go it alone on your big project. The 'Rockefeller Center,' you're calling it, right?"

"That's right," Rockefeller responded. "Not the most *creative* name perhaps, but, it will be my legacy, after all. Right smack dab in the middle of Manhattan. It'll be fantastic, regardless of the Opera pulling out." The Metropolitan Opera had decided to pull out of what was to be a joint financial venture in the Rockefeller Center, owing to the 1929 stock market crash and the ensuing Great Depression. "Besides, people see 'Rockefeller,' and they think success, they think progress. Am I right?"

"You're right, John, absolutely right. Which is why I came to you. I need results. I need a man I can count on to ensure that this nation progresses the way it needs to: the American way." Stimson glanced at Robert, then back at Rockefeller. His host got the hint and excused his servant, who bowed slightly as he backed out of the room, shutting the door behind him. Stimson sat himself in a leather chair facing Rockefeller's reading chair, and waited for the tycoon to seat himself before he would continue. Rockefeller paused for a moment, realizing too late that the shock of the unexpected visit had caused him to entirely forget to extend the household courtesy to his esteemed guest. Regaining control of his faculties, he nodded to Stimson, seeming to indicate an unspoken apology for forgetting his manners, to which the Secretary responded with a nod of his own, seemingly indicating his understanding and acceptance of the apology. Rockefeller eased himself into the chair in which he had so recently sat alone, ready to spend a quiet evening at home, away from affairs of business, politics, and the state of the nation. An evening that was now as good as lost.

"What do you mean, Henry?" Rockefeller started, realizing after sitting down that his interlocutor wanted him to prompt him for whatever purpose he had envisioned for this visit. "What, you want me to move investments to boost the market or something?"

"Not exactly, John." Stimson was biding his time, drawing out the conversation for dramatic effect, like an actor following a preplanned script. He pulled a silver cigarette case from his coat pocket. He opened it, pulled a cigarette halfway out, then looked up at Rockefeller, almost as an afterthought asking, "Mind if I smoke?"

"Please," Rockefeller answered, anxious to get to the point.

"You don't happen to have—"

Rockefeller's lighter was out, flipped open, and lit in his extended hand before Stimson could finish his sentence. Stimson dipped his head, cigarette pressed between his lips, to the flame, lighting his stick of tobacco and puffing briefly before leaning back in his seat, crossing his legs, and turning again to his host.

"I don't need to tell you that the economy is worse than it's been in a long while," Stimson began. "It's getting better, to be sure, but the general public isn't feeling the effects. The President's plans *will* work, but the voters aren't too keen on starving to death, or eking out some meager existence that's about as far away from the American Dream as they can imagine. And all the while, those damned Russians are touting all their successes resultant from their conversion to Communism."

"But that's only because they'd all but isolated themselves economically before the crash," Rockefeller interrupted, slightly indignant at the audacity of the Russian propaganda machine. "Communism, especially that rotten blend the Soviets are serving up, simply *can't* work."

Stimson smiled briefly, almost patronizingly, and nodded to the tycoon. "You're absolutely correct, John." A long drag on the cigarette, followed by an even longer exhalation, the smoke pluming slowly from his lips. "And it's likely far more rhetoric and flag-waving propaganda than actual results. What've we heard from the Soviets? Nothing but 'official' government reports and bureaucratic bullshit, espousing their noble ways and the productivity it supposedly gives them, and condemning the rest of us. So yes, it's probably a bunch of hooey, but me knowing that and you knowing that just won't cut it with the masses."

"If they would just use their brains—"

"They're too hungry to use their brains, John. They're focused on just one thing: results. They don't care about the long-term sustainability of a system if they don't think they'll be alive to see the long-term. They don't give a rat's ass for ideology if they don't see jobs, progress, and food. And yes, the magical results of Communism in Russia are probably completely illusory, but these are desperate times with desperate men, John. To millions of jobless, homeless, hopeless Americans, they are lost in a desert of desperation. Pretty soon, even the mirage the Soviets are shoveling will look pretty tantalizing to massive numbers of our own people."

"It's like the Red Scare all over again." Rockefeller looked genuinely concerned, realizing that the situation must be grave indeed to warrant this visit from the Secretary of State of the United States.

"Only without the 'scare' part," Stimson continued. "Japan's invasion of Manchuria is a problem, to be sure, but the real issue we need to be worried about is communist subversion, both in Europe and – God forbid – here in America. This could genuinely be a mass movement long before people have a chance to realize its inherent danger for the nation, both to our eventual economic revival and to the very ideals we stand for, and have stood for one-hundred-and-fifty years. And, by God, that we'll stand for one-hundred-and-fifty years from now, if I have anything to say about it."

"So what do we do, Henry?" Rockefeller sat forward in his seat, leaning toward the Secretary with genuine worry and rapt anticipation. "I'm assuming you've got a plan or something, am I right? Otherwise you would have called at the office to set up a proper meeting…" The oil baron's voice trailed off, ceding the conversation to Stimson as it began to dawn on him that, whatever purpose the politician had for coming here, it was probably something that he wouldn't want in the papers with the golden "Rockefeller" name on it. But he wasn't able to delve too deeply into these reflections and speculations before his guest began speaking again.

"Germany." He stopped, allowing the word to linger in the air, the name of the fiercely divided and volatile nation, the central European country that was once an industrial giant, that was a capitalist buffer between long-time American allies Britain and France in western Europe, and the Soviet colossus looming in the east. The country whose instability and frivolous lending and spending during much of the 1920s, mirroring the United States's own irresponsible business practices during the same period, was a crucial domino whose fall exacerbated the Great Depression's worldwide effects; in America, in Great Britain, in France.

"Germany?" Rockefeller inquired after a brief moment of silence. Stimson allowed this voicing of the country's name to resound a moment as well, sinking into the flame-hardened leather, the rich-stained wood, the age-musted books that surrounded them, the only witnesses to their late-night conversation, before continuing his carefully choreographed speech.

"Yes, Germany. Germany, as I'm sure you know, is on the cusp of civil war. The Depression may be ravaging us in the States pretty hard, but over there, it's absolutely appalling." Stimson stabbed his finger toward the window, his voice growing louder. "Those 'Hoovervillites' would count their lucky stars if they realized what the Germans are going through. Largely due to the same unscrupulous bankers who caused this debacle over here. That Treaty of Versailles..." He shook his head as he spoke through clenched teeth. "Goddamn Frenchies just had to have their reparations from a country that couldn't even afford to..." He stopped, blinked, and looked up at Rockefeller. "I'm sorry, just entertaining a little bit of 'if we only knew then what we know now...'"

He grew quiet, staring at his hands in his lap, illuminated by the soft lamplight, the cigarette's smoldering end flickering in shadow, a trickle of smoke trailing into nothingness. Whether or not this moment was orchestrated by Stimson in his meticulously planned proposal, the statesman's posture, expression, and demeanor appeared quite genuine. Slowly, he raised his head again and looked Rockefeller in the eye, his gaze solemn but passionate, pleading but firm.

"John, I don't want that to be us in five years; looking back on this moment in time and *wishing* that we had done something about this impending crisis. Wishing won't get anything done, and you and I both know that we are men of action. Hell, this nation is a *country* of action. We've always made the hard choices, the tough decisions, the risky moves that looked crazy to our contemporaries but paid off enormous dividends in the end." He looked past the desk, to the wall with the window looking out on the wintry night, the night where thousands upon thousands of families were shivering themselves to sleep with empty stomachs and desperate hearts. The wall on which a placard hung, displaying Thomas Jefferson's famous opening lines from the Declaration of Independence, the natural rights of man inherent in democracy, capitalism, and freedom. "The writing's on the wall, John, and it's moments like this that history will remember as the moments that changed the world, for good or for ill, by bold action or by cowardly inaction."

"Alright, Henry, I get it. You know me; if it's the best decision for our nation, I'll take it. Especially if things are as dire as you seem to think they are."

Stimson pressed his lips together, gazing briefly at the lamp, seemingly lost in its glow, before looking back to Rockefeller to drop the bomb he had come to deliver.

"Germany is a battleground, John. *The* battleground, perhaps, where the future of our nation – indeed, of the entire capitalist way of life – may be decided." He paused briefly, both for effect and to study Rockefeller's eyes. They were filled with concern and intent interest.

"The Weimar Republic is as good as dead," Stimson continued. "As it's gasping out its last, two factions are vying for power. Two radical political parties that are increasingly popular in this unstable climate. One of which will likely come away with the proverbial brass ring. One of the parties is the Communist Party. The other party is our salvation: the National Socialist German Workers Party."

Rockefeller snorted a laugh. "The 'Nazis'? With that Hitler joker, the one with the Charlie Chaplin mustache who shouts about purifying the fatherland or some such nationalistic rubbish?"

"That's the one, John." Stimson's demeanor was just as solemn as ever. Apparently, he saw nothing funny here. "They are the only party with enough popularity and staying power to beat out the Communists. But make no mistake, the Germans want, no, *need* change. Radical change. And they will find it in one of two places: the Communists or the Nazis. It's up to us to ensure that they *don't* find it in the Communists."

"And how do you propose we do that?" Rockefeller asked, all too sure that Stimson had come here tonight to give him the answer to that very question, and equally sure that he wouldn't like the answer.

"Technically, the Weimar Republic is still a democracy. Since the failure of the Beer Hall Putsch the Nazis tried to pull in '23, Hitler has vowed that there will be no more attempts to overthrow the government by force. So they've been running in elections, winning seats in the Reichstag, in local offices, that sort of thing. Did quite well year-before-last. The crash helped bolster their support, but it also helped the Communists. Now we can assume that the Communist Party has Soviet money backing it for the elections this year. And as we're increasingly learning here in our own country, money can win or lose an election. Britain and France are strapped for cash, still trying to rebuild their infrastructures from the War and to climb up out of the financial mess they're in. That leaves us, the United States, the last bastion of freedom and democracy, of capitalism and the American way, that the world has to offer. Of course, we can't do anything official. The public is so isolationist right now, and if it were to get out that the government was handing out money to German politicians while our people are waiting half the day to get a lump of stale bread and some watered-down soup – well, you can imagine how that would go over."

"And so you want *my* money for your under-the-table political gamble an ocean away?" Rockefeller demanded. "Is that where all of this is going?"

Stimson took a deep breath, almost a sigh. He had been deprived of his punch line, and the exasperated tone in which Rockefeller delivered it worried him about the fruitfulness of his visit.

"Yes," Stimson said. "In a nutshell, yes. We need –"

"Who's 'we'?"

"'We' is me and some very close colleagues of mine who would be doing the fieldwork. For all intents and purposes, though, John, 'we' could just as well stand for the entire Western world. *We* need to stop this Communist threat before it's too late. And to do that, we need to feed money to the NSDAP. Without this money, they might not stand a chance, especially compared to the Bolshevik-supported Communist Party. Hitler's an incredible orator, if a bit repetitive and base in his messages, and his publicity man, one Joseph Goebbels, is a master propagandist. With the right money, they can make things happen."

"Let's cut to the chase here, Henry. Bottom line: how much are we talking about?"

Stimson took a deep breath, exhaled, stared at his hands, took a deep drag off the cigarette, exhaled through his nose, and stabbed the cigarette out in the silver ashtray on the nearby table. Finally, he looked back at Rockefeller and answered.

"Thirty million."

"Thirty *million*? For crying out loud, Henry, I know I'm rich, but for Pete's –"

"How much good do you think that fortune will do you when the Communists take over, John? Huh? How much of this life do you think you'll recognize when your assets are seized, your companies nationalized, your ass sent out to the soup line with the rest of the poor bastards? The Bolshies win Germany, then the rest of Europe falls like a house of cards. And when that happens, it's only a matter of time before they get us, and then every one of our founding fathers, national heroes, and veterans who gave their lives for this country and what it stands for will be rolling in their graves."

"Good Lord, Henry…" Rockefeller got up and slowly walked around the room. He ran his fingers over the time-worn leather spines of his copious volumes of the wisdom and

entertainment of the ages, over the books and books of led-
gers, each representing investments paying off, risks taken returning high dividends, capitalism *working*. He continued his
little jaunt over to the window, stopping at the placard with
the immortal words of one of fifty-six men who decided that
the necessity of standing up for what they knew was right out-
weighed the risk of taking that step of faith into the unknown.
Hell, that was what he did on a daily basis anyway, wasn't it? A
businessman takes risks all the time. Sometimes they succeed
tremendously, sometimes they fail miserably. But that was just
the way of things.

But was this the same as a business transaction? There
were people involved, people's ways of life at stake. Lives in
America and abroad alike. And yet, Rockefeller reasoned, there
were lives at stake whenever a business deal succeeded or went
sour: the livelihoods of employees and investors and the families who depended on them held in the balance.

He finally made it to the window, the dark winter night as
bleak as the hearts of the countless destitute who inhabited it.
He put his palm to the glass, feeling the cold seeping through
the pane and into his very blood. Rockefeller didn't want to be
out there with the rest of the shivering poor, but at the same
time, he wanted a better life for them as well. And God only
knew how much things would get worse for him, for them, for
everyone, if the Communists should take over.

"I want it in writing."

Stimson started in his seat, his host's voice coming so un-
expectedly that it took him a moment to register what he had
said.

"In writing? Why?"

"I'm a businessman, Henry." Rockefeller walked to his
desk, setting it between himself and Stimson, and placed
both hands firmly on the back of the desk chair. "You don't
ask a man to make a thirty-million-dollar investment without

signing some documents. You know that. You guys throw around enough paperwork in your Washington bureaucracies, making things official and covering your butts. I want it in writing. The whole thing. How and where the money's going to be used, and why."

A brief pause. The silence hung thick in the air, a Mexican standoff between two powerful men deciding the fate of the world on formalities.

"All right," Stimson finally broke the silence, pushing himself from his seat with hands on knees and walking over to Rockefeller's desk. "One week from tonight? Same place, same time?"

Rockefeller glanced at the pocketwatch that rested in its stand on the desk, noting the time and subtracting the approximately twenty minutes that had passed since Stimson had first arrived.

"Done. Bring the documents for us to sign, and I'll move around some of the assets within my companies. It's winter, so heating costs are up and business is relatively booming. I should be able to hide the expense without a huge slump in profits." Rockefeller looked at something just beyond the walls of the room, briefly lost in thought. "I think this could work, Henry. By God, this could be even more a legacy moment than the building of my Rockefeller Center."

"Perhaps your Center will be a monument to this moment, to the world you created anew in this bold, history-making moment."

"To the world that *we* created, Henry."

"Yes indeed, my friend. Yes indeed."

The two men shook hands, effectively sealing their deal save for the formality of signing the contract, the Dossiers officially commissioning the Operation. And with that handshake and the subsequent signing of the secret contract between the two parties – the vast Rockefeller business empire and the

Office of the Secretary of State of the United States of America – both men had made a decision that they would soon come to regret for the rest of their lives. A mistake whose ramifications would haunt them to their graves.

Chapter 30

Manhattan

Present Day

"So Rockefeller's money goes to the Nazi Party," Wayne continued, "and on election day in July 1932, the extra funding helps them win more than double the number of seats in the Reichstag than they had previously. Beyond that, they were the most powerful party in the Reichstag, their 230 seats dwarfing the Marxist-leaning Social Democratic Party's 133 seats and the Communist Party of Germany's 89 seats."

Jon was shaking his head. "But then the Nazis *lost* seats when a special election was held that November."

"Yes, they did," Wayne said. "And the Nazis lost seats, while the Communist Party gained seats. In fact, the Communists and the Social Democrats together now had more seats than the Nazis. Marxism was winning again. So we had to intervene again."

Mara was still standing dumbstruck, her mouth slightly ajar as she struggled to take all of this in. Jon, on the other hand, needed to scrutinize every detail.

"But neither Stimson nor Rockefeller had anything to do with Hitler's rise to the Chancellorship. That was what really cemented the Nazis' hold on Germany. And that was the work of Franz von Papen, President Hindenburg, and Hitler himself."

Wayne looked troubled, as though fighting off some inner demon. "Every man has his price."

Jon's face blanched. "No, they couldn't have…"

"How else could you explain a respected nobleman like von Papen, himself a former Chancellor, throwing his lot in with Adolf Hitler? Simple. We bought him. Stimson went back to Rockefeller in November of '32. Asked for another million to finally ensure that the march of Communism stopped at the Rhine. Rockefeller agreed, but only in exchange for a second detailed contract like the one they had exchanged in January. The formalities taken care of, Stimson had his agents take the million into the heart of Germany to bribe Franz von Papen himself. One million of Rockefeller's dollars bought Papen's cooperation, and with it, a Nazi bulwark against Communism."

Wayne quickened his pace again, finishing the story that Jon already knew the ending to. "Papen convinces President Hindenburg that Hitler can be controlled if they just appease him with the Chancellorship. Hindenburg is in his mid-eighties and his mind is starting to feel the effects of old age. He acquiesces to Papen's request, ousting Kurt von Schleicher and appointing Hitler as Chancellor, the very position Hindenburg had denied him just five months earlier. The Reichstag fire in February allowed Hitler to enact Article 48 of the Weimar Constitution, granting him emergency powers that Hindenburg didn't argue with. Hitler and the Nazis consolidated their power until 1934, when Hindenburg died and Hitler proclaimed himself President and supreme leader, or *Führer*, of the land. And the rest is history."

Jon and Mara's faces were twisted into an expression somewhere between shock and incredulity, an expression they had worn for the past five minutes of the story. Jon noted the pause, realized the story had come to an end, and spoke up.

"So that's what this whole cover-up is about. Making sure people don't find out about our involvement with the Nazis?"

"That's it. What would you say if you knew that the worst injustices of the twentieth century, the most devastating war and the most widespread case of genocide the world has ever seen, if you knew that your country was responsible for putting those men in power? What do you think would happen in the Middle East, with our relationship with Israel, if it came out that the American government had indirectly abetted the Holocaust? Islamo-fundamentalism, homegrown right-wing and left-wing terrorist groups, our political and economic allies and enemies alike would all have a field day with us. 'Sorry about your countries getting decimated, France and Britain.' And Germany, for that matter. How do you think our position as a player in the world stage would look after that kind of revelation? We're talking World War III: the world against us. Or at least, that's... certain people's take on it."

Jon averted his wide-open eyes and exhaled sharply through his teeth. Mara still stared through Wayne at the wall behind him.

"But they couldn't have known that..." Jon's mind scrambled to come to terms with what he was hearing. "How do you know all of this? How do you even know us? How do we know you're not screwing around with us?"

"Because I'm one of the ones charged with keeping the conspiracy secret. I'm an agent with the Division."

"What?" Jon's exclamation was squeakier than he had intended. "You're charged with keeping the secret, and you just *told* it to us? And what the hell is the Division?"

Mara had regained enough presence of mind to watch the exchange of words, her face turning from Jon to Wayne and back again like a tennis spectator following the volleys of a match, but her eyes were still fixed wide-open with disbelief, her mouth slightly agape.

"One question at a time. I'll answer the second one first. The Division is the... project, agency, call it what you will, that Stimson set up in '41 to cover up his involvement – the country's involvement – in the events of '32 and '33 in Germany.

Stimson had gotten rid of the U.S.A.'s counterespionage division in 1929, famously stating that 'gentlemen don't read each other's mail.' But he quickly changed his mind on that, albeit not publicly. The Office of Strategic Services – the predecessor to the CIA – was established in 1941 while Stimson was Secretary of War. He managed to piggyback off of that and set up his own damage control unit. Its sole prerogative was to make certain that the truth about America's involvement in the rise of Nazi Germany was never made public." Wayne smiled weakly, as though musing to himself. "'Operation Phoenix,' he had called the original missions. Objective: make a strong, right-wing Germany rise from the ashes of the all-but-failed Weimar Republic to battle off the westward march of Communism. And it succeeded. A little too well, you might say."

Mara coughed nervously. Wayne glanced at her, then proceeded.

"When things went south, when all of our European allies were being devoured not by Communism but by the monster we had created, this war-mongering, power-hungry beast that was Nazi Germany, the original conspirators freaked. The phoenix had risen and was turning our allies to ash. Bad PR for Washington, if the truth got out. So, shortly after he was appointed Secretary of War by Roosevelt – the 'Communist sympathizer' who he had feared was going to sell out the country to the Soviets – Stimson set up an agency that would keep tabs on the any leaks about the mission. Seal 'em up real quick if any appeared. And seal 'em up they did. So the Division, as it came to be called among the very few who knew about it, shut the curious and the loose-lipped up – permanently. They called it 'information containment.' Basically, no one outside of the Division was supposed to know anything about the Operation – or about the Division, for that matter. Think McCarthyism, but inverted. Everyone knew about the McCarthy witch hunts, and in some cases, it backfired. What's a sure way to get someone to think about Communism? Talk about Communism, plaster it all over the news, vilify it in public proclamations and spectacles. And what does that do? Give it an allure, a mystique. Stimson chose a different route with his undesirable topic – nip it in the bud, quietly and irreparably."

"Michael…" Mara whispered to the stones of the floor.

"Yes, Michael was probing where too many had probed before. Probing quite effectively, actually. He got closer to the truth than most before he was eliminated."

"He was *murdered*, you sick bastard," Jon seethed.

Wayne frowned. "It's just the training lingo talking. Apologies."

"So if you're… one of them," Mara asked, finally looking at Wayne again, "then why are you helping us?"

"I haven't helped you yet."

"Alright then, why are you telling us about what happened? Why are you spilling your 'Division's' secrets?" Jon made air quotes as he said 'Division,' his tone faintly mocking.

"Because I want it to end."

"You want *what* to end?" Jon asked.

"The killing, the lies, the cover-up. It's a vicious cycle." Wayne looked to the face of Jesus shining in the window. "Christ Himself said that the truth would set us free." He turned his eyes back to Jon. "And only through proclaiming the truth can the killing stop."

"So what, we just go down to Times Square, tell Katie Couric about a government conspiracy to put the Nazis in power eighty years ago, tell her how they've been killing their own curious citizens ever since?"

"Not without proof, no."

"What proof is there? I imagine Stimson covered his tracks pretty well."

Wayne smiled. "He did. But Stimson wasn't the only one involved in the conspiracy."

"Rockefeller." Jon's eyes lit up. The map from Michael's notebook. He *knew*. Somehow, Michael had found out about the whole conspiracy. Or at least enough to connect the dots between Roger Blumhurst's suicide and Rockefeller's Manhattan properties. The emails, the phone calls, the newspaper articles. And everything on Michael's laptop. Even though Jon couldn't go through all of Michael's sources right now and see how he had figured out what he had, he felt a surge of pride at his brother's brilliance. And then he remembered that it was this very brilliance that had gotten him killed.

"Exactly. The contracts Rockefeller exchanged with Stimson – for all intents and purposes, the Dossiers commissioning Operation Phoenix. When Stimson created the Division, one of the first loose ends he tried to tie up was getting rid of those Dossiers. Rockefeller refused to give his up. He said that they were in a safe place, and that someday, at the right time, they would be revealed. Not during his lifetime, he was sure, but someday, the truth behind the biggest mistake of his life would come out. And his guilty conscience would be bared posthumously for all to see."

"Someplace safe…" Jon repeated, deep in thought.

"Stimson persisted in his attempts to get Rockefeller to turn over the Dossiers, but Rockefeller never gave them up – or the secret of their final resting place."

"The man owned half of New York. He could've hidden it anywhere!"

"And not just in New York, Jon. Ohio, Arizona, Illinois, Wyoming, abroad. The man had homes and projects everywhere. Not to mention his philanthropic ventures."

Something stirred within Jon's mind at this last statement, but he decided to file it away for later. *Don't show your cards too early*, he reminded himself. *Or in some cases, don't show them at all.*

"And this is the proof you spoke of?" Mara asked. "The proof that could end the killing?"

"Yes. If the Dossiers are brought to light, if the truth of Operation Phoenix is exposed and proven, the Division would have no further reason to exist. Its mission parameters would be impossible, and the killing would end. Michael would be the last. His death would mean something, instead of being just another name in a line of lives cut short, a line known only to the ones who killed them."

"But how in the world are we supposed to find them, if no one has been able to find them for more than seventy years?" Jon asked.

"You have something they didn't have. Michael's research."

"But we've been over his research. *He* didn't even know where they are." Jon pulled his brother's notebook from the backpack and turned to the page with the map of the city. Wayne's face gave the slightest impression of a smile at the sight of the marked map. "He knew it was Rockefeller, but he didn't know *where* he would have hidden it."

"No, but he knew who could help him find out."

"Who?" Jon and Mara blurted together.

Wayne gave his closed-mouth smile that might have bordered on patronizing. "Roger Blumhurst."

"What?" Mara said.

"But we've been... wait a second..." The gears in Jon's mind were spinning and gnashing like the blades of a blender. "It *was* you! *You're* the one who masqueraded as Michael and stole the envelope from Catherine Smith!"

"Jon, you're in a church, lower your voice," Wayne said in a maddeningly calm voice. "I didn't *steal* it so much as she gave it to me, but yes, I took it. I had to see for myself. And now, I pass it on to you." He pulled a yellowed envelope from his coat pocket and handed it to Jon.

"Why are you helping us? I mean, why are you even *with* the Division if you want to stop the killing? Aren't you just putting yourself in danger, too?"

Wayne sighed, looked at the holy images shining through the window, stared for a moment, lost in thought. Finally, taking a deep breath, he turned his gaze back to his interlocutors.

"I am. I've probably just signed all three of our death warrants, but somehow... somehow we can stop it. *You* can stop it."

"Why are you turning your back on your mission, though? On your job?"

"I'm not turning my back on that so much as I'm finally turning *toward* the truth. Toward the path that my own loved ones – who were also mercilessly taken from me – would have wanted for me." He looked back at the altar for a wistful moment, breathing deeply and steadily through his nose. Then, turning back to his companions: "Jon, Mara, what path would Michael have wanted for you?"

Mara stood silent. After a moment of quiet reflection, arriving at the obvious answer, Jon spoke first.

"He would have wanted us to find the truth."

Wayne smiled. "There you have it then."

"But," Mara interjected, "why don't you do this yourself? Why do you need us?"

"Mara, Stimson and his cronies at the Division have been searching for this thing for the better part of a century. Michael got further than any of them, except, perhaps, for Roger Blumhurst, but his being *in* the Division kind of gave him a bit of a head start. Our intelligence reports indicate that you, Jon, think a lot like your brother, and considering how close each of you were to him, the two of you may be the best bet the country has of finding out the truth before we have *another* seventy years of senseless killing in the name of 'information containment.'"

"Maybe you should have thought of that before you let Michael get killed," Jon shot back. Wayne just looked at him in response.

Jon shook his head. "So what," he said somewhat snidely, "you think we're the country's last hope or something?"

"Or something," Wayne replied, quickening his verbal pace. "I have to keep up appearances with my superiors, so I can't go traipsing around with you two, but I'll be watching, keeping an eye out for any threat."

"Any threat? Like the guy who chased us through Grand Central this morning?" Mara said.

Wayne tilted his head downward, his eyes narrowing.

"What guy?"

"The same guy that I got into a slugfest with at Michael's apartment a few days ago. The guy who seems hell-bent on seeing me dead. Latino guy, angry eyes, maybe five-ten, likes to run around in black chasing me."

"Shit," Wayne exhaled under his breath, his eyes on the floor.

"You know him?" Mara asked.

"Know him? Yeah, I know him. He's one of us. Perhaps the most fanatical of anyone in the Division, except for Director Greer himself."

Jon exhaled heavily, his eyebrows starting to quiver nervously.

"His name is Ramirez," Wayne continued. "Don't let your little scuffles with him thus far fool you. The man is good at what he does. Very, very good. If there's any one agent I wouldn't want after me right now, it would probably be Enrique Ramirez. When he sets out to do something, he doesn't stop until it's done. Including killing people. *Especially* killing people. I'll definitely try to keep tabs on him too. To neutralize him before he can get to you." He looked away again and cursed at the silent stone floor.

Jon and Mara stood in uncomfortable silence until Wayne lifted his eyes again.

"You two be careful, and work fast. Time wasn't on your side before. With Ramirez on your tail, you'd better really book it."

Jon and Mara nodded. Jon ran his finger over the edge of the envelope. Mara nervously rocked one of her ankles back and forth, back and forth.

Wayne furrowed his brow at them. "Um, class dismissed? Go already, and watch your backs."

"Thanks," Mara said hesitantly as she led the way out of the chapel.

Jon followed close behind. "Yeah, thanks for your help… I think."

"You're welcome, guys. Just don't let it be in vain. *Find those Dossiers.*"

"We will," Mara promised as they walked through the gate and into the cathedral proper.

***

Wayne remained behind for a few minutes, staring at the stained glass and mulling over his thoughts. He had felt in his element right then. It had been a long time since the high-school salutatorian and university honors student had interacted with other civilians in an encounter that didn't end with a body count. But then, this was a mission he could believe in, a mission so very different from the track-aim-kill missions he had been running for years. A mission that seemed somehow more human.

He realized that this was a supremely dangerous game he was playing, especially with the wild-card Ramirez thrown into the mix. Wayne Wilkins had infiltrated terrorist camps, stalked enemy warlords through insurgent strongholds, put his life on the line dozens upon dozens of times. But this time was different. The implication that this mission held for him, and ultimately for the nation, was unparalleled in anything he had done before. The danger of failure was unavoidably clear. This, more than any other operation he had engaged in, was a mission where failure truly was not an option.

He stood, pulled his GPS receiver from his pocket, and turned on the display. The intrepid young adventurers were just south of the west exit of the cathedral. Heading back toward the park. Wayne walked out of the chapel, around to the northern exit, out the doors, and into the growing shadows of evening. Finding a somewhat discreet nook in which to hide himself, he opened his cell phone and dialed.

"Greer," answered the voice on the other end.

"It's me."

"Wilkins, my boy. How'd it go?"

"Like clockwork. They took the bait. Hook, line, and sinker."

<u>Part Three – Phoenix Rising</u>

All that is necessary for the triumph of evil is that good men do nothing.
~ Edmund Burke

This is preeminently the time to speak the truth, the whole truth, frankly and boldly.
~ Franklin Delano Roosevelt

Chapter 31

Back in Central Park, Jon and Mara found a secluded spot off one of the jogger trails, a place where they could open the envelope and discuss their plans in relative privacy. They could hear the drone of car engines below them to one side, traffic backed up on one of the many roads that traversed the park, but it was out of sight from the grass upon which they were seated. Through the bushes, they could see the jogger trail – and any joggers that ran by – but the joggers would likely assume that the young pair had come to this secluded spot for *other* purposes, and keep moving down the path. Satisfied with their sequestered little glade, they sat on the cold gray-green ground as Jon pulled out the aged envelope and opened the flap.

The seal was torn, but the surface underneath – where the adhesive would have held the envelope shut – was fresh and white, a contrast to the rest of the envelope that told Jon that Wayne had likely been the one to open it. The first one to see its contents in half a century. And Jon would be the second.

Inside the envelope was a single sheet of paper, folded into thirds. Fragments of handwritten sentences were scrawled on the outside of the sheet. Jon extracted the paper, slowly opening the page. He noted a tear along one side, as though the sheet had been ripped from a bound book, perhaps a journal of some sort.

Mara leaned in for a closer look. "It looks like a diary or something."

Jon agreed. Both sides of the page were filled with relatively short entries, each dated and ended with a cursory initialing. What looked to Jon like *JDR Jr.*

"Is this…" Mara trailed off.

"I think so," Jon answered, his hands starting to quiver with excitement. "Journal entries from Rockefeller himself. No wonder Blumhurst made a big deal about–" He stopped talking, his eyes fixed to the page.

"What?" Mara entreated at his silence. She followed his finger to an entry, starred in the margin by a different pen, perhaps by Blumhurst years after Rockefeller had written the words.

"'*My punishment for using my power to try to help the people is the gnawing guilt that devours me from within,*'" Jon read aloud, "'*hidden from the world, borne in silence and suffered in solitude. His punishment was much worse, but he was eventually absolved. He points to the source of my anguish, the first of five.*'"

Jon and Mara looked at each other, the brains behind the surprised eyes and furrowed brows working in overdrive. A clue? Directly from Rockefeller? It was almost too easy. Jon pulled out Michael's notebook and thumbed through the pages. The pieces were finally coming together. On one page, Michael had written '*September 1957 – theft from mansion.*' Jon smiled. Somehow, his brother must have found out about the theft of this journal page from one of Rockefeller's mansions, and connected the timeframe with Roger's suicide and the envelope that the agent had entrusted Catherine Smith just beforehand. Such disparate pieces of the larger puzzle, but both Jon and Michael had long possessed a seemingly uncanny ability to see hidden connections where others saw nothing but white noise.

"'He points to the source of my anguish, the first of five,'" Mara repeated, her eyes locked on the paper. "Five sources of anguish?"

"I don't know. The big question is *who* he's writing about. Alright, we know the author is Rockefeller, right?"

"We *assume* so."

Jon rolled his eyes and shrugged in a conciliatory gesture. "Yeah. Well, let's just run with that assumption for right now. I don't think Blumhurst, Catherine Smith, and Wayne would get so worked up if it weren't."

"*Assuming* Wayne didn't make this up to screw with us."

Jon's tone was suddenly stern. "You got a better plan?"

Mara got quiet. "No."

"Nor do I." He shook his head. "Besides, if his story weren't true, why did he go through all of this instead of just shooting us?"

A pause. "I don't know."

"Fine. So what do we know about Rockefeller?" The question hung in the air for a moment, then Jon's eyes lit up. He reached into the backpack and withdrew the now-familiar worn red notebook. Flipping to the map page, Jon slapped the open notebook upon his lap, the Rockefeller journal page lying on his knee. Circles of ink stared up at him like unseeing unblinking eyes, famous properties all over the island of Manhattan that had some connection to Rockefeller. *Where did he hide it?* inquired Michael's handwriting, a question that had been passed on to his brother and fiancée.

"It's in Manhattan," Jon said, finally revealing what he had realized back in the Cathedral.

"You think so?"

"Michael thought so. And there are enough places here, places he would have felt were secure. *His* properties." Jon ran his finger from Rockefeller Center to the Museum of Modern Art, to the Cathedral of St. John that they had just left. "And places he had donated his millions to. Places he had donated land and real estate to. Churches, museums, parks, the UN Headquarters. Places that represented spiritual calm, higher callings, higher learning, everything he must've felt he had turned his back on. His own personal penance."

"Did he make *all* of his donations after 1932?"

"Well, no, but apparently that didn't rule them out in Michael's thinking. I guess if you endow a museum or church with millions of dollars, or if you founded the darned place, they'll pretty much let you go anywhere you want in the place. Hide things wherever and however you want."

"Money talks."

"That it does. If any man had his choice of hiding spots in the city in the 'thirties, it was Rockefeller."

"Which makes our job that much harder."

Jon grimaced. "Let's just work the angle we've got. The journal entry." He placed the page on top of the map. "So let's assume that he wasn't being more obtuse than necessary and talking about himself in some split-personality third-person."

"Agreed," Mara said with a hint of a smile.

"It was someone he sympathized with. Someone he related to. Someone who was punished for 'using his power to try to help the people.'"

"Abraham Lincoln?"

"Good guess, but I don't think they ever met."

Mara rolled her eyes.

"No, seriously though," Jon urged, "think Rockefeller. He's the author. What's important to him? Who would *he* be talking about?"

"I don't know, Jon. You're the history buff. You figure it out."

Jon pretended to ignore her jab and stared at the green of the copse that surrounded them. A car engine backfired on the road below, causing both of them to jump. They looked around in fear, then exhaled deeply. Not a gun being fired. They were safe for now. Then his eyes grew wide in epiphany.

"Fire! That's it!" Jon exclaimed in the most subdued voice his excitement would allow.

She looked both confused and excited. "What's it?"

"In Greek mythology, Prometheus was a Titan who defied Zeus and the Olympian deities by taking fire from the gods' home on Mount Olympus and giving it to man. A gift that he feels will help man, right? What does he get for his trouble? Zeus chains him to a rock and has an eagle pluck out and devour his liver every day."

"Holy crap," she said, a look of shock and disgust on her face.

Jon smirked. "Some thanks, right? Eventually, at the pleading of the other gods, Zeus lets him go after a few years of this torment, *absolving* him of his crime. It's Prometheus, Mara. *He's* the one who points to the source of Rockefeller's guilt."

"Whoa…" Mara sat wide-eyed shaking her head. "Wait, so Rockefeller means the *statue* of Prometheus? *His* statue of Prometheus?"

Jon stood, extended a hand to help Mara up from the ground.

"Mara, I think we have a date at Rockefeller Plaza."

Chapter 32

Dipped in twilight and peopled by a mixture of photo-snapping tourists, oversized shopping bags with the names of high-end retail outfits emblazoned on the side in conspicuous lettering, and diners patronizing the outdoor café at tables whose parasols protected those underneath from the rays of a now-absent sun, Rockefeller Plaza was a picturesque microcosm of Midtown Manhattan life. The ice skating rink, made famous by film and popular legend alike, was packed up until next winter, when the selection of the Center's famous Christmas tree would bring throngs from all over to dance upon razor's edge across the Plaza – or fall on their faces trying, laughing – in the shadow of that looming triangle of deep green and rich golden baubles. In its stead, the center of the Plaza was populated with pedestrians, diners, shoppers, with nary a Christmas tree or ice skate to be found. And though the iconic four-story *Tannenbaum* was absent, another icon presided over the Plaza – Paul Manship's famous statue of *Prometheus*.

Jon and Mara paused at the entrance to the Lower Plaza, a row of flowers and shrubbery lining the sides of the walk, the hustle and bustle of the scene seemingly unimportant in view of the statue. Immediately before them, a large granite marker held the famous "I believe" statements of John D. Rockefeller, Jr., etched for posterity in gold lettering that twinkled in the twilit ambiance. At the top of the display read the words, "I believe in the supreme worth of the individual, and in his right to life, liberty, and the pursuit of happiness." All but completely ripped-off from the *Declaration of Independence*, Jon reflected. But Rockefeller's gilded words continued on, declaring his lifelong beliefs in free enterprise, in religion, in the responsibilities that every man had to himself, to his family, to his country. And in the plaza below awaited a gilded monument of even greater importance.

Reclining on one hip, in one hand Prometheus held aloft a flame – his gift to the people gone awry. His other hand, outstretched and pointing to his left, Jon and Mara's right. His brilliant golden skin gleamed in the floodlights, water splashing from the fountain around him and providing contrast to the fire he represented. Fire. Water. Opposing elements. Tension and conflict. Exposed for all to see, the true meaning obscured from all. The signs of the zodiac encircled the rock on which Prometheus was affixed, representing, perhaps, the relentless march of time, the inability to go back and change mistakes, the months and years that Rockefeller had to live with knowing what he had done, knowing about the pogroms the Nazis were enforcing against the Jews and other groups considered to be *Untermenschen*, sub-human. Pogroms that grew more horrifying and extensive by the week.

Fitting, Jon thought, that it should be a figure from classical mythology that should hide – and reveal – his involvement in Operation Phoenix, considering the classical origins of the phoenix mythos.

They kept their eyes fixed on the statue as they walked down the stairs to the Lower Plaza. The unfeeling, unchanging expression; the vacant, removed eyes – the countenance of Rockefeller's kindred spirit and secret bearer betrayed no emotion of any kind, remaining in silent repose as he had for the past seventy years. To think that all this time, the secret, the way to dispel the lies and end the killing, had been right there under everyone's nose. One of the most famous sites in all of Manhattan – pointing the way to the truth.

But pointing to *what* exactly?

Crossing the Lower Plaza, Jon and Mara walked through the café and came face to face with the statue. A faint mist from the fountain blew into Mara's face and made her shiver. With the sun gone behind the distant horizon, the heat from the unseasonably warm day had begun to rapidly dissipate, and the hint of a chill already hung in the air. A sign of colder weather ahead.

The statue was obviously pointing – a postcard photograph could tell you that – but the object of his denotation was unclear. The pair agreed to split up and look around the area to try to ascertain where the giant bronze finger was pointing. Jon shuffled to his left, skirting the edge of the fountain, trying to line up his line of sight with Prometheus' left arm. He was too far below the statue to see from the right angle. Climbing back up the stairs and around to the left side of the statue, this time from above, Jon looked down the length of the golden arm, from the fingertip to what lay beyond.

The street? The flags of the world that lined the pavilion? Had Rockefeller hidden it in another *country*? Jon scanned the flags that seemed to be in the general area of the statue's indication: Mexico, Israel, Italy. Israel might make sense, seeing as the Holocaust – for which Rockefeller, in helping the Nazis come to power, must have felt at least partially responsible – was the main impetus for the creation of a Jewish state. But were these flags even here when Rockefeller commissioned Prometheus to be the guardian of truth? The State of Israel didn't even exist until 1948, a decade after the Plaza was completed.

Jon shook his head. He was making it too complicated. Was it a window *beyond* the flags? Past the double row of flags, across the street, the stone and glass building whose windows looked down onto the plaza? Was that part of Rockefeller Center, too? Did some room in that building have special significance? How could Rockefeller ensure that it remained safe, especially if it were leased to some business or…

Stop, he told himself. Too complicated again. Rockefeller wanted this to be found *someday*, by *someone*. Someone purposefully looking for it, looking for it in the right way, at the right time. He wouldn't have hidden it in some obscure place that would be more likely found by building renovators ripping up floorboards and tearing through plastered walls than someone following *his* clue to absolve *his* guilt. It had to be some place more permanent, some place more important to him. A monument or something. Like the statue itself?

Jon looked to his right. Three generations of a cheery black family stood at the top of the steps leading down to the Lower Plaza, huddled in their winter coats and nestled together. A young Asian man took the family's picture – two grandparents, four parents, and five kids. Another picture because one of the grandkids wasn't looking at the camera. Then one of the men in the middle generation offered to take the Asian man's photograph, who readily accepted and posed with his sprightly girlfriend, the couple clinging to each other, pointing behind them, visibly excited to be here. Jon couldn't see their faces from where he was, but he knew that in each of those pictures, every subject wore a grin; these pictures would be shown to family and friends, shared and laughed at over the years as they relived their memories of the vacation they took to New York City, the vacation they got their picture taken at Rockefeller Center.

And that's when it hit Jon. He was looking at it wrong. Beyond the symbolic road marker that Jon now knew it to be, it was also a world icon. It was a masterpiece, both in its aesthetic value and in its symbolism – double meaning though the symbolism did seem to have now. Maybe the statue didn't point *directly* to the Dossiers. Maybe it just *pointed*. To its left. To...

Bingo.

Of course, he thought. Another symbol of blame removed, of guilt absolved, of wrongdoing forgiven. To the right of the statue, just beyond Prometheus's outstretched arm, a hole

– roughly two feet square – had been cut in the polished granite wall of the alcove housing the statue and fountain. A similar hole mirrored it on the other side of the statue, but no golden finger pointed to that one. The right-hand hole had three pieces of granite set within – one long vertical section and two shorter pieces on either side. Four smaller holes remained around the inlaid granite. The design formed was one of the most ubiquitous symbols in the Western world, and one that Rockefeller himself would have been quite familiar with: the Cross.

Jon called to Mara, who was presently below him, checking out the angle that he had checked out earlier, and beckoned her to his side. He pointed to the hole and the cross.

"There," he said. "Behind the cross, in one of those holes."

"You think so?" As soon as Mara spoke the words, the lights set inside of those holes turned on, the darkness or the hour having set off a preset timer for illuminating the statue.

Jon smiled at the uncanny timing of the lighting. "The cross symbolizes hope, redemption, salvation from our sins and wrongdoings, right? Absolution from our mistakes, no matter how grievous. And the golden dude seems to be pointing in that general direction."

"Yeah, he does. One question though." Mara indicated the crowd that filled the Plaza with a sweeping motion of her hand. "How exactly do we go about *getting* whatever's inside with all these people around?"

Jon looked thoughtful for a moment, stroking the five o'clock stubble on his jaw.

"We don't," he finally answered. Mara looked surprised briefly before he clarified his statement.

"We come back when the people are gone. We come back tonight."

Chapter 33

Harrison Greer arrived in Manhattan at dusk. He could have flown or taken a train and not had to deal with the nightmare that was finding a parking spot in this city, but Greer had driven his black Lincoln Town Car instead. He didn't trust taxis, the subways stank, and he always, always needed to be in control. In a city of more than eight million people from every belief system, every nationality, every culture known to man (and several that, surely, hadn't yet been documented), there were far too many variables for Greer to rely on crowded public transit or on a cab driver who reeked of boiled lamb and body odor and only spoke three words of English. And of course, there was also the cargo that Greer carried in a secret compartment under the Lincoln's back seat – his trusted sniper rifle, a scope, a pistol, plenty of ammunition for both weapons, and a black sweatsuit and ski mask. These would soon be used to artfully kill both Jonathan Rickner and Mara Ellison. And though he would enjoy destroying these traitors to the nation, what he would truly relish would be aided by the tool that he held in his hand.

At every stop light, he flicked the lighter – an old-fashioned silver one with a flip lid that had once belonged to his grandfather, Walton Greer, the first Director of the Division. On, off, on, off. The flame was beautiful, and it would help him to finally purge the country of her dark secret. How proper that it would be through flame that this stain would finally be purified. How ironic that the truth about Operation Phoenix would quite literally be reduced to ashes, never again to rise up and threaten them. And how fitting that it should be the lighter of Walton

Greer, guided by the hand of his grandson, that would finally finish the mission started all those years ago.

Harrison Greer found a pay-by-the-day lot near Grand Central. After parking the car, he opened the secret compartment under the back seat, withdrew the pistol, loaded it, and placed it in his shoulder holster. You never knew what you might encounter in this city, and Greer wasn't about to take any chances. Especially not with everything he'd ever worked for on the line. He had all the proper documentation for a concealed weapon, which – signed by the Secretary of State herself – so he needn't worry about some two-bit cop giving him lip about it. As always, he had all of his bases covered.

Closing and securing the compartment, he locked his car and left the lot with his small rolling suitcase in tow. After he checked into his usual room at the Grand Hyatt – the luxurious five-star hotel just next door to Grand Central Terminal – he headed back out into the city. He found himself walking north as though his feet had a mind of their own, which ultimately, he didn't mind. As much as he hated not being in control of all the variables, there was something about this city – an energy, so to speak – that invigorated him.

Of course, this was also where the Operation had begun eighty years ago, when, in 1932, Stimson had met with Rockefeller just a mile or so north from where Greer now stood. This was where, in 1941, Rockefeller had denied Stimson's demand for him to turn over his copy of the Dossiers commissioning Operation Phoenix. Just to the southeast was the site of the United Nations Headquarters, which, in 1947, had been purchased with a small fortune donated by Rockefeller in unspoken penitence for unwittingly visiting upon the world the worst atrocities and most devastating war it had ever seen. Ten years later, in 1957, just to the south of the UN Headquarters, the Brooklyn Bridge was where Blumhurst had had some sort of crisis of conscience and derailed Walton Greer's plans. And here, today, Harrison Greer would finally finish that work. Truly this great city was inextricably tied to Operation Phoenix and its cover-up. How fitting that it would be here that the cover-up would finally be completed.

He had gotten another status report from Wilkins while on his way into the city. Apparently Rickner and Ellison had figured out something from what Wayne had given them. Clues of some sort left by Rockefeller. Clues that would eventually lead them – and Greer – to the final resting place of the Dossiers.

He had also gotten a curious phone call earlier that day from Ramirez. He was in New York as well. And although Greer secretly cursed himself for not thinking of using him as an asset in this way, he realized that the fear that Ramirez created in Jon and Mara was a definite advantage. That fear of impending death was lighting a fire under their butts that would have them not only afraid to trust anyone else – thus preventing any further information leaks – but would also make them move on toward Greer's goals much more quickly. Although he felt fine right now, Greer knew from his father's own battle with cancer that the sickness often gave no warning and offered no mercy. He had to finish this soon, and with both Ramirez and Wilkins moving their quarry closer to where he needed them to be, Greer had no doubt that this would all be over very, very soon.

Harrison Greer stopped short when he realized where his feet had taken him while he was lost in his thoughts: Rockefeller Plaza. The heart of the audacious Center that the self-righteous old tycoon had named after himself. He had thought that he knew better than Stimson, or indeed, the whole of the United States Government, in his refusal to give up the Dossiers. Hiding them away for later generations, leaving clues to their secret location; who did he think he was, a treasure-burying pirate? National security was on the line, and he'd refused to play along. And now, nearly a century later, the nation was still reaping the deadly consequences of his actions. As the loved ones of Michael Rickner could attest. And as the loved ones of Jonathan Rickner and Mara Ellison would soon be able to.

Greer stared out at the Plaza, at the families and friends dining in the terrace below, the tourists snapping photographs of the iconic site, the craze of New Yorkers shopping and wining and dining. All built on a lie. All built by a man who had done the unthinkable, and then been too conscience-stricken and cowardly to do what needed to be done after the fact. What his country had needed him to do. It was a wonder Greer's grandfather hadn't hauled Rockefeller himself in as a traitor. But then, when someone is an imminently public figure with more money than the government, arresting him on charges stemming from an explosive national secret was probably not an option. In truth, Stimson – and Walton Greer after him – probably had to walk a fine line between trying to reclaim the Dossiers and not antagonizing the tycoon to the point where his conscience would overwhelm his rational mind and opt to just spill it all to the press.

Greer glared across the Plaza at the entrance to the towering GE Building, one of the principle structures of Rockefeller Center. *Now it's finally come to this*, he thought, mentally challenging the long-dead billionaire. *Your secret versus my plan. You've bested us for seventy years, you old bastard. But your time is finished. Your breach of conscience will no longer haunt the Division or the future of our great nation. It's over, old man. Despite your best efforts, the Dossiers are as good as mine. You, Mr. Rockefeller, have already lost. And your final secret will soon be as dead as you are.*

Chapter 34

The chill in the air at dusk had evolved into a full-fledged biting cold by half-past midnight. Jon and Mara shivered in their coats, but recognized the advantage that the temperature afforded them. The less pleasant the weather, the less likely it was that someone would come into the area and interrupt their admittedly suspicious activities.

Since the area was now closed for the night, all the hustle, bustle, and special effects of the Plaza were now dormant. The once active fountain was now just a placid pool of water. The lights for artfully illuminating the statues and architectural features of the Plaza were now dark. *Prometheus* was draped in shadow, his bronze arm continuing to point as it had for decades, waiting for someone to finally release his maker from the secret that had consumed him until the end of his days. Those someones had finally come, dressed in dark shades of blue and green – but not black, for black-clad persons skulking around the Center at night just *had* to be up to no good.

When Rockefeller Plaza had closed for the night, barricades had been put in place at the entrances and exits to the area. Though they sent the message to passersby that the site was closed for the night, they did not present a particularly potent obstacle to the determined. After hopping over the barricades and sneaking past the sleepy security, Jon and Mara found themselves staring not at the centerpiece of the Plaza, but at the dingy and neglected hole next to the monument – captured in thousands if not millions of photographs taken by tourists and publicists alike, none of whom realized the gravity of what lay within. None except Roger Blumhurst, Jon Rickner, and Mara Ellison. One of the three was dead. And the other two were doing their best to keep from joining him.

Having gotten a closer look at the hole prior to leaving that afternoon, Jon had realized that it wouldn't be as simple as just reaching in the hole and pulling out Rockefeller's secrets. That would've been too easy, so of course it couldn't have been that simple. A small square of dull glass covered each of the holes, seemingly housing floodlights within. Moreover, the distance from the hole to the platform below it was far greater than Jon's height. Having Mara sit on his shoulders would be far too precarious an enterprise, and bringing a stepladder… that was simply out of the question. The idea was to look as inconspicuous as possible, and walking into the abandoned plaza in the middle of the night with a stepladder in tow was just asking for trouble. Luckily, the hole was only a few feet from the *top* of the wall in which it was set, so it could be reached, albeit with some effort and balance, from the Upper Plaza above.

Jon checked the small utility door on the opposite side of the wall from the hole. The door was too high on the wall, didn't correspond with the backside of the hole in the granite. Of course it didn't, he thought. Again, that would have been too easy. And, after seventy years, *somebody* would have definitely found it in such an often-used location. The only way in was from the other side. The difficult side.

Jon unzipped his coat and consulted his tool belt. The tools still bore the price stickers from the hardware store he had purchased them from a few hours earlier. Two screwdrivers – one Phillips and one flathead – and a small rubber mallet hung on the belt, which Jon now unbuckled and laid on the flat surface of the ledge. When leaning over the ledge with most of his weight on his waist, having a clunky tool belt with a screwdriver and a mallet between his center of gravity and a hard granite surface didn't seem like a desirable experience. Mara stood at his side, holding the beam of a penlight steady on the top-left hole, ready to hand him a tool from the belt at a moment's notice, like a surgeon's assistant. She would also be keeping a lookout for any potential trouble – from security personnel, police officers... or worse. Setting his feet firmly on the pavement, Jon graciously accepted Mara's wishes for good luck, and bent over the ledge, doubled over as far as his seventy-four inches would allow.

He had only gotten a cursory glance at the holes and their protective glass earlier this evening, when the Plaza was as busy as the main concourse of Grand Central Terminal, so he didn't know exactly how the glass was held in place. He only knew that it was in the way of his goal, and thus, it had to go.

"Flashlight," he said, stretching his torso flat – and up – and extending his hand toward Mara. She handed him the small penlight, and he relaxed his back muscles, allowing his weight to lower him back into position. The beam of the flashlight shone on each of the four smaller holes created by the cross and reflected back at Jon. On the first pass, Jon could detect nothing out of the ordinary in any of them, no bundle of papers, no cylindrical tube, no neat little box that might hold the prize that they sought.

"Phillips screwdriver," he said before sticking the handle of the penlight in his mouth, using his lips and teeth to keep its beam steady on the hole, thrusting his open hand up toward Mara. She handed him the screwdriver, which Jon quickly moved to the top-left hole, loosening the brackets that held the glass in place. The pane finally came free, and he handed it to Mara. He peered inside the hole, around the floodlight within – which, thankfully for Jon's eyes, was turned off like the rest of the lights behind the granite cross. He unscrewed the floodlight, removed it, looked again.

Nothing.

He blew a frustrated sigh from his lips. It had to be here though. If it wasn't, if there was nothing here... No, he couldn't think like that. He was still three holes from a dead end. Press on.

He replaced the glass, screwed the brackets tight – one of them *too* tight, cracking the glass. Started on the next hole, the top right, the one that, really, Prometheus's finger seemed to be pointing closer to than any of the others. Removing the pane, he took a deep breath, silently mouthed a brief prayer, and got to work on the floodlight. From above, heightened breathing and nervous scuffles of rubber soles on concrete reminded him that his assistant was excited, impatient, and cold.

The floodlight free and dangling by its cord out of the way, Jon shone his light into the hole. Still nothing. Zero-for-two. He felt his spirits beginning to sink.

He put the flashlight back between his lips and started to pull up the dangling floodlight, when the flashlight's beam reflected off something in the hole. Some surface that caught the light in a slightly different way. Jon started, almost dropping the penlight. He quickly lowered the floodlight again and took his penlight from his mouth.

Something was in there.

He could hear the blood pounding in his ears, unsure as to how much of it was due to nerves and exertion, and how much owed to the fact that all of the blood from the top half of his upside-down body was rushing to his head.

With his fingertips, he could touch the object. It was small, flat, boxlike, set almost flush with the left-hand wall, where the head of the Crucified would have been had the symbolic cross been real. The dull silvery sheen of old polished tin, a visual contrast to the gray granite around only if you were *looking* for something different in the hole, reflected off the flashlight beam, almost tauntingly. The object was *just* out of reach.

Jon grunted as he wriggled his body further across the ledge, his feet leaving the ground on the other side.

"Careful," Mara cautioned. So enrapt was she in the excitement – and danger – of Jon's endeavors, Mara didn't even notice when the security guard, making his rounds of the Center grounds, came around the corner of the GE building, spotted the pair of them, and started making his way toward them.

Down below, Jon perched precariously on the precipice, his fingers finally able to grip the lid of the box, which, of course, was stuck. Affixed somehow to the stone.

"Flathead." Mara traded his Phillips screwdriver for a slotted one.

He used his flathead screwdriver to attempt to pry the box loose. The screwdriver jammed into the gap between box and stone. Jon pulled on the handle. Harder and harder, trying to break the resistance of seven decades of inertia. The tip of the screwdriver slipped from the gap and Jon's torso slid a few inches further down the vertical granite face.

"Jon!" Mara cried, grabbing the bottom of his coat and helping to haul him back to the top.

Jon took a deep breath, grateful for the chance to still be breathing.

"Thanks," he said before lowering himself back down into position.

"You're crazy, you know that?"

"Hey!" came the voice behind her. She turned to see the beam of a flashlight pointed at her, the light bobbing as the security guard walked toward them.

"Cop," Mara warned Jon out of the corner of her mouth. Jon, penlight between his teeth, flathead screwdriver in hand, dangling within inches of the truth they sought, stiffened.

"No, make that rent-a-cop," she revised as the uniformed guard walked into the light at the edge of the Plaza, the patch of the security company he worked for visible on his shoulder. Jon kept working, wriggling the box until finally the box *opened*, a horizontally positioned lid separating from the box itself on a hinge. Not quite what he was going for, but he'd take it.

"What're you two doin' here this hour of the night?" demanded the guard. His demeanor was quashed, his uniform rumpled, head balding, and jowls sagging. Mr. Ace Detective he was not.

Jon plunged his hand in the open box, his fingers tracing the mostly smooth surface of the metal – save for one side that had more than its share of deep scratches – feeling around for whatever was inside. Something, anything. Nothing. No papers, no Dossiers. They must have already gotten to them… Just as he was about to give up hope, his hand brushed against a shape on the lid of the box. It felt textured and relatively warm, not smooth and cold like the tin or stone it was entombed within. He tugged at it, and it popped right off. A small dab of epoxy or some other adhesive was all that had held the object to the lid. Pulling the object from the hole, Jon knew from its shape what it was before he even saw it. Another cross.

Mara was stammering up above, unsure of what to say, caught off-guard and at a complete loss for words. Pulling his arm from the hole, he shoved the cross in his coat's lapel pocket, zipping it closed so the artifact wouldn't fall out.

"Hey, you, get up from there." Jon felt a tug at his pants leg accompanying the tired but irritated voice of the security guard. While dangling below, Jon had been considering how to go about this confrontation. Fight? He could probably take some rent-a-cop, especially if he caught him off-guard, but he didn't need the police hunting him for assault. Flight? He and Mara could probably outrun the guy, but they still might have the cops after them for trespassing. And besides, if there were something else in that box, he wouldn't be able to come back and look for it after this. When he finally pulled himself upright, a look of indignant consternation already painted on his face, Jon surmised that his plan just might work.

"'Get up from there'?" Jon began, throwing his hands into the air in a display of exasperation, the blood that had rushed to Jon's recently upside-down face presenting a convincing image of indignation. The guard took a step back, already adopting a defensive posture. Jon pressed ahead, taking a step toward the shorter man. "D'ya think I *want* to be down here in this freakin' cold tonight? D'ya think I wouldn't rather be home in my nice warm bed right now? But no, my supervisor calls me up at quarter-to-midnight, tells me to get my butt down here and fix these damn lights. I says can I just come in and fix it in the morning when my shift begins, and he says no. Maintenance," he continued, his voice growing more snide, "has to be done at night, when we won't bother the freakin' tourists. So here I am workin' my butt off for jack pay in the freezin' cold, and then Joe Detective comes and tries to start trouble." He shook the flathead screwdriver at the man, continuing his charade of exasperation. "What's the name of your supervisor? I oughta report you and your interfering with important Center maintenance work."

The security guard was visibly shaken, the lines in his face deepening as though his features were trying to retreat from Jon's verbal onslaught. But he didn't relent.

"Could I see your work order to verify?" he stammered, trying to maintain some semblance of authority.

"My work order? Didn't you hear me? I got called out of bed less than an hour ago. I just know what my boss told me; he must've forgotten to FedEx me the work order. Jeez." Jon fished his cell phone out of his pocket, and held it ready to dial. "What's your supervisor's name and number? And *your* name, too, for that matter?"

"Th- that won't be necessary," sputtered the guard, beginning to back away with his hands forward in a defensive gesture. "I'm sorry for interfering, just trying to do my job, you know. I won't keep you." And with that he briskly continued his beat around the corner and out of sight.

"Nice work, Jon," Mara said, admiration twinkling in her eyes.

"Meh," Jon said with a shrug. "Could've just as easily backfired. Michael tried the same thing with a security guard in a Viennese cemetery one time. Didn't work out so well. Landed us both a cell overnight until Dad managed to pull the requisite strings to get us out. We got lucky this time is all." He unzipped his pocket and pulled out the small wooden cross. "Doubly so, you could say," he added holding it so he and Mara could both study it.

It was a simple, unadorned object, two pieces of beveled and varnished wood dovetailed together in a cruciform arrangement. Jon turned it over, scrutinized it. There was nothing particularly strange about it. It still had a slightly woody odor, a daub of dried adhesive at the intersection of the cross pieces where the object had been affixed to the lid of the box, but no Dossiers, no clue, no message.

"That's it?" Mara asked expectantly. "That's all that was down there?"

"It was in a little metal box set in the wall. But yeah, that's all that…" He drifted off.

"What?"

"Gimme your camera," Jon said suddenly as he bent over the rail for another trip down.

"Jon, be careful, already. You fall, and you crack your skull open."

"I know," he said, taking the camera from her and shining the light in the hole. What if the cross wasn't the secret, but it guarded the secret? What if…

He set the penlight in the hole, its beam aimed at the box. Sliding his fingers into the metal enclosure, he felt along the tin walls until… there it was. On the side of the box opposite the cross-adorned lid, the side set into the left wall, Jon's fingers found the scratches he had glanced over before. Tracing some of them with a fingertip, he realized they were not just scratches, but *letters*. Letters etched into this secret hiding place decades earlier by Rockefeller himself. He pushed the camera into the opening, aimed it as best as he could, and took a series of photos, some with flash, some without. Different angles, different lighting. *That should cover it*, he figured, withdrawing the camera and scanning through the pictures he had taken. Without taking the time to register *what* the message said, the pulse of blood in his head making it difficult to concentrate, he realized that he had in fact captured the entire message of the box in the shots. Pulling the flashlight from the hole, he shoved the floodlight back into position, and secured the glass facing as well as he could. And then, just as he was turning the final screw, twisting his body to properly angle the screwdriver, he slipped down the ledge.

He gave a startled cry, but Mara had already grabbed his belt and was attempting to haul him back topside. After a few seconds of pulling and wriggling, Jon found himself safely back on top. Mara smacked him on the chest.

"Don't *do* that," she admonished him.

"Do what?"

"Scare me like that," she answered, gathering the tool belt and tools from the ledge.

"Sorry. I think it was worth it though," he said, holding up the camera and tilting it back and forth, its illuminated display of the box from below dancing back and forth in the night.

"You got it?"

"Yeah, but it's not the Dossiers, obviously. I think it's some sort of a clue or some—" Jon cut off midsentence and grabbed Mara's arm, pulling her into the shadows.

"What?" she asked in a hushed tone.

Jon pointed at another security guard approaching from a different direction, this one looking less haggard and pliable than the first.

"Let's not press our luck," Jon whispered. "Continue this at the hotel?"

Mara nodded and the pair snuck off through the Plaza under cover of night and onto the street, headed southwest toward the safety of their hotel.

***

Hiding in the shadows of a nearby alcove, the earbud of a long-distance listening device stuck in one ear, Enrique Ramirez shook his head. He was proud of himself for letting his hunter instinct bow to calculating patience, waiting for the bigger kill. Chasing the pair the day before had initially been a gut reaction, spurred on by his indignation at leaving Jonathan Rickner as a witness, which at face value was the biggest mistake of his career. Tonight though, he was patient, purposeful. For if what he had heard was true, something truly disturbing was going on. He would follow, verify, and take the necessary actions.

Which, ultimately, would result in the two things he had been going for all along:

The successful completion of the most important mission in the Division's history. And equally important for Ramirez: revenge against Jonathan Rickner.

Chapter 35

The small monitor in the elevator showed a talking head and a reporter in the field discussing the latest development in the Middle East, another dustup between Hamas and Israeli forces that left civilians on both sides devastated and neither side any further in promoting their cause. The news ticker underneath ran off headlines about North Korean missile launches, Iranian President Ahmadinejad's perpetual rhetoric about his country's nuclear program, another dip in the stock market, unemployment and foreclosure comparisons, further unrest in yet another Middle Eastern country, alleged corruption in the latest election in South Africa, a school shooting in Germany. Dire news, gripping news, news that sold. But news that happened in the world in which Jon and Mara, who watched the ticker and listened to the anchor's banter on the sixteen-floor ride up to their hotel room, lived. News that might have been different, for better or worse, had Operation Phoenix never come about. News that might be different, or at least, be looked at in a different light, after – God willing – the two of them found the Dossiers and exposed to the nation – and the world – the truth behind Operation Phoenix and the cover-up that followed.

Jon wondered if they really understood all the consequences of what they were about to do. He was lost in thought as he and Mara disembarked from the elevator and padded down the hallway to their room, both of them silent from the occupation of their minds and the fatigue of their bodies. Did they really know what all might happen after this missing piece in one of the critical moments of the twentieth century was finally put into place? Would there be public backlash? From their own people? From abroad? Who, besides them and the Division members, already knew what was going on, the killings of innocent Americans by their own government? How high up, and how far-reaching, did this conspiracy stretch its tendrils? They would, for all intents and purposes, be implicating their government in bringing to power one of the worst villains in recent memory, a man responsible for the deaths of over 10 million civilians, countless casualties of war, and the devastation of a continent. Given, America had also been instrumental in bringing about Hitler's downfall, but its cover-up of the facts for the past seventy years, and the loathsome way in which it had kept the truth a secret from its own people would surely complete its guilt in the eyes of the public. Might they be bringing revolution down onto their own country's heads by revealing the truth to the public? Might their cause, however noble, ultimately do more damage than it sought to prevent?

Jon slid his keycard into the slot on the door. A small green light, a whirr, a click, and the door unlocked, Jon turning the handle and leading the way into the room. With a flip of the switch, the room was instantly bathed in illumination, a comforting sight after the ardors of the day. A safe haven from the cold and dangers of the outside world, but not from the thoughts that haunted Jon's mind.

"Let's see the pics," Mara said, tossing her bag onto the bed and inching up to Jon's side.

Jon sat down on the foot of her bed, camera in hand, and flipped through the photos, Mara looking on. Some were too bright, some too dark. Some had been taken at such an angle that half of the message was out of the frame, while the angles of others had failed to capture the shape of the letters engraved in the metal. Two pictures in the middle of the inverted photo shoot were perfect – the message could be read loud and clear. It's meaning, however, was less obvious.

Her great bells toll, Chapel of Christ
Read right of saints and then shift thrice

"What the heck?" Mara blurted. "Some sort of poem?"

"Some sort of clue it looks like."

"Well, these certainly aren't the Dossiers."

"No, it's… hang on a sec," Jon said as he pulled out Rock-efeller's journal page. "'*He points to the source of my anguish, the first of five.*' Maybe 'the first of five' doesn't refer to five different sources of anguish, but five different markers, the first of which was the Prometheus statue?"

"Like some sort of treasure hunt or something? A clue leading to another clue and so on?"

"And so on five times, until—"

"The Dossiers."

"Exactly," Jon said, a contented grin on his face. "Five clues, five locations. The Rockefeller journal entry gave us the first clue, and here's the second." He waved the camera in the air. "The question is, where is location number two?"

"And with it, clue number three?"

"That's how I figure it." He suddenly looked wistful, staring off into space with a look of nostalgic satisfaction dancing in his eyes.

"What?"

"Huh?" he asked, yanked back from somewhere in the past and turning his attention to Mara.

"What were you just thinking about?" she pressed.

"Oh, sorry. I was just thinking about me and Michael growing up. We used to devise treasure hunts with puzzles and clues for each other. Be they around the house or the neighborhood, or in temple ruins near where Dad was working. One of us would find something cool, an ancient idol or something, then work backward, identifying key points, engravings on walls, a copse of three palm trees, whatever, and leading the other one of us from the starting point to the 'treasure' via encoded waypoints."

Mara smiled a tight-lipped but genuine smile, torn between happy memories and the knowledge that no new memories of Michael would ever be formed. "Then this should be right up your alley."

"Yeah, it should." Jon allowed himself one last sentimental smile, then turned back to the image on the camera's display screen. "Alright then, let's pick this puppy apart. *'Her great bells toll.'*"

"Her. Like a boat or something?"

Jon kneaded his bottom lip between his teeth, scratching at the stubble on his chin with his thumb.

"Could be a boat. Or maybe a church."

"Something big and impressive. It'd have to be to be personified as a *she*, right?"

Jon chuckled. "Yeah sure. But then this is a port city. And churches are ubiquitous here."

"Well, he would have wanted it to still be here whenever 'somebody' looked for the clues years down the road, right?"

"Yeah, someplace permanent, someplace safe."

"Kinda rules out boats then, doesn't it?" Mara concluded.

"Good point. Churches then."

"But most of the churches in the city have been around at *least* since Rockefeller's time, if not decades before. Which one would he have used?"

"Well it would have had to be some place that A: he had access to, and B: he felt some special connection to…"

"Wait a second. We've been looking at this all wrong."

Jon raised an eyebrow. "What do you mean?"

"Okay, we've been thinking that "her" is a personification of a great building or vessel or something." Mara smiled. "But what if it belongs to an actual person."

"An actual person? Like someone important to Rockefeller?"

"Like his mom," Mara said with a triumphant grin. "The Laura Spelman Rockefeller Carillon is the largest of its kind in the world. We learned about it in my Ecclesiastical Music course back in college. The carillon was donated by Rockefeller, in memory of his beloved mother, to Riverside Church here in Manhattan."

"Holy crap, why didn't I think of that?" Jon said, mentally kicking himself. "Rockefeller was a member at Riverside. It's where he attended services and everything while here in the city."

"It fits," Mara said. "It was important to Rockefeller for multiple reasons. And his donations and membership there would open doors for him to hide something there if he felt so inclined."

"Nice work, Mara," Jon said, giving her a fist bump. His face turned a little more somber before he added, "Michael would have been proud."

Mara took a deep breath as her eyes lifted briefly toward the ceiling. "Thus far, yeah, I think he would. Of both of us."

Jon allowed himself a quick smile before he returned the conversation to the task at hand. "Okay, Riverside Church is a big Baptist church up in Morningside Heights. I went there a few years back on one of my trips down from Harvard. Beautiful sanctuary. It's a little ways north of the cathedral we met 'Wayne' at this afternoon."

"Okay, we've figured out the first line," Mara said, shifting her gaze back toward the camera's display screen. "But what about: '*Chapel of Christ; Read right of saints and then shift thrice*'?"

"Well, I guess the church has a chapel called the 'Chapel of Christ,' or something similar." He pointed at the words on the screen. "'*Right of saints*,' maybe some sort of sculpture or painting or something. '*Shift thrice*' might be referring to moving your vantage point to see something hidden. Honestly, I don't know without seeing it. Which I guess we'll do first thing tomorrow?"

"Sound like a plan." Mara glanced at her watch. "Oh, crap, it's after two in the morning."

Jon automatically looked at his watch. *Well* after two, at that. "Alright then, let's get some shut-eye. You feel good about tomorrow?"

"Yeah. Well, I guess it's later today, but whatever. You?"

"Yup. We're gonna do this," he said, squeezing her shoulder in his hand as he stood up from her bed and started to move to his side of the room.

"Hey," she called with a quiver in her voice. He stopped, looked back at her. "Thanks."

"For what?"

"For everything. Michael always thought the world of you, spoke so highly and hopefully of you. He would be proud of you."

Jon's face twisted into something between a smile and a wince, moisture that portended tears glimmering in the corners of his eyes.

"Wow," he said, biting his lip. "Well, you're welcome. And if I couldn't have Michael by my side on this adventure, I'm glad I've got you here with me."

She smiled and nodded quietly. Then they shuffled about their late-night rituals of teeth-brushing and pajama-changing, too overwhelmed by tiredness and consumed by thoughts of the fast-approaching morning to talk any further.

Minutes later, as they both lay in their respective beds, the only light the dull illumination the moon cast underneath the curtains, Jon stared at the ceiling, his mind a pinball machine, too occupied with the thoughts bouncing around in his head to make sleep come easily. After about fifteen minutes of restlessness, listening to the soft slow breathing of Mara from across the room, Jon finally succumbed to an exhausted, dreamless sleep, praying that he would be prepared for what lay ahead.

Chapter 36

Wednesday

The tallest church in the United States, Riverside Church soars 22 stories above the streets of Morningside Heights, its Neo-Gothic form towering over even the high-rises surrounding it. The bell tower, visible from New Jersey across the Hudson River, houses the largest carillon in the world, 74 bells, including the 20-ton Bourdon, the largest tuned bell ever cast, rung to indicate the top of the hour for the hundreds of thousands living within earshot. This impressive, record-shattering carillon was named the Laura Spelman Rockefeller Memorial Carillon after the tremendous sum of money that her son, John D. Rockefeller, Jr., had donated to fund the church's construction. The deep resounding bass of the Bourdon rang overhead as Jon and Mara approached the entrance to the church, reminding them that, it already being eleven o'clock, they had gotten a rather late start.

Not wanting to deprive themselves unnecessarily of sleep or food, both of which would be needed for the mental hurdles they would have to tackle and for any more physical challenges – like evading Ramirez or dangling off the ledge of another Manhattan icon – they had slept until 9:00. Following a hearty breakfast at Lindy's, they had taken the Number 1 line north to the 125th Street Station, a journey of nearly one hundred blocks that had eaten up the rest of their morning. If Rockefeller's clues had remained hidden for the past seventy years, they could afford to stay hidden a few more hours while Jon and Mara prepared properly for their pursuit, they had surmised.

Once inside the imposing structure, the engine roar and horn honk and hustle and bustle of typical New York life dissolved away. The hallway Jon and Mara walked down seemed to be in a world of its own, a passageway between the secular and the sacred, between the stressful chase of this life and the reflective peace in the promise of the next. Down the hallway, and past the information desk, they climbed a stone staircase, following signs for Christ Chapel.

At the top of the stairs, two memorial placards set into the wall caught their attention. One was in memoriam for Rockefeller because of his "generous gifts" that "made possible the construction and endowment of this edifice" and his "personal devotion to the work of the church as a member, teacher, and trustee." The second was "in loving memory of my mother," the dedication by Rockefeller himself of the bell tower and carillon that would become the trademark of the church, donated in 1930, two years before he started down the ill-fated path that had, in turn, set both Michael and his brother on their own troubled paths. Truly, Rockefeller felt a connection with this church, a place where he would not only feel compelled to confess his secrets, but where he would also feel they were safe. But, perhaps more importantly, a place that respected him enough to give him relative free reign within the building, enough freedom to create and use a hiding place to conceal his darkest secret.

When Jon and Mara finally reached the Christ Chapel, they were struck by the even more peaceful, even more reflective atmosphere that seemed to pervade within the solemn Romanesque room. Jon had been to the main sanctuary a few years before – on a weekend sojourn from his undergrad days at Harvard – and in contrast to the soaring Gothic heights and elaborate stained glass of that room, this chapel was far more subdued. Perhaps Rockefeller felt it was more genuine, more personal.

The worshippers were few at this hour on a Wednesday morning. An elderly gentleman wearing a faded brown suit sat on the end of one pew, his head bowed either in prayer or in sleep. A young couple in their early thirties admired the artistry of the altar, the woman sneaking a photograph of the beautiful carvings every once in a while, then covering her camera with her hand at her side, as though she were ashamed to be taking snapshots in this sanctified place. Jon and Mara's entrance into the room brought the total number of patrons to five.

As the newcomers slowly made their way through the dimly lit barrel-roofed chapel toward the altar, the young man glanced at them, then back at his wife, who was still snapping covert photographs of Christ and the apostles. He grabbed her hand and lightly tugged, indicating that they should see what other wonders the magnificent building held. She took one last picture as she started to back away from the altar toward the entry door, then turned around and walked hand in hand with her husband out of the chapel, leaving Jon and Mara with the nodding old man, his head still bowed in what was starting to look more like sleep than reverence. Stepping closer to the altar, Jon and Mara began to study the artistry themselves.

High above the altar, a rose window stood sentinel, the Eye of Heaven keeping watch on this holy place. The stone altarpiece itself had all the iconography one would expect from an elaborately carved altar: Christ, the apostles beatified, the cross, worshippers and seekers, angels, the hand of God, a dove descending, lambs, and open scriptures, among other symbols and decorations common to religious sculpture. Two of the figures that caught Jon's eye were pointing, motioning with their hands. One, at the top left corner, pointed to the opposite side of the altar, looking over his shoulder at his companions to see that they understood. Another, the saint standing just to Christ's left, the viewer's right, also pointed, *away* from Jesus and toward the right-hand side of the altar. *Look over there*, the miniature stone figures seemed to be saying to Jon. And the legend spanning the top of the altar, boldly chiseled in all caps and sandwiched between two sun crosses, the aptly chosen words of Jesus proclaiming the very thoughts of Rockefeller and Rickner alike: "THE TRUTH SHALL MAKE YOU FREE."

"'Read right of saints,'" Jon quoted in a whisper to Mara, still eyeing the old guy with a slight suspicion. Mara caught his glance.

"I don't think we have to worry about him. Even if he did try something, I think you could take him."

Jon returned her teasing smile and nodded. "I don't know, though. He looks like a tough character. Old folks these days, they can be feisty."

The first part of a laugh escaped Mara's lips before the echo reminded her of where she was. "So right of saints, huh? *Which* saints, though? The altar's full of 'em."

"All of them?" Jon offered. "Let's just explore." He walked around to the right-hand side of the altar, eyes fixed on the sculpted figures and scrollwork, scanning left, right, up, down, trying to find anything that might be hidden in plain view. An aperture leading to some hiding place, a lever to reveal some secret chamber holding the next clue. *Shift thrice*, the last clue had said. Shift what? Was that crucial to finding the clue, or to interpreting it? Shifting one's vantage point? Shifting some mechanical device, a primitive combination lock that would betray its secrets when properly set? He glanced at Mara, standing next to him and scrutinizing the stonework with her eyes, looking just as lost as he felt. Turning his gaze back to the altar, Jon noticed all the *other* outstretched hands of the stone figures before them. Pointing not just to the right of the altar, as Jon in his knowledge of the clue was prejudiced to notice, but left, up, down, and any combination of directions, hands pointing, questioning, beckoning in every direction, in too many directions. Was there a pattern? Perhaps some path created by the hands, waypoints to a covert location imbedded in the sculpture. Starting with Christ, the most logical starting place, Jon surmised, he followed his hands… and already ran into a problem. Both of Jesus' hands were motioning in different directions.

Jon closed his eyes, shook his head and took a deep breath. He was going about this wrong. Rockefeller didn't design the altar, just, supposedly, hid some message here. Added something, maybe, but he had to work with what he had. And if the directions to the next clue were already hidden within the sculpture, why even have *Prometheus'* clue? No, he needed to focus on the clue he had. *That* was what Rockefeller had intended the seeker to follow.

"Jon," Mara's voice came at his side, startling him. "I might be grasping at straws here, but do those look like letters to you?" He moved closer to the wall she was staring at, her fingers tracing letters in the air between her and the ornately decorated pattern at the right-hand edge of the altar.

"Letters?" he looked hard. He supposed you *could* see letters there, much as animals and faces could be seen in clouds on a summer day, but…

"Right there. Q-L-W… um, V…"

"Mara, what did you just spell?"

"Uh, 'kluh-wuv'?"

"Do you have your camera?" he asked, inspiration suddenly glimmering in his eyes.

"Yeah," she answered, taking it from her purse and handing it to him. He turned it on and zoomed in, training the lens on the section of decorative edging Mara had been pointing to. He snapped a few shots, then checked the images, zooming in the display to more closely study the artistry.

"Ingenious," he said automatically.

"What?"

"Rockefeller, or whomever he commissioned to hide this, managed to hide these letters right into the natural shape of the carvings. Look," he said, showing her the zoomed-in image. "'Kluh-wuv.'"

"How about that. What does 'kluh-wuv' mean, though?"

"It's probably in code." Jon was snapping more and more pictures, making sure he caught every square inch of the carved border from top to bottom. He fished a pad of paper and a pen from his backpack and placed both of them on the rail of the prayer kneeler before them. The two of them went through every picture and wrote every letter they found in its corresponding position on the original border. Two lines of letters, relatively parallel and running down the side of the altar, were transferred to the paper. When Jon and Mara were satisfied that no hidden letter had evaded their detection, the letters they had found were:

PHGLHYDOXUJHOOKDVJLYHQLWVORVW
HQWRPEHGOLHVWUXWKDWJUHDWHVWFRVW

"Oh, well that helps!" Mara moaned.

Then they both jumped as the old man behind them began snoring. Loudly. Jon let out a deep breath. They were both on edge, and had all but forgotten about the old man. But at least now they had a little extra sound cover for their conversation.

"Don't forget the code," Jon said to her. "Look at the last few letters of each line. RVW. And the last clue was a rhyming couplet. It looks like a simple substitution cipher. Probably a Caesar cipher."

"A what?"

"Julius Caesar used them to relay messages to his commanders in the field," Jon explained, "encoding them to protect their sensitive contents should the message be intercepted en route. 'Shift cipher' is another name for it. You have the key, say A=16, and you would know that 'A' would be encoded as the sixteenth letter in the alphabet: 'P.' So every 'P' in the code corresponds with an 'A,' every 'Q' being the seventeenth letter, corresponds with a 'B,' and so on. It just shifts the alphabet a certain number of spaces to encode it, and you shift it back to get the original message."

"So what's the key for this one?"

"'Shift thrice,'" Jon quoted. "So instead of A=1, the message is written so that A=4. Shifting each character three spots back in the alphabet decrypts the cipher and leaves us with the original text. So the first 'P' becomes an 'M,' 'H' becomes an 'E...'"

"'G' becomes 'D...'" Mara continued.

"Exactly." He continued to scribble on the pad, rapidly deciphering the code. "Until we have this."

He held up the notepad for Mara to see.

MEDIEVALURGELLHASGIVENITSLOST
ENTOMBEDLIESTRUTHATGREATESTCOST

Mara's eyebrows shot up. "Wow. That's better."

"Add a few spaces in the logical spots, and... voila!" Jon showed her the new version of the clue, holding it so it caught sufficient glow from the dim lighting around them:

Medieval Urgell has given its lost
Entombed lies truth, at greatest cost

"Urgell?" Mara inquired.

"Some province or duchy from the days of yore, I'd guess. The key word is 'medieval.'"

"What, we have to go to Europe for the next clue?" Her eyes squinted in the dim light as her mood seemed to instantly sour.

"I don't think so. Remember, everything through the lens of Rockefeller."

"Wait, isn't there a medieval art museum in Manhattan?"

"Yeah, I think that's gotta be it, Mara. The Cloisters, property donated and funding provided by..."

"I'm gonna go out on a limb here, and say 'Rockefeller?'"

"*Ding ding ding!*" Jon smiled, reminding himself to keep his voice to a whisper but exuberant nonetheless. "We have a winner. I think our next stop is where the Metropolitan Museum of Art houses their medieval collection: The Cloisters, a little ways north of here."

Mara gave Jon a confident smile before the two of them walked as casually as possible out of the chapel, through the corridors and into the bright of day. There was still a chill in the air, but somehow, their excitement had managed to warm their spirits, as they realized they were getting closer and closer to the end of their journey, to the truth that they sought, to the ability to finally breathe easily again, knowing that Michael's memory was preserved and their own lives were safe.

Climbing onto the northbound subway when it finally arrived at the platform, Jon and Mara were so caught up in their victories and in the promise of more to come that they didn't even notice the dark-clad man who got onto the train one car down from them, pretending to study the day's *Times*. But in contrast to their obliviousness of his presence, not a word or motion of theirs escaped his attention.

Chapter 37

Lunch was conducted in a considerably breezier atmosphere than that of the previous day, buoyed by their recent discoveries and tethering their hopes onto the successes of the past twelve hours. Three codes down, two to go. And then: the Dossiers, the finish line.

Mara's chicken salad sandwich was already half gone, and the juice from Jon's Philly cheesesteak sandwich kept trying to dribble down his chin until he would corral the leakage with a swipe or two of his napkin. Despite their relatively recent breakfast, the pair had voracious appetites, devouring their sandwiches and their individual bags of Sun Chips at their window seat in the small streetside café.

This far north on the island of Manhattan, the terrain grew more hilly, the streets less of the rigid grid of the rest of the borough and more organic, more natural. Jon found the lush greenery and quick-rising topography somehow soothing. It reminded him of the Smoky Mountain retreat that he and his brother had shared a few years back when Michael was finishing up his undergrad at UNC. Peace, solace, no sounds but the twittering of birds eking out their carefree existence, the placid gurgle of a mountain stream meandering down the hillside. Here, it seemed as though the ordered chaos of steel and glass, of gray and grime in Midtown was a world away, a peaceful respite granted not by the closing of a church's heavy bronze doors, but by the dropping of nature's curtain to shield this last part of the city from the hubris and avarice of man.

"It's been a long time since we heard from Dr. Leinhart," Mara said between the swallow of one chunk of sandwich and the biting of the next. "You left him a message didn't you?"

"Yeah…" Jon said uncertainly, an unpleasant realization slowly dawning on him as he first patted his pockets, then dug in his backpack until he came up with his cell phone. He pushed a button to light up the display. "Aw, crap."

"What?" Mara asked, leaning slightly across the table.

"Seven missed calls. Three messages. The first one was yesterday afternoon." He looked up at Mara apologetically. "It's been on 'silent' ever since we went into St. John's."

"Oh, geez." Mara fished her phone out of her purse. "And I've got a few as well. I *never* forget to check my phone. I guess so much has happened and we've been so darn busy…"

He nodded. "Yeah, I know. Shoot. Well, at least we have a lot to update him on now."

Mara pursed her lips, raised and lowered her eyebrows. "Yeah," she said, seemingly bearing her share of the guilt.

Jon dialed his voicemail and listened to all three of Leinhart's messages. The first was a calm, cordial, just-returning-your-call type message. The second, left early that morning, had an audible tinge of fear and worry, was more rushed, felt more nervous. In the third, Jon could hear the shaking in the professor's voice, the almost stammered voicing of concern and pleading for a prompt return call updating him and letting him know that they were alright. The time stamp on the last message was just forty-five minutes before, so Jon felt there was a reasonable chance that the good professor hadn't died of a heart attack from worry in the intervening time.

Hanging up on his voicemail, Jon dialed Leinhart's number, keeping eye contact with Mara as he counted the rings in his ear. One. Two. The professor picked up halfway through the third ring, the sound of the line connecting followed immediately with his voice.

"Jon!" The man sounded like he was out of breath.

"Professor."

"Oh, thank God, you're alright," Leinhart burst in before Jon could say anything else. "I've been worried sick about you both." A brief pause, followed by, "Mara's still okay, too, right?"

"Yes, yes, Professor, we're both fine." Jon raised his eyebrows and rolled his eyes slightly at Mara, who giggled despite herself. "I'm afraid our search took us inside a church yesterday and, in all the excitement, I completely forgot to turn my ringer back on. Sorry for making you worry."

Distortion on the other end as Leinhart exhaled into the mouthpiece. "You don't know how worried I've been, Jon. I've discovered some pretty freaky stuff about your Mr. Blumhurst. I called in a favor to an old army buddy of my dad's. He's in his eighties now, but he served in the same outfit that Blumhurst did. Told me about the day Blumhurst was supposed to have died, and that something didn't add up, but every question he and his compatriots asked were stonewalled by their superiors.

"So Blumhurst's death was faked by the Army?" Jon asked, lowering his voice to a whisper as he glanced around the room for spies that weren't there.

"That's the way it looks. And if that's the kind of firepower you guys are going up against… I've been absolutely terrified for you both. For me, too. You realize you just about gave me a coronary?"

"Sorry, Professor. The excitement that distracted me…" Jon caught Mara's glance. "Distracted both of us. Well, for the most part anyway."

Jon brought the professor back up to speed – using code and euphemisms when addressing sensitive parts that might make any inquisitive ears in the café perk up and pay closer attention – telling him about the missing microfilm at the library, the chase with Ramirez, the meeting with Catherine Smith, the stolen envelope, the meeting with Wilkins, the return of Rockefeller's journal entry, and all their clue-finding thus far.

"We figure we've got about two more clues to go before we find the Dossiers," Jon said when he had finished the recap. "And then it's all over."

"You sound so jovial, Jon. If these guys are backed by the Army – or as this Wayne guy alleges, the CIA – you'd better believe they're not going to sit idly by while you ruin the grand cover-up they've kept going for all these years. I'd watch your backs more than ever, Jon. The closer you get to the Dossiers, the closer you're probably getting to danger. I'm particularly worried about this Wayne guy. It sounds like some elaborate trap to me. Have you had any contact with him since he gave you the journal?"

Jon paused, furrowing his brow. "No, sir, now that you mention it, we haven't."

Leinhart grunted on the other end. "I'd be awfully careful about who you trust Jon. Awfully careful."

"We will, sir. We'll keep you updated on anything else we find out."

"I'll keep working this end. And keep your phone on vibrate at the very least."

"Will do, Professor." Jon grimaced. "Sorry about before, and thanks."

Chapter 38

Enrique Ramirez, wearing a dark green sweatsuit, a matching stocking cap, and black wraparound sunglasses, walked
on grass-straddled paths through the park, the birds' singing
and chipmunks' chattering hardly registering in his ears. He
was pretending to shoot photographs of the area with a cheap
disposable camera, walking, stopping, looking around like a
tourist, walking some more. Pacing himself. Looking inconspicuous. And despite all of this seemingly intricate fakery for
the benefit of the other park visitors this afternoon, Enrique's
mind was miles away from the task immediately at hand. He
was focusing on the big picture.

He could hardly believe the audacity of Greer's plan. To
get *them* to do the legwork for them, to get *them* to find the
unfindable: the Dossiers that Rockefeller had hidden so well.
To gain their trust and exploit it for the inexorable gain of the
Division. And he could hardly believe he had been sidelined
in this, the most important hour of the Division's seventy-year
operation. *He* was the most skilled and experienced agent they
had. He couldn't stop kicking himself for botching the laptop
retrieval back in Washington, and yet he realized that, had he
succeeded in killing Jonathan Rickner, the Division would be
back to Square One in its search for the Dossiers. But despite
his inability to be the point man for this mission, Ramirez was
still a major player, and he would make sure everything went
according to plan.

No more mistakes.

Regardless of what had happened the previous weekend at
that apartment, Enrique knew beyond the shadow of a doubt

that he was a high-quality soldier, the kind of combatant that his country would have decorated with medals upon medals – if they had recognized he was still alive and in her service. But he had never done his job, either in the military or for the Division, because of the awards and recognition. Sure it felt good to have one's accomplishments, one's selfless service, recognized, but ultimately, it was his unyielding patriotism that carried him through each mission. Like most of the nation's career soldiers, he believed that his service in defense of his country was the most important thing he could dedicate his life to. And Enrique had dedicated his life to his country twice over.

Yet, at least by his standards, he *had* made a mistake. And that mistake had relegated him to an unofficial observer's post for the final reclamation of the Operation Phoenix Dossiers. And, in truth, it was as though the fates themselves had conspired to bring him to this point, mistakes and all. For, as Greer observed, he had already encountered Jonathan Rickner in the apartment; thus, he would never work as the agent of subterfuge that this mission called for. Perhaps he wasn't as subtle as Wilkins. He was a great killing machine, but gaining the trust of someone he would ultimately kill would probably have been a struggle. Yet at the same time, had he not made his mistakes, had he not been given a reprieve from field work in anticipation of the new post-Dossiers regime that he would usher in for the Division once Greer took his retirement, Ramirez would be on another assignment, somewhere, and thus unable to shadow Wilkins and his marks. And thus, he would have been completely unaware of the events that had unfolded in the past twenty-four hours here in New York, and the shocking implications they held for Ramirez, for the Division, and for the integrity of this mission.

He checked the GPS tracking device he'd procured from Division headquarters once more, and shook his head. He would have to call it in. If what he had seen and heard panned out, if what the tracking device was displaying wasn't a glitch of some sort, then there was a definite threat to the mission that Greer had failed to take into account. An element that could destroy them all. But he couldn't call prematurely. To make this sort of allegation, then to be proven wrong... No, he wasn't wrong. But he had to make sure of his proof if Greer were to believe him. And so he found himself here, trailing two very unsuspecting people as they made their way north through the park.

Ramirez moved past a copse of beech and ash trees to see a brown and white edifice, at once imposing and peaceful, rising from the hilltop ahead, perched like a monastery overlooking the surrounding countryside. He glanced to his left, caught sight of the Hudson River shimmering in the sunlight through the trees. He was near the center of Fort Tryon Park, one of the largest and most beautiful parks in Manhattan. Lingering again briefly while he maintained his safe distance, he then followed his quarry up the hillside toward the medieval-looking building, watching Jon and Mara enter one of the side staircases to the entrance to the museum known as The Cloisters.

Chapter 39

Climbing the narrow stone stairway that wrapped around The Cloisters complex, Jon felt as though he were climbing to an actual medieval monastery, nestled in the Pyrenees or the Alps, its residents sequestered in time and space for their holy purpose. The surrounding park, like the building itself and much of the collection within, had been donated by John D. Rockefeller, Jr. He had even purchased and preserved a hundred acres of the New Jersey Palisades across the Hudson River, so as to ensure developers would be unable to spoil the pristine view. Rockefeller had commissioned Frederick Law Olmstead, Jr., the landscape architect whose famous father had designed Central Park, to work his magic on the 67-acre plot of land that would become Fort Tryon Park, a private estate that had belonged for decades to various members of the city's elite, a plot of land that Rockefeller, as a member of the elite himself, was giving back to the American people. Everything about the area – from the architectural beauty to the surrounding greenery to the placid drift of the Hudson – was orchestrated to create an unshakeable feeling of tranquility, a retreat from the world. Yet another location Rockefeller would have felt safe for his secrets to find their final resting place.

The Cloisters was largely constructed from disused monasteries and other ecclesiastical buildings from the twelfth century through the fifteenth, brought over from Europe and reassembled right there in the park, sometimes stone-by-ancient-stone. Even within the building, doorways, stairwells, and frescos from various ruined churches around western and central Europe made appearances, complete with placards identifying their origins, the very bones of the museum as much an exhibit as the tapestries, reliquaries, and manuscripts that it housed. Spanning four centuries and much of Europe's lands, the medieval-themed collection had a tremendous amount of diversity in medium, artistry, and design. And somewhere in all that vast collection, an artifact from Urgell held the next clue.

After paying their admission fee, Jon and Mara grabbed a guide map apiece, scanned it, and – seeing how relatively undetailed it was with regard to individual pieces of art – headed to the bookshop to pore through the official guidebooks to the museum. There were several different books pertaining to the collection. Jon took one, Mara another, both heading straight to the index.

"Urgell!" Jon exclaimed in a subdued tone, cognizant of the shoppers and staff around the store. Mara looked at his book as he flipped back to the page the index had indicated. When he saw the image on the page, he turned his face to Mara, a triumphant smile in place.

"A tomb," Mara said, matching his smile as the words of Rockefeller's last clue clicked in place with the photograph of the medieval tomb from the Catalonian province of Urgell.

"It's in the Gothic Chapel," Jon said, already closing the book and hurriedly replacing it on the shelf.

Mara placed her book back in its spot as well. "Another chapel."

"It's good for what ails ya," Jon quipped as he checked his bearings on the map and charted the quickest path to the Gothic Chapel. "This way," he motioned as they exited the gift shop.

Jon found himself wishing he could spend more time in this building. The sense of peace, of quiet, was insatiably attractive to him right now. The chaos that had gripped his life for the past week was unrelenting, and he longed for the ability to just *be*. He felt sure that soon it would all be over, that the chasing after elusive truths and running from the wraiths of the Division would soon come to a close. If all went according to plan, he would have plenty of time to breathe. And if it didn't turn out like he hoped... well, having time to breathe easy wouldn't matter much if he couldn't breathe at all.

He pushed the thought out of his head as he led the way out of the building and into the afternoon sunlight. He had arrived in one of the five cloisters for which the museum was named, the enclosed pavilions housing gardens, fountains, and other landscaping elements designed to inspire and encourage quiet reflection of the soul. But with a bullseye on their backs and their own goal nearly within reach, neither Jon nor Mara could summon either the quiet of mind or the reflection of spirit that the admittedly beautiful cloister attempted to evoke.

The pair reentered the building after crossing the cloister, the blanch of the stone hallway draining something from their eyes that the lively green and blue of the outside had stirred. Jon motioned with his head, and they continued toward the chapel, steering around other patrons without missing a step. A few moments later, they caught their first glimpse of the chapel through the colonnade before them, the upper walls rising into view, the floor of the chapel itself a story below. The columns edged the balcony that overlooked the somberly reverent room, an air of spiritual mystery present despite the fact that the chapel was technically an architectural and artistic museum, not a house of worship, although most of the artifacts within had originally been constructed for ecclesiastical purposes. The stonework was darker, more somber, more sobering. The sun's rays illuminated the room through ancient stained glass, the windows lining the right-hand wall and forming a semicircle around where the altar would be. But no altar graced this chapel. Save for a few statues keeping watch at the far end of the room, the hollowed sanctuary was full of tombs. Sepulchers of lesser nobility from medieval Europe lined the walls, with more positioned down the center of the room. No velvet cordons or green carpet to distinguish this as a museum; this was, to all accounts, a crypt. The perfect place to lay one's darkest secrets to rest.

Almost immediately, Jon caught sight of what looked to be the tomb they were looking for, set into a shallow alcove on the left-hand wall and distinctly recognizable from the guidebook. It consisted of three tiers: at the top, an elaborately detailed relief depicting the decedent's funeral service; in the middle, the sarcophagus lid itself, was an effigy of the deceased count wearing stone robes and looking pious, surrounded by a sea of mourners; and below, the twelve Apostles stood in a line on the side of the coffin itself – six on each side of the centrally enthroned Christ, each in his own separate compartment like miniature altars to the beloved saints. It was almost as though the Apostles were laying claim to the precious soul that once resided in the corporeal form entombed within. Or perhaps guarding something else, something that the artisan centuries back never could have fathomed would be hidden inside. While the whole monument was beautifully and artfully carved, the ravages of time were apparent: surfaces worn dull by the elements and by the oils of countless hands, missing fingers, obscured letters, even saints whose heads had been broken off. Broken, but beautiful.

"There. C'mon," Jon said with an excited wave of his hand as he started to descend the stairs to the side. He and Mara reached the bottom floor and doubled back into the room, passing a middle-aged Arabic couple and their teenage son who were just leaving the chapel. They were now alone in the room.

" 'Sepulchral monument of Ermengol VII, Count of Urgell,'" Jon read from the display next to the stone coffin. "Sounds like we've got our tomb."

"'Ermengol'?" Mara repeated. "I would've hated to be him in school."

Jon stared at the tomb, at the stone angels and saints who watched over the deceased Count. Actually, many of them were headless, casualties of the ravages of time, abuses of war, and recklessness of humanity. Jon squatted next to the monument and began to inspect the carvings along its side. "Entombed within, right? But how do we get in? Surely we're not just supposed to take a crowbar to the lid right here in the museum?"

"Maybe there's some sort of secret lever or something?"

Jon looked at her. "I think you've been hanging out with Michael and me too much."

Mara shrugged. "Hey, government conspiracies, military cover-ups, Rockefeller's codes hidden all around Manhattan, I don't think a good old-fashioned secret lever is too much of a stretch."

Jon laughed. "No, I suppose not. Alright then, if I were a secret lever on this puppy, where would I be hidden?"

"This is a priceless piece of art, right?"

"Yeah, so?"

"So it would have to be hidden so not even the curators would suspect anything."

"Good point. So maybe the cracks and gaps left by your secret lever have been... My God, Mara."

"What?" she asked, squatting down next to him.

"When you're right, you're right," he said, pointing to what looked to be some sort of stone-colored cement filler around the edges of one of the foot-tall Apostles that lined the sepulcher's side. He wouldn't have noticed it had he not been looking for this exact Apostle: Peter, the disciple who had so infamously denied knowing or being associated with Christ three times at the Crucifixion – out of the same fear of the horrible consequences that Rockefeller himself must have felt. And, like Rockefeller must have dreamed of for himself, Peter was granted forgiveness for his hiding the truth out of fear and cowardice. Peter was easily recognizable by the keys he held – the keys to heaven that tradition dictated had been given to him, spurring the notion that the first person one meets when arriving in heaven is St. Peter as the realm's gatekeeper. "You want to do the honors of pushing the secret button?"

Mara beamed. "Sure." She placed her fingertips to the cold stone chest of the figure, took a deep breath, and pushed. It gave a fraction of an inch and stopped. When she released the pressure, the saint clicked back into place. "Well, crap," she said.

"Maybe it's supposed to be pushed in conjunction with something else. Otherwise it might be too easy for someone studying it or whatever to push it in without knowing what they were doing."

"Like what?"

Jon studied the line of saints again. "Like another saint. Like this guy," he said, pointing to another stone effigy that had a similar dusting of the filler around its exterior, the dusting once again so fine and close to the original color that Jon wouldn't have noticed it had he not been looking for a seam around this exact Apostle – the one holding his traditional symbolic emblem of a carpentry square, indicating his pre-calling profession as a builder. Thomas, the disciple whose famous demand to put his hands in the wounds of the resurrected Christ before he would believe that Jesus had truly risen – a request that he was soon afterward granted before he fell on his knees before Christ in penitence and was also granted forgiveness and more – had given the English language the idiomatic "Doubting Thomas." Jon chuckled softly to himself. These would be the disciples Rockefeller would have sympathized with: men who were endowed with a great privilege, screwed up royally, and were offered a second chance.

"On three?" Mara said, her fingertips already placed on the chest of her stone figurine.

Jon nodded.

"One, two, three." Jon and Mara pushed against the ancient stone, the filler crumbling with their efforts, the sound of stone grinding against stone resonating from within the monument. After the figures had tilted backward about two inches, a loud click, like the cocking of a gun, emanated from the tomb as the saints locked into their reclined positions. Half a second later, another click sounded, accompanied with another sound of stone rubbing stone, this one high-pitched and quick.

Jon and Mara's eyes met, speaking surprise, excitement, and triumph. Then they both started looking for what had changed, what "hidden chamber" had opened up, revealing the clue they sought. Mara checked one end of the tomb, Jon the other, both coming up short. He peered underneath the tomb, between two of the three recumbent stone lions that held the tomb off the ground. Just behind the depressed effigies of the saints, a small panel had opened, just large enough for Jon to fit his hand inside. He plunged his eager fingers into the aperture, fumbling around until his hand found a small tablet of stone, loose and resting inside the hollowed interior of the compartment. Withdrawing it, he looked at it and recognized the now-familiar couplet style of clue-leaving Rockefeller seemed to have favored.

"Got it," Jon said with a satisfied smile, looking up at Mara from his position on the ground. Then looking past her, to the columned balcony above. To the uniformed security guard who was glaring at them, two-way in hand.

"Hey, you two!" he shouted down at them. "Stay right where you are."

Chapter 40

Mara's eyes widened as they met Jon's. The jig was up.

Jon leapt to his feet and tucked the piece of stone in his pants pocket. They couldn't be detained. Not now. Not when they were so close. Not when they were on the hit list of a squad of government assassins. A night in lock-up could be their last night alive. They had to get out of here, alive and free.

The guard had briefly disappeared from view when descending the stairs, but was now approaching them, calling in his position – and the possible vandalism of the artwork by the two patrons he was currently approaching – on his walkie-talkie. He was about Jon's height, but with a slightly heavier build, a heavy born not of donuts and neglect but of hard work at the gym. His eyes held a determination that those of the beleaguered Rockefeller Center guard had not. And there was enough staff on duty in the museum to verify – or blow holes in – any story Jon might try to concoct. He couldn't take any chances with trying to bluff his way out of this one, but what he would have to do instead would be taking an even greater chance.

One shot. Make it count.

"I dropped my cell phone," Mara started, stopping her fabrication when she saw the guard's eyes flit to the monument, widening in surprise as they registered the depressed saints, flitting back to Jon and Mara under furrowed brow. Then he started to move the walkie-talkie back up to his mouth, and Jon leapt into action.

"Hey!" shouted the guard as Jon slammed his shoulder into the guard's chest, his hand grappling for the radio. The guard fell backward onto the floor, landing hard on his backside, wincing in pain as the impact with the cold stone floor shot up his spine. Clutching the guard's walkie-talkie, Jon ran up the stairs, Mara following close on his heels. Shouts of *Stop them!* from behind, out of sight, went largely unheeded, as most of the tourists and non-security museum staff were neither equipped for nor desirous of a potentially violent encounter with the two fugitives. Also working in Jon and Mara's favor was the fact that the facility seemed to be short staffed today, perhaps owing to the strand of flu that seemed to be making its way through the northeast the past few weeks. But, Jon realized, those lucky breaks didn't guarantee their escape; it only made the seemingly impossible slightly less so.

Once up the stairs and out of sight of the Gothic Chapel, Jon became conscious of every security camera that he saw, and many more that he didn't, the all-seeing vision of some thousand-eyed mythological beast from whose stone belly he and Mara were desperately trying to escape.

Pushing through a set of doors, they found themselves back outside in the sunlight, the columned porticos on all four sides of the cloister looking far too much like prison bars. Like the ranks of some impenetrable army come to hold them captive until Ramirez or whomever else the Division saw fit to send their way could come take their potshot at them, sitting ducks as they would be. Jon shoved the oppressive thought from his mind, using it to drive him onward and discarding it before his fear could paralyze him, becoming a self-fulfilling prophecy.

Turning the corner, they nearly bowled over a tour group being told about the columns, fountains, and other items of historic and artistic significance, treasures to which the two fugitives didn't even give a second glance as they cut a path through the crowd.

The pair darted across the plaza, through another set of doors and into the stone interior of the building, the arched hallways evoking more images of the intestinal tract of the great all-seeing rock beast whose labyrinthine bowels presented enough of a challenge without the guard who now pursued them through these corridors, without the shouts of fear that echoed inside Jon's head. As the doors were closing behind them, Jon caught a glimpse of the guard, red-faced with exertion and with anger, entering the cloister, looking left, right, then seeing the still-closing doors. He ran through the pavilion after them, alerting his colleagues as he shouted *Stop*, a cry Jon and Mara didn't care to heed.

"Keep going," Jon said, his breath trying to catch in his throat as he forced the words out. He and Mara picked up the pace, their brisk run turning into a full-fledged sprint. They slid and nearly fell into one another as they rounded the corner in front of the entry hall. Then they consciously slowed their pace as they passed between the two solidly built guards waiting on either side of the hall.

The walkie-talkie in Jon's hand squawked as a voice came through. "What's the ten-twenty on those vandals, Carl?" Damn. Somebody was looking for them. He glanced at the guards he'd just passed. They seemed oblivious to the sound coming from his radio – probably assuming it had come from their own units. To the right of the front desk was the back entrance they'd arrived through. Left led to the main entrance. Jon decided to take a risk. He grabbed Mara's wrist and yanked her to the left, using his eyes to ask for her trust, which the resigned expression in hers said she understood. He knew what he was doing. Or at least, he hoped he did.

"I've just sighted them," Jon huffed into the walkie-talkie in his best imitation of Carl's voice once he was halfway down the stairs, praying that his winded breathing wouldn't give away his bluff. "Heading out the back entrance. The girl's wearing a white sweater, guy's in a light green windbreaker." Mara shot Jon a look, her parted lips smiling even as they sucked in all the oxygen they could. The wardrobe he had falsely reported was a far cry from Mara's vibrant red long-sleeved blouse and Jon's navy blue jacket. Their footsteps on the stone beneath them produced an impressive clamor, echoing nowhere louder than in their own ears, each reverberation another footstep of the guards who were surely closing in on them. Unless they went for the bone Jon had thrown them.

The detour that Jon had yanked Mara on, the route that flashed in his memory like a photograph from his cursory examination of the map just minutes before, avoided the back entrance altogether, instead taking them down the stairs, past the bag check, and through a tunnel before finally exiting into the sunlight. They slowed down right before reaching the bag check desk, sure that a pair of young people running out of the museum at full tilt might throw up some red flags, even if their dark clothing was miles away from the description Jon had offered them.

After powerwalking past the bag check station – only now aware of his luck at coming in the side entrance and not being forced to check his backpack with the attendant when entering the museum, an oversight on the staffers' part that now seemed like a godsend – and down the long hallway of stairs, Jon pushed the door to the outside open and breathed deep the cool spring air, the air of freedom. Almost.

They picked up the pace again, jogging at a reasonably fast clip, when they heard the door behind them fly open, slamming against the doorstop as the red-faced guard, Carl, shot into the daylight. Blinking once, twice, he swiveled his head around quickly as though it had three settings: left, right, and forward, jerking between each in a split second. Over his shoulder, Jon could see that the guard had sighted them, shouting unintelligibly from behind and starting after them.

"Crap! He's still on our tail," Jon said as he accelerated across the street, Mara following his example. She had a fearful look in her eyes that reminded Jon of a cornered animal, the feral survival instinct that all the civilization in the world couldn't drive from the human race. And he wasn't sure that his expression was any more comforting.

Jon chanced another look over his shoulder. Thankfully, Carl didn't yet seem to have the rest of the guards rallying behind him, perhaps because the rest of the museum still needed guarding – and this could have theoretically just been a distraction so a second party could abscond with a greater prize – or perhaps because Jon's theft of the guard's radio had robbed him of the ability to describe the situation and the nature of the incident, something which Jon knew no one, save he and Mara, had any real idea of. But despite the apparent reluctance of the rest of the guards to join in the chase, it wouldn't take them long to begin their own pursuit. Now, though, Carl was on Jon and Mara's heels – keeping pace with them, not gaining, not falling behind, but the stitch in Jon's side told him that this wouldn't end well unless they mixed things up a bit.

"We... need to split up," Jon huffed between deep breaths of much-needed air. "Meet back... at the same spot... in Central Park?"

Mara nodded quickly, nervously as they approached an immediate fork in the path. "Be careful."

"You too," Jon said. They hit the fork, Mara turning left, back toward Fort Tryon Park, Jon turning right toward the road. He slowed his pace slightly, hoping to entice the guard to follow him and leave Mara to escape unharassed. A few seconds after the pair had parted ways, Jon chanced a look over his shoulder. The guard hesitated briefly, unsure, then turned to his right to follow Jon. Jon sighed between breaths, immediately wishing he hadn't, as his cramp worsened.

The path headed downhill. Steep, almost treacherously so. A makeshift stairway with narrow, uneven steps led down, down to his salvation, to his getaway.

The street.

A taxi waited at a traffic light. The flashing *Don't Walk* signal indicated that the light would change soon, that the taxi would be driving away, that his window of opportunity, of escape, was closing fast. And each step he took, trying to clear as many stairs as possible without breaking his ankle with a poorly aimed landing, each step required him to slow down, to navigate, to be careful. Given, Carl had to slow down, too, but Carl had backup. Carl wasn't on the run. Jon was alone and in flight. And his only ticket out of there seemed to be taunting him, the precarious descent preventing him from reaching his destination in time.

The light turned green. The traffic was too light to expect another taxi to come by in time. The taxi began to move south.

Jon saw his chance. The stairs continued down the hillside to the street. But so did the hillside itself, now running adjacent to the stairs. Jon chose the hillside, leaping off the path and scrambling down the dirt slope to the street.

Feet hitting asphalt, he ran in front of the yellow car and threw his palms in front of him, beseeching the taxi to stop. The vehicle screeched to a halt just inches away from Jon's kneecaps, the driver leaning out of his window to yell at him in typical New York cabbie vernacular. Jon ran around the side of the cab and hopped in the back, greeted with continued abuses about his mental capacity and the night-time profession of his mother. Jon responded by tossing three twenties over the front seat.

"145th Street Station, and step on it!" Jon shouted.

The cabbie eyed the money lying where it had fallen on the seat, snatched it up, and put the car back into gear.

"You got it, boss," said the instantly congenial driver as he gunned the engine, leaving behind an irate Carl, who was just breaking through the trees and stepping onto the sidewalk, empty-handed.

All the way to the 145th Street Station, Jon worried about Mara, about the repercussions of their actions even *if* they both got away. With each breath that he took to refill his starving lungs, he felt increasingly grateful for each ounce of precious oxygen. Like a terminal patient savors the taste of each meal, each moment of his family's company, Jon didn't want to take a single breath for granted. His last could be just moments away.

Especially considering the sinister-purposed man who was trailing Mara at that very moment, trusting her to lead him to Jon, the Dossiers, and their inevitable deaths.

Chapter 41

Harrison Greer surveyed the city from the 102nd story observation deck of the Empire State Building. He was alone, the chilly weather and constant winds at this height keeping most of the tourists at bay. He surveyed the city, a city built by powerful men, men with names like Woolworth, Chrysler, Vanderbilt, Morgan – and Rockefeller. Men with more money than any one man would ever need. Men who thought they were above the law of the land. Somewhere in this city, Rockefeller had hidden something that was rightfully the property of the United States Government. It was a national security threat, and he, Harrison Greer, was about to find it and destroy it. With the threat of the Dossiers eliminated, Greer would have completed the overriding goal of his father and grandfather. He could leave the running of the Division – if the Secretary of State decided that there was a need to continue the Division's mandate – to Enrique Ramirez, a man who had proven his zeal for the ideological security of this country many times over. It was almost a shame that Ramirez couldn't be alongside him in these final hours, finishing the mission together and passing the torch of the Director's office on to him. But that was not Ramirez's fate. He was not a man for subtle subterfuge; he was a prime killing machine. And that was why Greer had had to rely on a new recruit, Wayne Wilkins, to be his counterpart here, to drive their quarry into the trap that the Director had set.

Greer sighed as he caught sight of the skyscrapers of the Rockefeller Center complex stabbing into the twilit sky. It was almost over now. All that remained was for Wilkins to finish his mission, and the fruit that his family had been working toward for seventy years would be ripe for the picking.

As though by some sort of telepathic link, Greer's phone began to ring, the Caller ID identifying it as Wilkins's Division-issued cell phone. Greer glanced around to ensure that he was still completely alone, and answered the phone in the middle of the second ring.

"Greer."

"Status report, sir."

"Wilkins. What's the news?"

"They're making headway, sir. It looks like your hunch was right. They might be the ones to lead us to it after all."

"I thought as much," Greer said. "So when they find the Dossiers, they're going to give them to you as an employee of the National Security Archive, right?"

"Right. They think I'm a fellow truth-seeker who has the connections to get the Dossiers into the right hands to stop the killing and bring Michael Rickner's killer to justice."

"Excellent. And they don't suspect that the reason you know about the Operation is because you're one of us?"

"No sir. In fact, I told them that Michael and I crossed paths in our research, that I was sorry to hear about his death."

Greer guffawed into the mouthpiece. "Brilliant! Tug at their friggin' heartstrings, Wilkins. Great thinking, kid."

"Thank you, sir."

"I'll hear from you again as soon as anything new develops?"

"Yes, sir."

"Excellent work, son. I look forward to great things from you."

A pause, almost imperceptible. Then Wayne said, "Thank you, sir."

The line disconnected, and Greer stared out at the horizon, the daylight slowly giving way to the oncoming night. Wayne had nearly completed his mission. Everything was going swimmingly. He leaned toward the railing, his eyes shut in silent contemplation, soaking up the cool wind on his face. And then his phone rang again.

He pulled back from the railing and looked at the Caller ID. *Ramirez.* Curious.

"Yes?" Greer answered.

Ramirez's voice was tense. "Director Greer, we've got a situation."

Greer blinked. "I just heard from Wilkins, and he said everything was going according to plan. What's this situation you're worried about?"

"The situation *is* Wilkins, sir. He's turned."

Greer shook his head in disbelief. "Ramirez, what the hell are you talking about? There's no way one of my agents would turn traitor. I make sure of that personally."

"Well, Wilkins slipped through the cracks somehow. He fooled you. Apparently, sir, he's fooled us all."

"That's a hell of an accusation to be throwing around, Ramirez. What on earth would make you think that he's turned on us?"

"He's already found a journal page from Rockefeller himself."

Greer paused. "Who did? Rickner?"

"No, sir. Wilkins. He didn't tell you about that, did he?"

Greer swallowed, his forehead growing warm despite the cold breeze that blew against it. "No, he didn't. Does he still have it, or has he sent for someone to retrieve it?"

"Neither. He gave it to Rickner."

Greer's eyes grew large. "*What?*" Depending on what it said, the journal entry could have put the ball back in the Division's court, perhaps even removing the need to use Rickner. To have this new development and not even report in about it was suspicious at best, treasonous at worst. This was Greer's operation, and keeping him in the dark about finding a direct piece of evidence from the magnate himself was beyond unacceptable.

"Secondly, his cover story wasn't a cover story at all. He told them he was an agent with the Division. Named names and everything. I've overheard them say both your name and mine since they met with Wilkins."

"This can't…" Greer wanted to curse and fling the phone off the railing, but that would serve no purpose. He needed to stay in control. He always stayed in control of himself. And he desperately needed to understand and control this situation.

"And finally, the GPS transmitter you gave him. It's active?"

Greer tried breathing through his nose. "Yeah. He *said* he dropped it in Ellison's purse."

"Where does it say they are right now?"

"Hang on a second." Greer pulled his GPS monitoring device from his coat pocket. "Washington Square, in Greenwich Village."

"Then why am I staring at her right now in *Fort Tryon Park*. Six miles from there."

Greer pulled the phone from his face, as though the device itself were as loathsome as the words coming from it. His world began to tilt on its axis. He wasn't afraid of heights, but right now, he had the worst sense of vertigo, as though every pillar he had built his life's work upon was crumbling as his plan crashed down around him. He put the phone back to his ear and replied, "No. How's that possible?"

"I figure he dropped *your* GPS transmitter in the purse of some third party who's still tooling around the city. It would appear that Wilkins is tracking Rickner and Ellison through a transmitter of his own. He's gone rogue, sir. I'm sorry."

He grabbed the railing to steady himself. Everything had been going so right, and then…

"How do you want to play this, sir?"

Greer wished it weren't true. He prayed it weren't true. And yet, Greer trusted Ramirez's judgment over anyone's other than his own. If Ramirez wasn't one-hundred percent sure Wilkins had turned, he never would have phoned in his suspicions. And, Greer realized as he stared at the GPS tracker in his hand, the proof of something terribly amiss was staring him in the face. If Ramirez said Wilkins had turned, then by God, it had to be taken care of.

"Sir?"

"It sounds like Rickner and Ellison have been given enough of a push to find the Dossiers on their own now. You take care of Wilkins. I'll take care of the Dossiers myself. Contact me on my cell when you've gotten what you can out of Wilkins."

"Consider it done, sir."

Greer hung up and gripped the railing again, glaring out into the gathering dark. He was seething. He wanted to smash something. But he had to control himself so he could regain control of the mission. He had to channel that anger toward his all-important goal.

All of his plans for the endgame now lay in ruins. The betrayal had changed the whole setup. Wilkins could have described Greer's appearance, perhaps even shown them a picture. If they spotted him, or anyone they might suspect was him, the whole enterprise could be for naught. All his carefully-laid plans, the brilliant opportunity that fate had given him in the Rickner brothers, the decades of trying to finally conquer Rockefeller's last secret; all of it was now at risk, because he trusted the wrong man. Greer had never had an agent turn before. Nor had the Division itself. The closest it had come was Roger Blumhurst, who had, like Rockefeller himself, taken the coward's way out, neither having the strength to do what was required of him, nor the traitorous balls to go all the way and make public what he knew. But if Ramirez was to be believed,

then Wayne Wilkins had not only fallen off the path and protocols that Greer had dictated, he had also chosen to ally himself
against the Division and all that it stood for. Including the protection of this great nation from the horrible truth of Operation
Phoenix. Wilkins was now an enemy combatant in this war,
and Ramirez was better suited than anyone to tie up this very
loose end.

Greer turned his mind to the problem immediately at hand:
reclaiming the Dossiers and killing Jon and Mara without being detected and scaring his quarry off. He thought back over
what Ramirez had told him over the phone. He thought about
Rockefeller and his hidden secret. His mind honed in on a brilliant possibility that would all but negate any further betrayals
that Wayne might have orchestrated. A wicked smile crawled
its way across Greer's face. Not only would it work, but the revised ending to his plan was decidedly poetic. As well it should
be.

Within a matter of hours, the Dossiers would be safely in
his hands; Wilkins, Rickner, and Ellison would be dead; and
the truth would forever be safe from the scrutiny of the public
eye. Seventy years of searching were about to come to a head;
and Greer would have a ringside seat. He was director, screen-
writer, and lead actor all rolled into one. And after it was all
finished, he could retire and live out his final healthy days in
paradise with his beloved Lucinda.

As he turned back toward his hotel to gather what he needed for the final showdown, he lifted his eyes skyward.

*This is it, Dad, Grandpa. The end to your life's work. This
one's for you.*

Chapter 42

Upon arriving at the 145th Street Station, Jon thanked the cab driver, dove into the station, swiped his MetroCard and boarded the southbound train. The guard might have gotten a look at the taxi's number, a potential problem if he were to call it in to the police, so Jon had opted to just drive to safety, then let the anonymity of public transit ferry him the rest of the way. A nervous train-ride later, Jon emerged into the waning green-filtered sunlight of Central Park. Entering the park, he meandered along the paths, the sense of urgency gone, the fear that he would arrive at their agreed meeting place to find it inexorably devoid of Mara all too real. He tried to call her, but her cell phone went straight to voicemail. If something had happened to her… He couldn't bear the thought, especially considering how he had abandoned her in the park. Not abandoned, perhaps, but Jon knew he would feel that way if she got captured – or worse.

Eventually, realizing that Mara might end up waiting for *him* in the clearing, going through the same guilty routine he had envisioned himself dealing with, he made his way to the small clearing just off the jogging path. Upon his arrival, his feelings of worry and guilt came rushing back. If enough time had transpired for him to be worried about Mara waiting alone, then surely she should have had time to get here by now. At least, if she hadn't been detained…

Jon tried to push the thought out of his mind, giving the area a quick visual check to ensure that he was as alone as he needed to be. Satisfied, he fished from his pocket the small stone tablet he had taken from Ermengol's sepulcher, sat down on the grassy patch beneath his feet, and began to study the next clue, a task he had all but forgotten about in his flight from the museum, a task he felt could distract him from his worry about Mara.

The tablet was small, only about the size of Jon's index, middle, and ring fingers pressed together. Jon was amazed that it hadn't broken during his flight, immediately grateful for small blessings. The couplet inscribed on it resembled the one from the Prometheus statue, written in plaintext, presumably because it wasn't hidden in plain sight like the one at Riverside Church. It read:

> Hughes' Folly: the penitent pray
> The Saint of my plight eyes the way

Jon unconsciously mouthed the words as he read it a second time. Hughes' Folly. He knew this one. It was on the tip of his tongue. Why wouldn't it come? It referred to a church, he remembered, but anyone could have figured that out with the inclusion of words like "penitent," "pray," and "saint." Why couldn't he remember it?

Jon tilted his head back and looked skyward, a jet drawing its frozen contrails across the stratosphere, a line of white across a once-blue sky, steadily bleeding toward the orange of sunset. He knew why the name of the church wouldn't come. He was distracted. It would soon be dark, and still no Mara. He gave a little moan, rubbed the heels of his palms against his eyes as though to crush out this reality and wake up in another, one where the government wasn't plotting against its citizens, where he wasn't being chased by assassins, where Mara wasn't in lock-up somewhere. Where Michael was still alive.

As the jet disappeared behind the branches of the trees overhead, Jon found himself staring at the stream of frozen condensation left in its wake. Michael was gone, out of sight, but his memory, his impact on Jon's life and the lives of countless others, lived on. And Jon wasn't sure if that was a good thing or a bad thing right now. His feelings hung suspended in oblivion and numb to their surroundings, like so many ice particles dangling impotently miles above the earth. For the time being though, Jon surmised, a lack of any powerful – and likely overwhelming – emotion was probably for the best. Once the chase was over, once the task was done and the bullseye off of his back, then Jon could mourn his brother's death, could celebrate the life he had lived and the influence he had had. Then, and only then, could he finally begin to pick up the pieces of his life, to heal the hole in his heart that Michael's death had left, a hole Jon could not even start to acknowledge right now, for fear of the debilitating effect it would likely have on him. And if he didn't watch himself, he might end up joining Michael before he'd even had a chance to mourn him.

Saint. That word was key, he felt. But why? Jon's mind was working in slow motion, as though it had been dipped in tar, addled by some depressant he hadn't taken. Saint. Sometimes churches were named after saints. Saint of my plight. Rockefeller's plight. What saint would that be? But "Hughes' Folly," *that* pointed to the church, Jon was sure of it, even if the church's name continued to evade him. So the saint was inside the church? A particular saint. Inside the church. At the church where Jon worshipped, they didn't have saints in the church. Saints were respected but not revered in Protestant churches. Not in Protestant churches. Which left Orthodox churches and Catholic ones. Catholic churches.

Jon smiled as his brain finally made the connection he was looking for. Hughes' Folly. Archbishop John Hughes. He had been ridiculed for the site he had chosen in the 1840s for the building of the new Catholic Cathedral of the Diocese. It was way up in the boondocks of what Manhattan was then, and some had derided the choice of location as "Hughes' Folly." But today, it was not only one of the most beautiful churches in the United States, it was also right in the middle of Midtown Manhattan. St. Patrick's Cathedral, Archbishop Hughes's supposed folly, had been built on the outskirts of the town, but less than a century later, the city had moved its epicenter north, putting the church right in the heart of one of the busiest cities on earth.

Right across the street from Rockefeller Center.

Jon leapt to his feet with excitement, wiping the grass and dirt from his jeans. And paused. He couldn't go yet. Not without Mara. He pulled out his phone again and dialed her number. Halfway through her voicemail greeting, he heard a beep from his earpiece. He looked at it, hoping it was call waiting from Mara. Instead, it was his phone shutting off. The battery was dead.

Jon scrambled for ideas on how to contact her. He could leave her a note, but someone else could find it. Maybe even Ramirez. And she wouldn't be looking for a note. Or would she? If he wasn't there, maybe she'd have the presence of mind to… But Jon hadn't looked for a message when he had arrived to find the clearing empty. Now standing, he peered around the clearing in the deepening twilight, seeing nothing obvious or obscure. She hadn't been here yet, or at least hadn't left him a note. And just as he hadn't looked for one, she likely wouldn't either.

A jogger ran past, wearing a green sweatsuit and stocking cap, barely visible through the bushes in the dwindling light. Jon thought he saw the jogger turn his head in his direction, but the young scholar couldn't tell for certain. Either way, the man kept jogging along, and Jon released the breath he hadn't realized he had been holding.

A few moments later, a crack came from nearby, a twig breaking under a furtive footfall. Jon crouched and froze. Whoever it was seemed to be doing their best to avoid being seen or heard, biding their time as the sun sank deeper into the Hudson, as daylight, Jon's ally and enemy, drowned in the west. Was it Ramirez? The cars below and behind Jon seemed to disappear. The silence hung like ice particles in the stratosphere, unmelting, unmoving, Newton's first law of motion holding it in place until an external force chose to shatter it. And *how* would it be shattered? A gunshot? A fist flying from nowhere? A shout of "Freeze!" followed by a pursuit that would end poorly for Jon, one way or the other? Jon waited, waited, waited, his feet going numb beneath him, slowly growing conscious of sharp edges cutting into his palm from the tight grip he had on the stone tablet. Slowly, quietly, he relaxed his grip, slid the tablet back into his pocket, and wiped his sweaty palms on his jeans legs.

A rustling from the bushes. Had the moment come? The nearest lamppost was far enough away, through trees and shrubbery, to cast only a nominal glow toward the darkening enclosure where Jon stood. He moved his legs, gearing his muscles to pounce, although in which direction, toward or away from his would-be captor, he hadn't yet decided. It would all depend on what sort of face emerged from the twilit shadows.

"Jon?" The voice was entirely not what Jon was expecting, and, perhaps, exactly what he should have.

"Mara?" he called back. Mara burst forth from the shadows and wrapped her arms around his neck. "What happened?"

"I… I think I was being followed," Mara started, only slightly releasing Jon from her embrace, afraid that to let go would be to lose him again. "I've been trying to ditch him. I was waiting until I was sure he was gone."

Jon swallowed. "Was it Ramirez?"

"Could've been. I didn't get that good a look at him yesterday. I was heading back here and just got a strange tingling on the back of my neck, like someone was watching me. I turned around and there was a jogger running a little ways behind me, but not too terribly close. It's New York and people are everywhere, so I didn't get too suspicious. But the feeling didn't go away, so I checked again and again. And though he was never *right* behind me, he was always there, watching. I know he was tailing me. He was just very good at not being obvious. If I weren't so paranoid I probably never would have noticed him following me. I ducked around the corner of the old dairy up further north in the park here and broke into a run to put some distance between us. I was pretty sure he lost sight of me once I ducked into the bushes, but I wasn't sure, so I waited until I figured it was safe, then I climbed through the bushes to–"

"Mara," Jon interrupted, suddenly looking very serious, "what did the guy who was chasing you look like?"

"He was wearing lots of green. Dark green. Sweatshirt, sweatpants, stocking cap. What?"

Jon had frozen, his face etched with fear. "You sure he was following you?"

"Since we split up at the park, yeah, pretty much. But, like I said, I've lost him now. Why?"

"We need to go. Now." Jon grabbed her arm and started pulling her toward the jogging track, heading south, away from the northbound green-clad jogger.

"Jon, what's going on? And where are we going?"

Jon shot a look in every direction he could think of, staring into the encroaching darkness, daring Mara's stalker to show himself. No one appeared, and Jon continued to tug.

"I'll explain on the way, but we can't stay here. We have to finish this tonight."

Chapter 43

Wayne Wilkins stared at the phone in his hand, contemplating what he'd just done. He'd lied to a superior. He was disobeying orders, subverting a mission. Nothing like the soldier he'd always been.

And he loved it.

His plan mirrored Greer's – to a point. Point the Rickner brother in the right direction, keep tabs on his progress, and eventually, he finds Rockefeller's long-lost copy of the Dossiers. And then their paths diverged. Greer's plan: take the Dossiers, kill Jon and Mara, destroy the evidence, and the powers-that-be could rest easy knowing that the truth of Operation Phoenix was buried forever. Wayne's plan: exactly what he had told Jon. Free the nation from the guilt of the past, share the truth, work through the pain, and move on. No more killing, no more lies. Ultimately, it's what Rockefeller would have wanted. It's what Blumhurst would have wanted. It's what Ed and Martha Wilkins would have wanted.

Still, he was torn. Nine years he had been the country's dream soldier. Nine years he had served the nation flawlessly, following orders and obeying mission parameters. Today, he was breaking all the rules. But then, that man, that good-little-soldier, had died in Iraq. For better or worse, Wayne was a different person now, shaped by the very forces that had wanted to harness his cold killing prowess for their own purposes.

This was a difficult path to walk. Even without the niggling doubts in his mind, the battle of what he knew to be right versus what had been drilled into his head, this would prove to be his riskiest mission yet. Unlike the splinter cell missions he had run before, he didn't have any backup this time. In fact, his backup was now officially the enemy. An enemy he'd spent the last six months learning just how dangerous they could be.

But also, an enemy whose weaknesses he now knew.

Seeing this through, making sure that Jon and Mara found the Dossiers, that they were *not* killed, and ensuring that the truth got out; the odds were stacked against him, even more so than during his Green Beret days. But any time he started to doubt, any time he started to wonder if his own mission of redemption was worth pursuing, he reminded himself of the three innocent faces that he'd fed to the lions in a windswept valley in Iraq, of the four haunting screams that ravaged his ears even now, of the faces of his mother and father, of everything he knew and loved and believed about his country, and he knew he was doing the right thing.

The mission valiant, his resolve steeled, he was finally on a path that he felt was just. He only prayed he'd be able to see it through. Because now, the Division – comprised of the only people who knew Wayne Wilkins was still alive – had become his greatest enemy.

He smiled to himself as he started to cross the street, so caught up musing about the implications of what he was about to do that he barely avoided getting rammed full-on by the black Explorer that careened out of control and onto the sidewalk. He managed to leap out of the path of the drunkenly driven vehicle, but the left front bumper clipped him as it went past, pain shooting up and down his leg.

He cursed and limped out of the way. A woman yelped in surprise from the sidewalk. Wilkins waved her off. Told everyone in earshot he was fine as he continued on his way. He was on a tight schedule and couldn't afford to waste any time with accident reports, emergency rooms, or half-hearted sympathy. Wayne didn't exist, and couldn't afford to be caught up in something like this. Especially now. His injuries were nothing life-threatening. A bruised shin, a twisted ankle, maybe. But nothing could come between him and seeing this mission through.

And then, something did.

Something hard jabbed into his ribs, but even through the clothes, he recognized it as the barrel of a Glock. Standard issue for cops, muggers… and Division agents.

"Keep walking," came the voice at his ear. It was even, cold, and instantly recognizable.

Ramirez.

Chapter 44

Illuminated from below with dramatically placed spotlights, the dual Gothic Revival spires of St. Patrick's Cathedral soared overhead, pointing heavenward in a city obsessed with the here and now. The glass and steel skyscrapers surrounding the Cathedral dwarfed it in size, but for sheer majesty and architectural wonder, St. Patrick's obliterated the local competition. The Cathedral had been here decades before the business district had moved in, representing a God who had been around for eons before Man and his worldly pursuits. Its stalwart beauty in the midst of the fast-paced utilitarianism of the buildings surrounding it served as a constant reminder of the insignificant cosmic blink that was Man and his earthly kingdoms in the face of eternity.

Across Fifth Avenue, the towers of Rockefeller Center stood proudly in testament to the ability of Man to overcome in the face of adversity, to achieve beyond the limits of what could be expected, to aspire and endure. And yet, the Center's visionary and namesake had apparently felt humbled by the presence of the Cathedral, enough to leave in its trust the final clue to the location of his most-guarded secret, his deepest shame. A building on which Rockefeller – at least publicly – had not had much influence, unlike the other locations guarding his clues. He was a Baptist, not a Catholic. The Cathedral had been consecrated when he was just five years old, decades before he had inherited the fortune and power that allowed him to use philanthropy to open the doors of the city to him. But the Cathedral had somehow beckoned to him, the house of God an omnipresent reminder of the wages of sin, of guilt for wrongs he couldn't seem to forgive himself for. And, Jon knew, he had managed to use some of his far-reaching influence to hide something very dear to his heart inside this iconic structure.

Jon had explained the couplet to Mara on the way, the "Hughes' Folly" nickname once used for the Cathedral, the reference to the "saint of my plight" – the identity of which Jon had a hunch that he was anxious to prove. As they climbed the stairs leading to the west entrance, Jon glanced across the street.

The view would have been mutual. From the posh offices of the Center's towers, Rockefeller would have had a grand view of the cruciform house of worship, but the Cathedral itself, through its intricately crafted yet majestically powerful stained-glass windows and the triple maws of its bronze doors, would have provided an excellent vantage for staring into the tormented soul of the billionaire scion. God Himself could stare through rose window eyes and turn away in sorrow at the sin and cowardice of John D. Rockefeller, Jr., a man to whom He had entrusted much, of whom much was expected. And in the unrelenting stare of those unblinking eyes, Rockefeller had felt unworthy, feeding his already insatiable guilt. Hence, perhaps, his entrusting his most important clue – the final pointer – to that particular church, an unholy sacrifice in an unsuccessful attempt to absolve himself of the regret that ate away at him till the end of his days.

Through the massive bronze doors, Jon and Mara slinked into the vast sanctuary of the largest Catholic cathedral in the United States. As visually impressive as the outside was, the interior took their breath away. The distant apse looked like some sort of frozen waterfall, the semicircular enclosure dripping its narrow windows and ribbed arches from the ceiling, a celestial cascade from the fount of heaven. The altar, though not nearly as enormous as that of St. John's, still managed to evoke a sense of awe in believer and skeptic alike. And the high vaulted ceilings, rising more than one-hundred feet above all who visited the church, made one feel small, insignificant in the face of true might. A little like Jon and Mara were feeling now, although the higher power that was currently foremost in their minds was far less benevolent or just than the God worshipped here.

Jon glanced at his watch. 8:10. The Cathedral would soon be closing for the evening, and they needed to hurry if they wanted to finish this tonight. Which they did. More than anything.

"Let's see if there's an altar or something for St. Jude," Mara whispered to Jon as they started to head to the left-hand side of the nave, the line of altars – dedicated to various saints and other important persons and events of the faith – leading from the vestibule to the transept.

"St. Jude? As in the children's hospitals?"

"Yeah. Among other things, he's the patron saint of things despaired of, people in desperate situations who don't see any way out. Rockefeller would've definitely—" Mara stopped in front of the first altar. "Bingo." The Altar of St. Jude.

Jon looked at her for a moment. "How did you know that? About St. Jude."

Mara smiled. "What? I don't ask you how you know all the random stuff you've known to get us this far."

Jon continued to look at her expectantly.

She rolled her eyes. "I volunteered at one of the St. Jude's Hospitals back in high school. They told us about the origin of the name."

"Gotcha." Jon turned his attention to the altar, studying its artistry and design. "He 'eyes the way,' huh?" The bronze statue looked up, toward heaven, to the cross that stood atop the Gothic-styled white ciborium, the ornate cover of the altar. An army of votive candles stood guard on their racks in front of the altar rail, a box for offerings positioned to one side. Jon looked up, at the archway framing the altar. No encoded symbols, no hidden chamber revealed itself to Jon's well-trained eye. And remembering his tendency to look past the obvious, like looking across the street at Rockefeller Plaza and trying to find a hidden chamber at Riverside Church, he traced St. Jude's sightline back to what its eyes were most immediately fixed upon.

"It's the ciborium," he whispered finally, pointing to the arched shelter over the statue. "On the other side, I think. Where St. Jude's eyes are looking."

Mara kept her voice to a low whisper as well, conscious of every footstep and word that echoed through the massive cathedral. "Okay, but Jon, how would Rockefeller write or hide something on a Catholic altar? That'd be sacrilege, wouldn't it?"

"Not in his mind, no. This was his part of his offering to God, his penance, so to speak. Saying that, though he was but an imperfect man, he trusted that God would, in His time, do what Rockefeller could not: reveal the truth about Operation Phoenix."

He paused while a young brunette approached the altar, lit a candle, bowed her head in a quick prayer, crossed herself, and dropped a dollar in the offering box. After she left, Jon realized he had been holding his breath, and then he continued.

"Every other place was a place that felt safe to him, right? Special in some way. This church is special because it's so beautiful and so darned close to his greatest achievement – Rockefeller Center. And where better to place it than under the eternal gaze of the Saint who was the defender of those without hope, of those in desperate situations?"

Mara twisted her lips to the side, thinking, then inhaled.

"I guess so. But how in the world are we going to get over there?" she said, eyeing the railing and the candle rack.

"We're not," Jon whispered back. "I am."

Mara raised an eyebrow at him.

"I'm a head taller than you," Jon explained, "and judging by the height of that ciborium, you won't be able to reach it."

"So I'll just stand here and keep guard?"

"Close. Your job is to distract those guys." Jon pointed a subtle finger toward the three staff members who manned the entrance area, welcoming visitors, directing them toward requested features of the cathedral, and giving any information that they may request. "And those guys," he added, indicating a pair of security guards standing on either side of the vestibule.

Mara twisted her lips some more, scrunching up one eye as she drummed up a plan. "Okay," she finally said. "I've got it. I don't know how long I can keep them busy though, so be quick."

She strolled about halfway down the nave, turned and crossed to its south side, then walked back toward the vestibule. When a pair of pillars blocked the line of sight between her and Jon, she grabbed her leg and fell to the floor, moaning loudly in pain.

Jon winced. He could hear her groaning, and its subsequent echoes, as clear as day, and he knew that countless others, from visitors enjoying the reverent atmosphere to worshippers meeting God, were distracted by it too. But then, that seemed to be adding to the diversion, the staff trying not just to help the young lady with whatever injury she seemed to be afflicted with, but also to quiet her down so as to preserve the tranquil atmosphere of the Cathedral. Two of the staffers abandoned their posts to go offer assistance to Mara, the other staff member and the two security guards turning and watching from afar.

Jon was free to do what he needed.

He opened the gate in front of the altar and crawled under the candle rack, careful not to topple the latter over and bring down on himself a rain of molten wax, red-tinted glass, and metal bars, not to mention the inevitable cacophony that would result, thwarting his attempt to discover this last clue and likely landing himself in a cell for the night. Once through, he stood, looking behind him to see the staffers crowded around Mara, who had fallen where pillars and pews blocked any view of Jon's trespassing. He stuck his head inside the altar, a place no one's head had likely been since the message had been hidden some seventy years ago. He almost felt blasphemous, sticking his own head in a place of reverence, but, he told himself, it was not for his own glorification but rather that of the truth, a noble cause that Christ Himself would surely have supported. Jon's eyes swept the inside of the front of the ciborium, where St. Jude had kept watch for these many years.

And there it was. Hard to see unless you were looking for them, but the tiny letters were unmistakable. Even with the power he normally held, Rockefeller would likely have had to befriend one of the previous archbishops to get this sort of access. Perhaps he even confessed the whole of Operation Phoenix and its cover-up to the prelate, trusting in the priestly vows to keep his secret between him and God. Jon had found Rockefeller's final clue, but he had to hurry. He couldn't hold his position, bending backward behind the candle rack with his head inside an altar in one of the country's most famous churches, without being seen – and without falling over – for long. He whipped out his phone and used its camera to snap a series of photographs, checking the screen to make sure that all of the letters showed up clearly before leaving the altar. There would be no coming back.

Satisfied, Jon pulled his head out of the opening and crawled back under the candle rack, Mara's moans still echoing across the Cathedral. Sooner or later, one of those staffers was either going to call her bluff or go elsewhere for help. Jon had to be out of there before either happened. Or before anyone *else* noticed him. Luckily, the Cathedral seemed to be somewhat empty tonight, but that luck could only last so long.

His foot snagged on the crossbar beneath the candle rack. Votive holders clinked above as his leg jostled the whole apparatus. He paused, maneuvered his foot around the bar, and scurried through, shutting the gate behind him. Safe.

Now to save Mara.

Jon walked briskly over to the south side of the nave where Mara still lay and moaned, clutching her leg as she was doted on by the embarrassed staff members.

"Donna, are you alright?" Jon said in a stage whisper as he approached where she lay.

Mara blinked in mid-moan. "Keith? It's my leg again."

"Can you move?" Then to the staffers, "Can you help me move her to one of the pews? It's just a bad muscle cramp. Marathon-gone-wrong sort of thing from last month." Jon and a man in his early thirties helped her to the nearest pew and she sat, rubbing her leg, her moans ebbing away to a gracious nothing. Jon thanked the staff members for their help and apologized profusely for all the trouble, the staffers just grateful to go back to their posts in relative peace. Mara kept breathing heavily for a few moments longer to ensure that her sudden recovery didn't come under scrutiny, then looked at Jon.

"And?"

"Your incredible performance was well worth the trouble," Jon whispered. He contemplated leaving the church and heading somewhere more private, but time was of the essence. Wherever they went might take them ultimately further away from wherever the clue pointed, and with each minute that ticked past, their enemies could be closing in on them. He looked around him, and satisfied that their eyes were the only ones around, showed her the images on his cell phone's camera.

"Another code?"

"Yeah." As Mara looked at the images, Jon pulled out Michael's notebook from his backpack and turned to a blank page.

"Can you decode it?" Mara asked as Jon started transcribing the letters from the pictures.

"I think so… Here, look."

Mara leaned over to see what he had written:

HEAETADPPKESBOPLVKFHBLHEPHIVHEZTFHALAGPWPH
GMOVMSEWPAPAKNKPEPKBHPMGOADYAFHPKNFHFTCI

"O-key dokey, then," Mara said, her eyes wide, her face moving away from the page. She massaged her hamstring so as to keep up appearances for anyone who might've been suspicious of her earlier "injury." "I've got nothing."

"Well, we know from previous experience that Rockefeller was a fan of rhyming couplets. The last two lines don't have any of the same characters, so it's probably not a monographic substitution code."

"Huh?"

"Monographic, meaning each letter in the code refers to one letter in the original message. Like the one we found in Riverside Church. This one is probably digraphic, meaning each *pair* of letters in the code refers to a specific pairing of letters in the original message."

"And you can solve digraphic codes?"

"Well, there are different types. This one, though, I'd be willing to bet is a Playfair code."

"Play *fair*?"

"Not 'play fair' two words, but 'Playfair' the one-word name, like Lord Playfair, the guy who popularized them in the 1800s. You use a keyword to create a five-by-five table of the alphabet that serves as your key."

"But five-by-five is twenty-five," Mara reminded him. "There are twenty-six letters in the alphabet."

"I know. Playfairs either put I and J together, or eliminate Q. Seeing as there's no Q in the coded message, I'm gonna guess he went with the latter."

"So what's the keyword? 'Phoenix'? 'Division'?"

"I think he would've shied away from words that reminded him of what he had done. Wait…" Jon pulled the stone table from his pocket. "What about 'the penitent pray'?"

"A key*phrase*?"

"Yeah, it'd make decryption harder if someone were to find it and try to decipher it without the keyword. 'The penitent pray' isn't in the dictionary."

"True. Okay let's try it. How do these work?"

"You start your five-by-five square off with the unique letters of your keyword, meaning that only the first 't,' 'e,' 'p,' and 'n' get in." He scribbled in the notebook. "Which gives us:"

T	H	E	P	N
I	R	A	Y	

"And then," he continued, "we fill in the rest of the alphabet. Like so…"

T	H	E	P	N
I	R	A	Y	B
C	D	F	G	J
K	L	M	O	S
U	V	W	X	Z

"And voila, we have our key. Next, we have to break the code into the digraphs:"

HE AE TA DP PK ES BO PL VK FH BL HE PH IV HE ZT FH AL AG PW PH
GM OV MS EW PA PA KN KP EP KB HP MG OA DY AF HP KN FH FT CI

"And then we use the key to translate each of those digraphs into the original. For example, H and E are in the same row on our key, so we take the letter immediately to the left of each letter, giving us T and H. A and E are in the same column, so we take the letter immediately above each, giving us E and W. And T and A are in neither the same row nor the same column, so we take the two other corners of the rectangle they would form, the corner that's on the same row as the first letter being the first of the two letters from the message, and we get E and I." Jon fell silent as he deciphered the rest of the message, Mara quietly watching on in admiration at the way his mind worked.

Jon finished writing and pointed to the page. "And the decoded digraphs look like:"

TH EW EI GH TO NM YS HO UL DE RS TH ET RU TH UN DE RM YF EX ET
FO LX LO WM YE YE ST OT HE SI TE OF MY GR EA TE ST DE CE IT

"The X's are usually superfluous, simply added to give a relative position to double letters like 'EE' and 'LL' that can't be charted in a Playfair code, so we nix them and are left with:"

The weight on my shoulders, the truth under my feet
Follow my eyes to the site of my greatest deceit

"More following the eyes?" Mara said, but Jon didn't respond. Turning her gaze from the page, she saw him staring slack-jawed and wide-eyed at Rockefeller's last riddle. "What?" she asked.

"Oh my God."

"What?" she repeated, more urgently. "You know where it is?"

"Yeah. Oh my God. Of course."

"Jon, what? Where is it? Where are the Dossiers?"

Jon stood, shoved his cell phone and the notebook back into the backpack, and grabbed her hand, starting to pull her back toward the vestibule entrance. She stood and remembered to feign a slight limp to appease the sympathetic eyes that followed them to the doors.

"Jon, just tell me already. Whisper it if you have to, but I deserve to know. Where did he hide them?"

Jon pushed open the heavy bronze door and jabbed a finger into the night, pointing across Fifth Avenue to Rockefeller Center, to Lee Lawrie's statue of *Atlas Supporting the World*, bowed on one knee by the weight of his burden. Kneeling in penitence toward the majestic beauty of St. Patrick's Cathedral.

Jon's outstretched finger quivered as he pointed toward Rockefeller Center's famous statue. His voice shook as the single word nearly caught in his throat:

"There."

Chapter 45

Ramirez threw Wayne to the floor of the dark, cinder block room. About ten feet square, it was a disused storage room for some business that – judging by the silence that pervaded the room – was closed for the night. The door they had come through was made of heavy iron, veins of rust and the peeling remnants of an ancient paint job marring its face. The dirty concrete floor was strewn with old newspapers and broken beer bottles. A single light bulb, set high into one wall, cast a flickering yellow glow over the room.

Keeping his pistol trained on Wayne, Ramirez tossed a pair of handcuffs at the prone agent.

"Cuff yourself to the pipe," Ramirez ordered, motioning to a heavy iron pipe protruding from the wall, its other end buried a foot below in the concrete floor.

Wayne pulled himself up into a crouch and complied, his own gun, phone, and GPS monitoring device having been confiscated by Ramirez en route to this tomblike chamber. Once the cuffs were in place, he turned back to face his captor. "Ramirez," he said, forcing himself to keep his tone even and free from the nervousness he was beginning to feel, "what are you doing?"

"What am *I* doing? How about what are *you* doing? You who Greer trusted with this secret assignment. You who are trying to destroy everything we've worked for."

"And what is that? Killing innocent civilians? Burying the truth?" Despite Wayne's best efforts, he couldn't help the traces of indignation that crept into his tone.

"That truth should never have happened." Ramirez began pacing angrily, stalking up and down the room in front of Wayne. "If Rockefeller and Stimson had known what the Nazis would do, they never would have helped them take power in Germany."

"I agree. But burying the truth doesn't make its consequences any less real."

"It *has* to be buried. Do you know what would happen if this got out?"

"I had the training, too, Ramirez. Yeah, I know the Division's theory. But someday it *will* get out. And then what? You gonna kill everyone who watches that news special, who reads that article, who logs on to that blog? You can't stop this, Ramirez. This skeleton has to be brought out into the open so it can finally be put to rest."

"*Into the open?* The world would be clamoring for our head!"

Wayne shrugged, maintaining his collected demeanor. "For a season, perhaps. Some saber rattling, some angry denunciations, a whole lot of apologies, but I think the most damning thing is that we continue to hide it. We continue to kill for it. And as long as we do that, we will continue to be haunted by this shadow from our past."

Ramirez spat on the floor. "You're insane. You want to tell *them* about the Operation? About the Division?"

"*The truth will set you free,*" Wayne said in a hushed tone, as though speaking to himself.

"What?"

Wayne straightened his back against the wall. "Yes, Ramirez, that's exactly what I'm saying. It's our history. We have to deal with it – the good, the bad, and the ugly – together."

Ramirez gestured toward the door with his gun. "*Those people* get their panties in a bunch over Brangelina and Justin freaking Bieber and you think they can be trusted with *this*?"

Wayne kept his expression stoic. "I hope so. But it's not for you, me, Greer, or the Division to make that decision for them."

Ramirez shook his head in disgust, glaring with unbridled antagonism at his fellow agent. "That's where you're wrong." A buzzing sounded from his pocket. The agent pulled out the phone, checked the caller ID, and flipped the phone to his ear. "Ramirez. Yes sir, I've got him contained. Are you ready to move on the targets?"

Wayne grimaced as the conversation continued. Both Greer and Ramirez had come to New York to finish what he would not. And they now had the true GPS positions of Jon and Mara, who by now had to be nearing the end of their quest. Another wrench in his plans. Then, with a final look of disgust, Ramirez took a step away and turned his gaze from Wayne, as though the very sight of the traitorous agent was an offense to the mission that he and Greer were discussing. And Wayne's dark cloud grew a silver lining. In his arrogance, Ramirez had failed to remember that Wayne too was an adept agent. Just with different allegiances.

Wayne reached into his coat pocket with his free hand and procured a paperclip, which he proceeded to bend into a more useful form. Ramirez swiveled toward his captive, who palmed the makeshift lockpick, trying to continue looking hopelessly defiant. With another ashamed shake of the head, Ramirez turned away again to focus on the conversation. Wayne fitted the lockpick into the lock, waited for Ramirez's own voice to mask the sounds of his escape, and removed one handcuff, and then the other.

Unfortunately, all Wayne could hear was Ramirez's side of the conversation, but it was rich enough in information that he decided it would do. "Yes sir. St. Patrick's. Rockefeller Center? Son of a bitch. Yes sir, I'll be right over. One last thing to take care of." He hung up and started to turn when Wayne slid away from the wall, kicking out and catching Ramirez in the shin.

Ramirez cursed and dropped the phone as he staggered back, still standing. His shin wasn't broken, but Wayne figured it must've hurt like hell. Ramirez tried to level his gun at his opponent, but Wayne crashed into his side, slamming him into the far wall. Wayne pounded a fist into Ramirez's gut, then flung the handcuffs at the single flickering light bulb. With an explosive shattering of glass and phosphorus, the room was cast into darkness.

"God damn you, Wilkins!" Ramirez's winded and furious voice came from the dark. "Where the hell are you?" Ramirez still had his gun in hand, but Wayne knew that his opponent wouldn't risk any stray shots in this ricochet-prone cinder-block chamber.

Wayne strafed noiselessly, trying to circle around where he assumed Ramirez was. The concrete room's acoustics bounced sounds around like a pinball, making it all but impossible to accurately ascertain a sound's source. Which was what Wayne was counting on.

He tossed a beer bottle from the floor in the direction of Enrique's voice, leaping to the side as he threw it. An *oof* told him he'd hit his mark. He rushed, grabbing for the beltline. Where Ramirez had stuffed Wayne's gun when he'd confiscated it earlier.

Ramirez was closer than Wayne had anticipated, apparently having run straight toward the threat once the thrown beer bottle gave away his position. Their bodies collided, Wayne grabbing his pistol as Ramirez brought his own gun's handle down on Wayne's forehead. A gash opened up, trickling blood down through his right eyebrow. He clenched his eyes shut, fought on. In the darkness, his sight was useless to him anyway.

Wayne heard the click of a round being chambered, Ramirez's hand grasping at Wayne's clothing, trying to keep track of his target in the lightless room. Wayne thrust his gun-holding arm upward, knocking Ramirez's hand from his shirt collar. He grabbed Ramirez's other wrist with his free hand. The gun in Ramirez's hand erupted, a gunpowder flash temporarily illuminating the room. Wayne's ears rang with the concussion reverberating through the tiny room. But the brief moment of light gave him a target, and he intended to use it.

Wayne pulled his head back just as Ramirez wrenched his wrist free. He slammed his already bleeding forehead into Ramirez's nose. Ramirez cursed, both of his hands flying instinctively to his injured face. Wayne grabbed Ramirez's gun and ripped it free as he planted the barrel of his own pistol against Ramirez's temple.

Ramirez's cell phone began vibrating from where it lay on the floor, the screen's backlighting casting a crepuscular glow over the room. The look on Ramirez's face as he stared at Wayne could have curdled milk. His eyes burned with a fiery hatred, but he knew he was beaten. Wayne shoved Ramirez's gun into his own waistband behind his back, pulling his shirttail over the weapon. He reached into Ramirez's coat pocket, removed his handcuff keys, and pocketed them.

"You know the drill," Wayne motioned to the handcuffs and pipe that had so recently held him prisoner.

"Go screw yourself," Ramirez spat, the dim illumination from the floor making his hateful expression look truly demonic.

Wayne increased the pressure of the muzzle on Ramirez's temple. "Don't make me say please."

Ramirez trudged across the room, looking for an opening, a way to turn the tables, but Wayne gave him nothing. He squatted, and, glaring at Wayne, secured the open handcuff around his own wrist.

"Tighter," Wayne instructed, his weapon still leveled at Ramirez. Ramirez squeezed the cuff tight around his wrist, the clicks echoing in the empty chamber.

The abandoned phone's vibrations ceased for a moment, plunging the room back into darkness. Wayne took a step back, wary of falling prey to the same move that had gained him his freedom moments earlier. A cacophony of scraping and shuffling suddenly emanated from Ramirez's direction, but Wayne was powerless to do anything but back away and wait.

The phone rang again, the vibrations scuttling it across the floor. Wayne picked it up, answered.

"Ramirez, what the hell happened?"

"Greer?"

A pause. "Wilkins? What the hell are you doing?"

"What has to be done."

"What are you talking about? You know the mission. Stay the course, son."

"Sorry, Greer. Mission aborted."

He hung up the phone to angry protestations from the other end. He switched on the flashlight function, pointed it at Ramirez's face.

Ramirez spat a bloody glob of saliva onto the floor. "This isn't over yet."

"For you it is."

"You're a dead man, Wilkins. You and Rickner both."

"Sorry, Ramirez." Wayne reached the door, looked back. "I've got bigger fish to fry right now." Wiping the blood from his face, he shouldered open the door and stumbled into an abandoned alleyway, shutting the door behind him and sliding a heavy trash barrel in front of the entry to Ramirez's makeshift cell. He then staggered out of the alleyway and into the night, immune to the muted shouts and curses echoing behind him.

Chapter 46

The dark bronze statue gleamed in the floodlights that shone on its skin from beneath. In Greek mythology, Atlas, condemned by the gods to hold up the heavens in punishment for his rebellion, quite literally had the weight of the world upon his shoulders. In the statue Rockefeller had commissioned, Atlas' burden consisted of an empty orb constructed of several circumscribed rings, resembling the orbits of the stars around the earth as viewed by the ancients. Again, the symbols of the zodiac made an appearance, as they had around the Prometheus statue, the signs of the ages cast in metal and pressing their eternal weight upon Atlas' shoulders. His back to the rest of Rockefeller Center, he faced the Cathedral, but his head was bowed, his eyes downcast as though ashamed, as though too burdened by the weight he carried to look at something far holier than himself and the mark of sin that he carried. His left foot was firmly planted on the pedestal, while his right seemed to have slipped off, the knee nearly resting on the statue's base, although whether it was in a representation of penance or of eternal encumbrance, it was hard to say. For Rockefeller, they seemed to have been one and the same.

Jon and Mara ran across the street to the base of the statue, their eyes darting every which way, anticipating some sort of ambush from the Division – but their search found nothing suspicious. Perhaps the pair truly was several steps ahead of their seemingly omnipotent adversaries. Despite its fame and artistic beauty, no one was around the forty-five-foot tall statue, the passersby preferring the thoroughfare of the Fifth Avenue sidewalk to the recessed alcove, surrounded by the office buildings of Rockefeller Center on three sides, where *Atlas* was positioned. Which made the impossible task Jon and Mara had to undertake a little less impossible.

Upon drawing close to the statue, they immediately noticed Atlas' eyes. His gaze was fixed on the southeast corner of the base, the spot where his right foot would have been resting if it hadn't trailed behind him, dangling off the pedestal. His eyes not simply averted from the sight of the Cathedral but fixed on the source of his shame. Rockefeller's shame.

Jon shivered and noticed Mara was doing the same. And not just because of the chilly night air.

"He hid the Dossiers in the base of the Atlas statue?" Jon whispered to the night. "One of the most famous statues in the country?"

"Well, he did go for places with a good chance of long-term permanence. Sit a beautiful statue on top of it, developers in later generations are less likely to come along and knock apart the hiding place."

"True, but still… Right here, all along. Alright, so the question is, how do we get to what's inside?"

"Jackhammer?"

"No, I don't think so. Everything thus far has been possible for the two of us, with just some minor tools, screwdrivers and our hands."

"And our minds."

"Well, that's the point," Jon agreed. "It was our minds, our ability to reason, that Rockefeller wanted to test in getting here. Our desire to seek the truth against all odds, our ability to be rational and lateral thinkers. The ability to see and act outside the box of mutual paranoia that Cold War politics had created."

"Okay, then, let's use our minds. How do we get to the Dossiers?"

Jon absentmindedly scratched at his chin with his thumb, staring up into the somber eyes of the bronze Titan. He searched those eyes for some answer, some revelation that he might somehow be able to see now that he had proven himself worthy. The statue's face was an inscrutable symphony of gleaming light and recessed shadow. Jon half-hoped that some heavenly light would shine down from the night sky, the base opening of its own accord, revealing the Dossiers to the noble seeker. But he had no such luck. The statue just held his gaze, simultaneously seeming to wish to turn its eyes from Jon's and to ask him, plead with him, to free him from the bonds that had held his heart hostage for three-quarters of a century. His true burden was not the heavy, star-adorned metal loops soldered to his back, but the few sheets of paper hidden beneath his feet.

He walked around the sleek marble base, looking it up and down, scanning it for any cracks or crevices, any indication of how one might get to something inside. At the back, there was a small rectangular hole in the base where it met the concrete ground, but upon peering inside, even with the aid of his flashlight, nothing jumped out at him. Even if the hole did lead to the Dossiers, his arm would not fit inside, much less be able to maneuver around whatever final safeguards Rockefeller had placed around the site. And then he realized the significance of the hole.

"There's another base," he said suddenly.

"What?"

Jon looked around the area, toward the street and climbed up onto the corner ledge of the shiny marble base. Lifting himself up on his knees, he peered down past the upward-shining floodlights at the center of the base. He had realized that the hole at the bottom was a drain hole, meaning that there had to be somewhere for the rain to get trapped, some opening that ran from top to bottom on all four sides. And there it was. The inner base. The one upon which the statue was actually resting. A smaller, hidden, more secure one – constructed of cinder blocks and shame. The keep inside the fortress, where the king would store his most valuable treasures – and his darkest secrets. Jon looked around again, Mara watching him expectantly as he scanned the area, surprised that, apparently, no one seemed to care – or even notice – that he was climbing around on a world-famous statue.

He looked back into the gap between the two bases, squinting into the glare of the floodlights that shone upward toward the statue. The inner base was composed of concrete blocks cemented together with mortar. How was he supposed to get through that? He began to wonder if a jackhammer might be more practical after all. But of course, they'd be thrown in jail long before they got anywhere near the Dossiers. He was already skirting the edge of the law by just being up here. Taking heavy-duty power tools to national landmarks would be a fatal leap into illegal territory, not to mention shooting up hundred-decibel flares to every law enforcement agent in the area to come and arrest him.

He looked up at the statue. Atlas, looking down at Jon, held his gaze. There was something sad, something mournful in his countenance. Like a guilty man who has been punished beyond his crime. Burdened with a horrible weight. Like the mythological Atlas must have felt, the weight of the sky pressing down for all eternity. Like Rockefeller himself, the ramifications of Operation Phoenix growing more and more dire as Hitler's Reich grew, conquered, stole, destroyed. The unrelenting guilt from his unspeakable mistake. Knowing that his silence made him all the more culpable. Letting his mark on the city do the speaking for him, sharing a message no one had gotten until now.

Yes, Jon felt. *This place was special. Something was here. The Dossiers.*

He reached down into the gap between the bases, the heat from the glowing floodlights warming his forearm. He touched the cold concrete blocks, ran his fingers along the rough edges of the mortar. How could they get inside this? It was a solid pillar of load-bearing blocks, bearing a heavy – and important – load indeed. He was so close. They had come so far. Only to be met with an impregnable castle keep.

Jon clenched his jaw. He rapped his knuckles against the concrete cinder block in frustration. Then he paused, his eyes narrowing, widening, his jaw shifting. He rapped his knuckles against the block again. Moved them to the block above and knocked again. To the block below, the block to the left, listening with his fingers, feeling the vibrations and lack thereof, and drawing inferences from what they sensed.

"Mara!"

"Yeah? What is it?" she said eagerly.

"Screwdriver from last night. You still got it?"

"Um…" She rummaged around in her purse. "Yeah, I guess I do," she said, finding the tool and holding it up for Jon to take. "Oh, geez, and I've been carrying the mallet around, too. No wonder my shoulder's been hurting me today. I really need to clean this thing out."

"Mallet," Jon said, holding his hand out expectantly like a surgeon asking for a scalpel with a dying patient on the operating table. She handed it to him, asking him what he was doing.

"Getting those Dossiers, I hope," he answered hurriedly. He reached into the gap with both of his tools in hand, each arm in a different hole, feeling exposed, like a medieval prisoner in the stocks. Staring through the third hole and holding the tip of the screwdriver against the center of the block that had felt a little too hollow under his knuckles, Jon tapped the end of the handle with the mallet. He was conscious of the percussive metal-on-stone sound echoing, but whether it was just inside the outer marble base or in the whole of the U-shaped alcove, Jon couldn't say. Regardless, no one from the street seemed to be aware of his presence, apparently too caught up in their own little worlds – their rush home, to the hotel, to the show, the mad New York dash to the next thing in their lives – to notice the statue or the man who kneeled at its feet, perched six feet from the ground.

He hammered and hammered, moving the screwdriver in an X pattern in an attempt to weaken the stone before he breached it completely. The half-centimeter hole that a single puncture with the screwdriver would open wouldn't get the Dossiers out. If indeed they were inside.

A few minutes of tapping later, Jon and Mara both heard the beautiful sound of concrete cracking, crumbling. Mara looked at Jon, wide-eyed in anticipation. Jon glanced backward at Mara, a flicker of joy in his expression, before he turned back to the widening hole. Tap, tap, tap. Within moments, he had created a hole large enough to put his hand through. Feeling around inside the hole, Jon's fingers found a metal cylinder, closed at both ends with caps larger than the cylinder itself. He gripped it, tried to pull it out, and failed.

***

Across the street, perched on the roof of St. Patrick's Cathedral, Harrison Greer viewed Rickner's progress through the scope of his sniper rifle. He had climbed up fire escapes, belfries, and long-forgotten ladders on the Cathedral's periphery to get here. A combination of intuition, cell phone triangulation, and satellite imagery had served to locate both Wilkins and Rickner. This, right across from Rockefeller's most lasting legacy – Rockefeller Center – was where his family's quest would end. This was his moment.

Greer was already in position by the time Wilkins overpowered Ramirez – or whatever ended up happening there. It was too late to go back now. And though Ramirez might have been detained or killed by the traitorous Wilkins, they weren't the only assets Greer had in New York tonight. Jeff Berenson, a six-year veteran of the Division, was on his way to retrieve the Dossiers from where Jonathan Rickner would soon drop them. Greer would strike them down, Berenson would retrieve the Dossiers, Greer would verify them, and using his grandfather's lighter, Greer would destroy them once and for all. But right now, Greer was waiting, patiently waiting, until he was *sure* that they had located the Dossiers.

***

Jon widened the hole in the concrete with his screwdriver and mallet combo. Deciding that the aperture was sufficiently large, he again thrust his hand into its cold recesses, wrapped his fingers around the cylinder, and tried to extricate hand and dossier-holder together. This time, he succeeded.

"Got it!" Jon said triumphantly over his shoulder to Mara.

"Well, get down here already," Mara returned, her voice a mixture of excitement and fear. Jon slid down from his perch, and the pair of them looked at the cylinder in the reflected light of the illuminated statue. It seemed to be some sort of document tube, a smooth metal cylinder with a metal cap screwed onto each end. In their eagerness and elation, they abandoned their habit of withdrawing to some private quarter to study their latest find, instead opting to open the canister there in the alcove. They were as relatively alone here as they had been in St. Patrick's, and besides, their quest was all but over. But they had to know now: had they really discovered the Dossiers?

***

Squeezing a cramp out of his trigger hand, Greer maintained his unblinking surveillance of Rickner and Ellison, keeping his eye trained on the metal cylinder Rickner had found under the Atlas statue, analyzing every movement, every breath, the same question running through his head over and over again: had they really discovered the Dossiers?

***

Wayne Wilkins, cursing Ramirez for his interference, hobbled up the street. His arm throbbed, and his ankle injury caused him to limp, and he had to wipe a trickle of blood from his forehead every thirty seconds or so. All his injuries were impeding his progress toward what could be the pivotal moment of his career. But he couldn't afford to be late to the actual discovery of the Dossiers. His body ached with reminders of what would happen should he not get there in time.

Now, turning south from East 51st Street onto Fifth Avenue, Wayne Wilkins checked Mara's position on his GPS monitor. Still in the same place. Right across from the Cathedral. *Wasn't that Rockefeller Center?*

A stocky black man in a brown sports coat and khakis was stopped on the sidewalk in front of him, looking south toward the Center, his hand pressed to his ear. An earpiece? An agent? Wayne was new to the Division and didn't know all of the agents, but–

The man turned slightly, just enough for Wayne to catch a partial glimpse of his face in profile. Wayne cursed his luck. It was Jeff Berenson, another of the Division's top agents. How many did Greer have swarming the city tonight? Of course, if Greer was here himself, he was definitely pulling out all the stops. Tonight was to be the culmination of his life's work – and that of his father and grandfather before him. And Wayne needed to make sure that Greer's plans didn't come to fruition.

Berenson was an extraordinarily adept agent, but he was intently focused on whatever was happening at Rockefeller Center while attempting to fade into the city's backdrop and hadn't yet noticed his fellow agent's presence behind him. Wayne still had the element of surprise, something that he assumed, had the roles been reversed, Berenson would have already used to kill the rogue agent. If Greer had activated other assets within the city, chances were that they knew about Wayne's betrayal and that they had received corresponding shoot-to-kill orders. Wayne had one chance, but with the street and sidewalks full of potential witnesses, he had to be careful.

Wayne slunk up behind the man, trying to maintain a balance between stealth and inconspicuousness. In one fluid motion, he gave the man a chop to the back of the neck with the side of one hand, grabbing him with the other hand and walk-dragging Berenson's now unconscious body to the shadows of a nearby doorway. Wayne placed him on the ground, searched his body, and found a pistol and a small radio transceiver wired to which the earbud was connected. Wayne took them both, ruffled the agent's coat hem a little, and stood up to survey his work. There were still enough homeless in this city sleeping in doorways and on sidewalks that no one would pay Berenson's limp body any notice. And thanks to New Yorkers' propensity to mind their own business on the streets and elsewhere, no one had paid his smooth takedown any mind either. Mission accomplished.

As Wayne left Berenson's unconscious form behind and continued down the sidewalk, his years of special ops experience kicked in as something caught his attention on top of the Cathedral.

***

Jon turned the end cap as both he and Mara held their breath in expectation. The threads on the cap seemed to be endless, each turn that should have opened the tube leading instead to yet another turn. Finally, the cap popped off, and Jon and Mara locked eyes. She nodded slightly, her lips pressed tightly together.

They both looked at the tube in Jon's hands as he tilted it upward, the open end angled toward Jon's palm. Two sheets of paper, held in a rolled-up shape for decades, slid reluctantly from their round metal tomb. One glance at the signatures at the bottom, Rockefeller's and Stimson's, told without a doubt that they had uncovered the Dossiers.

After a relentless week of heartache and peril, their quest was finally complete.

***

The bitch had moved in front of the tube. Greer had lost his line of sight on the Dossiers, and he couldn't change his angle too easily from his high perch. He hadn't gotten a look at the Dossiers, documents that no one had seen for longer than he had been alive, but the way the traitors were hopping on their toes and hugging each other in celebration was all the confirmation he needed.

Fine, he thought, wiping the sweat from his brow with one hand. The girl would be the first to go. A thin layer of sweat had broken out on his palms. Not nerves. Anticipation. The singular goal to which his father and his grandfather before him had dedicated their lives was about to be accomplished. *This is for you, Dad*, he thought as his finger tightened against the trigger.

***

Wayne was walking more quickly now, forgetting the pain in his leg. There was no way he could be seeing what he thought he was seeing on top of the Cathedral. There couldn't be.

But deep down, as Wayne began to break into a stilted run, he knew that his eyes weren't deceiving him.

***

"We did it!" Mara exclaimed.

"Not so loud," Jon cautioned, laughing through his warnings. He was on top of the world. They had finished his brother's work, could now bring his killers to justice, and would now be able to live without fear of government agents chasing them across the city or murdering them in their sleep. Both of their faces were pictures of exuberance, smiling as though they had never smiled before. Unlike the towering Atlas overhead, a giant weight felt like it had been lifted from his shoulders. From somewhere beyond the grave, both Michael and Rockefeller would be smiling with bittersweet pride.

A sharp report sounded from the street, echoing in the skyscraper canyons. Pedestrians could be heard screaming, seen ducking. Cars screeched as their drivers looked about nervously, trying to ascertain the source of the gunshot.

Jon noticed none of these changes. What he did notice was the change in his and Mara's happy countenances: Mara's to one of wide-eyed shock, Jon's to one of abject horror. A crimson stain appeared on the right shoulder of her jacket, growing with each pump of her heart. Someone had shot her. Someone had shot Mara.

No. *No no no.* They were done. They had found the Dossiers. The good guys had won. And now someone, somewhere, was taking potshots at the victors.

He grabbed her upper arms as she started to lean forward, weakness and shock overtaking her body. She winced as the pressure from his hand sent jolts of pain through her nearby injury. He relaxed his grip slightly, but couldn't bring himself to let her go. This wasn't supposed to happen. Not like this.

They had won. End of story. Game over.

Yet right now, he felt like everything was about to be hopelessly lost.

***

It was what he had feared. Wayne had wished with every ounce of his being that it wasn't Greer himself that he had spied atop the Cathedral, but the muzzle-flash that had sparked in the night confirmed his fears. A handful of pedestrians were pointing toward the Cathedral's roof, but just as many were pointing elsewhere. The truth was, aside from that brief spark of the weapon discharging, it was almost impossible to detect Greer's form hidden among the Gothic crenellations of the Cathedral. Wayne ran faster, closer, into range, exchanging Berenson's gun in his hand for his own pistol – the only one he trusted for what he was about to do.

***

One down… Greer thought as he ejected the empty shell and chambered the next. Peering through the scope, he could see Rickner trying to drag Ellison behind the statue, the girl writhing in pain. *Damn it.* The wind currents in the urban canyons of Manhattan were different from those in his forest valley shooting range back in Virginia. His shot had only wounded her. In the shoulder, from the look of the crimson stain soaking through her blue sweater.

But ultimately it didn't matter. She was incapacitated. Berenson would be here any second to finish her off and claim the Dossiers. All that remained was to take care of the one remaining civilian witness to the horrible truth of Operation Phoenix.

He wiped the sweat from his palm on his knee. This was it. The moment of truth. The work of three lifetimes culminating in this one shot. He leaned forward, bracing himself on his knee, perched a hundred feet above the front steps of the Cathedral.

This time his bullet would hit true. This shot would put the final Rickner brother in the grave.

***

It was insane to attempt a shot at this distance with a sidearm, Wayne told himself, but he knew he had to try. He had his pistol at his side as he ran, then he suddenly stopped. Raising the pistol with both hands, he aimed at the figure sitting like a lethal gargoyle atop the Cathedral. Crazy or not, he had to take the shot. It was now or never.

The moment of truth had come.

***

"Mara," Jon called to the unresponsive face. She was still alive, looking at something far off, far above their heads, above the skyscrapers, above the stars. Her breath had grown short, rapid. She was losing blood fast, probably going into shock. *Oh God*, his thoughts screamed, *what can I do? What in God's name can I do?* He dragged her behind the statue, praying that the hulking Titan could protect them like it had protected Rockefeller's darkest secret.

And on the ground to the side, the Dossiers lay next to the metal tube, neglected and forgotten.

***

On opposite sides of the street, pressure was applied to the triggers of two different guns pointed at two different targets. Both men were shooting to kill.

***

Another gunshot rang out across the urban canyon, this one somehow different, as though it had been shot from a different location or from a different type of weapon. Mara's neck twitched with the sound. Jon's hand instinctively went to his chest, checking for the wound that he didn't yet feel. He knew that with serious injuries, you sometimes didn't feel the pain until seconds after the damage was done, part of the body's defense against incapacitating levels of pain. But the moments passed, and he felt no pain, found no wound.

But, curiosity getting the better of him and peering out at the street through Atlas' legs, he did see a strange sight on the roof of St. Patrick's Cathedral.

***

Greer coughed. Something warm and wet sprayed from his mouth, flecking his arms and his rifle with crimson. His eye started twitching, his whole face beginning to contort with pain. Somehow, *somehow* he had been shot.

No, it wouldn't end like this. It couldn't. He had an enemy of the state in his sights. He had to eliminate the target. He had to finish the mission.

He put his eye back to the scope, trying to focus through the pain, through the spasms. He was a good marksman. He was a good soldier. He was a patriot. He had to finish his family's work.

He coughed again, once, twice, three, four times, coating his forearms and knee in blood. He felt his strength ebbing away.

No. This isn't how it ends. I have to finish this. I can't quit now. I'm so close.

His knee slipped to one side, the torso it had been supporting toppling forward, over, down, down, down. He didn't see the horrified pedestrians gaping in terror as he fell, nor did he hear their shouts and screams. All he heard was the cool wind whistling in his ears. All he saw was the large American flag that hung to the left of the Cathedral's entrance doors, the southerly wind blowing the banner toward Greer, drawing his attention, the last thing he ever saw. But what filled his mind's eye was that of his father and his grandfather. He had failed them. And he had failed his country.

He whispered two words to the night wind: *I'm sorry.*

With generations-old patriotic thoughts in his mind and the stars and stripes in his tear-filled eyes, Harrison Greer fell ten stories to the stone steps of St. Patrick's Cathedral, his rifle still clutched in his hands. His body made a sickening splat, like a sack of tomatoes smashing against the pavement. The Star Spangled Banner fluttered overhead, two of the white stripes speckled with scarlet, expectorated blood from Greer's lungs as he fell, his very breath and blood given in defense of the nation he and his family had served for generations.

***

A wall of blurred noise surrounded Jon, screams and shouts that filled the area. He had expected a crowd to gather around the injured Mara, but whoever or whatever had just fallen from the Cathedral seemed to be a bigger draw. That, and the pedestrians' fear that the shooting might not be over yet.

"Jon!"

Jon looked up at the voice that seemed to cut through the haze. He recognized it. But he couldn't remember from where he knew it. Then the figure came closer, stepped into the light.

It was Wayne Wilkins.

Jon glanced at Wayne's pistol, still clutched in his hand. "Did you…?" he managed to choke out.

"*He* shot her. I shot *him*," Wayne explained, pointing to the bloody heap across the street to emphasize who he was talking about.

"Who was that…?"

"That was Harrison Greer. The Director himself. But even without him, the Division is still a threat. I don't know how many agents are in the city right now, possibly converging on our position." Wayne noticed a cell phone lying next to Mara. "Did you call 911?"

Jon looked at him with a blank expression. "What? No, I… no," he exhaled heavily, picking up the phone. "I will. I think she's in shock."

Wayne noticed the papers lying near the two prone youths. He stepped around Jon and Mara and bent to pick up the Dossiers. Though they wanted to curl back into the shape they had been hidden in, the papers were still white and relatively crisp – the airtight metal tube having protected them not only from prying eyes, but also from the decaying influence of the elements and time. He shook his head from side to side, pressing his lips tightly together. All this killing over these, a few sheets of paper. But, he thought, what he saw here was nothing compared to the millions upon millions who had died because of Operation Phoenix – and the Nazis it put into power – in the first place. As he stared at the signatures of Stimson and Rockefeller, Wayne couldn't honestly say that he wouldn't have been tempted to cover up what he had done, were he in their position. The best laid plans, even the best intended plans, going horribly, horribly astray. But he did know what he had to do now.

"This yours?" Wayne asked, picking up Jon's backpack from the ground.

"Yeah," Jon said, still kneeling on the ground, pressing Mara's hand in his, trying to get through to her somehow. He had propped her head up on her purse, trying to give her some measure of comfort from the cold concrete slab she lay on.

Wayne opened it, found the notebook, and slid the Dossiers between two blank pages toward the back.

"Do not lose those, do you understand?" His voice came quick, as though hurried, anxious. "You get those into the right hands. Congress, the National Security Archive, wherever. If this gets swept under the rug, nothing can bring down the Division. And you and I will be the next ones dead."

Jon wrenched his gaze from Mara's unseeing eyes. "Yeah, I got it."

"You swear it?"

"Yeah, of course."

"Okay." Wayne pulled a pistol from his waistband and handed it to Jon. "Ramirez's. Clip's almost full. He's out of the picture, but use this for protection until this is over."

Jon raised his eyebrows but took the weapon. "Thanks. But where are you…"

"Jon," Wayne explained, "I just gave St. Patrick's their own fallen angel, right on their blood-spattered doorstep. I can't exactly stick around right now." His ears perked up as the sounds of sirens, police and ambulance, started to reach them. "That's my cue." He turned to go.

"Hey, Wayne."

Wayne turned back toward Jon.

"Thanks."

Wayne smiled somewhat contentedly to himself, privy to some secret joy that he hadn't felt in a long while, and then extended his hand to Jon.

"Thank you, too, Jon," Wayne said, shaking his hand. "I'll see you around." And with that, Wayne Wilkins darted into the shadows, escaping into the dark embrace of night.

***

A few moments later, the block was filled with the screams of sirens and the flash of blue and red and white emergency lights. The EMTs unloaded a stretcher from the back of the ambulance and wheeled it over to Jon and Mara. They asked Jon some questions while they checked Mara, looked at her wound, her eyes, her state of shock. They loaded Mara up on the stretcher, refused Jon's demands that he be allowed to ride in the ambulance with her – *protocol*, they said – and took off for the hospital.

A police officer who had been waiting for the EMTs to finish their work pulled Jon to the side, gave him the typical routine about knowing that this must be a hard time for him, but he had to ask him a few questions. Jon's newly acquired firearm weighed heavy in the back of his waistband, a constant reminder of the danger in which he was still in. But the cop was heavyset and didn't seem to be Division material, so Jon decided that he could linger for a few moments more. Jon had initially thought about running from the scene now that Mara was safe, but a search of his person would turn up a concealed weapon for which he had neither permit nor registration. And he didn't need the cops putting out an APD on him while he still had unfinished business to attend to. It would be hard enough to finish this task with just the Division still on his tail.

So Jon answered them as best as he could, leaving out the presence of Wayne altogether, figuring it was plausible enough that Greer had shot Mara, then fallen off of his own accord. After all, he *had* been leaning off the edge of a precipice with one eye closed and the other pressed to a lens that screwed with his depth perception, his magnified sight telling his precariously balanced body that he was hundreds of feet from where he really was.

Why had Greer shot Mara? Don't most people who get up on bell towers or other high places overlooking populated areas with a rifle just fire at targets indiscriminately? Jon argued. He went through the motions, acting distant and removed, in shock from the whole experience so the officer eventually relented and decided that it seemed fairly cut and dry. On examination of the mangled body of Harrison Greer, they would manage to discover the bullet that Wayne had shot him with, but by that point, Jon would be back in Washington, driving the final nail into the Division's coffin.

The officer gave Jon his card and asked him to call if he remembered anything else about the incident. Jon murmured his consent, and the officer left. The body of Greer and the blood-spattered bronze doors and stone stairs had drawn a crowd that the cops were trying to cordon off with crime scene tape. A pair of news vans were arriving, satellite dishes elevated from the roofs so the affiliates could get in on the story for their evening news programs. Despite the commotion just a few dozen feet away, Jon felt utterly alone. Michael was gone. Mara was gone. Wayne was gone. Jon was on his own, alone against a faceless enemy that apparently still presented a very real threat to Jon. But he had a secret weapon. He had the Dossiers. And remembering Wayne's charge to him, he realized that he had another ally who was perfectly situated to help make the Division history.

Slinking off into the shadows before anyone else could question him further, Jon made his way west, leaving the scene of blood and death behind him.

Chapter 47

Upon arriving at the hospital where the ambulance had taken Mara, Jon was turned away – told that she was in surgery, that she had lost a lot of blood, that the doctors were doing the best they could, and that even if she came out of surgery all right, she wouldn't be able to receive visitors for some time. In shock over the events of the previous hours and cognizant of the hurdles and responsibilities that he had yet to face, he wandered the streets en route back to the hotel like a ghost ship, adrift with only the natural motions of the sea and wind to propel it. Although cognizant of his surroundings – always trying to walk with a crowd of people as protection – the beauty of the city's vibrant culture and nightlife was lost on him.

When he finally arrived back at the hotel a short while later, the cold of the night and the anonymity of the big city having lulled him even further into his surreal numbness, Jon had his plan fully formed in his mind. Tomorrow morning, he would head back to Washington. By nightfall, Operation Phoenix would be exposed, the proof revealed, the Division vanquished. *If* everything went according to plan.

The elevator ride up to the seventeenth floor, despite the half-dozen other hotel guests sharing it with Jon, felt desperately lonely. The Division had taken everyone else from him, leaving him completely alone to finish this, the lone knight against the hundred-headed dragon. *But only for a season*, he told himself. *Only for a short while longer.*

A deep-seated guilt sat on his shoulders like an old gnarled vulture. His brother's death – and Jon's "abandonment" of him beforehand – hung over him like an oppressive fire blanket, wrapping itself around his mind and spirit. He knew he wasn't to blame, but it didn't make the guilt go away. Indeed, in failing to protect Mara in Michael's stead – her falling prey to a bullet that likely had been intended for Jon – only served to deepen the sense of personal failure, the talons of the burdensome vulture of guilt sinking deeper into his being. This was not at all how he had imagined their victory to be.

The quiet, the unbearable silence that pervaded the seventeenth floor hallway was maddening. Like the audience in his life's drama had been shocked into speechlessness. A hush had fallen over the imaginary crowd in the background, rendered mute by what had just transpired – or perhaps in breathless anticipation of what was to come.

Upon entering his room, the stillness in the air grew even more repugnant to him. A constant reminder of Michael's death, of Mara's possibly fatal shooting, of Wayne's forced flight. A reminder that he was on his own. Luckily, his years of companionship with his brother, although cut far too short, coupled with the obstacles he had overcome in the past week, gave him encouragement. It was almost over. It was almost over.

Mara's suitcase lay to one side of her unmade bed, Jon remembering that they had left the "Do Not Disturb" sign hanging from their doorknob all day. The dent in her pillow where her head had rested was still visible in the overstuffed pillow. Her hairbrush, blow dryer, makeup kit, shampoo, face scrub, toothbrush – the bathroom was filled with toiletries and appliances that would not see any use tonight. Or for many nights after. And possibly never again... but Jon refused to entertain such thoughts. They were unproductive, simply serving to dig himself deeper in the mire that the night's turn of events had thrown him into. And, physically, mentally, and emotionally exhausted though he was, he had to take care of one final thing before he crashed for the night. Despite the late hour, he dialed

Professor Leinhart's number. He knew this would be a call the professor would gladly get out of bed for.

"Jon?" The voice on the other end was predictably sleepy, but infused with a sharp awareness honed by long hours of worrying.

"Professor, sorry for calling so late. Big news. Good news and bad."

"Bad news first?" Leinhart requested halfheartedly.

"Mara's been shot. A clean shot through her right shoulder. She was taken to St. Luke's Hospital, but I don't know how she's doing. They wouldn't let me see her. Apparently no vital organs or arteries were hit, but she lost a lot of blood and went into shock before the paramedics even showed up."

"Good God." The professor sighed a ragged breath on the other end. "I'm guessing this wasn't a mugging gone wrong."

"It was the Division. Apparently we were important enough for the Director himself to try to gun down." Jon swallowed, then added, almost as an afterthought to what really mattered, "He's dead now, though. Wayne took him out."

"Wayne, huh? He came through after all. I was half-afraid he was trying to play you, win your confidence or whatever and then take the Dossiers once you found them." Another heavy sigh. "Thank God for that, then. Well, come on, son, give me the good news already."

"I've got the Dossiers."

The professor laughed triumphantly, Jon having to pull his ear away from the receiver slightly at the sudden noise. "You got them? I knew you could do it. You know, your brother would be so proud."

Jon smiled wryly to himself. "I know, sir. I have the Dossiers, but I need to get them into the right hands in Washington somehow. I don't know who to trust in the government. Even people who aren't affiliated with the Division might want this information repressed. The President, Congress, everybody in the federal government could feel some real public backlash when this comes out."

"So you want me to use my connections with the National Security Archive to ensure that someone else doesn't bury the truth," Leinhart guessed.

"Yes sir. I know I've already put you in danger by bringing you into this…"

There was a slight whistling noise as the professor inhaled a long breath through his nose. "Not at all, Jon. I'm still alive and kicking. Your brother and Mara are the ones who've been burned thus far. We just have to do whatever we can to make their sacrifices not in vain. They're out of commission, but we have to carry on, am I right?"

"Yes sir, absolutely."

"I'd be happy to help. I want to. Are you coming back to Washington?"

"Yes sir, tomorrow morning hopefully. I'm going to catch the first flight back I can get."

"Why don't I pick you up from the airport?" Leinhart offered. "Eliminate the possibility of a Division agent posing as a cab driver and knocking you off when you're inches from the finish line."

"Well, I don't want to put you out. It's a Thursday, so won't you have classes?"

"Jon, I can *teach* history any day. Tomorrow, I get the opportunity to help *shape* history. For this, I'll gladly cancel my classes."

Jon smiled weakly. "All right then. I'll give you a call when I get my ticket so you'll know when to pick me up."

"Excellent. Congratulations again on finding the Dossiers, and know my thoughts are with Mara. We're almost done, son. Make sure you don't lose sight of the goal. And for God's sake, be careful. That one Division agent may be dead, but they're bound to have more after you, especially after they find out that he's been killed. Make it to Washington in one piece, and we'll put this beast to rest together. Take care of yourself, son, and I'll talk to you tomorrow morning. Or later on *this* morning, as it were," he added with a monosyllabic chuckle.

"Thank you so much. For everything. I'll let you get back to bed, and I'll call you later."

They exchanged goodbyes and hung up. Jon placed a bottle of cologne on the door handle, a hardback book underneath, ensuring that any attempts to jiggle the handle or open the door would wake him from his slumber. He also dragged the heavy sitting chair across the room and shoved it against the door to slow anyone who might try to get in. Part of him thought he should change hotels and book another room under a false name, but he was too drained to actually do it. Besides, he figured, he had survived foot chases with trained assassins and shootouts with rooftop snipers. If they found him in his sleep tonight, that was simply the worst case of irony he'd ever heard. He'd have enough ghosts to deal with tonight anyway.

Weary and broken, Jon dropped the backpack from his shoulders and placed it next to his bed, kicked off his shoes, and hit the lights. Still in his clothes, bloodstained jacket and all, he lay down in bed, tucking Ramirez's pistol under his pillow. He was asleep within seconds, plunged into dreams of cathedrals with fallen angels and of Mara dying in his arms, his hands drenched in crimson as the remorseful eyes of Atlas bore down on him from above.

Chapter 48

Manhattan and Washington, D.C.

Thursday

The next morning, Jon went by St. Luke's Hospital again. Mara, though out of surgery, was in a drugged sleep in the Intensive Care Unit. Her breathing was labored, assisted by oxygen tubes stuck in her nostrils, and her face was ashen. Jon squeezed her hand, hoping that she could feel his touch and realize how much he appreciated all she had done. Though they had never brought the subject up again, the assumptions he had taken from their argument at Del Frisco's – that she wouldn't have the mettle to see this through, that she had completely misunderstood Michael's passions – now seemed not only petty, but completely off-base. Her assistance in finding the Dossiers and her determination to accomplish their mission, even to the point of nearly dying at the Atlas statue, had more than proven that. It was with no small twinge of sadness that he reflected on what a great married couple Michael and Mara would have made had things turned out differently.

He left Mara's bags at the hospital and, after making a few last minute stops in the city and calling the professor with his arrival time, Jon boarded his flight to Washington. His sleep the night before had been a restless one, tossing and turning while chased by phantoms of the past and specters of what was to come, dreaming of missed appointments with Death and bullets with his name on them. Yet despite his lack of real rest, despite everything he had endured in the past week, his mind was sharp, focused. His plan was brilliant, and he couldn't afford to miss a step.

During the short plane trip, Jon kept his eyes open, alert, but refusing to read the novel he had in his bag. He focused solely on the task at hand, going through the details in his mind, over and over and over again. The ever-changing landscape below, the puffy whiteness that sailed past the window hardly registered. His world was in his mind, the unfolding of the near future that would be perhaps one of the most important junctures in American history, and, certainly, in Jon's life.

Professor Leinhart had warned Jon about trusting anyone once he and Mara had been thrust into a world of subterfuge and double-crosses, of government conspiracies and buried secrets worth killing for. But Wayne Wilkins, by all accounts weaving a tale that was almost too outlandish to believe, had proven true, his motives apparently in line with Jon's own. How differently the previous evening could have gone if he had *not* truly been an ally. Even if he had not arrived when he did. Just a few seconds later, and Greer's next bullet would have ensured that Jon and the Dossiers disappeared forever. Thankfully, at least in that instance, trusting someone else hadn't blown up in his face.

When the plane finally landed in Washington, the passengers gathering their belongings in anticipation of their imminent disembarkation, Jon was confident that his plan would work. From the plane to the terminal, from the terminal to Dr. Leinhart's car, from the car to the National Security Archive's headquarters at George Washington University. Barring a suicide bomber at the airport or a deadly car crash orchestrated by the Division en route to the university, there were few gaps between here and the end of his ordeal, the fruition of his quest – and his brother's.

Waiting for the aisles to clear somewhat before pressing toward the exit, Jon finally grabbed his belongings and left the plane, carrying his backpack on one shoulder and keeping his hand over the zipper as he walked through the crowded terminal. He kept a wary eye on everyone around him, studying their faces and their body motions for anything that might warrant suspicion – a furtive glance or a bulge inside a jacket. No one stood out. In studying their faces, however, he realized that behind their impassive expressions, their minds focused on families, work, relationships, bills to pay, the mundane and commonplace ordeals of life. In contrast, Jon, like Rockefeller before him, felt the weight of a nation's future upon his back. But, while Rockefeller merely refused to destroy the truth, Jon refused to let the lies live on at all.

Continuing his surveillance of the people bustling through the airport, Jon's eyes finally lit upon one face that *did* mean something to him, a face whose burden was equally less mundane, whose grave ordeal held implications that reached far beyond vacation plans and college funds. As Professor Leinhart caught sight of him and began to draw near with a tense smile upon his face, a nervous anticipation gripped Jon's stomach. The planning he had been going over in his mind for the past few hours was no longer simply a plan; it now had to be put into action.

"Jon," Leinhart said, placing his hand upon Jon's shoulder in a gesture of comfort. His eyes were tinged with red, as though his night had been restless, filled with worry, and the occasional tear. He sucked at his bottom lip, nervously nibbling the chapped skin between his teeth. His unshaven jowls sagged mournfully and his rumpled clothes looked as though he had slept in them. Jon realized that he was going to have to take the helm here also, but that was just as well. It was his plan, and he knew how to enact it. Leinhart just had to get him in the door. That, and drive him across town.

"Professor, you look like crap," Jon quipped. "No offense."

"None taken. I feel like crap. But the sooner we finish this, the sooner we can both rest easy." Despite his ragged demeanor, Leinhart moved to help Jon with his bags. "So we'll go to GW to get the Dossiers into the National Security Archive's system for starters?"

"That sounds good. You know how the system works better than I, so I'll trust your judgment there."

"Yes, I think that's best. I've already begun drawing up the paperwork to start processing it based on what Wayne told you. Background and whatnot. I haven't told anyone else at the University or at the Archive just yet. You never know where they might have spies."

Jon grimaced. "Too true. 'Reds in every closet,' huh?"

The professor laughed uncomfortably. "Yeah." He swallowed hard, his stubble-covered Adam's apple leaping, diving in his throat. "Let's just get this over with."

Leinhart led Jon through the parking lot to his car, the silver Audi shining bright in the sun. He unlocked and opened the passenger's side door for Jon, holding it open while he climbed in.

"I'll put your suitcase and backpack in the trunk," Dr. Leinhart offered.

"You sure?"

The professor nodded.

"Thanks. I'll hold on to the backpack, though," Jon said, setting the bag in the floorboards between his feet.

"As you wish." Leinhart closed the door, and Jon watched him in the rear view mirror as he unlocked and opened the trunk, heard bags moving around in the back as he shuffled around whatever else he had back there to make room. Jon buckled his seatbelt and closed his eyes, going over his plan in his mind once more. The calm before the storm, a storm that hopefully would never come. The last pep talk before the big game. The last meal before… no, that was a bad metaphor to use. His nerves were on edge enough as it was.

Jon heard the back door open behind him. He slowly opened his eyes, turned his neck slightly.

"Sorry. I've been meaning to clean out the trunk, but it keeps slipping off my to-do list. I couldn't fit your suitcase back there," Leinhart explained as he slid Jon's carry-on into the back seat. Jon grunted in understanding and closed his eyes again. A silent pause, as though Leinhart were thinking about something. Then Jon's eyes shot open as a strong hand wrapped a sickly sweet-smelling wet cloth around his nose and mouth. He could see the edge of the cloth at the bottom of his vision as he struggled against Leinhart's grip, wishing that, just this once, he hadn't buckled up.

As the too-empty parking lot began to fade to a chemical black, Jon found himself wishing he had taken the professor's advice against trusting anyone.

Even the professor himself.

Chapter 49

Rockville, Maryland

The first thing Jon noticed when he blinked open his eyes was his inability to properly focus, as though he were sobering up after a long, hard bender. The second was that he could not move his arms or legs, his wrists and ankles being bound to the chair he was seated in. He was powerless to stop the itching injection site where, Jon surmised, his captor – or captors – had administered a secondary sedative designed to keep him unconscious until he was securely bound and transported to his current location. Once his senses began to sharpen back toward normal, his brain began to register details about the room he was in, his surroundings both familiar and foreign to him. Oak paneled walls. Forest green couch. Black leather recliner. Coffee table. Old TV. Bookshelves filled with tomes whose title-embossed spines were still a blur to Jon's impaired sense of sight. He could tell it was the living room of a home somewhere, but he had never seen this particular room, been in this particular house, before. The room was windowless, although two hallways leading elsewhere in the house were visible: one to the left, one straight ahead.

He could recognize his bags on the floor across the room, their contents ripped from within and strewn about the floor by someone searching for something, but exactly what they were doing there, he couldn't say. Exactly what *he* was doing here, wherever this was, also remained a mystery to him. A mystery that started to gain some illumination, a weak wind beginning to dispel the miasmatic fogs clogging his semi-drugged mind, when Dr. Richard Leinhart, still wearing his rumpled clothing and looking more haggard than ever, came back into the room from the left-hand hallway, two sheets of Xeroxed paper clutched in his fists.

"Where are they, Jon?" the professor demanded in a weary, but urgent, voice.

"Where are what?" Jon asked, his head pounding as he forced the words.

"*The original Dossiers*, Jon!" the professor shouted, shaking the Xeroxed copies Jon had hidden in the pages of Michael's notebook. Leinhart grabbed Jon's immobile forearms and stared into his face with desperation. "Where are the Dossiers?"

Jon smirked, blew a puff of air through his nostrils in a private laugh. "They're safe."

"Safe where?"

Jon ignored the question. "You're working for the Division?"

"Yes. No. I'm working to stop the Division from killing anyone else. They contacted me right after you and Mara left for New York. I don't know how they found me, but they did. Look, the guy told me that they don't want you, they just want the Dossiers. They get the Dossiers, the killing stops. I don't help them reclaim the Dossiers – through you, of course – they kill you, they kill Mara, and they kill me. And who knows how many others until they *do* get them."

"And you believed them?" Jon spat on the floor, his dry mouth providing almost no saliva for his expectoration. "They shot Mara just seconds after we discovered the damned things. Would've shot me too, if Wayne hadn't taken the bastard out when he did."

"The man I talked to assured me that no harm would come to any of us if we delivered the Dossiers to the Division and kept our mouths shut."

"Bull. Their whole purpose is to kill, to protect this skeleton in the nation's closet. They've been going strong longer than either of us has been alive, and you really believe they'll stop once they've destroyed the one thing that could bring them down? Hell, that'll just embolden them further. Professor, the *only* way to stop the killing is to expose the Dossiers. You know that's the truth."

Leinhart's brow creased even further, his troubled eyes betraying the tumult of warring thoughts raging in his mind.

"No," he finally said. "Perhaps what you're saying is true, but we can't bring them down. Not anymore. They know about me. They know about you. They've probably got the National Security Archive under wraps, ready to pounce on anything we try to push through the system."

"We've at least got to try!" Jon exploded, leaning toward the professor as much as his restraints would allow. Leinhart backed up in defense, but only a little. "Mara and I have been out here busting our asses hunting down the truth, putting our lives on the line every step of the way, and you just want to roll over and play dead. Is that how you work, Professor?"

"Not usually," Leinhart said, his face hardening as he straightened up to his full height and stared down at Jon, "but in this case, I'll make an exception."

"Well, you knew my brother well enough to know he would never do that. And neither will I."

The professor stood there glaring for a moment, his eyes narrowed in frustration.

"Fine," he huffed, and turned to walk off to some other part of the house, disappearing down a hallway to the right. Jon sat there, racking his chemical-addled brain for what to do next, what he *could* do next. His brother would have been proud of his courage, his integrity in the face of stalwart opposition. Jon just hoped that it wouldn't land him in a premature grave like it had Michael.

The professor returned with a pistol, its black metal shining dully in the interior lighting. He didn't look like he had much experience handling a gun. Which potentially made him even more dangerous, especially when coupled with the visible nervousness that had seized the professor's demeanor.

"We can do this the easy way, or the hard way," the professor said, brandishing the pistol and making sure Jon was aware of its presence, and Leinhart's readiness to use it. "It's your choice."

Jon had to stifle a groan. The professor sounded like a walking movie cliché, his stereotypical bad guy line ringing hollow. The man wasn't a villain, Jon knew. He was just like Jon, a good person put in an impossible position. But that didn't mean he couldn't be just as dangerous to Jon's survival.

"Professor..." Jon started with a beleaguered tone.

"Tell me where the Dossiers are!" Leinhart bellowed with a ferocity that startled Jon. He pointed the barrel of the gun in Jon's face, then lowered it to his leg, digging the muzzle into his kneecap. "You have until the count of three."

Just like in the movies, Jon thought, Leinhart's villain performance pulling out even more clichés. But, even in the movies, those shattered kneecaps were devastating. Unoriginal lines and bad acting or not, the professor could really ruin Jon's day in the next three seconds.

"One..."

"What time is it?" Jon asked.

The professor looked surprised. "Why?"

"You'll see. What time is it?"

Leinhart checked the Rolex upon his wrist. "It's a little after six. The morphine kept you out longer than I might have hoped. Why the devil does the time matter?"

Jon chuckled to himself. Perfect timing. "That television," he said motioning with his head toward an old cathode-ray set across the room. "Turn it on. I want to watch the news."

"The news?" Leinhart repeated, a dumb look on his face. Then, seeing the renewed confidence, the gleam of some secret victory in Jon's eyes, his face grew ashen, a dark realization dawning upon him. He lowered the gun to his side and quickly crossed the room to the television, paying no attention to the remote control that sat in its cradle only a few feet from where he had been standing. Switching it on, he stood back, realized it was tuned to the History Channel, and finally grabbed the remote control from the holder, using it to flip to CNN.

"...conspiracy from the 1930s, using American money and government assets to give Adolf Hitler control of Germany..."

Desperate and wide-eyed, Leinhart flipped the channel to CBS.

"...according to recently unearthed documents that appear to have been signed by former Secretary of State Henry Lewis Stimson and billionaire businessman John..."

NBC also had their special report.

"...an alleged secret government cover-up program that purportedly targets its own citizens, supposedly having killed hundreds if not thousands of Americans since the advent of the Cold War..."

"What the hell is this?" Leinhart demanded, throwing the remote to the floor as the breaking news continued to be dispersed by the onscreen reporter behind him, eighty years of secrets and lies being exposed to an audience of millions. The professor was shaking with a mixture of rage and fear.

"I made copies of the Dossiers," Jon explained, a thin, victorious smile on his face as confidence came back into his voice. "Much like the copy you found in Michael's notebook. I took them around to different news studios in New York. And there are a *lot* of them up there, let me tell you. I gave them the entire story, showed them Rockefeller's journal entry that Blumhurst had stolen in '57, explained all the clues, and told them about the Division. And how it all tied into the very public and very dramatic shootings that happened at St. Patrick's the night before. *And* I told them that I would have another part of the story for them, a final conclusion, one that *you* were supposed to help me fix: the filing of the Dossiers with the National Security Archive. I told them that if I didn't call by five, they should run with the story at six. Ensuring that, if something happened to me, the story would still get out." He nodded toward the still-reporting TV. "Like it has."

"That's it. You've killed us. We're both dead." The professor's grip tightened around the pistol, his hand shaking noticeably. He brought the gun to his own head, pressed the muzzle against his temple as tears began to trickle down his cheeks. He dry-sobbed, looking from the TV to Jon to the backs of his closed eyelids, his breaths quick, rapid, like a terrified rabbit.

"Professor, don't," Jon pleaded in genuine concern. "It's over. We've won. Let it be over."

"*You killed us!*" Leinhart shrieked, his eyelids flying open to reveal the crazed eyes beneath. He swung the gun from his own head to point at Jon's. "You killed us!"

"Professor, please," Jon begged, struggling to keep his voice calm. "Think about what you're doing. This isn't you. You *know* this isn't you."

"Shut up," Leinhart shouted, his whole body vibrating as though shaken by some inner earthquake. "Just shut the hell up already."

Jon begrudgingly complied, afraid to do more damage by disobeying the wishes of the admittedly unstable professor. His breathing grew shaky, ragged, his eyes fixed on the cold, hollow barrel of the gun that stared hungrily at his forehead. He hoped, prayed that the last part of his plan, his final failsafe, would work in time.

The next sound Jon heard told him that it had.

Chapter 50

"Richard Leinhart, this is the Washington Metro Police." The megaphone-amplified voice from outside seemed to shake something inside the professor's eyes. "Come out with your hands up, or we will be forced to enter." Leinhart's gun remained trained on Jon's forehead as the professor's eyes twitched, as his face spasmed. A few seconds later, a loud bang from what Jon assumed was the front of the house, followed by shouts of "move" and "clear," told Jon that the police had breached the house.

Leinhart's hand continued to point the pistol at Jon, shaking more and more as his sweaty index finger tightened around the trigger. The crazed look in the professor's eyes grew more and more desperate, as though seeking some way out of a labyrinth with no exits.

"It's over…" Jon breathed, locking eyes with the professor and trying to quell his own shaking and calm his nerves. "It's over…"

A clamor at the entrance to the room, followed by a loud voice. "Leinhart, drop the weapon or we will shoot you!"

The professor gave Jon an apologetic look and moved the pistol to his own temple, staring into Jon's eyes the whole time. Jon mouthed the word "no," as the professor closed his eyes and tightened his finger around the trigger.

When the shot rang out, Jon slammed his eyes shut, feeling tiny droplets of warm liquid land on his face, on his hands. The professor screamed in pain… something he shouldn't have been able to do had he shot himself in the head. Jon opened his eyes again to see a groaning Leinhart lying on his back, bleeding from a bullet wound to his chest; behind him, a police officer's gun still trained on the professor for a second shot should the need present itself; a pair of cops walking toward them, kicking Leinhart's gun aside as they secured the suspect and tried to stop the bleeding while calling in EMT support; a fourth officer walking to Jon to free him from his bindings.

Jon blinked at the professor, who was sobbing in between blood-tinged coughs and raspy breaths of air. Then Jon turned toward the face of the female officer who had released him from his bindings and did a double take.

"You believe me now?" he asked Officer Mabry, smiling despite himself, glad simply to be alive.

"When I heard about what you'd done, I *specifically* asked to be put on the team that came to find you," Mabry said with a half-smile that hinted at a somewhat apologetic relief. "Smart thinking covering your back like that. When we got the call from the network, we just followed your cell phone's GPS here." She squinted as though suffering from some minor pain, shaking her head slightly from side to side. "Look, I'm sorry about not listening to you before. It seems like the bastard at your brother's apartment was a bit smarter in covering his tracks than we'd allowed for." She raised her eyebrows and shrugged. "Government conspiracy… who'd have thought?"

Jon smirked with one corner of his mouth. "I only *wish* it had been my overactive imagination."

"Well, at least you know the truth about your brother's death. And everyone else will know he went out as a hero, not as a coward."

"True," Jon said as Mabry helped him to his feet. One of the other officers was reading Dr. Leinhart his rights, but the professor cut him off.

"Jon!" Professor Leinhart gasped from the floor. Jon, shrugging off Mabry's requests to the contrary, hobbled over to him, unsteady on his recently unbound feet, and leaned down toward Leinhart's face.

"I'm here, Professor."

"Jon… I'm—" The professor coughed fitfully, spat a glob of congealed crimson on the carpet, and tried again. "I'm so sorry, Jon. I'm…" He drifted off, then submitted to his sobbing attacks again.

"I know," Jon said softly, gazing down at the man with something approaching pity. "So am I."

Then Jon Rickner straightened up, grabbed his backpack from the floor, and walked outside with Officer Mabry into the cool evening air, greeted with the stares of curious neighbors as he breathed in the satisfying freshness of freedom and justice.

At long last, it was over.

Epilogue – The New Beginning

What doesn't kill me makes me stronger.
~ Johann Wolfgang von Goethe

*Revenge is the sweetest morsel to the mouth that ever was
cooked in hell.*
~ Sir Walter Scott

The day of the funeral was beautiful, sunny and clear, with just enough wispy and fluffy whiteness to give the brilliantly blue sky some layering. Church bells rang in the distance, reminding all present that the deceased was, thankfully, in a better place. The morning sun shone magnanimously upon the private ceremony, the hilltop cemetery seeming somehow greener than a place of earthly repose should, especially in light of the sad occasion that had brought them together that day. The laying to rest of a beloved brother, son, lover, friend. The burial of Michael James Rickner, intellectual martyr and fallen hero, a man who would live on in the lives and memories of those who knew and loved him best.

There had been a large memorial service held at George Washington University, then another held at the church Michael and Mara had attended in Foggy Bottom, but this graveside service was only for those who were closest to the deceased. Three of those people were seated in the front row during the intimate ceremony. Jon sat in the middle; Mara – her right arm in a sling tight across her chest – sat to his right, fighting through the pain and the pain-numbing drugs to lock every nuance of this moment in her memory for eternity; and to Jon's left, the father of the deceased, Jon's father, Sir William Rickner – fresh from his archeological expedition in the Amazon Basin, his salt-and-pepper hair and beard seeming more "salt" than the last time Jon had seen him, his hastily pressed tweed jacket a far cry from its Savile Row brethren in his closet back in England – sat in a mournful stupor, jet lag and still-fresh shock numbing him into a quiet agony.

After the death of his wife, Sir William had grown closer to his sons – the last living vessels of Anna Rickner's adventurous spirit and compassionate determination. They'd traveled together, experienced life together, and tried to help each other through the pain. Now, however, Jon wondered if his father would reach out – and allow himself to be reached out to – or if he would retreat even further into his work, the pain of losing a second loved one too much to bear. Jon also wondered if the experience and the shared connection with Michael that he and Mara had would keep their friendship alive – or ultimately hold too many painful memories for the relationship to continue. Hopes and fears for the future notwithstanding, the three mourners – Jon, Mara, and Sir William – held hands throughout the ceremony, each drawing strength from the next, a chain of the bereaved, a sorrowful trio brought together in community by their unshakable bonds with Michael.

The pastor spoke at length about Michael, having had a strong relationship with him during the few years the deceased had been active in that church. The adulatory remarks and humorous stories almost brought a smile to Jon's lips, but the sense of loss was too great.

Jon was tempted to get up and talk about his brother himself. Especially to talk about what Michael had done in recent months, the courageous intellectual pursuit that had resulted in his murder. But he couldn't. For one, that would entail the breaking of the chain that he knew Mara and his dad, both physically drained and emotionally wrecked, needed even more than he did. But more importantly, any words he might say would ring hollow. He was fluent in nearly a dozen languages, but none of them had words that came even close to describing who Michael really was – at least to Jon. Perhaps before Babel, back when Man spoke in the tongue of angels, such words could be found, but no longer. Michael was far from perfect, but he was Jon's hero, friend, and the best big brother he could have ever asked for. And those who sat under that beautiful yellow sun that day, tears of heartbroken sorrow streaming down their faces as the heavy coffin was lowered into the earth, had been close enough to Michael to know the man's true character far better than any further eulogy could convey. Jon changed his mind: there was a language that could describe Michael – the language of the heart, the part that, despite Michael's impressive intellect and natural eloquence, was touched far more deeply in those who knew him.

Hours later, after the folding chairs had been cleared away and their occupants had left – Mara back to her doctor-mandated bed rest and Sir William back to his hotel room to sleep off his jet lag – Jon sat on the dirt-brushed grass at the edge of his brother's grave, talking to Michael like he knew he would return to do as often as he could – despite knowing that the corporeal form that rested beneath six feet of dirt and subterranean wildlife no longer housed the spirit that was Michael.

Jon didn't notice the figure that cautiously approached him until it was nearly upon him. He glanced up from the mound of freshly turned earth when the visitor grew close, squinting at the tall man silhouetted against the afternoon sun. His mouth broke into a smile as he recognized the man.

"Wayne."

"How are you holding up?" Wayne asked. He wore a black trench coat that belied the peaceful look on his face, as though some long-held demon had finally been exorcised.

"Alright, I guess. All things considered." Jon shook his head slowly. "I just never imagined life without him, and now that's exactly how the rest of my life will be."

Wayne took a knee on the grass at the other end of the grave. "And how's that, exactly?"

Jon tilted his head quizzically. "What do you mean?"

Wayne motioned toward Jon with an open palm. "I mean how do you figure life will be different without him?"

Jon looked at the grave, furrowed his brow in thought, then turned back to Wayne. "I don't know exactly. He won't be there to share it with me, for one."

"Okay, that's a given," Wayne said, looking to one side. "But how will *your* life be different without him?"

Jon shrugged slowly. "I guess it won't, really."

"Won't it?" Wayne creased his brow as he looked intently at Jon. "The death of a loved one is always a tremendous life experience. It almost always has some impact on our lives, but it's up to us as to how that impact takes shape. For years, I allowed my parents' death to shape me into someone I wasn't. I didn't know you before Michael's death, but I'd say you've already begun changing. From the moment you picked up your brother's work, sniffing out the conspiracy that had cost him his life to uncover."

Jon's mind flashed back to the first time he had picked up Michael's backpack and worn it as his own, assuming the mantle that had been knocked from his brother's clutches.

"But I would have done that anyway. Michael and I did this sort of thing… well, not *exactly* this sort of thing, but we explored and tried to solve ancient mysteries and stuff all the time when we were growing up."

Wayne tilted his head forward, eyes looking upward at Jon. "Had you done that *without* Michael before?"

Jon paused thoughtfully. "No, not quite like this I hadn't."

"Well, there you have it. For starters, at least."

Jon raised his eyebrows and turned his gaze to the freshly turned earth covering his brother's grave. He thought about the past week: his fears over losing his brother to Mara, actually losing his brother to something much worse, then overcoming his fear and sorrow to quite literally pick up the mantle his brother had left – not just in donning his backpack, but in finishing his work, in looking out for Mara, in *leading* the quest against unspeakable odds and truly gifted foes. And he had come out not only alive, but triumphant. No longer the follower or the sidekick to his brother, the experience had forced him into the Alpha Dog role, and he had managed to succeed where even his brother – his one-time mentor – had failed.

"Yeah," he finally managed to say. "It's almost like I… I don't know, absorbed some part of him into me when he passed."

"Well, one way or another, mailing the Dossiers directly to the National Security Archive under a false name while sending copies to the news media, Congress, and the Supreme Court was a brilliant move. No matter what happened to you, the story would still get out. Michael's mission would still be complete."

Jon smiled. "And I was kind of banking on the fact that I was out of sight right after Greer's death. If the other Division agents in the city didn't know for certain if I still had the Dossiers, I figured they were less likely to try to whack me without knowing if I had already passed them or their contents on – and to whom. And thank God, it paid off."

Wayne returned Jon's smile. "That it did."

"So what's next for you? Are you officially un-dead yet?"

"No, not yet." Wayne made a face. "And I'm not entirely sure that I want to be. The Wayne Wilkins who, according to the Army, died last year in Iraq, actually no longer does walk this earth. I might just start my life all over again entirely. Not quite sure what that would entail, exactly, but I'll figure it out as I go. I figure it'll be an adventure in introspection."

Jon laughed. "'An adventure in introspection.' Sounds like fun. Well, listen, if you ever need anything…"

"I'll definitely let you know. You too."

Jon stood up, pulled out his wallet, and gave Wayne a card with his contact information on it. "Keep in touch, alright?"

Rising from his kneeling position, Wayne took it and looked at the card. "Will do. Sorry, but my old job didn't exactly allow us to carry our business cards, so I'll have to send you mine when I get it."

They both laughed, shook hands, offered their respective thanks, and exchanged farewells. Wayne stood and started to leave, then turned back.

"One last thing: I think your brother would have wanted you to have this." Wayne unzipped his coat and extracted a long, slender object wrapped in green cloth. Jon took it from him and began to unwrap the object. At the first glint of steel catching the light of the setting sun, Jon knew what it was: Michael's rapier.

"Where did you find it?" Jon asked.

"Ramirez isn't the only one who can do a little breaking-and-entering. I had seen the police report you tried to file about the incident at your brother's place, and saw you mentioning the theft of the sword. So I found his car in a parking garage in Manhattan the other night after I'd shot Greer and left you with the Dossiers. I jimmied his trunk, and lo and behold: stolen property. So I confiscated it to return it to its rightful owner." Wayne squinted into the sunset, a cast of oranges and reds playing off his features. "I'd better go. I've still got one last ghost to put to rest before I can move on." And without waiting for a reply, he left in the direction from which he'd come, as mysterious as ever.

Jon found himself alone with his thoughts again. Wayne's words weren't lost on Jon. *Its rightful owner.* The sword had belonged to Michael, but this was yet another part of his brother that was being passed on to Jon. He chuckled to himself, holding his brother's heirloom with a reverence for all that Michael was, and all that Jon was becoming. He finally returned his gaze to his brother's grave and kneeled, his mind mulling over Wayne's encouraging thoughts.

Michael James Rickner was dead in the flesh, but Jon vowed that as long as he drew breath, he would never allow his brother's spirit – his love of his fellow man and of learning, his unwavering sense of right and wrong, his relentless pursuit of hidden truths and righteous justice – to die.

That would live on through Jon for the rest of his days.

***

Enrique Ramirez was late to the cemetery. He crouched behind a raised marble tomb, using the wing of an angel statuary to steady the barrel of his sniper rifle. Feeling the wind, watching his target, waiting for the right moment to strike.

The last week had been mayhem for Enrique. The two cops who had responded to the scene of his capture – likely tipped off by Wayne Wilkins sometime after he'd made his escape – were dead, shot in the head with their own guns before they'd even gotten him out of the room. But by the time he escaped, all he had fought for had already gone up in smoke. Greer was dead; Rockefeller's Dossiers on Operation Phoenix had been discovered, then later revealed on national television; and, to top it all off, his car had been towed, the trunk broken into, and the elder Rickner brother's sword stolen. Ramirez raced back to Division Headquarters at Langley, trying to salvage whatever he could of his charge, but then the State Department goons had shown up, beginning what amounted to a massive cover-up of the cover-up. They confiscated equipment, destroyed records, and rounded up all of the staff and operatives for debriefing – a debriefing Ramirez feared would end not with offers of new government posts or off-the-record bank deposits to buy their silence, but rather an indefinite sentence at some officially non-existent prison in a country that most U.S. schoolchildren couldn't find on a map. So Ramirez did the only thing he could do: he ran.

After planting false trails to Chicago, Marseilles, Vancouver, Buenos Aires, and Tokyo, he made his way to Denver, then took a circuitous route of back roads back to D.C. It would never again be safe for him in this country, and his next stop would be somewhere in Central or South America. Perhaps Venezuela or Colombia. Places with constant conflict could always use a man of his talents. But before he could make his last journey south, he had to take care of one last loose end up here. Even though the Division was dead and in the process of being buried by the State Department, Enrique had to put to rights the memory of Greer and all he had fought for.

Ramirez adjusted the scope, Jonathan Rickner's profile coming into focus. The young scholar was alone, as he had been since Ramirez had first set up his weapon. The entire cemetery was, as far as the eye could see, devoid of any other living souls, and Ramirez would soon snuff out his only other company still residing on this side of the beyond.

A gust of wind threw his aim slightly off-balance, and Ramirez had to stifle a curse. With the wind picking up as it was, any sound he now made could carry for hundreds of yards, alerting Rickner... or worse, any FBI agents that might *happen* to be in the area. But he had done an exceptional job of covering his tracks. So good a job, in fact, that he himself would have had a hard time cutting through the noise and tracking him to this quiet cemetery. Which would prove of paramount importance, since his next move would be to leave the country. Forever.

He got the sight fixed back on Jon's head, and paused. The young man's face was one of contentment, of all being right with the world. Or at least, of a resoluteness to get there. His brother had just been killed, and yet he was all but smiling. But then, perhaps it was just the renewed sense of life that surviving near-death experiences can bestow. *How deliciously ironic*, Ramirez mused, *that such should be the last thought he has before dying.*

Ramirez brought his body tight to the stock, his finger finding its ideal position on the trigger. His last kill on U.S. soil. He inhaled, slowly started to squeeze the trigger.

A report, muffled by a sound suppressor, echoed from behind him. He tried to turn his head, but his body was already doing that for him as he flopped over on his back, his rifle sliding harmlessly to the ground. He knew he had been shot, but he couldn't tell where. He felt light. *After surviving battlefields the world over, how horribly ironic to die in a cemetery in my own homeland,* his thoughts floated past, seemingly with no connection to his conscious mind.

The gunman was standing just a few feet away from Ramirez, plenty close enough to go for the headshot, but for some reason, he hadn't. Almost as though he wanted to confront Ramirez face-to-face, to personally redress some wrong that had been the longtime assassin visited upon the other man. A second muffled report sounded, and then another. A spume of crimson shot upward from his chest. His breaths came as blood-drenched gurgles, and he realized he was drowning in a field on a perfectly clear day. Drowning in his own blood.

For a brief moment, Ramirez focused his vision enough to see the figure standing over him, a mere silhouette against the deepening orange of sunset. The figure's gun flashed once more, but Ramirez couldn't hear the report. All he heard now was what sounded like a howling wind, or perhaps just the white noise of brain cells dying en masse. But the flash momentarily illuminated the face of his killer. And, although he no longer trusted his senses any more than he trusted that bright light he seemed to be floating toward, he could have sworn that he recognized that face.

That it belonged to Wayne Wilkins.

And that, for the first time since Ramirez had met him, Wayne was smiling.

Author's Note

In writing a book like this that blends actual history with speculative or fictional elements, an author is has done his job if the reader has difficulty separating what is real from what is not. Now that the narrative is complete, however, I want to set the record straight on what is real, and what is merely a speculative creation.

A word first on my setting: In an effort to be faithful to what is perhaps the most famous city on earth, I made several trips to New York to research the key locations for my novel. Experiencing the world in my characters' shoes; walking (and, at times, climbing) where they would; seeing, hearing, and smelling the city that is so integral to the heart of this story was a real inspirational treat, a vast living canvas where I could envision where my characters would go and what they would do (and, of course, where I could hide Rockefeller's secrets). All of the Manhattan locations – including the routes that my characters take through the streets, parks, churches, museums, train stations, and libraries of the city – are accurate and faithful to their real-world counterparts. In addition, all of the historical background about the key locations – including Rockefeller's associations with them – as well as the sites where Rockefeller hid his codes, are accurate (although the codes themselves are my own creation). If you have never had the pleasure of visiting the city of New York, I urge you to do so. It is a fantastic, vibrant place like no other I've seen in my travels, with a culture and soul exclusively its own, and its rich history is evident from every street corner.

Now, on to the history behind the mystery.

John D. Rockefeller, Jr., trying to escape the shadow of his eminently famous father (and the bad press that Senior had gotten for his strikebreaking and other actions against his company's workers), became one of the greatest philanthropists the world has ever seen, donating more than half a billion dollars of his vast fortune to various causes over his lifetime. He helped finance the League of Nations (the predecessor of United Nations, created in the wake of World War I), as well as donating over eight million dollars to finance the site of the UN headquarters in Manhattan. Riverside Church, the Cathedral Church of St. John, and The Cloisters museum, among many others in Manhattan and around the world, were all properties that either received significant funding from Rockefeller, or were at one time owned by the man. He even donated his 54th Street mansion (Chapter 29), which is now the site of the world-famous Museum of Modern Art (MoMA). His philanthropic legacy extends across America to Europe, Jerusalem, and beyond. But, even today, his most remembered contribution to the world, the crowning achievement for his legacy is still his Rockefeller Center.

The other historical characters mentioned in the novel, including Henry Lewis Stimson, Franz von Papen, Paul von Hindenburg, and, of course, Adolf Hitler, were based off of their real-life counterparts. The roles of Papen, Hindenburg, and Hitler in bringing about Nazi rule in Germany (except for the American bribes that I have Papen taking from Stimson's agents) are all based on historical fact.

There really were a number of top businessmen – German, American, and otherwise – who saw the strong right-wing rule of the Nazi Party as a boon. Although its infamous anti-Semitism was always a key component to Nazism, what drew many to their ranks was a longing for the days of German self-determination and empowerment – rather than the weak Weimar government that had been foisted upon them at Versailles in 1919. In the midst of the Great Depression, the gains that communism was making as a result of the public's damaged perception of capitalism, many business leaders whose power and way of life was entrenched in the capitalistic system saw a strong right-wing government as the best way to fight back. Here in America, there was even talk of a plot financed by Wall Street bigwigs to overthrow President Roosevelt in a Fascist coup (known today as the Business Plot), a plan that, because of its sensitive nature and its inability to move past the preplanning phase, was largely swept under the rug by contemporary sources. It was a volatile climate of warring extremes, each offering their own solution to the desperate challenges presented by ongoing economic, social, and ideological strife.

Ultimately, though, Operation Phoenix – the conspiracy between then-Secretary of State Henry Lewis Stimson and industrial tycoon John D. Rockefeller, Jr. to stave off the march of communism by helping to resurrect a strong right-wing government in Germany as a bulwark to protect capitalism in the West – is my creation. Would these two men have had the means, motive, and opportunity to have devised and executed such an operation? Most likely, yes. But did anything like this actually happen? That, dear reader, I leave for you to decide.

Jeremy Burns is a former educator and journalist who holds degrees in History and Computer Science. He taught literature, political science, creative writing, and philosophy at an international school in Dubai, and has traveled to more than twenty countries across four continents. When not exploring a new corner of the globe, he lives in Florida, where he is working on his next novel.

For more info about Jeremy and his upcoming projects, visit his website, www.AuthorJeremyBurns.com and his Facebook author page, www.facebook.com/JeremyBurnsBooks.